ALSO BY MARY GORDON

FICTION

The Liar's Wife

The Love of My Youth

The Stories of Mary Gordon

Pearl

Final Payments

The Company of Women

Men and Angels

Temporary Shelter

The Other Side

The Rest of Life

Spending

NONFICTION

Reading Jesus

Circling My Mother

Good Boys and Dead Girls

The Shadow Man

Seeing Through Places

Joan of Arc

THERE YOUR
HEART LIES

THERE YOUR HEART LIES

Mary Gordon

 PANTHEON BOOKS, NEW YORK

Copyright © 2017 by Mary Gordon

All rights reserved. MAY 1 6 2017,
Published in the United States by Pantheon Books,
a division of Penguin Random House LLC, New York,
and distributed in Canada by Random House of Canada,
a division of Penguin Random House Canada Limited, Toronto.

Pantheon Books and colophon are registered trademarks
of Penguin Random House LLC.

Library of Congress Cataloging-in-Publication Data
Name: Gordon, Mary, [date] author
Title: There your heart lies / Mary Gordon.
Description: First Edition. New York : Pantheon Books, [2017]
Identifiers: LCCN 2016038634 (print). LCCN 2016044808 (ebook).
ISBN 9780307907943 (hardcover). ISBN 9780307907950 (ebook).
Subjects: BISAC: FICTION / Literary. FICTION / Contemporary Women.
FICTION / War & Military.
Classification: LCC PS3557.O669 T48 2017 (print) | LCC PS3557.O669 (ebook) |
DDC 813/.54—dc23
LC record available at lccn.loc.gov/2016038634

www.pantheonbooks.com

Jacket design by Janet Hansen

Printed in the United States of America
First Edition

9 8 7 6 5 4 3 2 1

For Kitty and Steve Klaidman

Therefore where your treasure is, there also your heart lies.

—MATTHEW 6:21

PREFACE

In July of 1936, the Fascist army, led by General Francisco Franco, launched a coup against the democratically elected Republic of Spain. The great powers of the West—the United States, England, France, Germany, and Italy, signed a neutrality agreement, promising not to arm either side. Germany and Italy violated the agreement, providing arms and other aid to Franco's armies; the United States, England, and France remained neutral. The Soviet Union, which had also signed the agreement, provided arms to the Republicans—their only source of military aid. Thousands of foreign volunteers fought on both sides. The International Brigades and the corps of medical volunteers were organized by the Communist Party to join in the Republican struggle, although not all who participated were communists. The Americans who fought on the Republican side were known as the Lincoln Brigade. The left was split into two camps: the anarchists, who believed that social change must be accomplished at the same time as the war was being fought; and the communists, who believed that the war must be won before social change could be effected. Along with fighting soldiers, Stalin sent a cadre of secret police, who made sure that the Spanish cause was in league with his own.

Unable to resist the superior arms provided by Adolf Hitler and Benito Mussolini in the support of the Fascist army, the Republican forces surrendered in 1939. Franco became dictator of Spain and remained in power until his death in 1975.

THE SS *NORMANDIE*, 1937

GREENWICH VILLAGE, 1936

HE OFFERS HER a coat.

She takes it, making a cradle of her arms.

Shy, small, scurrying, he backs away.

She sees him take his place beside the man with the megaphone.

All of them are standing on the pier, some of them, like her, waiting to board the SS *Normandie,* pride of the French line, which will carry them to France. But they will not stay in France; it is Spain they're bound for. Medical volunteers, to serve the army of the Republic, to defeat the fascists, Franco's rebels, nearly a year after the coup against the democratically elected government.

The man with the megaphone is getting ready now to speak. Ben Gold, president of the Fur and Leather Workers Union.

She can't concentrate on his words; she is looking at the beautiful ship. The *Normandie,* the newest, the fastest, the most glamorous of the great ocean liners. She's glad it's the *Normandie* and not one she took with her parents. But it seems wrong: to be traveling on a ship famed for its luxury when they are not on holiday, they are going to Spain to work beside the men who are fighting for its freedom.

This is what the man with the megaphone is saying, but she can't keep her eyes off the three huge black-and-red-striped funnels, the three layers of what seems like a gigantic cake: dark blue on the bottom, the lacy center, rows of slender columns, glistening like packed sugar in the uninflected sun. The open top deck, gleaming silver, everything capped by a stiff equilateral triangle whose only purpose seems to be the support of red, white, and blue pennants that snap extravagantly in the warm spring wind. She's afraid there's something wrong with her—perhaps she doesn't deserve to be here—because only scraps of what the union president is saying get hold of her attention.

"Fellow workers . . . you will be victorious over the fascists . . . Our cause is just . . . a war not only of the proletariat against the capitalist . . . a war of the poor against the rich, the lovers of freedom against those who would enslave us . . . The people will prevail . . . the people of Spain and the freedom-loving Americans . . . men and women of courage."

He holds up a coat, which the small man beside him provided at a secret signal that Marian had not been able to make out.

"And so, to show you our support, the workers of our union, as a token of our esteem, present each of you brave ladies with the fruits of our labor. A fur coat for each of you, compliments of the Fur and Leather Workers Union. Wear them to victory—the victory of the people, the workers, the makers of a great new world."

She understands now why she was given the coat.

Marian strokes the rich, hot fur. Not mink, not sable, nothing like her mother's coat, which she had loved to put her face against, hiding in her mother's closet, breathing in the scent—part of the warmth, the darkness—of her mother's perfume: Ombre Rose. Rose Shadow. Rose Shade. What is this fur? Fox, perhaps, or muskrat. It is May and warm, but she puts the coat on. It would seem ungrateful not to wear it. She is glad to have it, although she's afraid that it will make her sweat. This fur does not smell of perfume; it's not possible, as it was with her mother's coat, to forget that this was once the covering of an animal, keeping it warm, keeping it alive.

Everyone claps and cheers for the man with the megaphone. Some of the women are crying. One says, "I never thought I'd have a fur coat, I never even dreamed of it."

Marian takes her husband's arm. "Ready?" he says. "You okay?"

"Never better," she says.

·

Because it's the most wonderful feeling in the world: to know that you're doing exactly the right thing.

That you're exactly where you're meant to be, which is also where you want to be, that you are nineteen, healthy, on the way to Spain to save the world. Married, free of your parents, and, if the marriage is a sham, isn't that part of the fun of it, a secret they can giggle over in their bed instead of making love? And, after all, they love each other; they're each other's favorite person in the world.

What a surprise, what a shock for her family. That Marian Therese Taylor, of the Newport and Park Avenue Taylors, is here on this ship with people she calls comrades. Now Marian Rabinowitz, wife of Russell, one of what her family nastily refers to as "the chosen people," her husband, Russell, former lover of her brother, dead by his own hand.

But she won't think of that now, she must not think of Johnny now. It's why she's here, with people who believe that there are more important things in the world than private life, that the large sorrows of the world are more important than the private sorrows, that the great murderous injustices are more important than the intimate and individually killing slights.

Never has she felt more alive, never has she felt more at home in the world. Words like exultation, exaltation are real now ... and she wonders, does she mean exaltation or exultation or both, does it matter which vowel is in the middle of the word if the feelings are so similar, as if your body had given up its heaviness and it would be quite possible for you to spread your arms and take to the air simply, as in her favorite dream, to fly?

She no longer agonizes about being a daughter of privilege; she is a worker among workers; she has skills that are valued. She is fluent in Spanish. Working with her Spanish teacher at Vassar, an Andalusian (her brother a doctor in Connecticut), Marian has compiled a Spanish-English dictionary of medical terms and made ten carbon copies. She is a fearless driver; she knows how to fix cars. Would she have been allowed to join the volunteers because of these skills? She knows that the most important reason she was approved is that she is Russell's wife and he is a doctor specializing in infectious diseases. She tells him she doesn't want to just tag along. He says the same thing to her that he says when she expresses her unease that they are traveling on a luxury liner. "You just have to stop questioning everything. The guys in charge know what they're doing, that's why they're in charge." He doesn't say who the guys are, but they both know who he means, the men at the head of "the party" who have organized the volunteers. *The* party, the only one deserving the definite article. The Communist Party: the only hope for the future of the workers of the world.

They make their way to the gangplank where the third-class passengers are meant to board. The man in charge, who has checked the others' tickets and told them where they should proceed, looks at their tickets and says, "There's been a change in your accommodations."

Marian is frightened. She knows how powerful her father is, how far his tentacles reach. Does he know somehow that her marriage can be declared invalid, on the most unassailable of grounds? How has he found out? Who did he bribe, what favor did he call in, to stop her?

"We're overfull in third class," says the sailor in his perfect French uniform, cocking his head, twisting his mouth into a sly insider's half smile, the company's resident Maurice Chevalier. "And so we have put you into what we call our 'interchangeable quarters.' What that means is they're first class on some trips, but if we don't have sufficient first-class bookings, they become tourist or even third class on others. As you see."

Marian looks at Russell, certain that within the next few seconds— she hopes not too insultingly—he will refuse. It is from him that she learned the horrors of class distinctions, of riches hoarded by the rich, kept from the ones who have to produce their wealth.

And so she can't believe what she hears him say. "Well, I guess this is our lucky day."

They make their way over to the first-class gangplank. She is trembling . . . and she doesn't know if it's from disbelief or anger. "Russell, how can you do this? It makes a mockery of everything we stand for."

"Look, toots, the last trip your parents took across the ocean was on the *Île de France*. The last trip my parents took was on a filthy ship in steerage. I'm doing it for them, to thumb my nose at everything and everyone who kept them down."

"I don't like it, Russell," she says, wondering if this will be their first disagreement as husband and wife.

"It's the privilege of the privileged to refuse privilege," he says, and once again, abashed by her heritage, she walks behind him to the bank of golden elevators, more glorious than the Waldorf's.

Despite herself, she is enchanted.

She knows that she's aboard a ship, but the word "ship" seems too real, too ordinary for what she sees around her; sometimes she feels like she's part of a movie, where the madcap heiress flees an arranged marriage or the plucky working girl dances up just this kind of staircase, spinning away in a final swirl promising a life of endless days of bliss, free from the anxieties of 1930s Depression life, glamorously rebellious, secure but unconventional.

Everything the brochures promised has come to life. The three-deck dining room that boasts it is "longer than the hall of mirrors in Versailles." Unlike the *Île de France,* which her parents favored, everything on the *Normandie* is modern: the Lalique chandeliers, the series of geometrical patterning on the floor and walls, the angular, not quite comfortable chairs, the murals painted on glass of lolling asymmetric goddesses whose limbs, not really human, might be the parts of some complex hyper-efficient new machine. The fabulous food: lobster, roast lamb, a pastry cart that could mark the wedding celebration of a prince, a display of cheeses that she craves as she does not crave the sweets—she samples them, Boucheron to Stilton, accompanied by old port. The exquisite wines, the pervasive scent of French perfume and French cigarettes: she decides that since she is there, she will enjoy it all, because soon, soon, there will be no comfort, no elegance, only the horrible sights and smells of war.

She is particularly fond of their room. Two generous-sized beds with a longhaired white rug between them. At first she worried: did they know that she and Russell didn't really sleep together, had never shared a bed? Then she tells herself she's being ridiculous, and she's grateful for the crisp, sweet-smelling linens, the soft pillows, the shower with water that shoots out from its four walls, the extra washbasin enclosed in a door so if one person is in the bathroom the other can use the sink.

For the first day and a half, Russell is in high spirits: he never seems to be without food or a drink in his hand; he takes his book—a novel by Vincent Sheean—into the conservatory, full of wild and cultivated flowers, fountains, live birds.

"Imagine hearing songbirds on a ship," he says, twirling her around, putting behind her ear what she is afraid is some rare specimen he should never have taken from the conservatory.

But by dinner of the second day, he does nothing but complain. The people look like pigs. He is going to be sick from the endless rich food. Their music disgusts him: watered-down Broadway show tunes, played by third-raters who'd be happier with Victor Herbert.

"The difference between all this"—he makes a sweeping gesture, as if he would throw the whole of first class overboard—"all this and third class, it's unbelievable," he says.

"I didn't know you'd gone down there."

"Of course I did. Do you think I forgot why we're here?"

"Do you think I did?" she says. "You were the one who wanted to stay here. Either stay here and enjoy it, Russell, or do something about it."

"I'm going upstairs to talk to the men putting the chairs away."

She decides without him: she will request that they be moved back to third class. She understands that she can do this and Russell can't because she has the experience of assuming that people who are known as "employees" are paid to do what the people who pay them want done. She even knows who to speak to: the purser. In the pockets of her cotton slacks, she puts fifty dollars, part of the money she got selling the diamond watch she was given for her eighteenth birthday. She wears Johnny's watch now. She puts the fifty dollars on the purser's desk and tells him that she and her husband prefer to be in third class, and she's sure there is some couple who would be happy to trade places with them. She knows that someone unused to servants would feel that she had to explain their actions. She knows that she doesn't have to, that if her request is made with just the right hint of insolence, the right tone of command, no explanation will be required.

Russell walks into their room, rips off his tie, and throws it unlovingly on the chair.

"We're moving," she says. "We're moving to third class tonight."

"What did you do, you little stinker?"

"Don't ask, just say I'm the best little wife you could have imagined."

"You're the best little wife I could have imagined. Which is, by the way, not saying much, my darling."

They embrace and dance around the room. Like newlyweds. Which, in fact, they are.

Now, in third class with their comrades, he's happy. Once again, they are best friends. He praises the music: not like that crap from those guys dressing up in monkey suits, he says; Ernie, the guy with the banjo, he's the real thing. He and another man with a guitar sing songs about the heroes of their fight: "A las Barricadas," the 5th Regiment, the 15th Brigade. "If You Want to Write to Me, You Know Where I Am." And almost any hour of the day or night some group can be counted on to break into "The Internationale." The songs have urgency: life and death, eternal love, devotion to a cause, devotion to a country, with each note something at stake, something that cannot be questioned. In first class they are dancing to "It's De-Lovely," "Too Marvelous for Words," "The Merry-Go-Round Broke Down."

Now she is sharing food with people her parents would be appalled by. She's amused by the difference in the first- and third-class menus. One offer on their third night's dinner: roast turkey, buttered corn. Is this a kind of French snobbery, a sign of contempt for the poorer Americans they know make up the bulk of third class? It doesn't matter; the buttered corn is delicious. Perhaps, she thinks, it's the French butter. Only one dessert is provided: fruit and vanilla ice cream. Perhaps a nod to any Europeans who might be traveling: a cheese course, but one cheese only. Port Salut. She and Russell live like cubs in the small cabin—sleeping back to back, enjoying, once they get over the strangeness, the shared animal warmth. On the ship, she is Russell's wife, the girl who made the medical dictionary.

She is proud of Russell, of the part he takes in the endless discussions. He never allows the conversations to veer off from the press of circumstance; he is impatient with the infighting among Stalinists and Trotskyites. His explanation for why he is here, why he's a communist, comes in the form of a story. He says that he is a communist because communists show up. When his family was evicted, the communists—his mother's colleagues in the hatmakers' union, the ones who refused, as she did, to compromise with the bosses—arrived and moved their furniture back into the apartment, daring the landlord to throw them out again.

The others speak only of ideas: "We are here to fight fascism before it spreads. We are here on the side of the workers. The dictatorship of the proletariat: factories run by unions, collectivized farms."

Russell says that he refuses to discuss Russian collectivization because none of them have been to Russia to see it firsthand, and most of them have never been anywhere near a farm.

Never before has she so clearly understood the limitations of being a daughter of her family, the product of twelve years of Catholic education: Marymount School, Fifth Avenue; the Convent of the Sacred Heart, Noroton, Connecticut. Then Vassar. Before Vassar, she had never had a non-Catholic friend; except for Mrs. Chamberlain, the librarian, she had never had more than a passing conversation with a Protestant. With all her heart, she believed in the rights of Negroes. She had stood up to her brother when he had said that jazz was the music of the jungle and the brothel. But she had never spoken to a Negro. Now a Negro woman has chosen them as table companions, chosen Russell, really, because they worked together when Russell volunteered at Harlem Hospital, where Rosalie Compton was a surgical nurse. Rosalie Compton makes Marian shrink into herself. She is grand and impatient; for a while she called Marian "little girl." But she doesn't anymore; despite herself, she's impressed that Marian produced the dictionary. She asks Marian for help with Spanish; they laugh because Marian knows the Spanish word for "autoclave." "I bet that's something you didn't think you'd be knowing six months ago," Rosalie says.

Before Russell, Marian had never known a Jew.

Now she is married to a Jew . . . does that make her a Jew? Certainly, it means that, if asked, she will declare she is. She will not say, she will never say again, that she is Catholic. The Church is the enemy, the Catholic Church. On the ship, they rail against it almost as much as they rail against capitalism. "Crush" is the word they use most often. Everything the Catholic Church wants to "crush." Unions, democracy, freedom of thought. See who they are in Spain: the handmaid of the fascists, urging from the pulpit that reds be killed, tortured in the name of the Church. They make up lies about priests being killed, nuns being raped. No priests have been killed; no nuns have been raped. Marian is ashamed of who she was, who her family is. Thankful that she is Marian Taylor Rabinowitz, a name not obviously associated with the Catholic Church, like Murphy or Kelly. She doesn't want anyone to know who she was, where she came from. She makes Russell swear not to tell.

She doesn't know what it means to Russell to be Jewish, what it means to any of them. She is close enough to Marge Kaplan, a phlebotomist whose husband is a dentist and who still considers herself a religious Jew, to ask her what it all means: it's so different from what it means to be Catholic.

Marge says, "I don't know what it means to them. If you ask me, they have no idea what being a Jew means, what they even mean by it. They want to pretend it doesn't mean anything; they'd do anything to get away from it. Pinchus Kaplan becoming Pete Cole . . . Irving Feldman becoming John Fox. But for most of them, you can't have two of them in the same room for five minutes without one of them saying the word 'Jew.'"

One day, a beautiful clear day when it is almost possible to forget they aren't traveling to a holiday, she and Russell are on deck. She asks him what it means to him to be a Jew.

Russell says, "You know what it means to be a Jew when an anti-Semite lets you know."

Anti-Semitism. She knew about it, but it didn't strike her forcefully until the night of her brother Johnny's first Juilliard recital.

The light makes lozenges or diamonds on the water's surface, each separate, bounded, with no impulse to connect or merge. She wishes her mind would refuse that impulse to connect; the past comes to her, but she doesn't want it, not the past of her family, particularly not her father or her brother Vincent.

Johnny's recital. Her brother Johnny. With his usual sweetness, he had selected a program that paid homage to people he loved: for their father, the first sonata from Bach's *Well-Tempered Clavier,* for Reverend Mother Labourdette, the Chopin she always asked for when he came to collect Marian, the Étude op. 10. For Marian, a loving nod to their childhood, Schumann's *Kinderszenen* . . . and finishing the program, his love letter to Russell: Copland's *Three Moods:* "Embittered," "Wistful," "Jazzy."

She saw that her father wept straight through the Bach; he had tears in his eyes while they waited for Johnny in the lobby. "My son has done me proud. He's the real thing. I'll think of that Bach on my deathbed."

She saw her brother Vincent open his cigarette case, light two, offering one to his fiancée.

"Quite wonderful in its way, although I wish he hadn't tarnished it with the Copland. Forgive me, but I'm out of patience with the claque of crybaby cosmopolites, awash in their self-pity, oh boo-hoo, poor

me, the school of Proust and Freud, my mother didn't kiss me good-
night so I developed asthma, my mother preferred my father to me
so I had to kill him. Crying in their beer, no, not beer, beer would
be too forthright a drink for them, shedding precious tears into their
absinthe or whatever rabbinically approved decoction is the latest
fad."

"You're suggesting that this is a Jewish tendency?" Russell said, standing perhaps a bit too close to Vincent.

"Well, Mr. Rosenberg, you must admit there is a certain identifi-
able tincture," Vincent said, stepping backward.

"It's Rabinowitz, and it's Doctor."

"So sorry. I'll be sure to take two aspirin and call you in the morning. But for now, goodbye, Father, Mother, how proud you must be,
but Edwina and I are making our way to what I'm sure will be a rather
swell party."

Vincent linked his arm through his fiancée's, and Marian shivered.
She always imagined that the touch of Edwina's bare flesh would be
like the touch of a freezing iron railing against an ungloved hand.

Father Cunningham, the latest of what Marian told Johnny were
"Daddy's pet Jesuits," wiped his mouth with an exquisitely white
handkerchief.

"That young man is wasted in this century. He belongs with the
great eighteenth-century wits: Congreve, Sheridan. He has a tongue
of gold."

"That young man is eaten up with bitterness and he will spread
his bitterness wherever he goes," said Reverend Mother Labourdette,
headmistress of the Convent of the Sacred Heart at Noroton. "I know
vile insinuations when I hear them; my mother is a Jew, and so, under
the Law of Moses, I am, too."

Two red spots appeared beneath her cheekbones, as if someone had pressed two hot coins into her flesh—the sign, every Noroton schoolgirl knew, of Reverend Mother's wrath.

"Strange words to hear from a Madame of the Sacred Heart," Father Cunningham said.

"As I've been in the order forty-five years, Father, I would say I am more of an authority on what is strange for a Madame of the Sacred Heart to say and what is not."

"Oh, Reverend Mother, a hit, a hit, a palpable hit. Or, perhaps, knowing your antecedents, I should say, *touché ma mère*. But I can't joust with you. I am an old man and must be up for the six-thirty Mass."

"I'm terribly sorry, Russell. I would like you to know that not all of us are like this," Reverend Mother Labourdette said.

"I think that you are not. I believe you're the exception. But thank you. I couldn't have done it. They think they can say anything, any anti-Semitic garbage, as long as it's cloaked in gentility. I hate it, and you always look like a fool if you confront it. They'd say it's part of your fevered Jewish imagination."

Reverend Mother put her hand on Russell's arm. "Don't let Johnny know you're upset. This is Johnny's night. We have to do everything to make it perfect for him."

She and Johnny had a special fondness for each other. Everyone knew Reverend Mother was a pianist; sometimes she could be heard playing fierce music when the others were at dinner: Rachmaninoff, Liszt. But she always asked Johnny for Chopin. "Your brother is a gentle, gentle soul. I worry for him," she had said once to Marian. "I'm very glad the two of you are so close."

Mother Labourdette would probably not be happy that Marian is on her way to Spain. But Marian would never have told her. If she had urged Marian not to go, it might have made her hesitate. As her father's request had not.

It was easy for her to reject everything having to do with her father, with their family. More difficult was the rejection of the values of the nuns she loved and was drawn to. But she did not believe in God. She had been told he was a God of love, a God who looked out for the sparrows, but the world was too full of terrible things for her to believe it. She had tried, tried to pray as Mother Kiley had taught her to pray—for the poor, the suffering of the world. "Lay their sufferings at the foot of the cross of the suffering Christ," Mother Kiley had said. But that, she felt, would be of no help to the poor. She had tried going with Phyllis Curren to the Catholic Worker. That had been tempting; she was drawn to Dorothy Day, to her fierceness, her dedication. Russell and Johnny had taken Phyllis and Marian to lunch at the Plaza afterward and Phyllis had said, "They're very nice, but they seemed tied to worldly pleasures. I'm sure Dorothy wouldn't approve of spending all that money on a lunch when it could have been given to the poor." What Marian heard was: Dorothy Day would not approve of Johnny. She did not go back to the Catholic Worker.

Her father had begged her not to go to Spain. He had arrived at the Patchen Place apartment two days before she and Russell were to sail.

She was shocked to see him at the door.

"What are you doing here?"

"I hear you're going to Spain?"

"How do you know?"

"You're my daughter; you should know a man like me has ways of finding things out."

"I'm sure you do. You always have."

"I'm begging you, Marian. I'll give you whatever you want, I'll let you go wherever you want, if you won't do this mad, this wicked thing."

"I don't believe it's mad or wicked."

"Marian, this is your immortal soul we're talking about. An eternity of torment . . . should you die fighting for the enemies of the Church, that is what you'll earn. We have had our differences; I often think your mother and I left you alone too much, you and Johnny. I regret that now, but you are my beloved daughter, and I always admired your guts and your brains. It's eternity we're talking about, Marian, don't risk eternity to make a point against me and the rest of the family. Don't you see, the reds hate all that is good and beautiful and valuable and true, everything that the Church keeps alive in the world, they will tear it all down in favor of a sewer way of life in the name of justice, but it isn't justice, it's vile envy and self-indulgence."

Her father's eyes blazed; his thick curls, plastered against his skull with brilliantine—almost incandescent with the urgency of his message. How handsome he is, she thought against her will. She walked over to the mantel and picked up the photograph of Johnny.

She handed it to her father, pleased to see him flinch. "There is nothing you can say to me about a father's love. His death is on your head."

"I was trying to save his soul."

"Trying to save his soul, you took his life. And I will ask you to leave now before my husband comes home. I wouldn't want to upset him."

She closed the door, then moved to the couch, her head in her hands, the old Johnny gesture. Despite herself, she understood her father's terms. Eternal life. Eternal damnation. If she believed as he did, would she have acted the same? But she would never. She would never. She would never harm anyone she loved. Not for any idea in the world. Because, if she knew anything from her prayerful days, she knew that, if there is a God, he honors love above everything.

· · ·

She grips the deck's polished brass railing as if to stop herself falling in, falling over. But it's too late, she should never have allowed them, the first memories; she should have cut them off, closed the sluice-way fast, fast, because now there is no closing it, the water is too high now, the current is too strong, no force of hers can any longer hold it back. So often now, two noises fight for prominence in her boiling brain. The *beep beep* of the alarm: close the sluiceway, do not let the water in, don't think, don't think of that, and covering it over, so the alarm is only just audible, the roar of the breaking wave. You must remember.

She knows she should turn her back on the seductive ocean, with its all-too-available associations, find Russell, help someone with Spanish, wash her hair. But to banish the memories is to banish her brother, to leave him to the charge of the faceless, insubstantial sway-ing dead, who have no purchase on the history of one who is, to them, one only among many. If she refuses memory, she has refused him; she will not allow him to wander abandoned. It is one of the rea-sons she is here, so that her actions will be so entirely demanding that she will not be able to remember, therefore not guilty of the crime of banishment. But she will be with him now.

October 1, 1936, only seven months ago. How is that possible?

She has just taken the train from Poughkeepsie, the first time since she's been at Vassar that she has found the time to visit Johnny in New York. She still can't believe that there's no one whose permis-sion she has to ask; she'll be away for the weekend and has to notify the dormitory, but no one can tell her she can't go or ask what is tak-ing her away.

Before Vassar, she had weekends in New York, stolen weekends of cigarettes and cocktails and jazz, away from the Convent of the Sacred Heart in Noroton, Connecticut. These were made possible because of Johnny's best friend, Russell, who is a doctor and sends a letter to Reverend Mother saying that Marian is under his care, undergoing an experimental treatment for her allergies. Does Mother Labourdette know that it's a hoax? Perhaps she does and doesn't care because Johnny always comes to Noroton to accompany her, and Mother Labourdette is very fond of Johnny. Marian guesses that Reverend Mother prefers Johnny to her parents, his Juilliard shyness to her parents' bluster, their triumphalist pomp.

On this bright day in October, for the first time in her life, she thinks she looks splendid. It began as a lark, a favor to her roommate, Gwen. Gwen is going to major in Art History; she's crazy about Merovingian stained glass, but to relax, just for fun, she says, she loves designing clothes. She enjoys matching outfit to personality, or her fantasy of personality, which the object of the fantasy is obliged as her friend to assume, later even to wear. She calls Marian "Maid Marian" and always links her to Robin Hood. "You are gamine, but you don't want to be *too* gamine, and, for God's sake, never cut your fabulous hair." She shows Marian the drawing she's been working on in secret: a narrow skirt of a rusty, gold color, a long jacket, sea to olive green with a velvet collar of chestnut brown. The hat: part of the Robin Hood joke, boyish down to the jocular feather. She invites Marian home to Boston for the weekend where she will buy the fabric and where a dressmaker she knows will "whip it up in a couple of hours." While she's doing that, they'll concentrate on shoes. Marian demands that they be shoes she can walk in easily; Gwen insists that they find something to draw attention to her legs, "which are, dearie, your best feature, as you are entirely without *embonpoint*."

Marian has never paid much attention to her clothes. The ethic at Noroton, never stated by the nuns because it never needed to be stated, was to pretend you were above all that. Only the foreign girls rebelled, but silently. Particularly the ones from South America, one of whom, thrillingly named Lupe, was Marian's particular friend.

Marian was determined, when it came to fashion, to be nothing like her mother, whose clothes made her appear breakable, or her sisters, whose tailored suits and dresses seemed, Marian thought, a kind of armor, impermeable, plated. Every detail of her mother's wardrobe suggested that nothing could be asked of her; everything about her sisters made it clear that no one must dare ask.

Marian's new friends at Vassar, who are political or scientific, pretend not to be interested in clothes. But they make an exception for Gwen's creations because they are not fashion but art, because the Boston dressmaker is Italian, and Gwen hinted (they were eager to believe her) that she had some connection to Sacco and Vanzetti, and, therefore, they would be putting money in her pocket, not the fat pockets of the owners of department stores, possibly their relatives, whose names they can't bring themselves to speak.

Marian is going to surprise Johnny. On the train, she thinks of the pleased look, the delighted look that will come over him when he sees her in the apartment; he has given her keys, she'll let herself in to heighten the surprise. The day, she thinks, is as crisp as a just-ironed cloth. The gold clocks at Grand Central please her especially, striking just the right note of formality. She is a little too warm in her new outfit, but she enjoys the heat that makes its way through the stiff felt of her new hat.

She'll walk to the Village. Johnny isn't expecting her, and why waste a perfect day?

As she walks up the stairs, she hears Billie Holiday's voice, and she's sure it's coming from Johnny's apartment. "You'd be so easy to love." She starts singing along as she puts the key in the door, expecting to see his delighted face. But, instead, she sees him dancing, dancing with a man, his friend Russell.

At first, the oddness of what she sees makes her want to laugh. They must be rehearsing for some kind of skit. But then she sees: they aren't trying out steps for a comic performance. They're dancing as a man and a woman might; they're dancing as lovers.

Homosexuality. It's something she's heard of vaguely but never given much thought to. Girls had crushes on other girls; girls had crushes on nuns. And, of course, she has heard of Oscar Wilde; one of the English nuns told them that she prayed for him every day, or prayed *to* him, because she was sure he was in heaven.

As she stands in the doorway of her brother's apartment, ugly words defile her mind: deviant, or, more kindly, invert. And then fag, fruit, fairy, queer. And then no more words. Johnny faces her, horrified. She can't bear it; she turns and runs down the stairs, and he follows her, shouting, "Sweetheart, wait."

She allows her spine to collapse. She allows herself to fall against him and to put her head on his shoulder and to weep there, as she always has, because he is the one who allows her to weep. Tears are forbidden in the Taylor family. Her father said to her once when she was crying—she couldn't have been more than six—"Never let me see you crying, and never let me hear you cry out because of pain; even when you're giving birth, you must not cry out in pain. The noble thing is to keep silent." Only their aunt Dotie, who keeps to her room and drinks herself into a sweet stupor to forget the loss of her young husband killed in the First World War, only she allows tears. "Tears are sacred," she says. But Johnny and Marian cannot allow themselves more than to half believe her.

Of course she will follow him upstairs. Of course they will talk. Of course she will try to understand. Because he is the only one in the world she really loves, the only one who allows her to believe that she is capable of love. Because of him, when she thinks herself cold-hearted or unnatural, she can say, "I have a brother whom I love." She has been able to say this since her earliest memory.

They are the two youngest of a family of nine. The accidents. The afterthoughts. Half orphans, raised by servants. One night, when they were both drunk, they admitted it to each other: "We were lucky to be brought up by servants instead of our parents."

So how could she run away from him, run out of the door of his building onto Patchen Place? Run to what? An abyss? A terrifying place of utter aloneness. No, of course she will be with him. They walk up the stairs, leaning on each other, weeping, as they were forbidden to do.

Russell is standing by the window, playing with the cord of the Venetian blind.

"Perhaps you should have called ahead," he says.

She knows he's trying to make things normal, trying to make a joke of it, turn it into a small, social embarrassment.

"Russ," Johnny says. "She would never have had to call ahead. It's who we are."

"Well, she knows who you are now."

"I wanted to tell you, but not while you were at Noroton. I thought, Well, when she's at Vassar, that will be time enough."

Johnny sits on the couch, his long, beautiful hands dangling between his open knees. Russell sits beside him, and then Johnny holds his head in his hands.

She knows that gesture: he feels helpless, he can't think of anything that will be of the slightest use.

She has known since she was seven that she is, of the two of them, the stronger.

Russell hands them all drinks, but Johnny puts his down untasted on the coffee table. He grabs his sister's hands. "I just don't know what to say, I just don't know what to say. Will you forgive me?"

"Oh, for God's sake, Johnny," Russell says. "You don't need to ask forgiveness for being who you are."

"You're the one who needs to ask forgiveness, Russell," she says. "These are by far the worst highballs I've ever tasted."

The three of them laugh more than Marian's words warrant. They know their laughter is forced and excessive. And that no more needs to be said.

"All right, then, I'll take you to the Plaza," Russell says, "since I'm the only one gainfully employed. Grab your hats. Only, you, don't brag about stealing from the rich and giving to the poor."

"Don't you like my feather?" she asks, girlishly twirling around.

"Mad about it. Seriously, those colors are great on you. Good style."

"My roommate Gwen designed it. Johnny, whatever you do on your own time, for God's sake, take one of my friends to at least one dance. Or they'll think I made you up."

"What about me?" Russell asks.

"Oh, Russell, you're much too old."

Because they never talk about it, she has to understand things on her own. She has little enough sense of what men and women do in bed to try to modify it to make a picture of what two men might do. She's sorry that Johnny won't have children, but then, if he'd become a priest, he wouldn't have had children, and everyone would be thrilled.

They love each other, she tells herself, not even knowing fully what *that* means, as Johnny is the only person she has ever loved.

"You're going to have to be discreet, old thing," Russell says. "No late-night confabs while you're making fudge. We could end up in jail, you know."

"Russell, there's no way you can have grown up Catholic and not know how to keep secrets, not know who to tell what, not know how to lie," Marian says.

"And they say Jews are the ones with the brains," he says.

Back in the dorm, she talks about drinks at the Plaza with Johnny and his handsome friend, the doctor who wrote her notes that got her out of school on weekends. She hints of a growing mutual attraction between them. She says Johnny will come for a visit soon, maybe for the next dance.

The thought of Johnny in jail terrifies her. The thought of her family finding out terrifies her most of all.

And two weeks later, it almost happens.

There is a knock at the door, and Marian, answering in her pajamas, is horrified to see her brother Vincent there. Johnny and Russell are in their bedroom; she sleeps on the Murphy bed.

"Fancy seeing you here," she says, stalling for time, hoping he doesn't see her hand shaking.

"Aren't you going to invite me in, little sis?"

"It's not my place."

"Where's our brother?"

"Sleeping."

The bedroom door opens. Johnny and Russell, wearing only pajama bottoms, stand in the doorway.

Vincent pushes his way past her. She sees the joy, the energy in his shoulders, in the fabric, grown electrified, of his perfectly cut jacket, russet tweed. The color, she thinks, of dried blood.

He is hardly inside the door before he hisses his insulting words. "Sodomites. Filthy sodomites. You are an abomination before the face of God."

She notices that the words he uses are archaic, as if the lack of modernity were an inoculation, placing him apart, protecting him from the poison he is about to approach.

Johnny does the worst possible thing. He cries.

But Marian's body produces not tears but an icy coldness. The fighting animal's cunning.

"You're the pervert, Vincent," she says. "You're the one with the disturbed mind. Can't you see the situation? I'm spending the weekend here. What the hell did you expect them to do? Usually Russell sleeps in the Murphy bed. But what would you have, Vincent? Did you want me to sleep in the bed with my brother? Or with some perfectly strange man?"

He is the trapped animal now. She sees his skeleton gradually sink with defeat. But then the family eyes meet, the bright blue only Johnny has failed to inherit. She employs the family smirk. She lights a cigarette.

"I didn't know you smoked. What would the sisters say?"

She doesn't, in fact, smoke, and she doesn't put the cigarette to her lips, only holds it, the only weapon she can think of, twirling it in the air, hoping it looks dangerous.

"You've lost track, Vin. I'm not with the nuns anymore. I'm at Vassar. But what would your friends, the stylish Jesuits, think of your style if they knew you came banging in here like some Prohibition cop because of your fantasy of, what is it they call it, a fevered brain?"

Her heart is beating fast, but her hands have, thank God, stopped trembling.

"Don't you think it's time you were on your way, Vinnie?" she says, knowing he hates the nickname. "Or is it Vince?"

He doesn't bother to reply. He leaves the apartment, slamming the door as if he were erasing some sort of record.

Johnny is weeping, but Russell is on his feet. He takes her in his arms and lifts her in the air. "You've got the balls of a brass monkey, kiddo," he says, and makes coffee, which he serves black with a shot of whiskey. She doesn't like the taste but appreciates the gesture.

She sits on the couch and takes Johnny in her arms. "He's a bully, but, like all bullies, he has a stupid streak."

"Vincent isn't stupid. I'll never be safe from him."

"You're safe with me, honey," she says. And Russell says, "Johnny, you've got the two of us on your side. I would say you're as safe as houses."

"Houses only seem safe," he says. "Houses can be blown up. Burned down."

"You're being maudlin," Russell says. "Let's go to the movies."

Marian can't pay attention to the movie because she's too frightened; she knows Johnny is right. Vincent isn't stupid, their father isn't stupid, and they have resources that she and Johnny, doubting their ultimate value, will never have. And she knows that those resources can be called on at any time and used against whomever they wish.

For a while, they try to believe that Vincent will leave them alone, that Marian has shamed him. She comes down from Poughkeepsie every weekend in November. Russell takes her shopping; they go to jazz clubs, they hear Ella Fitzgerald. On Sunday nights, they see her off on the train with flowers, and the girls in the dorm are suspicious, a bit envious, of her veiled comments about the doctor whose specialty is infectious diseases.

The Taylors will be away for Thanksgiving, which they never celebrate, considering it a Protestant holiday. Instead, the Feast of St. Nicholas, on December 6th, is celebrated, a special Mass is said, and whichever priest is currently in her father's favor sits at the head of the table. Her father always carves a goose, not a turkey—infinitely superior, her father insists, although Marian finds it too greasy for her taste.

Russell and Marian and Johnny make a turkey for their own small Thanksgiving. "Only you two would consider a Thanksgiving turkey a rebellion," Russell says.

They drink glass after glass of Châteauneuf-du-Pape, and Johnny makes up a song, the chorus of which goes, "Screw the goose, we love the turkey."

The next weekend she stays in the dormitory, worrying that she's neglected her work. Late Saturday night, Gwen answers the phone and says it's Russell. The doctor they assume to be Marian's beau. "He sounds alarmed," Gwen says.

"Oh, Russell sounds alarmed if there's bad weather in Boise," Marian says.

"They've got him," Russell says, and the alarm is genuine. "Johnny's in jail. Your brother or your father, I don't know who, hired a private detective who trailed him to a bar we go to. The bar was raided tonight. I was supposed to be there, but I had to stay in the hospital because one of my patients took a sudden downturn, or I'd be with him. Jesus, Marian, Johnny's in jail. He'll fall apart."

"Where are you, Russell?"

"I'm home. I'm trying to get hold of a lawyer."

"There's no way I can get to New York tonight. The last train's already gone."

"I'll drive up and get you."

"You don't have a car."

"I'll borrow one. I'll get there somehow."

He arrives three hours later. She tells the dorm mother there's a family emergency, which no one questions: Russell shows his medical credentials. They drive through the December fog straight to the police station. They are told that Johnny is no longer there; he has been released into his father's custody.

"My father's in Cuba," Marian says.

"Afraid not, doll," the desk sergeant says. "He came right down here from Park Avenue as soon as he got the call."

"What call?"

"Not my department, sweetheart. Your brother was pretty shook up. Your father and your brother practically had to carry him out of here. I guess he's not the manly type."

"And I guess you're not the human type," Marian says. "I only hope that when someone you love is in trouble, you'll be treated just as you've treated me."

"Well, I see who wears the pants in your family," he says.

Russell takes her forcefully by the arm and whispers in her ear, "It won't do any good to sock him."

"It would do me immense good."

"You have to keep cool for Johnny. You have to be cool to protect him from your family."

She shakes herself like a dog getting out of a lake. Russell drops her at the Park Avenue apartment.

"If you need it, you have the key to Patchen Place."

She nods, but in her mind she is already in the family living room.

Vincent and her father are sitting in the two red brocade armchairs that flank the fireplace.

There is a fire blazing; they are drinking brandies; they are playing chess.

"Where's Johnny?"

"And hello to you, little sister."

"Where is he, for God's sake?"

"I've heard he has a lovely view of the river."

"What are you talking about?"

"Payne Whitney," says her father. "It's how I got him out of jail. I told them he had suffered a nervous breakdown, and his presence in that depraved place was a sign of his insanity. They agreed not to press charges because Dr. McNamara kindly arranged to have him admitted tonight."

"Daddy has consulted the best men in the field, and the consensus is that homosexuality is a form of insanity; the experts believe that shock treatments and some forms of medication are the only hope for a cure."

She runs in the direction of the door.

"Hold your horses, sweetheart," Vincent says. "You can't see him tonight. But don't worry. He'll still be there tomorrow."

"But I won't stay another minute with the two of you. The two of you are monsters. I wouldn't want to breathe the air the two of you have contaminated with your hatefulness."

Her father trains on her his famous baleful stare. "Have three months in a secular institution made you forget everything you stand for, everything we taught you to believe, everything most sacred to the Church and decent society?"

"If that's who you are, yes, and I thank God for it. Although, if it's your God, I won't even invoke his name."

She knows that she will never be the daughter of the house again. How is it possible, she wonders, that I feel nothing for these two but hatred? Flesh of my flesh. Bone of my bone. There were times she loved her father, admired him, enjoyed him. But for Vincent, she had never felt anything but fear and, later, fear mixed with contempt, most lately contempt only. What are we as a family, she wonders, that they can contemplate with perfect ease, sitting around the fire with their brandies and their chessboards, the ruination of a son and brother, the exile of a daughter and sister. Sure that it is done in the name of God. Because *they* know the truth. It is *their* truth, *their* property, *their* patrimony. It allows them anything; they can do anything in its name.

I do not love my father.

   My brother is a monster.

   Who am I?

   I am the one who saves the brother whom I love. I am the youngest, the strongest. I will not allow them to prevail.

She takes a cab to Patchen Place.

"They've committed him," she says, not taking off her coat. "He's in Payne Whitney."

"Jesus Christ. Your father must have set the whole thing up. Arranged the raid, then used his connections to make a deal. So Johnny can be turned into a zombie, so he can't be called a queer."

"They'll say they've done it so he won't lose his soul. Oh, I know just what they'll say. 'Better a man lose his life than his immortal soul.'"

Because Russell is a doctor and has friends at Payne Whitney, they are allowed to see Johnny the next morning.

In ten hours, Johnny has become someone she can't recognize. The beautiful grey eyes that always seemed to her like pebbles seen through the water of a clear stream are blank now. He can hardly focus. His smile is defeated. The overwashed pajamas he is wearing are too loose; they hang off his slight frame. His slippers are paper. He keeps falling asleep.

Russell speaks to the doctor in charge of the case and comes back to the room where Marian and Johnny sit holding hands. Marian doesn't let go of her brother's hand, even when he falls asleep. She's never seen Russell look so angry. He indicates that Marian should walk down the hall with him.

"They're going to give him his first shock treatment this afternoon."

Marian grabs Russell by the wrist so hard he pulls away and shakes his arm two, three, four times. "You've got to stop them, Russell. You're a doctor."

"Doctor, lawyer, Indian chief. I've got a lawyer on the case, but it seems your brother will be sent to jail unless he's given shock treatments."

"I'm sorry," says a nurse, not looking the slightest bit sorry. "We have to prepare your brother now."

"Prepare him for what?" Marian hisses. "Prepare him to have his mind destroyed?"

"I'm afraid, young lady, that you are overwrought, and we require an atmosphere of calm for our residents."

Johnny looks at them with a glance of stupefied desperation.

"We'll do everything that can be done. We're going to get you out of here," Russell says.

"So long, kids," Johnny says. "I'm awfully tired."

Marian goes to the hospital every day. She informs Vassar that there is an emergency, and she will have to be excused for the rest of the semester. The dean of students, hearing the words "Payne Whitney," with which she is all too familiar, is sympathetic.

"We'll be here when you're able to come back," she says.

Johnny now seems like a cheerful, dim child. Occasionally, Russell loses patience when he tries to remind Johnny of some happy memory and Johnny looks vague and says the sentence that is his most frequent: "I'm awfully tired."

After a week, they're told that Johnny will be allowed home for a few days in order to organize the things he will want to have with him for his prolonged stay. Because of Russell, because there will be "a physician on the premises," the doctor in charge releases him into Russell's care.

Russell makes childish, comforting foods, macaroni and cheese, blancmange, French toast for breakfast with real Vermont maple syrup.

The morning of Johnny's second free day, Russell kisses him goodbye. "I've got to go to work for a few hours. I'll leave you with the kid. But hers are the best possible hands."

"Her hands are beautiful, Russell, don't you think?" Johnny takes Marian's hands and turns them over twice, three, four times. "I always said she had the most beautiful hands. When we were little and I was upset, she'd put her hand on my forehead, and it always seemed so wonderfully cool. But sometimes there was grease under her fingernails, because she liked tinkering with cars. She loved cars. We loved our chauffeur, Luigi. Our father fired him because his brother was a communist. Our father did that, didn't he, Marian? Or am I getting it mixed up? I get so many things mixed up."

"No, you're absolutely right. I remember trying to argue with him, telling him that Luigi wasn't a communist, that his daughter was a nun, a Sister of Charity. And Daddy said, 'Thank God she, at least, has been saved.' But he wouldn't believe that Luigi wasn't involved. He said he was suspicious because Luigi never went to church. 'They hate the Church, they hate the truth, lies are what they love: they are the children of Satan, the father of lies.'"

"I suppose he really believed what he said. I guess that makes it better."

"Better than *what*? Our father has a lot of blood on his hands. Probably more than we know."

"Well, I've got to get some blood on my hands, that's what pays the rent," Russell says. "I'll be back early for cocktails."

It takes Johnny a very long time to shower and dress, but Marian is happy to see him spruced up and shaved, his hair combed, in grey flannel trousers, a light blue shirt, a blue-grey sleeveless vest, even a tie: a darker blue, solid, unpatterned. He hands her a piece of paper. "Listen, my love, I'm sending you out on a shopping spree. I need you to buy me some things at Abercrombie and Fitch. Lots of pajamas— elastic waist, no drawstrings, they think we'll hang ourselves with them. Try to find some slippers that aren't hideous: look for ones that are the most unlike Dad's that you can possibly find. A bathrobe. Don't let them talk you into a monogram, and, for God's sake, no paisley, you know I can't stand paisley, and I've been told I look best in blue."

She's happy to see him so animated. He hands her his wallet. "And stop off at Saks and get something nice for you. Take your time, don't worry about me, I'll be great."

She enjoys shopping at Abercrombie; it's so comically serious, so obviously about durability rather than fashion. When she buys the pajamas, the salesman says, "We had a call today from a woman who was complaining that the pajamas she had bought her husband had worn out. I asked when they'd been purchased. She said they were a wedding gift, so she guessed it was 1912. My supervisor said we should replace the pajamas immediately; we pride ourselves on being indestructible."

She doesn't know whether the salesman is telling her this because he thinks it's funny or because it's a point of pride.

At Saks, she treats herself to a pair of fur-lined ankle boots, the cuff a beautiful, soft black. It takes the salesman a long time to find the right pair; she wants the boots she's seen Myrna Loy wearing in a movie whose name she doesn't remember. Finally, he produces the boots of her dreams, and Marian leaves with a sense of her own discrimination and perseverance, her boots under her arm, Johnny's clothes to be delivered.

"YOO-HOO, Fashion Plate," she calls, closing the door with her foot, feeling the part of an actress in a screwball comedy.

He doesn't answer. She assumes he's sleeping, but she's eager to show him her new boots. She opens the door to his room.

He is hanging from a rope tied to the light fixture on the ceiling, the chair beneath his feet kicked away. She rights the chair and stands on it. She slaps the soles of his feet, as if he has fallen asleep and this will wake him up. "Johnny, wake up, Johnny, wake up," she screams over and over. And then she goes silent and steps down from the chair.

Her first thought is a concern for the problem of getting him down. The rope is thick; that's the first problem. She goes into the kitchen and gets the sharpest knife, the one they used to carve the Thanksgiving turkey, can it only have been a few weeks ago?

She believes it is essential that he not fall to the ground, that his face not be injured, that his beauty not be marred. She stands on the chair once again. She must saw through the rope carefully, so she won't hurt him by cutting his neck. She saws through the rope. What she doesn't reckon on is that, when the rope is cut, the body will be attached to nothing. She is holding him around the waist. The weight of his body knocks them both over, and they fall to the ground, he landing on top of her. Heavy. Dead weight. For a moment, she doesn't want to move, doesn't want to leave him lying on the floor.

Then she begins screaming. But her father's voice comes to her: "You must never cry out." She turns her brother's body on its back and covers him with a blanket. She phones Russell, who arrives, in seconds, it seems, with an ambulance.

They say nothing. They stand by the body, holding each other, rocking back and forth, a parody of a slow, amorous dance.

The ambulance drivers say that they can't take the body until the police arrive, and when they do, they enter the room slowly, tentatively, not at all like the policemen in movies. A minute later, they are followed by Marian's father.

He removes his hat and stands over the dead body of his son.

"Coward," he says. "He was never anything but a coward."

"Make him leave," Marian screams at the policeman. "Make him leave. He has no business being here."

"I have all the business in the world. I'm his father."

"You're his killer."

He turns to the ambulance drivers. "I believe my daughter has experienced a terrible shock. Perhaps you could administer a sedative."

"We're not doctors, sir," one says.

"I am," Russell says. "I'll take care of her."

"Just like you took care of my son," Patrick Taylor says through his strong, large teeth.

"We should get out of here," Russell says.

"I'm not leaving," Marian says. "I'm not leaving my brother alone with him."

And so they stand, like ice figures, until the medical examiner comes and Johnny's body is taken away. The absence fills the house, and Marian feels she will go mad with longing for the dead body of her brother. Her father says nothing as he follows the policemen down the stairs.

Then Russell hands her an envelope. "It's for you." He holds another in his hand, and puts it in his pocket.

"Where was it?"

"On the kitchen table. I didn't want it confiscated as evidence."

On the outside of the cream-colored vellum envelope, she sees her name in the beloved handwriting. She slits the envelope with her finger, making a ragged, inelegant opening: something Johnny would never do. But she can't imagine asking Russell for a letter opener.

She wants only to look at the black marks on the cream-colored paper, as if they were calligraphy in an alphabet she doesn't understand. She doesn't want to read the words, if reading means taking in, interpreting. These are the last words he will say to her, the last of him in the world.

My dearest girl:

I am so sorry that it will be you who finds me, but I must do this now while I am alone for the amount of time I need. Life is not good enough for me to live it. I have calculated the balance. Sorrow and suffering make up 90% of life. Joy or happiness, the other 10. But the materials aren't equal or even similar. Sorrow is rock, bedrock that forms at the bottom of the soul and cannot be dislodged. Happiness, joy are winds, unstable, fleeting. They have no durance. Sorrow is made of stuff that endures. My heart is burdened. Forgive me, my dearest little sister, I have thought of the pain to you. But asking me to live is like asking someone whose hand is in the fire not to pull it out. I must pull out my hand. You will have a rich life, I know it. You have always been the stronger of us two. The braver. Goodbye, brave girl. If I had another life,

I would save it, just for you. But I have only this one life, and
they are about to steal and destroy the thing I value most: my
mind. When they are done with me, there will be no more
music. I will be unable to concentrate, and concentration,
endless concentration, is what a musician needs. I would stay
alive for you and Russell if I could, but it is too difficult. Father
has always said I was a coward; he must be right. But I have
always loved you fully, purely, and above all things. I close
with this, the best of a coward's love. I know that it will hurt
Russell that our love was not enough. But love is not enough
when you no longer believe that you are real. I am unreal and
a coward, and they are about to take my mind. I hope that
somehow you and Russell will be a solace to each other.

Marian reads these words and knows that the life she has thought
of as her life is over now, that the person she was is dead, as dead as
her brother, and she wonders who she will be, how she will know
herself, by what name she will be called that she can answer to, what
the flavor will be of this thing she once called life, that she will have to
live, although right now she has only one wish: to be with her brother,
wherever he is. But he needs her now, to keep his memory, the true
image of him, which she must fight now to preserve. Fight against the
two enemies: forgetfulness, distortion. He has always needed her. She
is the stronger one. Which means, she supposes, that she is required
now to live.

•

She feels a hand on her arm, not gentle but not unfriendly. It is Marcia
Leavitt, almost a friend, a nurse from Pittsburgh.

"There's a meeting in the dining room now. Of all the women. You
need to be there."

"Yes, of course," Marian says, not saying what she would like to say: *Thank you, thank you,* she wants to say. *You have pulled me out. You have set me on dry land.*

There are twenty-four women on their way to Spain on the ship, and they are gathered in the dining room, six tables of four. Marian is grateful that Marcia Leavitt has saved her a place.

Ruth Lipsky, head nurse of the largest hospital in San Francisco, stands and claps her hands for silence. "Ladies, shall we all agree that, before we leave, we will present to the workers on the ship the lovely coats that our comrades, the furriers, have so kindly given us? It will be better not to have fur coats in Spain, and we will be bringing happiness to the wives or mothers or sweethearts of the workers who have made our journey so pleasant."

All the women clap. Not one disagrees. How wonderful they all are; Marian has never met people like them. Her new friends are the most wonderful people in the world. Once again, she knows the rightness of her choice in a new way, from the happiness she feels, the sense of rightness in her skeleton, in the sparkling nerves at the tips of her fingers. She is with people who look closely at the suffering of the world, with people who take the ideas she had, the vague ideas of a privileged girl, and make them real, turn them to actions.

But a few days before they land, Ruth says, "Let's face it, girls, the coats are falling apart."

Marian didn't want to admit it; at first, she wore the coat on deck in the early mornings or when the sun went down, all the girls did, and then, one by one, they stopped. No one spoke about it, but Marian assumed that what had happened to her coat had happened to the others'.

It is three in the morning, and she wakes from one of her dreams of Johnny. Not one of the frightening ones; a sad one this time. She's learned that she must, must get out of bed when the sadness over-takes her, or there will be no hope of getting back to sleep. She's taken to walking on deck; it's lovely there, watching the stars, the moon reflected in the ocean, making a path of light whose end stretches past the horizon. Her sadness stays but takes its place among the other sadnesses of the world, of all people who have mourned.

She moves to the closet to throw on some clothes; she doesn't want to turn the lights on, doesn't want to wake Russell. She reaches for her fur coat, which she will wear over her pajamas. She feels for her shoes.

Then the sole of her bare foot touches something that makes her scream in fear and disgust. She jumps back onto the room's one chair. Russell wakes. "What the hell?" he asks. She is mortified that he has discovered the one fear she has not been able to keep back: she has been horrified by rodents ever since, in her uncle Bill's cabin in the Adirondacks—she was eight or nine—she bent down to get something from the bottom drawer of a dresser and a mouse jumped out at her face. Since then even the sight of a rodent turns her into the kind of girl she has always despised. And now Russell knows.

"There's a mouse in my shoe."

He turns on the light, walks to the tiny closet, and takes her sensible brown penny loafer in his hand.

"Not a mouse, sweetheart. Nothing living. I'm afraid it's your coat."

He hands her the coat. She sees he's right.

The fur is falling out in patches, as if it had caught some disease on the ship.

"Go back to sleep," she says. "I'm going up on deck."

"Another dream?"

"Another dream."

He kisses the top of her head. But she sees that he's ready to fall back to sleep, and she's glad. Maybe he'll think he dreamed the fur in her shoe. Maybe he'll forget it. She won't mention it.

·   ·   ·

She throws the clump of fur into the ocean, so distressed that the kindness, the generosity of the furriers has come to this. And what of the plan of presenting fur coats to the workers on the ship, the lovely idea of giving them something they could use to surprise their sweethearts, their wives, their mothers? A lovely idea disintegrating, like the clumps of fur thrown overboard when no one was watching.

"I wonder what the hell animals they used," Marcia Leavitt says when Ruth acknowledges the problem with the coats. "Maybe they collected dead cats or sick rabbits."

Irene Rothman bangs her hand down hard on the table. "Our comrades did what they did from the nobility of their hearts, from their devotion to the revolution. Remember, you are here because you are on the side of the workers."

"I'm here because I'm a nurse," Marcia says.

The way Irene Rothman looks at Marcia frightens Marian. Growing up in her family, she knows a hunger to punish when she sees it.

"Enough, girls," says Ruth Lipsky. "Bring your coats here tonight, all of you, just after midnight. They will be redistributed."

At midnight, stealing away from their husbands' beds—those who have husbands—they drop their coats in a pile, saying nothing to each other, and then silently make their way back to their cabins, hoping they've not been seen.

No one wants to ask what Ruth Lipsky meant by "redistributed." They will present a united front.

Because they are united, in their devotion to the idea of a great new world, in their devotion to the cause of Spain.

AVONDALE, RHODE ISLAND, 2009

MARIAN won't hear a word against her granddaughter.

She's fond of her daughter-in-law, but Naomi, Amelia's mother, can be harsh. It's the other side of her remarkable gift for organization, the dark by-product of the fuel that powers her accomplishments. When she says to Marian, "Amelia's just so indecisive. It's not that she's lazy, no, I would never say that. It's just that she lacks—well, I don't know what to call it. Maybe *force*."

And Marian says, "Well, is it all so wonderful where it's gotten us as a species? Force."

And Naomi doesn't argue. She knows she won't win and, at ninety-two, Marian is just too old.

Amelia moved in with her grandmother a month after she graduated from UCLA. It seemed natural that when she graduated with no idea of what she would do next, she would move to Rhode Island to live with Marian, who was ninety at the time, but strong and vigorous, who welcomed the prospect of her granddaughter's moving in with a delight that made her clap her hands and say, "Oh, goody"—and she was a woman who would not ordinarily have taken up the words and gestures of a child.

Amelia lived her college years in a happy haze, majoring in Spanish because she'd lived in Mexico, gone to a bilingual school, and was so nearly fluent that she didn't have to work hard to do well in her classes. She made many friends and had a few lovers, not through any sense of urgency, but because sex seemed to her a kindly and pleasant thing to be doing, generous and enjoyable. When a man, a boy really, seemed to be wanting more from her—time, exclusive attention— she slipped the leash of her coupling and ran gently off, like a night creature who has found herself mistakenly spending too much time in daylight. Her friends remarked on her extraordinary ability to leave men with no residue of hard feeling. Occasionally, she would be accused of not really caring deeply for anyone; this accusation was usually leveled at her by a woman who had confided in Amelia and not been rewarded by return confidences of equal weight.

It wasn't that she failed to make deep connections. She loved her mother, although she occasionally found her "just too much"—too fast, too strong, too certain, too determined. She had loved her father with a clear, pure love that had run through her life like a stream; his death had neither frozen it nor clogged it. If his love was a stream, his death, when she was nineteen, had been a wound made by a cold knife that had pierced her through and through; she could feel, whenever she called up his face, the raw, tender place on her left side. Now he was gone, and there was one other person she could love with that kind of clarity. She loved her grandmother.

Marian was co-owner of a nursery, a large greenhouse with a half-acre growing field behind it. Her partner, Helga, was the same age as Marian. They insisted on coming to work as they always had, but they needed more and more help, although they hated admitting it. Reluctantly, they hired a young man—not so young by Amelia's standards, at thirty-five—a Nordic god who eats up all his summer wages on his long winter surfing holidays. Marian has grown very fond of him; Helga, despite her early misgivings, grudgingly admires him; both are dependent on his energy, his strength.

Helga fled Nazi Germany with her lover, Rosa. Rosa was a ballerina; Helga worked with her father in a factory that manufactured something Helga didn't like to talk about. She wasn't Jewish, she didn't have to leave, but Rosa was her love, and it was clear Rosa could not survive without support. If you wanted support, you would go to Helga; it was obvious from her posture, from the way she ate up the world with her long strides.

For fifty years, Helga and Marian had worked together, shoulder to shoulder. Partners in business. Dearest friends.

It is understood that Amelia will help in the nursery. But, in fact, she doesn't like working with plants. It isn't the hard, physical labor that she minds. She quite likes the digging; she enjoys dislodging deep stubborn rocks and roots. Nor does she mind getting her hands dirty. What she can't bear is the uncertainty, not knowing whether what you have planted will prosper or perish. The vulnerability of what goes into the ground hurts her. Storms could destroy it, cold rather than heat, dryness rather than the required wetness. Animals: deer, squirrels, chipmunks, overly greedy birds.

She is not, in any way, a person of faith. What small gift she had for it was crushed when her father died of the pulmonary hypertension he'd suffered from for years. A new procedure was performed; they were offered the possibility of a miracle. For a while, he seemed better. But there was no miracle; he died, suddenly, when she was thinking he was better than he had been for some time.

She can't focus on her work in the nursery because she worries for every seed she puts into the ground. Her habitual recourse when she's distressed is to become vague. When she helps her grandmother, she forgets where she is, loses things, can't remember what she has just done, doesn't hear when her grandmother says, "Bring this here," or "Carry that there," or "Water that gently at the roots."

Her grandmother sees it all. "This work doesn't make you happy," she says to Amelia during the first summer. And Amelia weeps hot tears of shame. She can't bear to disappoint her grandmother, and she knows it's a failure of her own spirit, a failure to connect, that has marked, and will go on to mark, her life.

But her grandmother doesn't seem upset. "You see, I understand. There are things one just doesn't have an appetite for. My family couldn't understand that I didn't love horses. It made them angry. But I loved other things. I was just crazy about cars. I learned how to drive early; I learned how to fix them. And, rather late, I came to love planting things. But you must never pretend to enjoy something you don't enjoy. And you must believe me that you'll find what you're meant to do. So I'll ask for your help when I really need it. Meanwhile, look for something else."

She works with her grandmother and Helga until the first frost. Then she takes a job in a bakery in Westerly that's trying to cultivate the business of the summer people and the folks who commute to Providence and the weekenders from New York. The Wildflower Bakery serves lattes and cappuccinos and espressos and each morning produces healthy muffins and unhealthy croissants and tarts and cakes and brownies and cookies: chocolate chip, oatmeal, peanut butter.

No one remembers when Amelia started doing the cupcakes.

She's often bored in the slack period between nine and eleven; she thinks the idea came to her then. There is a bowl of ordinary butter cream frosting on the counter. Rachel, who graduated from Brown six years earlier and works on large metal sculptures in her studio, an abandoned warehouse overlooking the canal, had been making a birthday cake for the child of one of their most regular customers. Alongside the large bowl of white icing on the counter are smaller bowls of pink, yellow, and blue, with which Rachel had filled pastry bags and created yellow, blue, and pink rosettes, squeezing the paste from a bag that ended in a pharmaceutical-looking nozzle. On the opposite counter are the cupcakes that Amelia is meant to frost with chocolate and then top with colored sprinkles. But she decides on a whim to frost the tops of the cupcakes with white frosting and rosebuds, bluebells, and buttercups squeezed from the pastry bag.

Rachel is amused. "Let's put them out and see what happens." All six of the cupcakes are bought within ten minutes of the entrance of the lunchtime crowd. Rachel encourages Amelia to branch out. On a trip to Providence, Amelia invests her own money in candied violets and silver leaf. Rachel sells the cupcakes at what they both believe is the exorbitant price of five dollars. People seem willing to pay. It becomes a fashion at gallery openings or official functions or up-market celebrations to serve cupcakes from Wildflower Bakery instead of a large cake. They're written about in *The Westerly Sun* and *The New London Day*. A reporter from *The Providence Journal* makes the trip. The Wildflower Bakery becomes, in its small way, famous, and Rachel knows it's because of Amelia. She offers to make Amelia a partner, but Amelia says no. "I feel guilty profiting from your talents," Rachel says, and Amelia blinks and smiles because the idea of profit from cupcakes seems funny to her and as far away as Andromeda or the North Pole. "At least let me give you a good raise," Rachel says, and Amelia blinks four times and says yes, that would be very nice.

Amelia never wants to eat the cupcakes. It isn't the taste of them she likes, it's the look of them, or the way people enjoy looking at them before they eat them. People say, "Isn't it painful to spend so much time on something and then have it disappear into someone's mouth?" And she blinks and says, "No, you see, that's why I like it."

If anyone asks Amelia—which they often do, she's twenty-four now—what exactly she's interested in, which means, what is she going to do with her life, when is she going to settle down to real work, preferably a real profession, she never says what she really means: "I'm interested in decoration."

Because she knows if she says that, she'll be misunderstood. They'll think she wants to fix up rooms, match drapes and slipcovers. Find the right sofa, the right lamp. But that isn't it. What she likes is adding little decorative touches. She doesn't want to make things; she thinks there are already too many things in the world. What she wants is to leave a mark that's a kind of greeting, friendly, encouraging. A mark with no future so she doesn't have to worry about its fate. By which she means its eventual destruction. Or its placement among the unloved objects of the world: resented, hidden, out of sight.

This was something she had learned not only from her father but from her mother. Her father was a potter. In his studio, she saw the stacked, unwanted pitchers, bowls, plates, mugs. At her mother's word, buildings were torn down, others put up. Urban planning, it was called. Her mother was an "urban planner." But she didn't like telling other children what her mother did, because she would have to say "mostly she gets things torn down." Her mother explained that some things got old, and they were not only ugly but dangerous, and they had to be torn down so that new, beautiful, safe things could be put up.

And so, it seemed wrong to devote any hope or love to things that were meant to last. Either as with her father's unwanted pots gathering dust in the basement, or the buildings her mother had torn down, they lasted too long. Or sometimes they were destroyed for no reason, or for reasons that were wrong, sometimes the most beautiful pots fell off the shelf and broke, or someone complained that her mother was responsible for the destruction of a treasure.

She waits till her mother comes for a visit to tell her that, in fact, she isn't working with Marian in the nursery, but in a bakery decorating cupcakes. Her mother makes that sucking sound that she makes when she's trying to keep back words that she knows will only make things worse.

"Don't take advantage of your grandmother's hospitality," she says.

And Marian snaps, "Oh, for God's sake, Naomi, it's not the Ritz, and she's not an indentured servant."

•

Marian knows that when she was younger, Naomi's age, fifty-seven, she might have been impatient with Amelia or someone like her. But she's ninety-two. One thing she knows about herself: with age, she got kinder.

It's certainly true that Amelia can be vague. She doesn't like saying what she thinks, or she'll say what she thinks if it can be understood as mere description: something that has no more weight than other descriptions. But her vagueness seems to Marian a desirable lightness; her seeming to skim over the surface of the world seems beautiful, like a bird skimming over the surface of the water. Vague. *Vague*, the French word for a wave. That's how Marian experiences Amelia's vagueness, a warm wave sluicing her tired skin, a wave that passes over dry stones and shells and turns them luminous and lovely. Sometimes, you think she's not seeing anything, and then, it's as if you're riding on a train at daybreak. You look out the window; at first there is only an unimposing greyness and then, gradually, a strange landscape shows itself, its lines sharper precisely on account of its recent invisibility.

She came to a new and, she believes, valuable understanding of Amelia when she was reading one of her hundreds of gardening books. She reads gardening books as some people read romances: now they're her most common reading; she doesn't really want to read anything new, certainly nothing that requires a radical recalibration of her understanding of the world. Gardening books and Trollope: that's her reading now.

She had been reading idly, thinking of planting something whose name as well as its properties had taken her fancy. When she turned the page, she found a section describing a plant that captured her imagination. "Love in a Puff," this one is called.

"Love in a Puff," she read. "Cardiospernum. Heartseed."

"Their color is so light," the writer went on, "it seems almost an illumination. The papery husk opens too easily. As it matures, the seed is joined to the plant by a thick attachment that is precisely heart-shaped. And the scar left behind when the seed frees itself is a beautiful, creamy white."

Love in a Puff.

Cardiospernum.

Heartseed.

Illuminated, fragile seeming yet containing in itself a black-and-white hardness—hardness, in this case, suggesting its most positive meaning: durability, something that can be counted on to do its work, to last. The separation that leaves behind a beautiful, heart-shaped scar.

Birds skimming over the water. Hidden landscapes. Waves. Plants. What is it about Amelia that makes Marian believe she can only be understood indirectly, using phrases that start with "like" or "as"? Similes. Similitudes. The direct view is not the true one, only a series of connections to other things helps her to understand her granddaughter better, she likes to think, than anyone else. This understanding, she believes, must be the truest form of love.

She tries to convey this when she says to Naomi, "Don't worry about Amelia. She's got something, maybe we haven't seen it yet, that's going to help her make her way."

And Naomi says, "Well, you're right, we haven't seen it yet. I guess we just have to believe."

"Blessed are they who have not seen and have believed." Marian stifles these words, will not let them escape her lips, Jesus's words to Doubting Thomas. So often, the echoes from a lost faith, a faith willfully and violently discarded, bob up, float up, unbidden, unwelcome, the flotsam and jetsam of a vanished way of life.

•

March 25th is one of the first days that can properly be called spring. It's been a hard winter, hardest on the old women: Rosa, the youngest, is eighty-nine. Marian and Helga, who have lived much of the last fifty years outdoors, have hardly been outside. Like dogs leashed almost beyond their endurance, they demand a walk, demand that Amelia drive them to the beach.

It is late afternoon. The sky is bluish violet; smoky clouds, thin as eyebrows, Amelia thinks, dissipate in the pastel air.

"The air has a chill," says Rosa, who was not entirely eager for the walk.

"Like a glass of ice water with the ice just taken out," Marian says. "My favorite kind of weather. Nothing has really begun, and so nothing is in the process of being over."

And Amelia thinks, with pride, I am descended from a woman who says things like that.

Walking up the dune, Amelia feels that they've entered a new climate. The chill in the air that Rosa and her grandmother spoke of seems to have disappeared. She feels the suggestion of a fog around her eyes; she watches the sky grow smokier, turns to the west, and watches what seems like a hole in the clouds grow larger, as if the sun had burnt it through.

Helga and her grandmother have gone ahead; Amelia allows Rosa to lean on her arm. She watches Helga's back and her grandmother's. They are a bit ahead, and if she didn't know them, their identities would be unclear. They seem to her not quite real, characters in a story, illustrations from a children's book. Nothing that she sees seems far; if there is disconnection, it can easily be bridged. There's nothing, she thinks, that can't be swum to.

She looks out over the inlet; the islands make a gap through which, in high season, boats sail. But there are no boats now, only this sense of an opening to an entirely desirable invisibility. Despite the heat that travels down her spine from the climb up the dune, Amelia knows it's winter. The beach grasses are dry, the branches of the squat rosebushes show uncomfortable-looking prickles that she knows would pierce her skin. The conifers are rusty, unbalanced by the winter winds.

She can hear the water, but the landscape seems more desert than seacoast. Having grown up in seasonless southern California, she never quite believes in seasonality. It always surprises her. Why should she believe that, by June, the beach roses will be pink, the grasses lush and green, then a metallic silver when the sun catches the drops of spray on their new curves?

Now everything is dormant, and she finds the dormancy restful. Nothing is being used. The only visible boat has been abandoned; it's a hull only, on its side, tied to a rock near the shore. She can't imagine that anyone will ever come for it, that it will ever sail again.

The fog thickens, and Helga and Marian disappear over the dune. Amelia can hear the sound of bells; she often hears them, but she can never remember their sources. She knows she's asked her grandmother, and her grandmother has told her, but it's the kind of thing she can't keep in her mind, and now she's embarrassed to ask again. She likes to believe that those bells signal the possibility of rescue.

At the top of the dune, Rosa asks if they can take a moment's rest. Amelia looks through the gap between the islands. She's never known what the islands are, if anyone lives there, what they're called. She likes it that the separation opens to an unknown destination; the unknown, rather than being frightening, seems to offer a possibility leading to something whose rightness she can sense but cannot see. Meme will go there, she thinks. Someday I'll lose sight of her as I've lost sight of her on the far side of the dune. She will be off somewhere, far off, a place that I can't follow. I must believe she will be happy. I must believe that it will be all right, as my father is happy, as for him everything is all right. Tears come to her eyes, and the islands blur, then come together, and then separate. Rosa sees her tears and leans more closely into Amelia's body, and she, too, is weeping. The tears are pleasurable to them both, coming easily, releasing something into the heavy air.

The wind has picked up. Amelia sees that Helga and her grandmother have crossed over the dune to the more sheltered part of the beach. The water there is nearly waveless; near the shore, there are pools of calmness and, in them, pastel reflections: blue, pink, violet—girlish colors, Amelia thinks. She looks at Rosa, her thin hair in its chignon, her rose-colored scarf, her pinkish lipstick. Her sunglasses: their rims a violet pink. She is still girlish, Amelia thinks, and I am probably, in all their minds, still a girl. Perhaps even in my own mind. She wonders when she will no longer think of the word "girl" in relation to herself.

Rosa and Amelia have caught up to Marian and Helga, who are standing at the foot of a high dune.

"I don't like this wind, let's continue alongside the lagoon," Helga says.

Amelia walks with her grandmother. Helga and Rosa link arms.

Something is going on in the lagoon.

"Whatever is that?" Rosa asks.

A man is standing in a canoe, wielding a paddle against a swan who flaps his wings with real, aggressive intent.

"I've always heard that swans could be dangerous, but I've never believed it," Marian says. "That fellow must be doing something to provoke him."

"Someone said a little boy had his arm broken by a swan in another part of Watch Hill," Rosa offers tentatively.

"Nonsense," say Helga and Marian, in unison.

But it's impossible to deny this swan's attempt to hurt the man in the canoe.

"I wonder if he is protecting something," Helga says.

The swan flies off and settles in the water.

"Look at him," Rosa says. "Something has made him ashamed."

"I don't think birds feel shame, my dear," Helga says.

Marian walks closer to the water. "Whatever are you doing?" she shouts to the man in the boat. She has never lost the diction, the timbre of privilege; always, her voice has been one that assumes it will be listened to. But Amelia knows that if anyone suggested that to her Marian would react with furious denial.

The young man in the boat takes his cap off. Amelia thinks he might be ready to bow. "It's an environmental project, ma'am. The mute swans here are overpopulating, and they're a threat to the native species, particularly the wild geese. The swans are overeating the various flora, so they're starving out several other species and upsetting the ecological balance. They're not native, you see, the swans, they were imported when this place was first turned into a resort, and they're very clever, very cunning, so they've pushed the natives out."

"Whatever were you doing with that paddle?" Marian asks.

"Well, we're approaching the nest so we can addle the eggs."

"'Addle,'" Helga says. "I don't understand that word."

"If we can get to the eggs and just shake them a little, or sometimes coat them with mineral oil, or just puncture their shells, the mother will sit on them, but they won't hatch. This controls the population without any harm to the adults. They only lay eggs once a year, and if you can control the eggs for one year, you've controlled the population for that whole year."

"Control," Helga says. "Oh, yes, your kind is very fond of control."

Rosa stands behind her, looking frightened.

"Control usually means the use of some kind of force against a weaker creature," Marian says. "I would say your brandishing the paddle is proof of that."

"Ma'am, I'm a wildlife specialist. I've devoted my life to birds. I don't do this work so I can hurt them."

"And yet," Marian says, "you are."

"It's a controversial enterprise," the young man says. "You're welcome to come to our headquarters and read our literature."

Amelia looks at the young man. He's blushing; he's beginning to stammer. She feels sorry for him. She feels sorry for the swan, looking so abashed. She's worried about Rosa. She's worried about the Canada geese, whose flight she loves to watch, their strong V such a sign of ardent, steadfast progress. She likes what she's heard about them, that every flock has leaders by turns, that the lead bird, the one at the narrow point of the V, only leads until she's tired, and then she's replaced. She likes what she's heard about swans, too, that they're monogamous, that the males are involved in the incubation and rearing of the young. She wishes they'd never come to this place, that they'd walked somewhere else, or at some other time. But she knows what her grandmother would say: "You can't pretend not to have seen what you've seen."

She remembers seeing a swan dead by the shore, stretched out, its whiteness sullied by the sand, its neck no longer beautiful in its length, but snakelike in its deadness, not suggesting dance or flight, but an excess, an asymmetry, an imbalance. Its beak was orange and ugly; its dead black eye stared: baleful, accusing, stupid. She had wanted something, someone, or a huge wave to take the bird away, out of her sight.

For a moment, no one speaks, and the young man twists his cap in his hands in what seems to Amelia an almost clichéd show of unhappiness. She doesn't know what will come next, but she knows that Helga and her grandmother won't let go. Until something has happened upon which they have left their mark.

Marian is all for driving immediately to the wildlife center at Kettle Pond to protest in person what they've seen. Helga says they're better off "doing their homework," which means they'll need Amelia.

Although Amelia is hardly adept with computers, Marian and Helga are so easily frustrated when they go on the computer that they refuse to use it for anything they consider important. Rosa has never even turned one on. The three women will spend some days in the library first; there, they are comfortable, particularly in one room they are all fond of, with a stained-glass window of an Indian in a canoe, oak-paneled walls, and carved refectory tables for reading and writing.

A week later, they've organized a thick folder. Helga spreads it on her dining room table; Rosa has made a leek and potato soup. She doesn't sit with Helga and Marian at the table; she carries things back and forth from the kitchen, and Amelia stands at the stove, stirring zabaglione, which will be served with raspberries Helga froze the summer before.

"How to think about this," Helga says, "without being sentimental. The damn swans, all the romance around them, all that encrusting of the dim romantic past."

Amelia hears the sound of breaking glass. And then a scuffling of chairs, and then the sound of weeping.

"Don't you hear it, don't you hear it, what they're saying about the swans? Doesn't it remind you of what they said about . . . about us . . . ? Don't you remember when I danced the swan, and then we had to leave, they wanted to destroy me, they wanted to destroy us all, it was the same things they said about us, what they're saying about the swans: we were clever, we were exotics, we were stealing the natives' proper birthright."

Amelia has seen it before: Rosa's past can descend on her, crashing around her, and she is lacerated by the shards. Helga's life has been devoted to protecting her. She says something in German and Rosa quiets down.

"They hate what is beautiful," Rosa says. "The brutes of the world, they hate what is beautiful, what they cannot buy or sell or put to use."

Marian stands up. "Well, we're not going to let them, are we, honey? We're going to keep the beautiful birds safe."

And so begins the organizing of the usual willing few, the signs, the picketing of the wildlife sanctuary, contacting the local newspapers, the local television. The three old women carrying the beautiful posters Rosa made: art nouveau swans surrounded by teal-colored reeds and mauve beach roses. The three old women shaking their fists, Helga and Marian shouting, Rosa politely murmuring, "Save the swans."

Amelia feels sorry for the workers at the wildlife sanctuary. Alongside the three striking old women, they can only seem coarse and callous. Amelia has grown fond of the young man, Scott Ricardi, who stammers and blushes when the microphone is put in front of him. She believes that he has a point. She also believes that the old women have a point. She doesn't know who she believes is right. But she knows she will stand with her grandmother.

One night, Amelia expresses her disquiet to her grandmother. It is the first warm night of the year, and she has unwisely opened a window, but she can't bear to close it—that seems such an unhopeful gesture.

"Of course, I know what you mean," Marian says, "but I learned a very long time ago that if you wait for the perfect action, you'll never act. In a situation like this, all you can do is the least bad thing. And be truthful about the cost of what you've done, of what's been brought about, or allowed to come about, for which, you must also understand, you are responsible. And besides, ideas aren't things that float in the air, they're connected to people. So, for Rosa, there is no question: the swans represent the whole of her past to her, what was destroyed, what she lost. And the sides are no longer equal, because someone I love weighs in on one side."

Amelia sits on the floor at her grandmother's feet. She puts her head in her grandmother's lap. I will never be as good as you, she thinks, as wise, as courageous. I will never be the woman you are. I may never be anything but some version of a child.

"Meme, I only hope I can be like you someday." She has always had only one name for her grandmother, the name from her childhood—Meme, pronounced *may-may*, which later seemed appropriate because whatever she asked her grandmother for was easily given.

Marian, not gently, moves Amelia's head from its position on her lap. "Nonsense, you don't want to live the way I've lived. You don't want to make the mistakes I've made. You don't want to cause the harm I've caused."

"Harm?"

"That's for another day. I'm rather tired."

Amelia is curious, but she won't ask anything. For as long as she can remember, her mother has told her that Meme doesn't like to talk about herself, that Naomi knows very little about her background. "That generation has a fetish for privacy. They resent any intrusion on it."

And she knows that when you live with someone, it's important to know what not to ask.

SPAIN, 1937–38

LANDING AT LE HAVRE, Marian and Russell board a train, still in the company of comrades, to Paris. They will stay in Paris for five days, and Russell is delighted, because he's never been abroad. But Marian's been abroad too many times with her parents, and she doesn't want to be anyplace where she has been with them. This is a new life, a new way of being alive; to be seeing the sights she saw during the old life is a penance, an encumbrance. She tells Russell it is her first time, too, and she pretends she's seeing things only through his eyes, and she believes she isn't lying when she says she's never been to Paris because the person who went to Paris is not the person she is now; that old self, that old body, that old skin covering the old heart, heavy and full of anger and sadness: she has sloughed all that off. That sort of lie is called, in the language of the catechism, a "mental reservation." So, for example, if, when the Fuller Brush man rings the bell and asks, "Is your mother home?" and, knowing your mother is home, you say, "My mother isn't home," if you say in your mind, "She isn't home to you," it's not a sin. Because you have made what is called a "mental reservation." But all that is her past; now she is named Rabinowitz, and she is going to Spain to save the world from fascism. She is not her parents' daughter. Perhaps she has never been.

They travel with two English journalists to Valencia. First by train to Toulouse, and then by bus over the Pyrenees, then to Barcelona, then they will be met and travel by truck or jeep or some other kind of motorized vehicle to Valencia.

They make their way over the Pyrenees. She thinks she has never seen a more beautiful place. The sea comes right up to the mountains, and, more than ever, she knows she is right to be here, to do what she can to save this beautiful country. She tells herself to look closely, to remember a landscape unravaged, because soon she will be seeing nothing that has not been ravaged. She hopes for a time when she won't have to be telling herself what to think, what not to think, what to remember, what not to remember. A time when there will be no time for thought: only one action after the other, each one important. She is here because there is a war, a war in which one side is the side of justice and one the side of brutal greed.

They arrive in Barcelona, and there is no more exaltation; there is horror at the sight of the devastated children wandering a bombed-out city looking for parents, old people looking dazed, carrying all their possessions in a tied-up tablecloth. One old woman carries a teapot as if she is looking for a safe place to put it down. Marian sees another kneeling in what must have been the courtyard of her house, digging for something with a silver fork.

There are barricades everywhere. The streets are full of rubble, covered with a rust-red dust the color of the inner organs of animals she refused as a child ever to eat.

Now the arguments she heard on the ship become not trivial but life and death. Literal life and death, because everyone talks of people they have seen killed: anarchists killing communists, communists killing anarchists. There are anarchist cafés in which some of her friends insist that the structure of everything—work, art, love—must be changed or else you will only replace one form of oppression with another. In other cafés, Stalin is toasted, and the anarchists are suspected of being secret allies of Franco. Most of her friends are communists; she meets anarchists who also seem like friends, but the communists call the anarchists enemies and the anarchists call the communists tyrants. "Feverish" is the word that comes to her mind when she listens to conversations. All of them begin benignly: friends are toasted, the fascist name is mentioned, and everyone spits on the ground. But the good spirits gradually heat up, and this frightens her: We are all fighting the same enemy, she thinks. Why, she wants to ask, why are you wasting time on what are only family squabbles?

But she says nothing because she is a woman, a wife, an American, and she has just arrived. She wonders whether it happened when she became someone's wife, that she became reluctant to speak, she who always prided herself on saying the difficult thing, who was not afraid of standing up to anyone, saying her piece, holding her ground. Or is it that, here in this world where so little now is comprehensible, she has become the docile child she never was?

Russell isn't silent; he has no patience with the anarchist argument. He's with his fellow communists: "We're fighting a war, for Christ's sake," he says. "The other things will follow when we win. If we win."

"Don't you see," says a young man named Juan, with small hands and feet that do not match them: they are large and clumsily booted. He has just bought them drinks. "Don't you see, here we have created a worker's paradise; see, no one is dressed in suits or high heels, no one calls anyone Señor or Señora, everyone is wearing simple, comfortable clothes, there is no more tipping. And by the way, my dear American friends, I would get rid of those hats."

"Why?" asks Russell, impatient, indignant.

Their new anarchist friend Juan begins to plead. He has tears in his eyes. "Please, please don't wear those hats. This is a very anarchist city. People can be shot for wearing hats; it's considered a sign of bourgeois hierarchy, a betrayal of the new worker's state."

·   ·   ·

That night, they walk hand in hand through the ruined city, carrying, not wearing, their beautiful hats.

Russell's mother's matching hats. She made them herself. Her wedding gift.

Perfect hats.

What a lot of hats Russell had ... many more than she did. But, of course, his mother was a hatmaker. And he cared about clothes much more than she did. She teased him about it, and he made fun of himself. "Beau Brummelberg," he said. "The Jewish Marxist dandy."

Shantung straw, Russell's mother had said, foldable. She wanted them foldable so they could be packed easily in the one bag they would take to Spain, could be carried in their pockets when they got there. "It will be important when things are really grim to have one beautiful thing, one elegant thing that you can put on, get courage from. Wear them in good health; I'm proud to call you my daughter," she said.

They were married in city hall in their matching hats. Only Russell's family was there; his sister and brother-in-law were the witnesses. When they got home to Patchen Place, Russell insisted on carrying her over the threshold, and they giggled at the absurd spectacle. They were a little drunk; they took everyone out for steaks and martinis.

When they walked in the door, they saw the letter from Marian's father saying that she was disowned, and her only place in his life was in his prayers. They put the letter in the big amber glass ashtray and set fire to it, and Russell made them more martinis, and they fell into bed laughing: this was their wedding night.

"Do you think Juan might be exaggerating about the hats?" Russell asks now.

"Let's not take the chance," Marian says.

The next day, they walk to the beach. At the shore, they stand on the seawall. They take off their perfect hats, their beautiful hats. They kiss their hats goodbye and throw them into the sea. They watch them floating for a minute, so jaunty and playful, as if they're just going for a little swim, and then, suddenly, they are gone. Marian cries, although she loved the hats less than Russell did, and Russell says, "Forget it, toots. It's our first sacrifice for the cause."

She is exhausted and numbed by the ride in the truck over the rough roads to Valencia. This is where her real life will begin; she doesn't have time to worry about comrades fighting among themselves as she did in Barcelona. Now she will be helping Russell treat the wounded in the hospital named after the heroine La Pasionaria. Marian likes the idea that the name of the hospital brings to mind: the Hospital of Passion, the Passionate Hospital. Bobbing up is the flotsam of an old, violently discredited life: the Passion of Christ. Which she will not allow to penetrate the surface of her brain; it is an infection that must be drowned, burned, or cut out.

She never learns, because she doesn't know whom to ask, what the hospital was before it was a hospital. A school? A convent? Something institutional, the large open windows letting in sometimes too much sunlight—you don't want to see too clearly what you have to see, the wounds, the ruined faces.

The largest room, a ward with nearly a hundred beds, iron bedsteads next to one another, as in a dormitory. But here there are no healthy sounds of schoolchildren, here there are cries of pain, groans of despair, cutting through the air in several languages to say, "I'm dying, I know that I am dying." A room but almost not a room, in any case a room like no other room: behind the beds there are glimpses of diamond-shaped, indigo tiles; the floors are tiled, too, but the patterns are obscured by a hundred feet, by beds, by medical equipment. And always there is something that must urgently be done, so the eye cannot afford the luxury of simple looking. Only sometimes when she is on night duty and the room is silent, except for the moan of someone whose pain has outstripped sleep, does she say to herself:

This is a room something like other rooms; here is the ceiling, the walls, the floor. But then a moan transforms itself into a cry and she has to get a nurse, who comes rushing.

The stink from gangrene is the worst. And then, the unbearable sights: guts open to the air, sores putrefying with maggots in them. Worst of all is the exhaustion, the bone-crushing exhaustion, exhaustion like a magnifying glass that enlarges and distorts, the constant ache behind the eyes, the lids demanding to be closed and the struggle against them: no, you will not close, you will not close. If she falls asleep doing something essential, the consequences will be enormous. For days she longs for sleep as someone might long for water or food or love, which she has never yet longed for, as she has never been in love, has never been seriously attracted to anyone because she has known almost no possible men. Her brothers' friends are bullies or brutes, or the nice ones are on their way to drinking themselves to death. Johnny's friends, whom she occasionally dreamed over, never seemed interested in her in that way, and later she would understand why. And after Johnny's death, she believed it impossible that her heart would ever open to anyone again.

Besides the physical exhaustion, there's the exhausting rage at the shortage of supplies, the having to make do against impossible odds: operations done when the power goes out, which it often does, by everyone making a circle with flashlights or, when the batteries run out, with candles. Rewashing bandages until they fall apart, having to ration sniffs of ether so the men have respites only from unbearable pain, and she thinks perhaps that is worse: the shock of reawakening.

And hunger, something she never imagined for herself, a hunger so fierce that food becomes not only an obsession but a terror. She dreams not of sex or of flying but of food: she dreams of the new bread their cook baked in her parents' kitchen in Newport; she dreams she lifts the white towel from the warm loaves and strokes them, as she would the flesh of a lover or a child.

She fears most of all that she will do something unforgivable for food: suppose she fights a child for a crust of bread, suppose she steals a piece of cheese from a dying man. Oddly, oranges fall everywhere, carelessly, as if what happens to the ground they grow in is of no concern to them. You pick them up from the street; often they are bitter or half rotten, but you salvage what you can, and you are very, very grateful for the fallen fruit.

She has had very little training, a course in first aid. She trains with the young Spanish girls, girls leaving their villages for the first time. One of her skills is her fluency in Spanish; she doesn't tell anyone it's because her father moved the family to Argentina for two years, thinking he might invest in beef cattle, bringing back with them to America two servants: a gardener and his wife, who would be their nanny. She loves Pablo and Jacinta; she keeps her Spanish up out of love for them, choosing to study Spanish rather than French in the Convent of the Sacred Heart in Noroton, so she makes friends with the Spanish-speaking girls, who are considered a bit overexcitable, a bit louche. She will never say: I learned Spanish from my servants. No one needs to know, because it is a new world, everyone is equal now, there are no servants and masters, no rich and poor. Everyone is the same; everyone is equal. The girls' hands smell wonderfully of oranges, but they apologize for it, for coming back from picking oranges from the trees around their houses, which are still, miraculously, intact. They think it is more honorable to be learning to bind the wounds of fighting men than to be picking oranges, which anyone might do, anyone not devoted to the revolution, to saving the world.

The bombing: another new way of being alive, a new way of being alive that is impossible to make sense of, because time means nothing that is in any way familiar. Everything seems to be happening at once; events pile up on top of one another like the stones from the destroyed buildings. Always your mind is tumbling over itself; you forget what came first, whether you saw the boy with the green eyes screaming for his mother on Tuesday or Wednesday. She wants to write to her family: I have seen what liars the fascists are; they say they never bomb civilian sites, but I can tell you they do because today I saw a line of children waiting for their ration of milk and bread, laughing, pushing and punching each other like other children, and then the bomb fell on them and I saw spilled milk on the pavement, rose colored, mixed with blood, loaves of bread beside an arm, an amputated leg. And always people running, running holding their children, old people trying to run to something, from something. They lie that the city of Guernica was not bombed by them, but set on fire by anarchists, a bold-faced lie, my family; the planes are German, they are Hitler's planes. But Marian knows what her father would say: anything is better than godless communism. Always the two words yoked together "GODLESSCOMMUNISM": no separation possible.

She is doing many different things because she is trained for nothing. Mostly she carries stretchers. And was it a Tuesday or a Wednesday that she saw the child with its head on its dead mother's breast, a girl child, maybe four or five, her skirt up around her head so you couldn't see her face, but you could see the sex, so vulnerable, but lovely, a little cleft, like a clean, washed-up shell. Marian couldn't bear that people would be looking, so the first thing she did, before she checked the pulse (though she knew the child was dead), was to pick her up gently as if she were her mother, or as if she were reassuring the mother, and then to pull the child's skirt down so she is modest in her death, so she will not be looked at in a way that dishonors her further. But what's the difference? She's a dead child, a murdered child, what's the possible meaning of honor? But she will not let the child be shamed in death.

Was it the same night, or another night, that they all went to the café, everyone who worked together? It was full of ordinary people, families with children. Do Spanish children ever sleep? she wonders. When do they sleep in peacetime? One little girl sat in her mother's lap. In her hair, there was a blue ribbon, elaborately tied, though the child had hardly any hair at all, and the material of the mother's dress was so thin that the word that came to Marian's mind was "sleazy"; that is the sound for what the cloth looks like. It could just fall apart or be ripped in a second. The husband said to Marian, "What upsets my wife the most is she can't get any thread now to mend the baby's clothes, and the baby is active, she is tearing up all her clothes." Old couples held hands as if to reassure each other that it's worth surviving. Courting couples kissed with a desperation that seemed almost like anger. The waiter said to her and Russell, "Americans love ice in their drinks. I have got some ice." And he produced two grey, corrugated ice cubes and some whiskey.

The door to the café opened, and a man walked in singing in German. He was carrying another man on his shoulders; the man had lost his legs. Everyone toasted them.

She learns that it is better if the bombing is at night because then it can seem unreal, almost theatrical, but in the day, you have to see the faces and the frantic running, from something, to something, you never know what. But to say it is better is the consequence of needing to believe that horrors are relative: that an instant death is better than a prolonged one, that a night raid is better than a daytime raid because at night you cannot see the faces. But a nurse named Jo from Montreal hates the night raids more. I know, she says, that for the rest of my life I'll hate bright white lights.

There are moments of what could be called normal life. Even an entertainment committee, which organizes dances in which the young Spanish girls dance with each other and the pale northerners, unabashed at not knowing the steps, hold each other, bobbing up and down like rowboats on a choppy lake. On some streets, you can see into houses whose roofs have been blown off, whose windows have been shattered. She sees a woman watering a plant; she sees a canary in a blue painted cage. A dressmaker, hungry for customers, rushes out onto the street when she sees American nurses, saying, "Angels of Spain, let me make for you something lovely," and thrusts on them fashion magazines, a decade old.

Marian and Russell even play bridge with other couples. There are only two couples close to their age; one is an English couple, a nurse and a dentist. Marian is very fond of Lydia Wentworth; without speaking, they recognize they were both privileged girls. Knowing that she will understand, Lydia says to Marian one day, "When I think of how hungry I am all the time, how I'd eat almost anything, I remember when I was in boarding school in France and I refused to eat French cheese; I would go into the woods and vomit it up every time. I asked my mother to tell them I would only eat cheddar. They wrote back to my mother, 'When she is with you, she is yours. When she is with us, she is ours.'"

This is the only time Lydia says anything specific about her past. Her husband, Len Wentworth, is the son of a miner, the first in his family not to have gone down into the pits; he is a man as silent as Marian has ever known. She works hard to resist the temptation to confide in Lydia, to tell her the truth about her marriage, but she is loyal to Russell; if he is not really her husband, he is really her closest friend.

"It's a good thing there are only two couples allowed in a bridge game, because the Wentworths would never agree to sit at the same table with the Levins," Russell says one night after the Levins insist they have drinks after the game.

If the Wentworths are a near caricature of British reticence, the Levins enact, daily, suspicions about Jewish volubility, Jewish volatility. Katie Levin has no trouble talking to nearly everyone about Sy's sexual problems. She says she just asks everyone in case they have advice: Sy is a premature ejaculator. When she approaches Marian, she stops herself and says, "Of course, you were probably a virgin when you married Russell. You probably have no experience at all." Marian would like to say, "I still have no experience. I am still a virgin."

Katie is a singer; she has lived in Spain for more than a decade, studying flamenco music. Sy is a neurosurgeon, trained at Johns Hopkins. Katie is given to fits of weeping and then fits of gaiety, to which, despite herself, Marian feels drawn. Gaiety is hard enough to come by; whatever the source, it seems, in its rarity, a valuable commodity. Katie says that her most prized possession, which she has held on to despite everything, is three washcloths. "One for my face, one for my armpits, one for my nether parts. I insist on fastidiousness. What I mean to say is: I insist on not stinking." And Marian worries, for the first time, baths or showers being a luxury, if, in fact, she stinks.

Marian and Russell worry about Sy's dramatic changes of mood. He is a brilliant surgeon, but occasionally Russell covers for him, on those days when he says he is unfit to operate and would not trust himself with a scalpel. Like his wife, he is not reluctant to speak about his past, about the circumstances of his conception. His parents were Russian and in one of the endless pogroms his mother was raped by a Cossack and infected with syphilis. A rumor was circulating at the time that pregnancy could cure syphilis; dutifully, his father impregnated his mother and Sy was born. Of course, the pregnancy and the birth were no cure, and Sy grew up beside an invalid mother who died when he was ten, and a father whose depressions ended in his years in a mental hospital.

Marian finds Sy endlessly interesting. He speaks seven languages; he knows music and physics and ancient history; he gets bored with conversations that don't veer from the political. He makes Russell laugh; one night he sings a song in a mock Yiddish accent: "Oh the cloak makers' union is a no-good union ... The right-wing cloak makers and the socialist fakers are making by the workers double crosses." Another one, all in Yiddish, called "Shiker Is a Goy," is about a drunken Christian who pisses in the window of a Jew's house. Marian sees Sy's vulnerability, as she saw Johnny's, and she is frightened for him; she wishes that Katie were more dependable, less prone to name-dropping—her father is a theatrical agent in New York.

Marian and Russell assumed that Katie and Sy are married, but one day they ask if Marian and Russell would accompany them to the American embassy in Madrid so they can be legally married. "There's a good chance I'll die here, and I need her to be married so she can collect my life insurance," Sy says.

They don't enjoy their time in Madrid; shells fall everywhere, sirens pierce the air the whole time they are there.

But their return to Valencia worries Marian and Russell for the Levins in a new way. The most die-hard party members castigate them for insisting on a bourgeois marriage. Sy is warned that his irregularities have been observed.

"Sy is almost determined to ruin himself," Russell says when Sy makes a remark after Marty—the French commander of the International Brigades, known to be an intimate of Stalin's—insists that all the women wear regulation nurse's uniforms, instead of the comfortable overalls they have adopted. "I thought this was a war, not a fashion show," Sy says.

Russell takes his arm and says, "Let's get out of here, pal," and the two couples take themselves to a café, where Sy can rail in what they hope is relative safety, and Katie fixes her makeup using a small gold compact she always seems to have with her.

Despite the horrors, sometimes there are moments when the beauty of the world, the miracle of drawing breath, can pierce her, and some rind is pulled back, some skin exposed, vulnerable, like the skin after a burn. And she feels her eyes filling with tears simply because she is alive, with tears for the Spaniards she works with, full of ideals, giving everything, and the others from all over the world, giving up their lives for what they know to be the truth.

She and Russell go to the railroad station, which has, miraculously, not been bombed.

It presents, despite everything, the possibility of holiday pleasure: the murals made up of small mosaic tiles. Flowers, fruits, women carrying baskets on their heads. The windows are Moorish in shape; the panes are midnight blue, separated by stark white mullions. Columns support the ceiling: lime and peach with gold borders. The roof is glass—a crystal palace—and the light it lets in always seems joyous.

"You see, Russell," she says, "this is why we're here, because there is something good in human beings, something that wants ornament, that wants blue glass and pink and green tiles that turn into flowers, all that work, just to say life is good."

"There was money for it then," he says. "Maybe it should have been going into the mouths of the workers."

It's the only time she gets angry at him. "Why do you have to smash the hopeful things? Why do you have to spoil the moments that let us make sense of being alive?"

"It's who I am. There are things I refuse to forget."

She knows what he means: so often she makes herself forget what happened to her brother, and she knows that underneath the forgetting there is a remembrance that is her life.

And so she walks the streets of Valencia without Russell, because she can't stand to hear what he says about the buildings: she loves them; she's lost too much; their lives, their work are too difficult; she won't allow these moments to be stolen from her. Even by the person she loves most in the world, the only living person she can say with any truth she loves at all.

It is her first time walking alone in a city. Even in New York, she always seemed to be accompanied. She didn't love Park Avenue, with its looming luxury. (*Ours is the penthouse. We have a rooftop garden—our own park. But then, the whole avenue is really a garden, isn't it?*) Her love for downtown was a public love: faces, gaits, smells so various, demanding to be shared. And in the cities she traveled to with her parents, she was overdressed, overwatched, overlectured: everything was pointed out, nothing left to her own eye to choose. Look at this—no, not that, *this*. Here she can mourn and shudder at the horrors she has just come from seeing. The orange trees, the posters proclaiming the triumph of the workers; these are hers, no one need tell her how to understand them. She loves even what would seem unworthy to be loved: the whores with their overly made-up faces, offering caresses in the name of the revolution; the children, much too young for it, selling sugar water that would quench no thirst. Because she has worked here as she has worked nowhere else, she has a right, she believes, to inhabit this city as she had no right to inhabit anything that might suggest the Taylor wealth, the Taylor privilege. In this horror-stricken city, she has, for the first time, placed herself at home on earth.

She understands why Russell dislikes the *modernista* architecture. If what pleases you are the spare lines of the new buildings of New York, the lacy facades of Valencia would seem at best frippery, at worst trash. Perhaps none of the comrades would approve if she said she enjoyed the half-mad rococo facade of the Ceramics Museum: gods lounging in extravagant indolence, bruisers curled in on themselves like sleeping babies, draped in girlish leaves and lace. They would point to the striking beauty of the skyscraper, the rightness of Bauhaus. But why, she wants to ask them, why do you have to choose? Can't you be thrilled by the Empire State Building and also love the Ceramics Museum? She wants to tell them that they remind her of her father and his implacable insistence on orthodoxy of taste. She wants to tell them: Don't you see it is the cause of sorrow? Saying,

If this, then not that. Why, she wants to ask, can't you have some of both? But she knows that, when life and death are at stake, you can't afford that kind of soft middle. Of course, she knows that the decorative richness of the ornamented buildings is based on slave labor. She supposes that knowledge should render them to her unlovable. But it does not, and there is no one with whom she can share her troubled loves.

Particularly not her love for the smiling stone angels on the cathedral facade. She doesn't love the cathedral's interior, and she hasn't the slightest shred of anything but rage-filled aversion for the Church as an institution. But the angels, the calm saints, their impassive, half-smiling faces: is it wrong for her, in her daily exhaustion, in her despair at the suffering she has been able to do so little to assuage, is it wrong to look just for a moment at those cool, sweet expressions and to believe that someday, it will all be over, someday, life will go on in a way that these stone faces might recognize?

Above all, there's no one she can talk to about what she feels when she goes into one of the churches that have become a hostel, sheltering people who have lost their homes in the bombings or the fires after the bombings, in the chaos of everything blown up. The churches have been opened up to these people, and of course it is a good thing, of course it's right that the endless side altars should become miniature apartments where families can sleep and eat together, of course it is right that the altars should be covered with all available food—never enough—set out there so people can take what they need back to their small alcoves or to the pews they have turned into beds. Of course it's good, of course she's glad. And yet, she's troubled by the incessant noise. Once she came into a church looking for quiet and found it had been turned into a stable. She saw a horse eating from a bucket on the main altar; she stepped over dung on the cool, stone floor. Of course it was good, of course it was right, and she knows she's wrong to feel this sense of loss, that a whole category that, without her knowing it, had been important to her—the sacred—is quite useless now, entirely gone.

•

Russell is becoming more and more difficult, more and more irritable. He's lost his dark humor. She tells him about the signs the new earnest Welsh head nurse has put up in the wards, which caused her and Lydia Wentworth a fit of almost punishable giggles. "Promiscuous use of adhesive tape can lose us the war." And he looks away, as if she were speaking a dialect he no longer cares to use. Even a few hours stolen by the water seem to bring him no pleasure. A day of swimming along the gentle coastline is ruined for him by a story told to them by their Valencian driver. As they pass through a woods, the driver says, "My uncle, who owned a factory, was shot here by the anarchists. My other uncle, a socialist school teacher, was shot in the same place by the Nationalists."

When Marian praises the calm waves: "It's so different from the fierce Atlantic waves," Russell says. "Perhaps the people have sucked the ferocity out of the air and taken it into their own lungs."

The endless political arguments get to him in a way they don't get to Marian because she never takes part in them herself. When she says, "Honey, we have so little free time, don't waste it on fights that no one can ever win," he walks out of the room because they don't like to disagree, their lives are too difficult for private quarrels. "Let's get an *horchata*, let's walk to the beach," she says. And he says, "You can't escape from things, Marian, you can't run away from the truth."

But she doesn't agree with him that it is wrong to want a little respite from the fatigue punctuated by terror, if only to refresh yourself so you can be better able afterward to be of use. She is most frightened when she seems far away from her own body, watching herself from a precipice, seeing herself straddling a cleft of rock that is widening, and she won't keep her footing, she will fall through, she knows it—any moment, she will fall into the abyss, and, from the precipice, she sees herself falling through. She can't always locate a central core that she can name with certainty as herself; there's too often a distance that she can't traverse between her body's actions and what she can only call her understanding, who is doing that, what are they doing, who is this Marian, I can say a name that I have been told is mine, but it's not real, Marian could be anyone, she could be anywhere, where is she, here, what do you mean by here, what does that mean, something that is different from there, but they are words, and words have no meaning. When she tries to ask what does meaning mean, she is farther away from the core than ever. Only once, the question helped because she answered it in a way that satisfied her: meaning is connection. But perhaps there is no connection, perhaps she is alone in the universe and she will spin and spin in a large, buzzing fog that will never allow her to come to rest, to know herself as herself.

It terrifies her to be that far from herself, so far that it becomes too difficult to return to the world of meaning. The sense of unconnectedness frightens her most. That is why she needs quiet, respite. It's why she's sorry that the churches now are of use for feeding and for shelter rather than what she would once have called recollection. To re-collect. To collect the flying, buzzing pieces dangerously far from the central core. To recollect, she needed silence, solitude. But it is impossible to come by, and, after all, why not, it is a time of war. It's why she's here, to help those who are struck down by doing the actual fighting: of course there is no silence, there is no time, and never enough equipment, enough electricity, water, never enough of anything, so how could there be time to say "I" or "Marian" or to search for the solid core or to fear its disappearance? None of that

means anything when you are breathing in the nightmare of suffering animals, but they are humans, these animals, and they suffer as
humans because they know they are dying, but they bleed and stink
and cry out as animals, and they always need something, there is
always something she needs to be doing, it is a relief from the buzzing, the spinning away from the central core, and so, in some ways, a
relief. And yet, she needs respite.

But Russell will not allow himself respite, and so she walks by herself and seeks it on her own. It makes her lonely. But she would rather
be lonely than bereft of respite.

Russell is tortured by a combination of remembrance and forgetting.
He wants to talk endlessly. Why isn't he as exhausted as she is? He
works as many hours, but when she comes home, all she wants to
do is sleep, or what she wants really is a bath, or to wash her hair, but
that isn't possible, there is no spare water for baths or hair washing,
and he wants her to listen to his talking. Don't fall asleep, don't fall
asleep, honey, this is important, it's important to me. I'm so damn
disillusioned, he says over and over, I'm so damn disappointed in
everyone involved in the whole damn mess, and she wants to say:
Russell, this is a time of war, disillusionment and disappointment are
minor sorrows, remember, we wanted to forget minor sorrows, our
own sorrows, our personal sorrows. She is thinking of Johnny, but
she doesn't believe he thinks about Johnny anymore; he wants to finger the wound of his disillusionment, his disappointment.

And then he falls in love.

She knows what he does in the nights he goes out without her, cruis-
ing the harbor for young men. They don't speak about it because,
although they are officially married, he knows very well that she is

still a virgin, has experienced nothing more than a few chaste kisses from boys for whom she felt nothing. And both of them are uneasy because of the ghost of Johnny; she hopes he doesn't know that it bothers her that he should be with anyone else, that what she believes most deeply is that his proper posture should be a lifetime of endless mourning, endless consecration to the great beloved, the great beloved dead, that this is a privilege she envies him, but a privilege she cannot, must not, ask him to take on.

And then one night, he comes in late, a little drunk, with an unmistakable air of satiation, and he lies on the bed next to her. She can smell a different kind of sweat, not the sweat of labor she knows so well. "Honey, I can't help it. I'm in love."

She leans on her elbow and looks at him, not knowing what she wants to say, not knowing what she feels, but knowing what is expected.

"That's wonderful, Russell," she says.

"Can you believe it, sweetheart, he's an anarchist, and you know how I feel about anarchists, what crap it is to be talking about transforming the social system when you're trying to win a war against people who out-arm you ten to one. One of God's little jokes, right, but after all, isn't this a country of God's little jokes, or big ones, but here I am, in love with an anarchist. And, of course, I know, I'm not a fool, he may just want my money, but he says he loves me, and why shouldn't I believe him for now? He's terribly young."

"How young?"

"Nineteen."

"I'm nineteen."

He rolls over on his back and laughs. "Well, you see, it's perfect. My wife and my lover are the same age."

She pretends to laugh, but she's frightened because she doesn't know what it means, for her, for Russell.

"I want to meet him, Russ. If you love him, I want to meet him."

"What a girl you are. Johnny always said it, 'She's one in a million, my sister, the best of the best, the pearl of great price.'"

She remembers a song Johnny made up for her when they were little: "Marian's a pearl, she's a pearl of a girl, she can spin, she can twirl, like a duchess or an earl." And she said, "An earl's a man, Johnny," and he said, "Whoops, well, you see, you're better than anyone."

It's happened; Johnny's entered the room. Perhaps, she thinks, that's good, I don't have to pretend not to be thinking of him.

"You have some time off tomorrow. We both do. Okay if we meet for a drink in the square? You and me and Eugenio?"

"Of course," she says. "I'd like it very much."

But she knows that "like" or "dislike" are words that are much too simple for what she is feeling. What will happen if she loses Russell, if he moves out of the room, where they can be alone, where they can be safe together, say anything to each other, where there is a place for Johnny, where he, too, is safe?

They walk hand in hand to the square. Piles of rubble are everywhere, and yet some café owners have set up tables in the midst of the rubble because it's summer and the sky is still blue until ten o'clock. Russell is uneasy; he's afraid Eugenio won't come, that it will be too much for him that Russell has a wife, that he will disapprove on anarchist grounds, or sexual ones.

And then, Russell raises his arm, and Marian sees the boy raise his arm in response. How can Russell, who is so muscular, so large, embrace this slight young man without fear of crushing him? This boy whom he must outweigh by fifty pounds. Does he think of Johnny's body, which was smaller than his but recognizably similar in mass, as belonging to a different category from this young boy— Eugenio is his name?—who is running up to them, full of smiles, skimming over the rubble in his patched khaki pants and shirt, apologizing already, twenty feet away from them, for his lateness.

"*Da nada*," Russell says. His Spanish is rudimentary, but improving, and he apologizes for his limited language to his lover but says that Marian is fluent, and now they will really know what the other is saying.

"Maybe that will not be so good," Eugenio says, smiling expansively. Two of his front teeth are missing but that takes nothing away from the power of his smile, his thorough loveliness, the fineness of his bones. Yes, Russell, I understand, she wants to say. I understand loveliness.

They drink quickly. The beer is weak, and Russell keeps ordering more; Eugenio talks about his hometown in Saragossa and how the republic will win, the workers will triumph, the seas of Spain are the most beautiful in the world, the mountains the most grand, his pride in being a part of POUM—the Workers Party of Marxist Unification—and, with every other word, "The fascist pigs, the fascist pigs," and Marian says they should all spit together on the pavement at the mention of the fascist pigs.

She's more than a little drunk, exhausted, ill-fed: it doesn't take much. She raises her hand to cover her eyes from the sun's late but strong rays, soaking into the stones of the cathedral.

"You see, Eugenio," she says, "I like you very much, and we don't know many anarchists, Russell and I, my husband Russell," she says, giggling, and Eugenio punches Russell in the arm, and Russell covers his face in burlesque shame. "So, I'm going to ask you what I've always wanted to ask. Why do you burn the churches? Why did you burn down the cathedral here?"

And he says, with real seriousness, "We didn't burn the main altar. It was just the vestibule."

Marian laughs, and Eugenio laughs, and Russell orders more beer.

"They were so bad to the poor people, the ordinary people; they were always on the side of the rich; they told us it was a sin to join a union, everything was a sin except if you were rich, and then nothing was a sin. The anarchists were the only ones who really stood up to them, all those fat priests. I didn't feel I was really a man until I got my own priest. We'd captured the fascists in the town, the mayor, the banker, the biggest landowner, and the priest. We weren't drunk, but we felt drunk with our own triumph, and we said to them, the four of them, 'Okay, run, we'll give you a head start,' and they ran like the cowards they were, and we ran after them with our guns and shot them as they ran. I got the priest. We all went into the café and had beers, and they drank to me and said, 'You got the prize, you bagged the real game.'

"We'd just left their bodies in the woods, we didn't want to do them the honor of burying them, we wanted them to rot as they had let the poor around them rot, and my friend, Luis, he was the wildest of us all, he said, 'I know what we'll do with the carcass of the pig priest,' and we went into the woods and took the priest's body and stripped it and hung it on the hook in the window of the butcher shop where the butcher had hung the pigs and the sides of beef."

He is laughing, and he expects them to laugh, but, quickly, he sees in their faces that they're horrified, they aren't laughing. What is that look on his face? Surprise, shock, a sudden comprehension? Then he smiles that smile that dazzles despite his toothlessness, and he says he has to go to the toilet and runs off clutching his stomach.

Russell and Marian say nothing to each other. They order more beer, and the sky begins to lose its brilliance and turn inky. After a while, she says, "Honey, I'm kind of tight. I have to go to bed. You wait for him here."

"Sure," he says. "See you in bed," and they laugh, as if this were a joke they could never get tired of, because they need something to hold on to, something familiar, something that makes sense.

She tries not to think about what she's just heard, she tries not to see a human carcass hanging from a hook in the butcher's shop. She runs home as fast as she can so she can be asleep, because, as always, she is exhausted, and she wants to hear nothing, to see nothing, to think of nothing.

Russell comes home stinking of cheap beer. She's never known him to be as drunk as this, but he wants to talk, once again, he wants to talk. He wakes her when all she wants, all she yearns for, is more sleep.

"How can this be, how can this be, that a person whom I know to be basically decent can do something like this and laugh about it?"

"I don't know, Russell," she says. "I don't know. I don't understand anything anymore. It's a war . . ."

He grabs her by the shoulders and shakes her. "What are we fighting for, though, tell me, what are we fighting for? Even if we win— which, of course, we won't—but even if we win, who will be left to be in charge that hasn't lost their minds to this insanity? Why are we doing this, who are we doing it for?"

"For the Spanish people, for all the wonderful people we work beside every day. What you're talking about . . . it's just a few, just a few young men driven crazy by crazy circumstances, by centuries of injustice."

She only half believes what she's saying, but she is determined that he will believe.

"No, my love, it's not a few, so many of them, so many of them, Eugenio . . . my comrades justifying God knows what . . . the fascists painting words on the wall: 'One Hundred Years off Purgatory if You Shoot a Red.'"

"I didn't even think you knew what purgatory was," she says, desperate to lighten the tone.

"How could I have been with Johnny and not known about purgatory? Every time we made love, he'd say, 'Do you know how many hundreds of years in purgatory I'm going to have to spend for this hour of heaven?'"

Johnny is in the room again, and she is free to invoke his name. "Johnny wouldn't want you to give up."

"Johnny's dead," he says, turning away from her. "We don't know what he would want, and how can you say, without feeling the mockery, how can you say that a suicide wouldn't want you to give up?"

She will not allow him to speak of Johnny in this way. Now having been insulted, the ghost must be allowed, or ordered, to withdraw.

"I'm sorry," she says. "It was my fault. It was bad of me to ask about the burning of the cathedral; I'd drunk too much, and you know . . . how I can get."

"No, I don't. I've never seen you drunk."

"Well, usually, I just shut up because you and our friends are always arguing about Trotsky or the NKVD or collectivization or something I have no idea about. I'd like to talk, but usually I'm not given the chance."

"Well, *mazel tov*," he says. "You certainly made the most of the opportunity."

"Yes, of course what Eugenio said was terrible, but it's not the whole story of what's been done with the churches. Even the cathedral here. Remember, Russell, they've taken the paintings from the Prado and hidden them in the basement of the cathedral, they let people in to see them, workers who would never have gotten to see a great painting in their lives, there are concerts in the churches, free for everybody . . . Mariposa, you know the girl that's so good at taking blood, she told me she'd never heard an orchestra before. It isn't all one thing, Russell, it isn't all madness and horror. Think of Julio's family making us that paella with the last food they had, think of Antonio, the surgeon from Galicia. Think of all the people fighting and dying against tyranny. That's not nothing, Russell," she says, "it's not nothing."

"No," he says. "It's not nothing. But it may not be enough."

It is impossible, after this, to break through Russell's pessimism. She knows he's right. The possibilities of a Republican victory seem increasingly remote. Franco has cut a swath right through the middle of Spain. Sy talks about the NKVD—the Russian secret police—who he says are "crawling all over Valencia like bedbugs." He becomes increasingly obsessed with the secret police. And Katie, prone increasingly to fits of hysterics, leaves for America. Sy asks to be sent home to America, but his requests are denied; if he leaves, he will leave as a deserter. Somehow, from a source never determined, rumors circulate about his incompetence. Nevertheless, he is forbidden to leave.

A young Spanish man arrives one day asking for Dr. Levin. Hollow eyed, disheveled, pacing up and down waiting for Sy, he is the embodiment of desperation. When Sy appears, he embraces the young man. "Coco, my old friend," he says in Spanish. Then he begins speaking Russian. The young man gestures to Sy that they should speak outside.

Sy comes back and says they should all meet in his room later that evening. He looks wild; his hands are trembling.

Russell and Marian knock on Sy's door. He is pacing up and down; he gestures for them to sit on the bed. "I met them in Baltimore," Sy says, "when I was training at Johns Hopkins. This young man, the one who was just here, José Robles is his name; his father is José Robles too. The father not only translated American writers, he also provided translations of the writers of Soviet Russia. We'd sit next to each other at political meetings; we met to speak Russian. When I first arrived in Valencia, I contacted the Robleses; we had an evening out. I was worried that José Senior was speaking too freely about what he had learned in his job translating for the Russian generals.

"I never got a chance to see him again, I guess Katie took up all my time, what little time I had after the hours I worked. And now, just now, his son told me he was taken away by 'some men,' he doesn't know who, they weren't wearing uniforms. They haven't seen him for a week; when José asked at the Soviet military headquarters, they told him his father was being 'interrogated.'"

Sy frantically asks everyone he comes across in Valencia what has happened to José Robles. He is told to stop asking: that some things are not to be looked into; that Robles is probably a fascist spy.

"He's no more a fascist spy than I am. He was much more an ortho-dox Marxist than I ever was," Sy says.

One night, men, saying they are there in the name of the republic but offering no other credentials, take Sy away. No one knows where he is, and Russell becomes frantic, as Sy was frantic about Robles, and is told the same thing: Don't question. He is a fascist spy. He will be given a fair trial.

But Russell will not stop asking. Marian is terrified at his obsessive concern, at his sensitivity to slights, his over-vigilance about what he calls "the worst elements in the party."

"What can it mean, what can it possibly mean . . . that people who don't identify themselves take people away, no one knows where. Robles hasn't been seen again. He's probably dead . . . who knows how, who knows where. And they could easily do the same with Sy."

"Don't say that, you don't know that . . . you're getting hysterical like Katie," Marian says. She hears her father's tone in her own voice: "You must never cry out."

After a week, it is whispered: Sy has been sent home; he is a danger to everyone; he has been declared mentally unstable.

And then, there is the evening of the radio broadcast, which every-one gathers to listen to, as there is only one radio. They meet in the hospital lobby, though even there the reception is irregular and faint. There are desperate efforts to get the Republican radio through the fascist jamming. One boy from Brooklyn, tall with light, curly brown hair, can pick up the loyalist signal when no one else can. He fiddles with the dials, he pounds the top of the set; he moves it an inch here, an inch there. The voices come and go. But, too often, it is jammed by the Nationalist stations and then come the horrible voices. That night, the loyalist signal disappears, replaced by the voice of Queipo de Llano, the fascist general in charge of Seville. He is a drunken braggart. Impossible to believe that he is human as others are human. The sickening, mocking singsong of his voice. Taking pleasure in naming the names of his targets, describing what he will do to the families of his targets. "I will take the skin off the backs of their wives and children and turn them into purses and wallets. I will sit in a café, drinking beer, and, for every sip I take, I will raise my hand, and ten reds will be shot down like the pigs, the dogs they are, dogs and cloven-footed beasts. We are the real men, and we will show you what red-blooded men can do to those red faggots who won't fight to the death as we will. Red red red, *rojo rojo rojo. Sangre sangre sangre,* blood blood blood."

Marian knows that when there are words like this in the air, and they enter your brain, all doubts about the righteousness of the comrades are nothing. The infighting, the cover-ups, the incompetence, the inefficiency, the bloodlust that you know are part of the people who are on your side. You must not forget what side you're on.

Then, some of the young men listening to the broadcast jump to their feet and raise their fists above their heads. "We'll show them who the faggots are. We'll make them kneel and suck each other's dicks. Then we'll cut their balls off and make them wear them as faggot necklaces."

She sees something in Russell collapse. She sees it and hopes that no one else does. He has been warned by another doctor, a Scot, who is also homosexual—or queer, as Russell likes to say—to be discreet, that he can do as he likes but needs to be careful not to be seen. Yet Russell still seems unprepared for the comrades' ugly words; they shock and hurt him, and he keeps saying, "What a fool I was, I believed things would be different with them, I believed them when they talked about human freedom. But they only mean freedom for people like them. They're no different from the fascists."

"Of course they are, Russell, you know that's not true. Of course they are. They aren't perfect—they're not good to women either. They think they have a right to fondle our breasts, they pretend we're equal, but they don't mean it for a minute, they only let me drive an ambulance when there's absolutely no one else, they don't believe women can drive as well as they can although I can drive rings around them. But to say they're no different from the fascists—for God's sake, Russell."

But he isn't listening to her.

It is only a few days later that he tells her he has decided to leave.

"Come with me, honey, please. We can live in the Village; we can get a dog; you can go back to Vassar, you can take the train into the city on weekends, you can become whatever you like, you never have to see your family. They can't get to you. You're my wife."

But she says no, as he knows she would. She wants to stay. Because in America, she is Johnny's sister, Marian Taylor, daughter of the Taylors of Park Avenue and Newport. Marian Rabinowitz is a joke in America, a joke she will have to live a humiliating life to keep alive. No work, no plans. Here she is needed. Here she knows what she does is important. And if she dies doing important work, it's better than living with emptiness. Why should she not put her life on the line? She has no connections. In America, the sham marriage might become a shackle. She and Russell might grow to no longer love one another. And that she could not bear.

"Sometimes," she says, "in terrible times like this, the best you can do is the least bad thing. The thing that does some good, or at least the least harm, or at least alleviates some harm."

"As long as you can live with the consequences of what you've refused to look at clearly. As long as you know that you're responsible for whatever that brings about, that you're responsible, too."

"That's the way you think, Russell. I don't think like that. That's not who I am."

"I wonder, I really wonder, because you know I love you more than anyone in the world, and yet I have no idea what you'll become."

"Become when?"

"Whenever it is that you become whatever it will be."

·

Everyone who works with him gathers what food there is for a party that he does not want, and none of them ask why his wife is staying behind; it is a time when questions are better not asked.

He'd been worried that his request to leave would be denied, as Sy Levin's was. But he is not stopped; he is thanked for his service.

"More and more," Russell says, "things are done arbitrarily and no one feels a responsibility to explain what's being done."

When he leaves, everything changes. People don't know what to do with her; she has always understood that she's been given a place at the hospital because she is Russell's wife. Some of the Spanish nurses resented her at first because she had no training, but her fluency in Spanish gave her an advantage over some of the English speakers who were better trained. They learned to accept her because she is strong and tireless, good at setting up IVs, adept at carrying stretchers, able to drive an ambulance if men are scarce. And the young Spanish girls who have no more training than she does come to her as an adviser, complain against the Spanish nurses to her, and the nurses know it. She also knows that some of the hard-liner comrades were aware of Russell's doubts about the party; somehow, they knew he'd been involved with a young anarchist. How much, she has often wondered, were she and, particularly, Russell, under surveillance, and by whom? And so, she can't think it is an accident that, two weeks after Russell leaves, she is asked if she'd be willing to transfer to another hospital. Malvarosa, near the shore, the hospital not for those just off the battlefield, not the place for life-or-death surgeries, but the place for the fixing of broken bones, for convalescence, for those with infectious diseases who have to be kept alive but apart from other patients.

The hospital of Malvarosa, she soon understands, is one of those slightly romantic places for the sick that seemed to spring up all over Europe before the Great War. It was built for sick children, particularly children with tuberculosis, built by the sea in the belief that putting sick children where they could breathe the sea air would help their diseases. Probably it didn't, Marian thinks, but she hopes that being in a lovely place did something; she hopes that at least it made them happy for a small stretch of time.

She doesn't question her new placement. She's relieved to be away from the true believers and from the constant political theorizing, arguments that, she feels, are sapping the small reserves of energy left after the impossible demands of her work. But she has come to understand that, for some people, the arguments are a source of energy, not a diminishment of it. For her, it is just one more reminder of the endless talk at her family's table that always made her long for nothing but silence.

She is driven to the new hospital in an ambulance, accompanying a patient with a broken pelvis. She helps carry the stretcher, says goodbye to the Spanish aides and to Lydia Wentworth, who has been transferred to the Teruel front. Marian helps carry the stretcher to the patient's new bed in the new hospital and walks slowly around the place that will be her home. And she thinks: How odd that I find it beautiful. *Beautiful hospital.* How oddly the words fit together. The place has an almost theatrical glamour: a set for a play whose theme is the healing power of the sun and sea. Gothic arches, green-tiled roofs, ornate cornices, high rooms through which the air blows calmly, thin white curtains billowing in the sea breeze. Chandeliers with crystals like diamonds; somehow, despite the demands of the sick, young women stand on ladders, polishing the crystals of the chandeliers. The floors, the walls, even the risers between the stair steps are covered in yellow and blue tiles with a pattern of acanthus leaves. She thinks of the railroad station, how wonderful it is that humans take the trouble to ornament, to design, to use color for no reason but to bring joy.

While she waits for the head nurse to explain her duties, she examines the photographs on the portion of the walls painted ochre above the tiles. Children on the rooftop, posing self-consciously for the photographs, children unused to being photographed, looking— what? she wonders. Grateful, frightened, hopeful, ashamed? How many of them survived, how many are fighting in the war, and on which side? The hospital was called St. John of God before the election of the Republic; now it is Asilo Sanatorio Hospital Popular. She's glad for the change; she hopes the children weren't made to confess to sins they couldn't have committed in order to be given the care they needed to save their lives. Or perhaps the nuns were kind. There are no pictures of the nuns who must have been the nurses here among the parentless children.

Finally, her duties are explained to her by a reluctant-looking doctor, Ramón Ortiz. Spoiled priest, she thinks, using the family term for someone who should have been the priest, had all the attributes of the ideal priest, but failed to answer the call. She sees by his hands that he can't be old, but his hair is thinning and his spectacles add to his prematurely old, therefore clerical, look. "Stout," she thinks, is the word for his physique: short, solid, not fat. The look in his eyes is regretful, on the edge of defeat but not succumbing. Everyone is on the edge of defeat; it is January 1938, and only a fool would believe the war is going well.

Ramón Ortiz points out the dormitory and advises her to rest until the morning. "After which, Señora Rabinowitz, there will be no rest at all. Walk by the sea while you can."

He shakes her hand, and she notices the dry width of his palm.

Asilo Sanatorio Hospital Popular. There is pain here, even ruin, but not everything suggests that the most likely outcome will be death. The groans and cries of the wounded might just have a termination that is something other than the grave.

No one here spends their free time arguing about the conditions in the Soviet Union. Sleep here is possible; occasionally, the wounded walk by the shore, their heads bandaged, their tended limbs relearning their first use. Here, she is not Russell's wife, and no one asks about a husband. She lives not as half of a privileged couple, but as a single woman among other single women. There is exhaustion, hunger, but a bit more freedom, a bit more time, and something of the atmosphere of her old school, however disguised. She makes a friend, Carmen Hernandez, and she has not made a real friend since Johnny died, since her identity had become that of Johnny's mourner, joined to Russell by their joint vocation. Carmen is a Spanish woman, younger even than Marian—seventeen—and like her an untrained volunteer.

They are tearing up old ruined sheets to make bandages of them. One of the sheets, besides being threadbare, is seriously stained: blood, or some unacceptable effluvia . . . it doesn't matter. But as they shake out the sheet, they both notice at the same time that the shape of the stain is exactly that of a cross. And they both start laughing. "*Milagro*," says Carmen, "Veronica's veil." "No, the stigmata," says Marian. They cross themselves; Carmen kneels before the sheet. "You see," she says, "we have the blessing of God upon us. Take that, you piece of shit Franco. Where is *your* miracle sheet?" They hold out the sheet to the other women, and everyone is beside themselves with laughter. "Stop, blasphemers," says Carmen, putting the sheet on her head so it looks like a nun's veil. All the women put sheets on their heads, pretending to be nuns. Marian does too. And with sheets on their heads, they sing "The Internationale."

After this, she and Carmen seek each other out. One of the convalescents has taken Carmen's fancy, and one night Carmen asks if Marian can take her place: she has—she uses the English word—a "date," which she pronounces *day-tay.* Thrilled to be part of a secret infraction of rules that probably don't exist, Marian agrees.

The next morning, taking up the tone she would have used after a dance at the Convent of the Sacred Heart, Marian asks Carmen, "How was it?"

"Disappointing," Carmen says. "I could hardly get him to shut up about collective farms."

One of the patients who has family living nearby provides Carmen, in great secret, with two eggs. She takes Marian behind the hospital and shows her the eggs, as if they were stolen diamonds. "I know I should share them with everyone," she says, "but I don't want to. So this is my idea. Not quite in the spirit of the revolution, but I hope you'll go along because you're on night duty. You boil the water on the paraffin stove they use for sterilizing, boil it in this pan, and just slip the eggs in when everyone is sleeping."

"But how will I get water without anybody noticing?" Water is scarce, and clean water is stored in large covered jugs in the center of the ward.

Carmen looks unhappy for a moment. "I hadn't thought of that," she says. A smile breaks over her face then: sly, larcenous. "Wine," she says. "We'll boil them in wine."

Marian is frightened; if they are caught, they will be shamed publicly, called greedy, accused of threatening the war effort. But the imagination of a freshly boiled egg, which she has not had for months; the joy of a comradeship that is real, not a political fantasy; the reminder that she is still young, lively, something other than a machine in the service of the war effort—all these are irresistible.

She tells the head nurse to grab some sleep; everything is quiet, she tells her, I'll call you if you're needed. Gratefully, the nurse lies down in the ward's one empty bed. Marian, looking over her shoulder like a cartoon burglar, opens the sack in which she has carried the small pot, the wineskin, the two precious eggs. She sets them on the stove. She dips the eggs into the bubbling purple, carefully, so as not to crack them. She times them: seven minutes, she thinks, seven a magic number, a number of good luck. The eggs have turned a lovely shade of mauve, almost like dyed Easter eggs. She wraps them carefully in a bandanna and puts them in the sack. She opens the window above a grassy patch and empties the pot of hot wine, then places the stained pot facedown into the sack.

She wakes the head nurse, who thanks her and sends her home to sleep.

Marian knocks on Carmen's door. Sitting on the floor, they peel the eggs, eating them with great slowness, acknowledging their preciousness.

"Ah, we've sinned," says Carmen, a look of satisfaction, almost rapturous, on her wide face.

"But we don't believe in hell anymore, or even purgatory, and there's nobody to confess to."

"Except each other," Carmen says.

"I absolve you, my child," Marian says.

"*Ego te absolvo,*" Carmen replies, making the sign of the cross in the air.

"What bad girls we are," she says.

They kiss each other on the lips. Marian tastes again the rich yolk, the ascetic white, the faint intrusion of the harsh red wine.

·

Marian discovers that, despite his serious look, Dr. Ramón Ortiz likes to make jokes. He orders a film to be brought to the hospital for the staff to watch: the Marx Brothers' *Duck Soup*. He introduces the film with words that might be considered punishable in the hospital La Pasionaria. "In this movie, there are four Marx brothers: Groucho, Harpo, Chico, and Zeppo. Not appearing is the fifth Marx brother: Karl."

Everything between them begins because she and Ramón Ortiz are the only two who don't smoke. This makes them figures of fun, especially when Dr. Ortiz seriously tries to defend himself. "I have enough poisoned air around me when I deal with suppuration." One day they meet walking along the shore; all the others are sitting on the stone benches of the hospital grounds, smoking. They walk together in silence, not knowing how to speak to each other, and the walk seems not like a walk but like a regimen ordered for their health. At first he is official, taking the tone of a supervisor evaluating her work.

"You have several qualities that I appreciate very greatly," he says. "You are willing to do anything, however disagreeable or humble. You have a great facility in inserting IVs, which is invaluable. Most important to me is your fluency in Spanish. It is a great relief not to have to search for a word in German or English, of which I have very little."

She has never been good at accepting compliments; she's always thought it was because so few were provided by her family.

"What I'm really good at is driving and fixing cars. But the men don't want me to drive an ambulance because I'm a woman— somehow it seems unladylike to them. So much for the transformation of society," she says.

The doctor relaxes; his shoulders lower, his pace picks up. "Where did you learn such good Spanish?"

"Oh, here and there," she says, uneasily, unwilling to say, "I learned it from my servants."

"Tell me the truth," he says, "you worked in a Mexican bordello."

Another daring joke, so she dares to be daring in return and says, "How did you guess?"

"Easy," he says, and pats her arm, causing a small shiver of pleasure, unfamiliar, therefore vaguely shaming.

Somehow—it can't be an accident—when she is taking a break, which she uses to walk along the shore while the others smoke, he arrives to join her. They always begin walking in the same direction, turning left, with their back to the harbor, because this way for a little while they can forget there is a war. When they turn around they have to remember: the harbor, repeatedly bombed, presents its ruination in a way they cannot avoid.

Carmen teases her. "I think you should start wearing lipstick when you go for your walks now, because it is such a coincidence that Dr. Ortiz always just happens to be there when you are."

"Oh, stop it," Marian says. "He doesn't know I'm alive."

"I know when romance is in the air," Carmen says.

"And I know that you love seeing things that are nowhere."

Ramón Ortiz is the only one she has ever heard speak about the political situation in a measured way. "No one in Spain has ever wanted to listen to a reasonable solution, compromise is betrayal for them, is death, everyone, right and left, young and old, they think they're El Cid riding on horseback with a raised sword, leaving their enemies in the dust, in their own blood. We were so happy when the Republic was elected, but we made mistakes, we made mistakes because we were so desperate to weaken the power of the Church. We had to weaken it, but we were too rash. We made it illegal to be married or buried in church, and people want to be married and buried as their ancestors were. Why, why is my country so in love with destruction? Every time I hear it . . . on the right and the left, all the words of blood, of fire, I want to say: Please, you are burning yourselves up, you are letting your own blood, please can't you move slowly, can't you see that things will take time. But no, they have to be the Great Crusaders. In the end that will be our downfall, because whoever wins will be drenched in blood. And because in the end reason won't matter—the fascists are armed by the worst people in the world, and we are armed with sticks and rocks and shovels."

He teases her about being the only foreign volunteer he's met who's Catholic. "What are you doing here, don't you understand the Generalissimo is preserving the Holy Church?"

"It's my only vanity," she says, "the one thing besides my Spanish—which I learned in the Mexican bordello. It's that, because I was brought up Catholic, I understand more of what's going on than the others, particularly the Americans. I understand the rhetoric: the shedding of blood, the promise of eternal reward. And I understand their taking the side of the rich, because my house was always full of priests with their fine white hands and the fine white linen towels my mother always provided for them, and the fine china in their fine rectories, and their small, consistent cruelties in confession when some poor soul confessed to something they could never dream of . . . It was always something sexual they were cruel about, some unfortunate girl getting pregnant, some mother of seven using contraceptives. They didn't care what you did, you could kill someone while you were driving drunk, you could beat your wife to a pulp, and they'd be oh so ready with forgiveness. But some poor wretch of a kid gets pregnant—they'd shame her until she wanted to die."

She expected some kind of sympathetic leaning toward her as a result of what she'd said, but, instead, she sees something happening to his whole physical being. His low compactness suddenly thins and sharpens; what was a dependable rock has become the flint head of an arrow. And his voice, always so low, always with some tone of regret or apprehension, suddenly goes high and cold.

"You think you understand, but you can't possibly understand. You're American, and you can't possibly understand the absolute power they had, not just over your spiritual life, but over the bread in your mouth and the earth under your feet. You think that because some priest was hard on somebody in confession, because some priest liked fancy china and silver, that you understand. But you can't, the way they would stand by while people starved, the way they would persecute people for something as simple as joining the union, threaten people with hellfire for joining the union, rail against teachers from the pulpit, and, from the same pulpit, defend the landowners who were literally starving the people. In America, it would not be possible to do what they are doing right now in the Nationalist zone, passing out forms that people have to sign, swearing they've gone to confession and communion, boxes in the church to collect them, and if your form isn't in the box, it's perfectly all right for someone to shoot you on the street.

"No, you have never seen what we have seen in this country. A priest with a rifle in his hand saying, 'Shoot, shoot the animals, all reds are animals,' calling from the altar for a massacre, for the holy sacrifice of shedding blood for the great cause, God's cause, God's cause against the devil's. You talk about cruelty in confession, but, in America, there is no one urging some young man, probably ignorant as dirt, to shoot a red in the name of the Virgin Mary. And you have never seen, as I have, a priest encouraging a young man to shoot a pregnant woman because, that way, there will be two fewer reds. You've never seen priests standing next to armed soldiers who are herding prisoners, herding them down to the shore to shoot them, one at a time. Quite a leisurely thing, they took their time about it so the priests could offer absolution to anyone who wanted it before being shot, and some poor souls asked for it, just in case it might save them from being shot, and, who knows, maybe some of them really still believed. But whether or not they believed, they were all shot, and the priests, thinking they're acting like some picture of Jesus on the rectory wall, blessing everyone, the butchers and the butchered, blessing everyone as the soldiers pour gasoline over the ones they've just shot, setting them on fire, just in case, just in case they're still living, and then the priests walking home calmly to their dinner and their evening devotions."

She knows there's nothing she can say. She's humbled, and yet angry, because, in his rage for the public horrors, there is no place for what the Church is responsible for in the private life of her and her brother. But isn't that why she's here? To say that the public horrors must take precedence over the private.

As suddenly as his body thinned and hardened, it relaxes now, not softening, but no longer pointed, no longer a weapon. He is not exactly relaxed, but the engine of his rage is idling now. He leans toward her and moves back, then forward again, taking her hands.

"Forgive me, I don't always speak like this, but, you see, in some ways, it is, to me, the worst thing that they act as they do in the name of what should be the most sacred things in the world, what is precious to ordinary people, they have made it impossible to do simply what should be the simplest things in the world: to marry, to bury your dead, without fear or rage."

She wants to forgive his outburst; once again, she's been reminded of her position of privilege, a position she has always hated and worked to be rid of. But it cannot be shed like a mink given happily to a beggar. His country has suffered; hers has not, and has, in fact, refused to put its weight on the scales of relieving the suffering they are witnessing every day. Her country stands back and watches, complacent, compassionate, or complicit . . . Does it matter if you simply watch? But she will not allow him to say that she hasn't seen what she has seen—it was the demand made always by her family—even if it is a small part of a larger something, and not the whole of it. It is nonetheless true, and she won't let him, in the name of a larger suffering, say that what she has seen isn't there.

"I understand what you're saying, but I want you to understand something, too. I understand that they have it in them to be killers because they killed my brother. They made it possible because he loved men instead of women—does that shock you, does it disgust you, as it shocked and disgusted them?"

"Of course not, of course not," he says. "Do you think I have never lived in the world?"

She nods, hoping she can believe him, but feels pressed to go on. "They made it possible, even necessary, for my family to believe they could commit every outrage on him until he preferred to die rather than live with what they had in store for him. Then they refused to bury him in consecrated ground because he was a suicide. A suicide whose blood was on their hands."

He kisses her hands, which he has all the time been holding.

"You must forgive me."

And, not knowing where it comes from, she says, "You should know that I'm not really married. Well, I am, but the marriage isn't real. My husband was my brother's lover, and so I am, as the law would have it, intact. Not really married, not even in the eyes of American law. Not even in the eyes of the Church."

He drops her hand, as if holding it after her confession is a defilement of her purity.

They sit on the pebbly beach; she feels the cold stones underneath the inadequate material of her dress, and he says, "Well, since you are a virgin, I suppose I must ask your permission to kiss you."

And so it begins—what, despite the horror of the times, she can only call her romance.

She has been in Spain less than a year, and, in that time, so much has happened that she can no longer say with certainty whether she is the same person who boarded the SS *Normandie* in New York, who was given a fur coat that disintegrated, who threw a hat into the ocean with a husband named Russell, a husband who never touched her. And, having been brought up in a family who rarely touched, she is newly born into a world where skin is more than a covering for the vulnerable organs. Kisses, caresses, the longing for another body, this alongside the bloody, excruciating deaths she's seen, the bombed streets, the starvation—how can this be the same body that boarded the ship in New York? The body she has, until now, believed she was born with.

Lovemaking. Making love. She does think they are making something, something that has never existed in the world before. And, in the midst of it, the despair because the news of the war is dreadful, no one can believe their side will win. The disastrous battles of Teruel, the Ebro, ill-conceived, impossible to win because it is not possible— why does anyone on their side think it is?—to prevail against the weapons, the planes, the tanks, the well-functioning guns, the protective helmets, provided by Hitler and Mussolini. From Madrid come reports it is impossible to make sense of: confusing accusations, then counteraccusations. Defeatism is the worst thing one on the Republican side can now be accused of. The president travels to France, then resigns. Indalecio Prieto, the secretary of war, said to be the only decent man in the government, suggests that everything is lost.

Yet in the midst of the exhaustion and despair, the simple joy of two bodies, young and still, against all odds, lively and healthy, astonished at each other, saying how has this miracle happened in a time when no miracle seems possible, how has this miracle happened: that you are mine.

She adores his body, although she would have said that he was not her type. But what was her type, free as she was of all experience of real male bodies? She would have said she liked the Gary Cooper "type," tall with a loping, slow-moving walk, deliberate gestures, nearly mute. There is nothing slow and deliberate about Ramón. His hands make chopping motions when he talks; he is incapable of moving slowly. Her lover is—she has to say it again—stout. He is shorter than she is by two inches. His hair is thinning although he is only twenty-five. When he is upset about something, he pulls his hair out, as if to act out his words, "I could tear out my hair." He is helpless without his eyeglasses. Without glasses, he has the unironic eyes of an adoring dog. With glasses, the adoration turns to pure attentiveness.

She loves the dark hair that covers his body. "Let me nuzzle your pelt," she says. And he says, "'Pelt' is a word for beasts, so if I am the beast, you must be the beauty. My long-legged American beauty."

Their lovemaking is time stolen from the sick, whose needs are endless, in his room that smells of the sea but is infested with black beetles. No one questions that they leave his room together in the mornings. It is a time of war, everyone is way beyond that, although she's sure they wonder to themselves what happened to her husband.

Mi amor
My love
My darling
Mi tesoro

•

She has lost more than twenty-five pounds in the months she's been in Spain, and her periods are so irregular that she never even expects them anymore. One morning, when they're making love, she tells him he needs to be gentler with her breasts. He is hurt. "When am I ever anything but gentle?"

He teases her that she's getting a sweet, round belly; no longer my American string bean.

And then, alarmed, he says, "When was your last period?"

Not catching on to the alarm, she says, "God knows."

He says, "I can't do a gynecological exam on you, that would be grotesque. But I want you to see Marguerite. I think it might be possible that you're pregnant."

"No," she says, "no, no, it can't be." The private horror drowning the larger public ones.

Marguerite, an obstetrician in France, whistles and says, "Five months, I think."

Ramón pulls at his hair, and she says, "Don't tear out your hair; you don't have that much of it."

He says, "It's too late for an abortion. I won't have you risk your life . . . not in these conditions."

They wonder if the condoms they were using are, like everything else provided by the Russians, or the leftovers of the West, not of the first quality.

They know this to be a disaster. They face it with a dull resolution. There is not one second in either of their minds or hearts of the slightest joy.

And she is someone else's wife.

"This is the least of our problems," he says. "Republican officials aren't fussy about that sort of thing."

They marry in the mayor's office. Carmen is their witness.

"I seem to be fated not to have a church wedding."

"And you are no longer entitled to wear white."

"From virgin to bigamist. A great title for a trashy novel, don't you think?"

"Great," he says. "Brilliant."

. . .

He writes to his parents to tell them he has a wife who is expecting a child. His father writes in the script of one unused to writing: "I wish you and your new family good luck." And from his mother, in perfect copperplate, words that come close to a curse: "As you have not been married in the Church, I cannot recognize this as a marriage. At least promise that you will have the child baptized."

He hasn't said much about his parents and passes her the letters without comment. They do not speak of them again.

Except for their moments in each other's arms, increasingly infused with desperation as the situation of the war becomes more desperate, it is the darkest of dark times. The International Brigades leave: what could be more a sign of hopelessness? Supplies become even more scarce as the Russian provisions arrive less and less frequently, and are less and less abundant when they do arrive. Many of the medical volunteers leave when the Internationals leave, so the hospitals are more and more short-staffed, but one supply that never slackens is the wounded.

And then Carmen, who has arranged to meet a beau in Valencia, does not return. She bought a new pair of high-heeled shoes, which Marian warned her would be a nightmare on the Valencian cobblestones, but she said she didn't care; she didn't have Marian's long legs, so she needed high heels so she wouldn't look like a fat cow. Marian and Ramón hear, in the distance, the noise of a prolonged raid, and when Carmen isn't on the ward in the morning, Marian runs to Ramón and says, "She didn't come back, she didn't come back last night."

Carmen is not seen again; and there is no way to find her body, or the pieces of her body, in the bombing wreckage. Marian wants to go into the city to search for her in the rubble: she would recognize her, she knows she would; she would be able to identify her new high-heeled shoes.

Ramón holds her. He tells her it is not possible, what she imagines. She knows that he is right. Her friend, everything about her friend, is lost for good.

Her pregnancy is barely visible, and she feels almost nothing but disbelief at the prospect of a child. No one remarks on her condition. Occasionally, Ramón urges her to rest, but he himself is too pressed to watch over her. And, although he urges her to get off her feet, he prefers her to anyone else as a surgical assistant, and so she is there when it happens.

He is operating on a soldier who has suffered a compound fracture of the femur, the bone grotesquely protruding through the infected flesh, looking more like a spoiled roast unfit for the oven than a human limb. Is it because they're both tired, or because the gloves are inadequate? One of the jobs she used to be in charge of before, when there was time enough, people enough, was the blowing up of the rubber gloves used by the surgeons to make sure there were no holes. But it is a job that has been done away with, for lack of people to do it, and a splinter of bone pierces Ramón's skin.

Everything happens with terrifying speed. By nightfall, he has collapsed and taken to his bed. He is drenched with sweat, his body convulsed with shaking chills. He begs for water, he is given it, he vomits it up, and begs for more.

"The wound was septic," he says to her in one of his last lucid moments. "And I am septic now. Bring a pen and paper."

Without saying the words to her—"I am dying"—he writes to his parents. He tells her, "You are only weeks away from giving birth. It's too late for you to go home. You must go to my parents. My mother will be harsh, but she will take you in. My father will be kind.

"*Mi tesoro,*" he says, "how can I be leaving you like this?"

By morning, he is delirious, calling for her but not understanding that she is there, that it is her hand he holds. By afternoon, he is dead.

·

Like a gleaner, this shock gathers in all the other shocks that she thought had been absorbed.

Dr. Bethune, in charge of the medical personnel in Valencia, arranges for a truck to transport her to Ramón's family in the village of Altea, also in the province of Valencia, but fifty miles north. The roads are nearly destroyed, but she doesn't worry that the roughness of the ride means her child will be in danger. Her child is nothing, someone she doesn't know. Ramón, whom she knew and loved, is gone. There is only numbness. She knows now that she was wrong to believe that public suffering could eclipse private sorrow. Rather, the two shed a garish light on one another, bathing each other in a lurid glow. The war is lost, the fascists will triumph, her brother is dead, her beloved Ramón is dead. There is no one whom she loves who seems able to stay alive.

They reach the village. The truck drops her off. The driver, forgetting himself, tells her to go with God.

There is no color in the things she sees. The steep streets with their dark, sharp stones, the extreme whiteness of every wall, the wrought-iron gates in front of every window, the old women in black sitting in their open doorways. She's grown used to raising her fist as the sign of greeting; she must unlearn that. Now she makes her fist knock lightly on the door; but then she notices the door knocker, in the shape of a pineapple. The Ortizes' door is not left open, like the doors in which the old ladies sit, but Señor and Señora Ortiz must have been waiting behind it, because the door opens a second after her knock.

And there they are, the parents of her beloved. Her in-laws? Señor Ortiz's face is marked with the scars of some pox; it might have been smallpox or the more innocent chicken pox. His face is pitted; his eyes, though kindly, are forced into a squint on account of his scars. His shoulders are stooped in what she guesses is his customary posture, a posture of apology; he seems apologetic for the air he breathes, as if he isn't sure he has the right to claim it for his lungs. She recognizes the thinning hair of Ramón—his father's head is as bald as Ramón's would have been had he been allowed to age. She sees, even marred by the scarring, Ramón's thick lashes, his tender, doglike eyes. He takes Marian's bag, then takes her hand and presses it; the kindness makes tears come to her eyes. He steps into the street to make room for his wife.

A stone woman. An iron woman. A high, masculine forehead and thick, black hair collected at her nape in a bun so thick Marian can't imagine any cool air penetrating it. Her dress is of coarse black wool. Her eyes are heavy lidded, a part of what must be, Marian sees, an attitude of general refusal, showing itself in her refusal even fully to open her eyes. Refusal, too, incised in lines on each side of her surprisingly fresh, full mouth, in the perfectly cut fineness of her nose, in the dark circles like punishing thumbprints below her eyes, as if she has refused, even, the proper amount of rest. She is taller than her husband, and her frame is larger. Ramón, Marian sees, inherited his father's height and his mother's broad skeleton.

Señor Ortiz shows Marian to her room, Ramón's old room, monkish: a single bed with an iron bedstead, a grey wool blanket, a small table (his desk, she thinks, the place he read and wrote, therefore precious), a black gooseneck lamp. "I am glad that you know Spanish," Señor Ortiz says. "I hope you will be comfortable. I hope that you are well."

The mother says almost nothing. She provides a thin towel, tells Marian she may rest if she likes, that dinner will be at nine, not much, a thin soup. "It is a time of war," she says.

Does she imagine this is something Marian doesn't know? Does she imagine that Marian doesn't understand that the mother begrudges her every spoonful of scarce food?

Ten days of near silence except for Señor Ortiz's comments about the weather and inquiries about her health. The midwife, also nearly silent, comes once to examine Marian and to say her time is close. She's right; the pains begin—shocking—but what did she expect? She expected nothing, and, having seen so much pain, she is, somehow, surprised that she is experiencing what she has seen others experience so often, and is humbled by the ordinariness of her experience. She remembers her father saying that when you're in labor, you must not cry out, and she remembers being angry with him for that, sure that he was nowhere when her mother went into one of her endless labors, somewhere far away from any cry, preparing to give out cigars. But now, she thinks, it is somehow important, in honor of the bravery of the wounded men she tended, the dying men, not to cry out.

Fifteen hours, and then the final tearing push. "A boy." Healthy, he is taken from her, washed, given back. She puts him to her breast. She feels for this new person . . . nothing. Because she has been, since Ramón's death, unable to feel.

No one asks her what the child will be named. Señora Ortiz says, "He will be named Ignacio because he was born on the Feast of St. Ignatius of Loyola, a great Spanish saint, a great soldier of the Church. I suppose you would prefer to name him Marx or Lenin."

"Ignacio is fine," she says. She has no impulse to argue. She turns away and says to the wall, "Ignacio, Ignacio," but the words have no resonance; they are absorbed into the plaster of the wall and disappear. Bitterly, she thinks: My father would be pleased. Ignacio, Ignatius, hero of the Church Militant, the Church Triumphant, which she knows will triumph now against everything she believes in, every idea she treasures.

Again and again, she puts the baby to her breast, but he howls in enraged frustration, because her milk is not coming in. Señora Ortiz, with grim satisfaction, takes the baby away after two days and says, "We will give him to Luisa down the street, she has a male child. You have the red poison in your breasts, the child must know it. I thank

God it will not be his first food. Luisa knows how to be a natural mother. It is clear that you do not."

Marian passes the baby to his grandmother, with no will to resist. You're right, she wants to say, I don't know how to be a mother. Everything I once knew is of no use to me. You're right, she wants to say, I don't know anything. I don't know anything at all.

AVONDALE, RHODE ISLAND, 2009

ON AUGUST 14TH, when Amelia comes home from work, her grandmother is in bed. It isn't unusual for Meme to take an afternoon nap, but today, at three, when Amelia stands at the open doorway of her grandmother's room, she sees that Meme isn't just napping. She hasn't been up all day. The covers are drawn up to her chin, she's still in her nightgown, her hair is in the single braid that Amelia has almost never seen: her grandmother unplaits her hair first thing in the morning and pins it in a knot at the nape of her neck.

"I'm a bit under the weather," Meme says, holding her hand out, and Amelia hears, for the first time, a wet, deep cough. It frightens her. She grew up with illness, and her instincts had been sharpened: she can tell a dangerous symptom from a trivial one.

She would never have thought of herself as "the child of an invalid," although, from the time she was nine, she understood that her father was fragile, that he needed to spend some days in bed. On those days, she made sure she was quiet because those were the days he needed to sleep and sleep. But because he loved her so much, because he so craved her company, he woke himself up so he could be with her. Despite the days in bed, and the days when his breath was short and labored, frightening to hear, despite the visits to the doctors and the trips to the hospital, her father was always hopeful and always, it seemed to her, in good spirits. She never thought of her childhood as blighted by her father's illness. Illness was simply a frequent guest, unwelcome but so regular that it came to be taken for granted. She knows that, underneath the countenance of equanimity that most people see when they look at her, there is a layer of vigilance that can rise to the top at a moment's notice: a servant who lives in the basement but can be summoned, at the touch of a button, to the living quarters.

Amelia phones Helga to suggest that they take Meme to the doctor's together. Meme has the habit of not listening to people if she doesn't like what they have to say. She waves her hands in the air as if she were brushing away an irritating insect and goes her own way, doing what she wants, believing what she wants to believe. But she doesn't do that with Helga. She always listens to Helga. Amelia understands that it's because of something Meme once said about her friend: she faces things.

What was the opposite of facing things? Turning your face away? Turning your back?

Amelia imagines that her grandmother divides the world into people who face things and people who don't. What's remarkable is how many of the people she loves would probably be counted by her as people who turn their face. Rosa, for example. The Nordic surfer god at the nursery, Josh. And—what did you call it when one of the people is ninety-two and one in his eighties—her boyfriend? Her lover . . . but probably there was no more sex. Graham, who had loved her for nearly thirty years, unable to be with her openly for twenty of them because he was married to a hypochondriac—who finally, as Amelia's mother said, had the good manners to glamorously die. Graham, Marian's lawyer, the lawyer who defended people who got arrested for protesting (Marian and Helga among them), but he was so sweet, so soft-spoken, that Amelia couldn't imagine him in court, facing down judges and opposing counsel. And she knows that her grandmother, although she loves Graham with unshakable devotion, doesn't take him quite seriously. And Amelia knows that he knows it, and allows her, in his love for her, to underestimate him. Once, before

Amelia moved in with Meme, she'd heard her grandmother say, "The reason I like living alone is that if I find a hair in my soup, I know it's mine." Graham was in the room, and Amelia worried that he might find this wounding. But he only laughed and said, "Well, I can literally say, Marian, that I missed out on something by a hair."

Her grandmother probably doesn't think of Amelia as someone who faces things. But she had faced things: that life could take from you the person you most valued. I have faced it, Meme, she wants to say, I knew my father would die early, and when it happened, I never pretended it wasn't terrible.

And so she understands that Helga will have to be the one to insist that her grandmother go to the doctor.

Dr. Anderson, who was Marian's doctor after she moved to Avon- dale in the 1950s, has been retired for five years. His practice has been taken over by a husband-and-wife team. Helga and Marian will only see the wife.

"She's the brains, he's the beauty," Helga said once.

"I believe he's very good with computers," Marian responded. She is always tender toward handsome young men. "And he has humility."

Humility is a quality that Amelia knows her grandmother admires. Sometimes she uses it to explain the fate of someone she likes—the Nordic god surfer Josh—who might be considered unsuccessful by the larger world.

The doctor has insisted that Marian and Helga call her Annie. Mar- ian does; Helga does not.

"Annie wants to see me tomorrow morning."

"We'll pick Helga up on the way."

Both Marian and Helga have given up their licenses, wisely no longer trusting their eyesight. Amelia knows that one of her most important jobs—besides helping with computers—is driving Marian and Helga. Railing against the paucity of public transportation, they organized a group called "Elders Need a Ride." They traveled to Providence; they saw the governor. A limited bus service had been organized. They considered it a victory, although neither of them ever uses the bus, because it runs at inconvenient hours and never seems to go where they want.

Amelia and Helga sit in the waiting room while Marian sees the doctor. When she is paying her bill at the counter, the doctor catches Amelia's eye and makes the sign for a telephone, holding her thumb against her ear, her pinkie to her lips.

Amelia sees that the trip to the doctor has exhausted her grandmother. She suggests a nap, and Meme doesn't reject the suggestion, as she normally would (she allows herself naps, but only if they're her own idea). This alarms Amelia, or, rather, increases the volume and duration of the continuous low buzz of her alarm.

When she's sure her grandmother is asleep, she phones the doctor.

"I don't like the look of the X ray, but I'm not a specialist, so I'm sending her to the hospital in Westerly. We'll schedule her for an MRI. She might fight me on this one, so I'm counting on you and Helga to make it happen. Of course, in the end, it will be up to her."

"Of course," Amelia says, wondering how she can make her grandmother have an MRI if she doesn't want one. She never understands how anyone can make anyone do anything. She calls Helga, but Rosa answers the phone.

Rosa's voice is so tender, so willing to express or expose whatever she's feeling, withholding nothing, as the voices of everyone else have learned to withhold. Amelia heard this even as a child, the extravagant sweetness, like a chocolate filled with an additional treat—pineapple, marzipan. Even as a child, it worried her, Rosa's enactment of too little self-protection, too much eager need.

"Helga has told me that your grandmother will be just fine."

"We hope so, yes," Amelia says. It has always been that way: Helga protecting Rosa, Helga keeping things from Rosa. It's possible, Amelia knows, that Helga will be angry with her for having said, "We hope so," instead of, "Absolutely, yes."

"Annie says we have to convince Meme to have an MRI."

"It will be so," Helga says. Amelia hangs up the phone, feeling stronger because she and Helga will be facing this together.

But Marian doesn't resist the idea of an MRI. Helga says, "I am relieved that there is no need to argue." She mispronounces words only rarely, only when she is under stress. Amelia notices that she pronounces the word "argue" as if it were a French word, a word of one syllable, *arg.*

As they drive to the hospital, Marian says to Amelia, "You have to understand. I have no wish to die. Even at my age, I haven't had quite enough of life. I'm greedy for it."

"And I'm greedy for time with you. All the time in the world."

What could that mean, she wonders as she says it: all the time in the world? How much would that be?

She wonders if her grandmother has the same thought because she says, "Not all the time in the world, but as much as we can." She kisses Amelia's hand with small, dry kisses, leaving behind the print of her red lipstick. "Cherries in the Snow"—Amelia knows that's its name. It's a name, an image, she has always loved, always connects with her grandmother.

Marian disappears behind a blond-wood door with a small window at its center. She waves, as if she were boarding a train.

"Don't go, Meme," Amelia wants to cry out, as she had cried when her grandmother left to fly home after her visits to California. But she knows that what she really wants to cry out is, "Don't die." The thought that, perhaps soon, her grandmother will be going through a door and will not return falls on her with the weight and shock of thoughts that are always there, but somewhere out of sight, above you—and now fallen on your head, preventing understanding. She waits until she's sure her grandmother is well inside wherever she's going before she allows herself to cry. Helga says nothing but passes Amelia a cloth handkerchief, snow white and perfectly ironed. In one corner, Helga's initials have been embroidered in red. Amelia thinks it's likely that Rosa did the embroidery.

Two days later, the pulmonologist's office calls and makes an appointment for the same afternoon.

"That can't be good," Amelia says to Helga.

"We don't know yet. Don't talk like that to your grandmother."

But when Meme comes out of the doctor's office, Amelia and Helga can see that the news is not good.

"The doctor wants to see you," she says to them.

The doctor tells them that Marian will have to be checked into the hospital for a lung biopsy. "The biopsy will be tomorrow," he says.

Marian asks Amelia to pack her suitcase. "For some reason, I find the prospect too fatiguing."

She directs Amelia to the suitcase underneath her bed: a small, anachronistic-looking rectangle of navy-blue leather with a border of white. At her grandmother's direction, Amelia packs a blue cotton nightgown and a pair of white cotton socks. She's embarrassed to be handling her grandmother's underpants, whose plainness saddens her: large, androgynous, white, they could belong to anyone before or past the age of sexual allure. But what did she expect? Satin bikinis? A black lace thong? She hates thinking about her grandmother in this way.

·   ·   ·

They keep Marian overnight in the hospital, and in the morning the doctor phones Amelia to set up a meeting immediately after her discharge.

He uses the word he has to use. Cancer. The word hangs over their heads like a vicious, shining hook. He says it is useless to make time predictions, but Marian's great age is on her side. Amelia hates him for using the words "great age."

They drive home in silence.

Marian sits in a chair at the dining room table. She hasn't said a word in the hour and a half since they left the doctor's office, and Amelia, following her lead, has been silent. Marian has the day's mail in her hands. She opens a large brown envelope with the letter opener that has always fascinated Amelia: ivory with a series of parading elephants on the handle.

The letter is from the Department of Fish and Wildlife.

Marian puts on her glasses. She seems, Amelia thinks, to be taking a very long time to read the letter. She takes her glasses off. She puts them down beside the letter on the table. She rubs her hands over her eyes, roughly, back and forth, as if she were trying to rub something out, erase it slowly, deliberately, once and for all.

"They're starting the egg-addling program again."

"Oh, Meme, that's awful. But we won't give up."

"We will, my dear. We will. It's over now, it seems," she says, rubbing her eyes again. "It seems my disappointments have caught up with me."

Amelia doesn't know what to say: "disappointment" is a strange word to use on the day you get the news of your impending death. A middle-range word, not grand, not tragic, someone failing to show up for a rendezvous. She looks across the table. Meme seems to be waiting for her to say something.

"I didn't know you were disappointed."

"Yes. But it's something I've always tried not to think of."

Amelia wants to say to her grandmother, So that's how you've dealt with the troubles of your life, by forgetting what you've lost. I can't do that, she wants to say. For me, it is already much too late.

·

Marian has decided against chemotherapy: why despoil the last days of her life? She has outlived most of her friends. Each loss was like the slow erosion of a chalky cliff, the pressure of some heavy foot that caused a gradual, steady crumbling until, at the bottom, there is a pile of irregularly shaped pieces, some large, some smaller, negligible, some of them, some seeming the evidence of a calamity. There was the first death, larger than the others and of a shape that could not be duplicated. There were no similarities between the first death and what could be called the other deaths. Or were all deaths just the first death replayed, lighter in tone, but taking the harmonics from the great original? The first death, the most terrible. The truest beloved. Johnny. Shocking because she was young, and it was unexpected, and she saw it, and it was his own hand that brought it about. She forces herself to believe in immortality, against all reason, because she must must must see her brother again.

She feels fortunate that there is no one alive whose life will be made unbearable by her death. It is a luxury that there is no one for whom she has to go on living, for whose sake staying alive is a responsibility, a duty reluctantly but stoically carried out. When she dies, there will be sadness, yes, but not the sadness that destroys, that blows apart the wish to live. She knows, and realizes it's a sign of her prosperity, that two people, Helga and Amelia, will mourn her; their lives will be (but not for too long and not with an irreparably deep cut) marked by grief. Or, perhaps, there are three people, or even four. Rosa and Graham. But each of them have loved others more intensely. Rosa could not live without Helga, and Graham could not go on living if he lost his son. "I couldn't live without Alex," he has often said. But having lost the first, the irreplaceable, she knows that it's always possible to go on living; it isn't the loss of the beloved itself that brings one to the point of death, it's the blotting out of the appetite for life, the distaste for any possible action.

But Helga is incapable of inaction. Helga, beside whom Marian has worked for fifty years, digging, planting, fertilizing, watering, fretting, and celebrating. What would she have done without Helga's support? Poor Helga, who could never be allowed to die.

One death she would not be able to survive. If Amelia died before her—an accident, an illness—the shock would literally, Marian believes, bring on her own death.

Although she knows her death will not destroy Amelia's life, she worries about its impact. Rather than being toughened by her father's death, Amelia seems permanently, perhaps not weakened, but made fragile, and Marian feels that, having achieved the unseemly distinction of having outlived her son, Amelia's father, she has a greater responsibility than the ordinary grandmother for protecting her grandchild from the blow of her death.

She phones Naomi. Naomi weeps when Marian tells her the news of her diagnosis, and Marian is surprised. She'd thought Naomi was tougher than that. Together, they had faced Jeremy's illness and death; she doesn't remember Naomi weeping once in all that time.

"It's just that somehow you were always one of those mountains I could look to and say, 'Well, it's there, I'm all right.' I always felt with you I had a strong accompaniment. I will feel much more unaccompanied when you're gone."

"Well, you have Amelia. And that's why I called, because I'm worried for her."

"Amelia is stronger than you think."

"I thought you were the one who said she lacked force."

"Force and strength aren't the same thing, Marian. You know better than that. You were always such a stickler for the right way of describing things. She doesn't have force, but she's not weak. It's partly her looks, you know how it was with Jeremy, they look like they can't stand up to a strong wind, but there's something deceptive about that, almost a part of their modesty, keeping their strengths in the shadow. Let her help you, Marian. Don't be afraid to lean on her."

·

Amelia and her grandmother are doing dishes together after an early supper. Marian doesn't have a dishwasher. She stands at her sink, a sink whose very inconvenience pleases her: its plain, unmodern whiteness, its shape—a long, shallow, rectangular basin—and its brass taps. Amelia stands beside her, drying the dishes with a white towel bordered by a thick red stripe.

"The days are shortening," Amelia says. "I don't like that."

"I'm dying, Amelia," Marian says. "I don't like euphemisms, and I don't like evasions. We have to be practical. I'm going to need your help."

"Ah," Amelia says, as if she suddenly understood the answer to a mathematical problem or had found a map hidden underneath a couch, behind a chair. "The most important thing, Meme, is to tell me exactly, and I mean exactly, what you want. Or maybe the most important thing is to tell me what you don't want."

What Marian wants, to her surprise, is to give up domestic responsibility. Each morning, she wakes defeated by the prospect of preparing food, sweeping the floors, doing the laundry. She is shocked at how little it takes to tire her, and the prospect of incessant fatigue frightens her as the prospect of her own death does not. Fatigue brings back a time she doesn't want brought back. And she dreads a future of endless requests that might become a burden to her granddaughter. Her granddaughter is young. The young should not, she believes, be burdened by the old.

She is astonished at how little she has to say to Amelia, how easily her granddaughter understands what needs to be done, how deft
her movements are, as if the whole business of keeping up the house
were a dance to which she had, for years, known the steps, and has
been just waiting to perform on stage. Marian takes to waking at four
knowing that Amelia has to be to work at five. What a pleasure it
is, drinking Amelia's delicious coffee, eating the muffins she brings
home from the bakery every night. Marian doesn't like to tell Amelia that she really doesn't enjoy the cupcakes. They're too sweet, too
uninflected in their sweetness, and Marian only likes sweets when
they include a contrast: something bitter, or neutral, or spiced.

It's clear to Marian that Amelia much prefers making soups and
stews to presenting a meal centered around meat or fish.

They agree to eat only the meat sold on a farm owned by friends
of Amelia's; she is content that the animals had a good life, weren't
fed unnatural things, and were brought to their deaths as easily as
possible. Most often, though, Amelia and her grandmother eat soups
and stews whose main ingredients are vegetables, beans, and obscure
grains, many of whose names Marian has never heard. In late August,
they gorge on melons. They spend a whole day making pear tarts,
intending to give some to Helga and Rosa and some to Graham. But
then, reveling in their own greed, they decide to share with no one.

"Can you make a nice supper for Graham on Wednesday night?" Marian asks. "He's going to come and talk seriously to us, God spare us."

Amelia makes a ratatouille with the overabundant eggplant and
zucchini and a chicken with roasted potatoes. To make up for their
earlier greed, they make more pear tarts, packing several away for
Graham to take home.

Graham, whatever else he is to her, is Meme's lawyer. And so if
he wants to talk about something serious, it's probably Meme's will.

What, Amelia wonders, is the right food for the discussion of a will? The pre-death banquet, the rehearsal dinner?

Usually, the three of them would play Scrabble, at which Marian is surprisingly bad, Amelia shockingly good, Graham occasionally winning. "That's because it's not really a game about words, it's about spatial relationships," Marian once said. She seems to have, for some reason Amelia can't grasp, a stake in understanding Graham as a charming fool.

"Meme, you can't be illiterate and win at Scrabble," Amelia said, solicitous about Graham's feelings even in his absence.

"I suppose," Marian said.

"No Scrabble tonight, my ladies," Graham says now. "We're here to talk about your grandmother's plans and the details of what she wants after she passes."

"I'm not passing, Graham, I'm dying. When people say 'passing,' all I can think of is passing gas."

Graham laughs. "Okay, my darling, when you kick the bucket, buy the farm, go into the wild blue yonder . . . how's that?"

"Much better," she says.

"The long and short of it, Amelia, is that your grandmother doesn't have much in assets, almost nothing. She's leaving her share of the nursery to Helga—I wouldn't be surprised if it eventually comes to you, but never mind. For right now, what she has is the house, and that will be yours."

"But if you want to sell it," Marian says, "you don't have to feel like you're dancing on my grave."

"I wouldn't sell it, Meme. I love this house."

"Yes, you think you love it because you've never had to take care of it. But that might prove to be a burden, and a legacy should be liberation, not a burden."

· · ·

Her grandmother is right. She will have to think of the house in a new way, the house that she has loved so easily, with such clarity, as she has loved her grandmother easily, clearly, the house and her grandmother, inseparable in her mind, what she thought of when she had to think of the word "home."

Home in the way that the house in Westwood doesn't seem to be. She wasn't a child there; the family lived first in Palo Alto, when her mother was in graduate school, then for five years in Mexico City, where her mother followed her mentor, a Mexican urban planner, who then relocated to Los Angeles, to which they followed him again. Through all those changes, every summer she came to Meme's house, where nothing changed, where everything was always as she had left it, waiting for her, enclosing, limited, and sweet.

If her grandmother's house was her grandmother, the Westwood house was her mother. She wonders if it is only women whose houses become their bodies, or whose bodies become their houses. The Westwood house had nothing to do with her father's body. Her father seemed barely to inhabit it, although he spent many more hours in it than her mother did. He stayed at home with Amelia while her mother was out saving a city, many cities, some of them thousands of miles away. A studio was set up for him in the basement; his kiln was there, and shelves and shelves overfilled with pots, vases, plates that he brought to craft fairs and flea markets, hoping they would sell. Amelia always went with him, collecting the money for the sales that were always far more rare than she hoped. She would leave each craft fair, each flea market, saddened for herself rather than her father. Her beautiful, gentle father, to whom it never seemed to occur to be ashamed or disappointed. Whistling, making up songs as he repacked the pots, the vases, the plates, each carefully, each like a loved young animal, and lifted the heavy crates into the van. Not seeing the disappointment on his wife's face when she asked, "Had a good day?" His reply was always, "Good enough," and he'd tell her about the wonderful conversation he had had with the person who bought the vase, the mug, the plate.

Everything in the Westwood house had straight lines; Marian once said to Amelia of her mother, "She only knows one way of proceeding: straight ahead," and she knew her grandmother was right. The house had been designed to be earthquake proof and energy efficient. Amelia understood that the house was considered enviable, although she'd never met anyone who said they envied it. It was admirable rather than lovable . . . as her mother was admirable, but also lovable, because, in her headlong straightforwardness, she sometimes crashed straight into what she didn't see. Amelia would never say she didn't love her mother; her mother was a bulwark, a shelter, a defense against the hostile elements. And after her father died, she found a new reason to admire and love her. She learned from her mother's mother only then that Naomi had wanted to be a singer. She said that Naomi had had a "fine contralto"—only after her course in music history did Amelia know what that meant. Only then did Amelia ask her mother why she'd given it up. Naomi explained that she knew Amelia's father would always have trouble making a living, and that she knew she didn't have the "fire in the belly" that a career as a singer required.

Amelia thought that was a troubling image: fire in the belly; it sounded unpleasant, but her mother made it sound desirable. Amelia knew she had no fire in her belly. And she didn't feel it in her grandmother, either. No, Meme was a warm lap, a curve that had a space for things, for something that might never come into being and that certainly had no name. Did that mean she loved her grandmother better than she loved her mother? She wouldn't consider that for a minute. But she knows she has always been more comfortable with Meme. With her mother, you always felt you had to be sitting up straight; her mother always seemed poised for something, the next new thing. She loved new things; it's why she was good at her job.

But nothing in Meme's house is new; nothing has hard edges; you can rest anywhere. Everywhere she goes in her grandmother's house, she feels safe. By safe, does she mean comfortable? That, she has always feared, is not admirable.

The house in Westwood is large and wide and open; the light always seems to Amelia too much of all one thing. In Meme's house, the light can change in seconds because of the movement of a cloud or the swaying of a branch, or even mysteriously at high noon in mid-summer. Each object in the house absorbs the light, softens, divides it—as with the brass pokers by the fireplace that give off a series of bronzed reflections—landing somewhere unexpected: falling on the brown corduroy of the easy chair, the white china dog that serves as a doorstop at the entrance to the living room.

She thinks that maybe the light in the California house is too much of all one thing because the house prides itself on its unified openness to the world. Nothing is hidden—except that it is. Everything you need is behind the doors of the built-in cabinets that present to the world only a white matte plane: there aren't even knobs or handles. You press a door at a particular place, and then a revelation occurs. There it is, what you are looking for: pencils, pens, glasses, dishes, books.

But in Meme's house, nothing is only one thing. Each room is divided into sections, even the small bedrooms upstairs—really, as her mother has pointed out, not a separate floor but an attic—take their shape from the relation of the walls to the roof. When she was small, she would count the number of sections dividing the walls and ceilings of her grandmother's bedroom. When her parents vis-ited, she slept on a cot in her grandmother's room, and, until she was twelve, she asked if she could stay there even after her parents had gone, which Meme always allowed. Later, when Amelia took geom-etry, she learned that the shape of the room was trapezoidal, made up of a series of larger or smaller trapezoidal panels of dark wood.

All the windows are made of small panes of wavy, unclear glass divided by mullions. When she was a child, Amelia thought "mullions" must be the wrong word: mullions sounded like something you ate, something in gravy, savory, melting in the mouth. Each year when she arrived, she counted the separate panes of glass: twelve in the front window of the living room, sixteen in the rear, twenty in each window of Meme's study. She was always afraid that when she was gone, something might be added or subtracted. But nothing ever changed, and the opposite of a fairy tale, the very lack of transformation—that she had gone away, had grown, had lived her life, and it had stayed the same—rendered it, for her, magical.

Most magic for her were the panes of red glass that bordered the front door. Each year, Amelia sat there for hours, looking out at a world grown wonderful. People would pass on the street; they were not themselves, however, but bejeweled royals. Cars were carriages transporting precious cargo. Trees were precious, too: their leaves were rubies. It was then that the word "precious" itself became precious to her. She understood its meaning: what she would give things up for, what she would hold fast, whatever came.

The objects in Meme's house seemed much more valuable to her than the objects in the California house, although later she learned that, in fact, they were not—that the black pyramidal sculpture in the living room, the brown-and-grey Indian blanket in Westwood were much more costly than the blue-and-rose Turkey carpet in her grandmother's bedroom and the blue-and-white plate that hung on the kitchen wall. She thought it therefore wonderful that things were left around in Meme's house, not a sign of crowding or disorder but of a friendly willingness of things to be of use. But so many of the things she liked weren't really of use, unless you counted comfort and the pleasures of familiarity useful. The piano that no one played; a window of frosted glass in her grandmother's bedroom that revealed only the dark hallway that led to the bathroom. She had felt hurt on the house's behalf when her mother spoke of a slice of the room she and Amelia's father slept in as "wasted space." To make it up to the room, Amelia asked her grandmother if, when her parents weren't using the room, she could make it into a space where her dolls could entertain each other, serve each other tea, lounge and read. Her grandmother, of course, agreed.

The California house never seemed to have any smell, except the smell of a hard-won cleanliness earned by the various cleaning products leaving behind the serious proof of a job well done. Everything in Meme's house had a scent that seemed to blend into all the other scents. Even the bathroom had a smell of a soapy, nourishing dampness, as if the afterthoughts of mildly scented baths had saturated the white walls with an unassuming essence that was proof of nothing.

The kitchen smelt of Meme's cooking; she baked bread every week, and she hung herbs from the ceiling to dry. Often the smell of sage pervaded, or lavender or thyme. When Amelia was a child, she associated the word "sassafras" with her grandmother's kitchen, not knowing what it was—but it sounded like the name of the smell she met every time she opened the kitchen door.

Nothing in her grandmother's house is exactly even or straight. The living room floor slants dramatically, the staircase lists a bit to the right. When in high school Amelia read a poem by Emily Dickinson, "Tell all the truth but tell it slant," she thought of her grandmother's house. She has never felt out of place in this house, as she always has in the house in California; she's more comfortable with the limitations of the architecture of the East. This is the house she belongs in. And now it will belong to her.

What will it be when Meme is no longer in the world? Will the house take up the job of her presence, will it take over the job of unquestioning protection that has always been Meme's job?

But when her grandmother dies, it will no longer be Meme's house; it will be hers. She will be the owner. Perhaps what had charmed her will be a worry. She will have to think of things like gutters and foundations and sills; she will have to monitor the smells for signs of mildew; the sound of rain on the roof—always so comforting—will it be a source of agitation then?

What does it mean to be a homeowner at twenty-four? No one her age she knows owns anything. Will it make her a different person, older than she wants to be, older than she's ready for? Is Meme right, is this gift in fact a burden?

No, it's what she needs, the required push out of an endlessly prolonged, prolongable childhood, the collision with the real. But the house will make her someone she does not yet know.

She wonders if her face, which is not good, she knows, at rendering itself illegible, has revealed her anxieties, because Graham says, "You're not on your own with all this, Amelia. I'm good with everything connected to houses, legal and physical, and, of course, Josh will be around to help if things need fixing, or fixing up."

But you're old too, Graham, she wants to say, and how will I pay Josh, or suppose he moves away, or something happens when he's on one of his long surfing holidays?

She smiles the smile—her father's—that she knows is meant to please whomever she directs it at, to please without promising anything specific, only a general good outcome, a sense that everything will turn out fine.

"This is wonderful. Thank you, Meme. You know how much I love this house."

When Graham leaves, it's ten o'clock. Amelia turns out the porch light when she hears his car door close; she sees the moon, a fingernail in the blue-black sky. The stars, she thinks, are brighter than they've been for months, scoured by the first chill of September.

She and her grandmother clear the dishes from the table. Amelia tells Meme to go to bed; she'll be happy to see to the dishes.

"I guess I'm an heiress now," she says.

"An heiress. Well, that's something I gave up; I probably could have been pretty well off now if I hadn't been disinherited."

"Disinherited." A word from another age, burnished, encrusted, dusted over with unlovely pollen, toxic-looking spores. Something in the word presses a spring in Amelia's mind, and words come out of her mouth before she can locate their source.

"Speaking of inheritance, Meme, you've kept some of my inheritance from me. And I want it."

"What's that?" Marian asks, waiting for the punch line to one of Amelia's rare, mild jokes.

"Your past," Amelia says. "I don't know who you are."

SPAIN, 1946

THE DAY BEGINS as all the others have begun. Five knocks. Insistent, accusatory. No words. She almost forgets that words are customary. "Good morning." "It's seven o'clock." "The sun is shining." "Rain today."

Each morning, the same thought first: "Johnny, if only I could be with you. But I am not like you—brave. I can't think how to do it. It seems much too hard. The details are beyond me. Everything is beyond me. Everything has been lost. Ramón, my great beloved. The war. Our dreams. The people we fought beside. The ones we loved."

She wakes each morning envying the fortunate dead, freed of the burden of living, the demand that one foot be put before another, one breath taken, then another breath. Free of the horrible pretense of being human when it is no longer possible to say what being human means. The constant dissimulation of pretending to live a life.

The pull of the bed. Hard, narrow, the rough blanket. The thin pillow. The coarse sheets. Nevertheless the one object of desire. The only lovely thought: When will it be time to be here again, in bed? The yawn: voluptuous. The single joy: the giving over, the giving in.

No matter how much she sleeps, she never wakes rested. Her dreams will not release her from the images she carries: her brother, hanging from a rope; a child's leg in his ration of bread and milk; the child whose sex she covered to spare its shame; her friend Carmen buried under rubble, her graceful foot in her new high-heeled shoe. Ramón, writhing, begging her to slake a thirst that nothing she could do would slake.

Always she wakes in fear. She knew fear in the days of the war, of course, but this was a new kind, a different flavor. The fear she felt during the war was a fear of something definite: an enemy that could be named and, more important, shared. Weapons that could be seen. Now this is like a duel with invisible weapons. A duel with a vapor, a fog, a poison gas that might or might not be inhaled at any moment. But hidden within the fog, the faceless one who threatens, "I will take everything, everything that makes you know yourself."

In war, a death, a reasonable death, was not unthinkable. And to try to avoid it would be to betray what you were there to do. But she would do everything she could to avoid this faceless one. He risked nothing, and you were nothing to him. What was the right word for the punisher who risked nothing, the enforcer of the law? The punishment not death, but something worse. Torture, imprisonment.

Often she tells herself that she is not afraid of death. She imagines it as something relatively quick. But torture and imprisonment are different; they can go on and on. For years. There are whispers, there are rumors. The war has been over for seven years. People disappeared, others were released and sent home, broken, unrecognizable. Hidden by frightened family. Unaddressed. Shunned. Pilar takes pleasure in repeating the rumors. Shaking her finger under Marian's nose. Do you understand that we are keeping you safe here? That you must do exactly as I say, not just to save yourself but to save your son.

And that is another kind of fear. She fears her child. She fears him most for what he makes her understand about herself.

She cannot bear to touch him or to be touched by him.

How quickly he was taken from her. Only days after his birth. She didn't have the strength then to resist. She believed they were right to

take him from her when her breasts could not produce the nourishment he needed to stay alive. She still believes it now. There is nothing of hers that would be, to this child, her child, of the slightest use.
There is only one thing she can do for him: if she can keep herself
from the attention of the authorities, she might keep him from being
taken away, the child of a Rojo—placed, who knew where, given a
new name, never seen again.

For his first six months she barely saw him, and when she saw him
she was discouraged from holding him. "The smell of you would confuse him," said the woman who nursed him, who Marian believed
knew far better than she did, having already nursed seven strong sons.

Marian knew nothing about babies. She had never even held one.
Always, she had been the youngest.

She was frightened, always, when she held him, and probably he
felt it; from the beginning, he screamed when she took him in her
arms. She was always afraid of dropping him, because she was weak,
weakened from the hunger that plagued them all, and not nursing the
child she felt she had no right to ask for more food than anyone else,
even though she had just given birth. But she knew that the woman
of the house, her mother-in-law, mother of her beloved, begrudged
her every bite.

She didn't want anyone to touch her. Her skin was dry and flak-
ing, she felt its cover insufficient, like an old overused envelope that
might disintegrate at the slightest touch. And so when she held her
child, she felt the pressure of his body was a danger to her. When she
walked with him, she wanted to put him down almost immediately.
His weight oppressed her; she felt his health, his strength, not with
pride, as a mother should, but as a crushing force that might, quite
easily, rob her of breath.

Every morning she forces herself to get up if for no other reason
than to diminish the fear. But there is nothing to get up for. Nothing
to look forward to. Opening the door to the dark hallway, making

her way through the sitting room, a jungle of obstructive furniture. A dim light from the gas lamp, but there is nothing she wants to see.

The tomblike closeness of the Ortiz household makes her scalp itch; her ribs press against her lungs like the tines of a fork. She longs to rip the pictures from the walls: the bleeding Christs, the bleeding saints, the bleeding bulls. In her bed, she hatches elaborate plans to smash the picture above the blood-red brocade sofa, the picture that is the pride of the home, Pilar's prize. In it, a child—Pilar—sits on what must be the same sofa, in what must be her First Communion dress. White, ruffled, a wide satin sash bisecting her unbending trunk; a veil, topped by a wreath of flowers. It must have been one of the first things Pilar told her, one of the only things: that the photograph commemorated Pilar's winning of a diocesan competition. In the whole diocese of Valencia, Pilar Ramirez answered correctly the most questions about the catechism. She was given, as her prize, a medal, which she holds out to the camera, almost belligerently, as if she's daring someone anyone to take it from her. Her face has taken on what will be its characteristic expression: a closed, aggressive smugness, the challenging proud mouth, the thick censoring eyebrows. On one side of her is a bishop, bald, with black glasses that seem too large for his narrow face and thin fingers that seem too delicate to bear the heavy weight of the Episcopal ring. On the other side of Pilar sits the parish priest, his hands folded on his lap, his feet planted indecisively on the dark floor: is he ready at any moment to leap to his feet, to fall to his knees to kiss the bishop's ring? On one side of the bishop, Pilar's mother in an elaborate black mantilla; next to the parish priest, her father, dwarfing both clerics, his chest puffed out, his brush cut bristling.

She remembers Ramón talking about the Spanish love of blood. *Sangre, sangre, sangre,* she can hear him saying. Nearly all the pictures in the Ortiz house have something to do with blood. The Sacred Heart, blood shooting out in diagonal needles from what seems like a pimento in the center of the Savior's chest. On the wall above a small round table on which a candle inside a red glass has been placed—not a painting, but what she first thought were framed slats. But then, Ramón's father, also Ramón, showed her with pride that if you tilted your head one way, you saw Jesus's head, crowned with thorns, blood streaming into his half-shut eyes; tilt your head the other way, and it was Jesus scourged at the pillar, his bloody back torn open by the grinning soldiers' whips. She didn't hate this picture as much as she hated the photograph of the child Pilar—she was always willing to be gentler in her judgments of Ramón than of his wife. He showed her the only kindness that came to her anywhere in the house; even the servant girl seemed an extension of Pilar's implacable contempt. Marian couldn't begrudge his delight in the marvelous trick picture he so proudly showed her. She didn't need to close her eyes against it, as she had to close her eyes against the photograph of Pilar, surrounded by her family, the clergy, her medal clutched in her gloved hand. And against the image that greeted whoever came into the front door: the huge photograph of Franco, framed in gold.

The house was always dark, and she often barked her shin on the overlarge furniture. She knew there was no space for her anywhere in the house. It had been made clear to her, not gently, that she was in every way incompetent. Incompetent in all the ways that went into making a proper, even an acceptable, woman.

The preparation of food was entirely beyond her. Once, the servant Lucia was ill and, with her customary pleasure in humiliation, Pilar said, "Perhaps you could take on some of her work?" But how was that possible? Marian's eyes fell with despair on the open fire where food was prepared: the implacable black hook from which the huge soup pot hung. The grill, supported by two brackets on squat legs. "What, have you never cooked before, my lady?"

She had to tell the truth: no, not really. She does not say, although it is obvious that this is what Pilar understands, that she was brought up with servants. Sent to boarding school. Then college. Then the war: she was better at carrying stretchers, at driving ambulances, at assisting at surgery; cooking was left to ordinary women. Acceptable women. Which she was not. She knows she is not an acceptable woman. A daughter of privilege. A little sister. There is no place for her in any normal home.

"At least you can set the table. At least you can sweep the floor." Grateful that she is of any use at all.

Soon, she is told that she is incapable of caring for her son. She is home with him all day, warned against going outside, she might say something to someone, she understands nothing, she has no idea what word could land her in prison, her son in the orphanage. But being alone in the dim house all day adds to her overwhelming fatigue. The only children's books here in the house, he cannot bear to look at: they are pious, saccharine. There are almost no toys. A few empty spools denuded of their thread, and something that looks like a sock, but the servant who knit it tells her it is a monkey. She feels foolish sitting with her son on the floor making the monkey hop, dance, scratch itself, and the child looks at her as if to say, "You are a fool."

On one of the first warm days of spring—Ignacio is two and a half—she decides that she will walk with him down to the sea. The Ortiz house is at the top of the hill; there is a glimpse of the sea from the plaza that surrounds the church—only steps away from the house—but to get to the water, hundreds of steps must be descended, then climbed to return. She takes her mother-in-law's warnings seriously: she vows to herself that she will talk to no one; if someone tries to engage her in conversation, she will turn to her child, whisper something to him, point to something on the ground.

Ignacio does not like walking. After a few steps he whimpers and asks to be picked up. He is a large child, heavy for his age. She tries to cajole him to walk by himself, but he refuses, and she can carry him only a few steps before she feels exhausted. She tries to make it a game: I'll carry you while I count to fifty, then you walk while I count to fifty. Then she realizes that numbers mean nothing to him; he is confused and begins to cry.

When they reach the shore, she would like to lie down and rest; the exertion has undone her. But she has forgotten that this is not one of the sandy beaches of her childhood; stones, not sand, lead to the water. Ignacio cries that the stones hurt his feet; he wants to go home, he is cold, he is hungry. They are at the shore only fifteen minutes before she gives in to him, agrees to take him home.

But it didn't occur to her how difficult it would be to climb up the hundreds of stairs leading from the sea to their home, which is at the highest point of the town. Holding her heavy child. She tries to make him walk up the stairs with her, tries to think of some way it would seem like play to him, but he loosens himself from her grasp and lies down on a step in the middle of the staircase. She cajoles, she wheedles, but he will not move. She crouches, lifts him, promises to carry him all the way home. But after a few steps she is out of breath, and her limbs have lost all strength. She tells Ignacio they must take a rest. He screams that he needs to go home.

From nowhere, from everywhere, women appear at the top of the staircase. "Are you all right? Is the child all right?" they cluck, squat officious hens; but their concern, she sees, is not uncensoring.

"Yes," she says. "I just need to rest a bit before carrying him."

"You are a big boy," says one woman, the age of his grandmother. "You can walk on your own, can't you?"

Ignacio opens his mouth in what Marian thinks will be a scream, but instead he bends over and on the stairs deposits a half-dollar-sized puddle of brown vomit.

"The little one is sick," the grandmother says, no longer dreaming of urging the little one to walk.

"I will get my son," she says. She disappears into one of the white houses and then comes down the steps to them, holding the hand of a huge boy—a man—who is clearly puzzled, and, Marian sees, perhaps not completely right in the head. At his mother's order, he lifts Ignacio, and the grandmother says, "Walk ahead of him, don't worry, he's a good boy; he's slow, but he's a good boy, show him where to go and he can help you."

Marian thanks the circle of clucking mothers, grandmothers, and leads the tall boy man up the hundreds of steps. Ignacio is silent all the way but looks over his carrier's shoulder with what Marian thinks is a victorious, a sated look. When they get home he says that he is hungry, and she feeds him bread and orange marmalade, preserved last year. She prays that he will agree to a nap after lunch, which means that she can sleep, and sleep is all she longs for.

At supper Pilar says, "Well, you made a spectacle of yourself today. Why did you take him out? I told you not to take him out. And if he catches cold now, whose fault will that be? You know how easily he catches cold."

It does not need to be said, it is so clearly understood by Marian, Ramón, even the child: You have failed; you are not to be trusted.

And finally, only weeks later, Pilar, the hanging judge, gets all the proof she needs.

Marian doesn't know how it happened. She was sitting on the hard, unaccommodating sofa—horsehair, she knows, is what it's stuffed with and always, sitting on it, she feels she is sitting on a bony and resistant nag. Ignacio was on the floor in front of her, rolling the spools back and forth, the sound of them repetitive, soporific. She was trying, she knows she was trying, not to let her eyes close. But it happened, of course, it must have happened, she fell asleep.

And then she wakes, terrified. Ignacio is not on the floor in front of her and Pilar is in the house, shaking Marian by the shoulders, leaning over her, her face feverish with outrage.

"Useless good-for-nothing! You allow your child to wander on the streets. Two and a half years old. Thank God he had the sense to make his way to my brother's home, where they know how to care for children."

How had it happened, that he had made his way out of the house? The heavy wooden door had not been closed; the weather was warm, and only a beaded curtain separated them from the street. But there was no excuse. She was to blame. She supposed she should be grateful that he had made his way to the house of his uncle.

·

Pilar's brother. José Ramirez. Merchant. Black marketeer.

In Marian's dreams of Spain before she'd ever seen it, there had been no place for the Ramirez family, who were neither stoic and warmhearted peasants nor haughty hidalgos. They were the bourgeoisie. Their importance in the town was outsized now in this time when scarcity was the chief currency. Only Pilar in the pharmacy could provide relief from pain, only José could make the difference between bare survival and the normalcy of prewar domestic life. All holidays were in his hands; without him there could be no celebration.

If Pilar was a woman of stone, José was the gnome villain of a fairy tale, his lightless eyes, his oversized potato-shaped nose and chin as sharp as a knife blade, his hunched shoulders, as if he were always counting coins in a secret cellar, bending over his treasure in the dark. When she thought of him, Marian wished that she could call up the old categories of sin, because she believed he was a great sinner, watching his neighbors starve while he guarded his treasures of oil, ham, olives, eggs, locked in a back room with a key he kept always on a chain around his waist, selling them at ten times what they were worth.

Hunger. Starvation. They were not descriptive words, they were conditions that could lead to death. One day when Ignacio was sleeping and she went down to the kitchen for a glass of water, Marian saw the servant Lucia slipping some pieces of cheese wrapped in a cloth down the front of her dress. She turned and looked at Marian with a look of pure hatred. "This is for my family. You must understand. I am not a thief. My niece almost died because all she had to eat was grass boiled in salt water; when they were lucky, they made a dinner of carob pods. And the *señora* has more than she needs, you all have more than you need."

"I would never say anything, never," Marian said. "You can trust me."

"Trust," Lucia said, snorting. "We have learned some things about trust that cannot be unlearned."

If Marian imagined that she would make a friend of Lucia, or at least an ally, she was wrong. The woman seemed to grovel even more to Pilar, and to cut Marian with a more marked coldness, as if she could not forgive Marian for placing her in the position where she might have to be grateful, or relax her suspicions, or risk the safe berth she had as the servant of the sister of the black marketeer.

They huddle together, the Ramirez family; José's house is fifty yards from Pilar's, his shop another fifty yards from his house. The house, even more overstuffed than Pilar's, is presided over by the strapping blond wife, the contrast between her and her husband so clearly comical that it seems like one of those jokes that lost its flavor by being repeated too often. How proud he was of his wife's largeness, her blondness, as if it were a particularly clever investment he had had the sense to make at a time when good buys were to be had by the perspicacious. "Beef on the hoof" were the words that came to Marian's mind whenever she saw Inez: the thick muscular calves, the high heels she always wore drawing attention to their strength, their heft. At family dinners, Inez sat always at the head of the table, across from the gilt-framed mirror; she could scarcely take her eyes away from her own reflection to pass a dish, to lift a fork to her lipsticked mouth.

And yet, like Pilar, both of them icons of flourishing female health, each had only produced one child. She often wondered what Ramón, her husband, had thought of his cousin José. Blond, and heavy like his mother, his largeness had loomed, whereas his mother's kept its place in the closed circle of her coiffed and corseted self-invention. He lived for the days when he could put on his blue Falangist uniform and parade, holding a flag, following the priest who raised the cross, following in his turn the Falangist officer who carried the banner with Franco's picture.

José and his wife worked in his father's shop. Ana was a country girl, a distant cousin whose face always expressed a kind of willed puzzlement, a desire to give way. They lived next door to José's parents and were the producers of the treasured girl child Fernanda, six months older than Ignacio. Fernanda of the golden ringlets, whose feet were never, it seemed to Marian, allowed to touch the ground. To serve her seemed an honor all the family vied for, and Pilar made her own contribution to this worship, placing Ignacio beside her: the princess and the crowned prince, her consort.

A sister of Ana's—Rosa was her name—had been brought in from the country to care for Fernanda while Ana worked in the store.

Rosa shared her sister's look of bewilderment, but whereas working behind the counter had dyed Ana's self-effacement with a shade of commercially based pride, Rosa scurried around like an animal unused to its new habitat, and abased herself in front of Fernanda as if she were the *infanta*, who could send anyone afraid to the gallows for any infringement, real or imagined.

It is to the house of the princess of the golden curls, the house of unlimited food and warmth, the house where he is prince, his great-uncle's house, that Ignacio makes his way, opening the door and walking out while his mother sleeps, her feet still on the floor, her head supported by the hard back of the brocade couch.

And so they appear before her, judge, jury, hangman. Pilar, her brother, his wife and son. The princess being carried by her father, Ignacio in the arms of his grandmother. Sucking a caramel, his eyes heavy with sleep and sugar. It has been decided, no one questions this, that he will spend his days with little Fernanda, prince and princess, waited on by the country girl who feels honored to be allowed to perform the task.

"Now you can stay in your bed and sleep the whole day long," Pilar says.

For a moment, Marian would like to thank her. Sleep all day long. Never wake. What could be better, what could be more wonderful?

•

In the depth of her shame a light enters, as dim as the vigil light in front of the trick picture that changes if you move your head.

A few weeks after it has been decided that Marian cannot care for her child—weeks in which she has done almost nothing but sleep and sit in her dark room, thinking of nothing—her father-in-law knocks on her door. "I was wondering if, since you will be more free in the daytime now, perhaps you could work with me in the store," he says. "It would be of great help to me if you could speak to the customers, help me with the money."

She is touched, and she knows this is an act, not just of kindness but of courage. What is more precious than the offer of a life preserver from a drowning man?

"I would like that very much, Ramón. But what would Pilar think?"

Both of them understand that Pilar, the stone woman, the iron woman (he is an ironworker, but he has no strength to bend and shape the iron of his wife), has for both of them nothing but contempt. The only question: does she desire to punish Marian by a thoroughgoing imprisonment inside the house, or will she say, by her refusal to put her weight on one scale or another, You are nothing, you are nothing, nothing you do is of the slightest consequence to me.

"She said it makes no difference to her what you do."

•

Marian had thought that perhaps having a destination that she had some obligation to reach might give her energy. But the air of the streets is of the same poisonous quality as the air of the house. As if a two-headed monster dwelt on the top of the near mountain, breathing over every inch of the town. The two heads, inseparable from the massive trunk. One head, the Church; the other the Caudillo. Caudillo, Franco's chosen title, leader, head, selected so that he might match the Führer or El Duce. Only they had disappeared, and he was everywhere.

It is never possible to feel free from surveillance. It is in the air: the lungs take it in like silicate; no one breathes naturally for years. Children are warned to trust no one; parents, out of love for their children, conceal the simplest details of their past. Children are beaten for asking questions they can't imagine are worth a beating. Because families are divided, no one feels safe, even at family gatherings. People speak, habitually, in whispers; people cover their mouths with their hands to make the slightest transactions. When Marian is working at her father-in-law's shop, she has to ask people to repeat their orders several times, their voices are so low, or they are speaking behind their hands, whispering: *Can you fix my gate; my window latch fails to close properly.* These are the only words spoken to her by the people of the town; she has been warned by Pilar against speaking to anyone, and her father-in-law has explained to her that it is an accepted belief that "no good ever comes from speaking to a stranger."

So she gets used to being unaddressed at church, and even at the movies shown in the parish hall. The movies, the one occasion for shared release. The people of the town flock to them with an avidity that surprises Marian, coming from America, where movies were one of the many entertainments available even to ordinary people. But in this town, they are the only entertainment; in the colder months, they are the only source of steady heat. Even here, no one is free from the all-seeing eye of the Caudillo. Each film starts with a newsreel praising Franco and his achievements. When his face appears, everyone must stand and salute him.

The censoring arm of the Falange controls what films can be shown in Franco's Spain. The majority of the Spanish films are either a version of operetta, where the girl and boy overcome obstacles to marry with a final duet mingling with the songs of birds, or rural, particularly Andalusian, romances, in which cheerful peasant boys and girls fight poverty to achieve perfect happiness while the townspeople happily dance. Popular too are historical epics chronicling the glories of Spain. A particular favorite are the ones recounting the expulsion of the Moors. Then there are the religious dramas: noble missionaries risking brutal torture and death at the hands of savages. *The Miracle of Fatima,* the most popular film of 1943, dramatizes the appearance of the Virgin in Portugal in 1917, with three brave peasant children enduring the disbelief of the bishop to spread the Virgin's words: Communism is the greatest evil the world has ever seen. Sometimes the two genres—the heroic past of Spain, the saint's life— are blended. San Ignacio de Loyola, the dandy, the soldier, who finds Jesus while recovering from a wound earned in battle. Santa Teresa— nothing to do with the Bernini Marian remembers from her trip to Rome: no ecstatic swoon, only a rigid insistence on the denial of all pleasure, her insistence that the nuns go barefoot. Marian notices what she thinks is a fetishistic emphasis on the saint's lovely feet.

The two American movies permitted in the town are *The Song of Bernadette*, celebrating the Miracle of Lourdes, and, incomprehensibly to Marian, Alfred Hitchcock's *Rebecca*, dubbed so that even the pleasure of sophisticated filming is denied her. She does not listen to the dialogue; she concentrates on Laurence Olivier, who she believes is saying something wonderful in English, something else she is denied. She goes to the movies because it is a way of getting out of the house, and in the darkness she can close her eyes and sleep.

There is one required destination: she has to be seen in church, at the very least each Sunday for Mass. There is no way for her to keep herself from it. Over and over, Pilar warns her, hissing into her ear, as if it were a precious secret, "You must be seen in church. They suspect you of being a Rojo, and they will have no trouble taking you and the child away forever." The Guardia, visible everywhere and nowhere, make it impossible for her to doubt her mother-in-law. The Guardia Civil, always imported from another region, always strangers, unplaceable. Everything about them becomes the furniture of nightmares: their patent leather tricorner hats, their stiff photogenic uniforms. Once, two of them tried to join a group of boys playing soccer on the beach—perhaps an innocent request. But the boys, seeing them, lost their zeal for playing; they ran halfheartedly, they let the ball go always to the Guardia, then trailed off, one by one, leaving the two Guardia to kick the ball back and forth to each other.

Three times a day, prayers are broadcast everywhere in the town from a loudspeaker—a gift of the mayor—that is attached to the walls of the church. The morning Rosary. The evening Vespers. At noon everyone must stop what they are doing and pray the Angelus.

Angelus Domini nuntiavit Mariae.
Et concepit de Spiritu Sancto.

The Angel of the Lord declared unto Mary.
And she conceived of the Holy Ghost.

The Angelus: the words of Mary and the Angel, when she is informed that she will give birth to the Son of God. The source of thousands of paintings: the lovely girl, the swooping angel with chaste or flamboyant wings. But here, the words ricochet like bullets against the stark white walls of the houses, they crash against the black cobblestones of the steep streets; the flowers trailing up the walls do not absorb them; nothing softens them; the blatant light of noon magnifies them, they root themselves, as straight as spears thrown down into the dry-packed earth.

Now the Angelus and the response to it are a way of keeping track, grounds for possible punishment. The Guardia patrol the streets at noon, they write something in their books—no one knows what—if they see someone not stopping work or a conversation to pray. The possible uses of this information are imagined, feared, never to be verified. What is known: people have disappeared, people have been imprisoned, and no one is told why.

Even the seasons of the year seem to be in their charge.

Summer is time for special surveillance; the Guardia in their uniforms, the priests in their cassocks, patrol the beach making sure that no women are wearing immodest bathing suits. Eventually, the beach is cordoned off into two sections: one for women, one for men. Two holidays mark the hot months: July 18, the anniversary of the beginning of the Civil War; August 15, the Assumption of the Virgin—both days in which the Falangists in their blue, their trumpets and their drums, insisting that everyone attend and think of nothing else. Any lack of enthusiasm, even a moderate response, can be a danger.

Autumn, the Feast of All Saints, the Feast of All Souls, the martyrs for the faith prayed for, the hundreds of thousands killed at the fascist hands erased, their deaths a blank or a blot: no grief for their lost souls permitted.

Winter, when the poor freeze because there is no fuel, the starving are given gifts in the name of the Three Kings, but no, it is not permitted to say anyone is starving, because the Caudillo protects his beloved child, Spain, as Joseph, foster father of the Lord, kept watch over the child Jesus. It is one of the few times when Marian misses America: she wishes they had a Christmas tree; she loved the smell of pine in the cold air, the ornaments packed in tissue paper, the candles on the tree in the middle of the huge dark hallway. She'd had no use for Santa Claus, but it would be something of a relief to see his image here, something outside the ring of authority that is the Catholic Church.

Spring is the worst. A season of enforced public observance, from Ash Wednesday straight through to Pentecost. The Lenten missions, the visiting preachers railing against the dangers of dancing, "torture of confessors, favorite fare of the Devil." Never absent from the words of the pulpit, the demand to thank God for the Caudillo, to pray for his success: "You must be grateful to Franco and his government and must ask God to illuminate them and give them comfort so they can continue with their work of enthroning social justice. I ask you to look at poverty and all trouble from the perspective of the divine, because if you look at them in this way, they will seem smoother to you and you will extract from them all the treasures of eternal life they contain."

The operatic climax of Holy Week, the penitents that terrify Marian in their Ku Klux Klan hoods; the flagellants, venerated for the shedding of their own blood by whipping themselves on the shoulders or the back. Good Friday: an orgy of accusation against the Jews, a prayer for their conversion woven into the charge of their murder of Christ.

And May, the month of First Communions. The girls like little brides, the boys in white, cadets in training, preparing themselves for the honor of serving the Generalissimo, white satin sashes crossing their chests, marking the place that will one day be taken by what she learned was called a "Sam Browne belt" (she doesn't know what the Spanish call it; she is afraid to ask), which the Caudillo wears beneath the jeweled crucifix that transects it.

•

This is why today Pilar's knocks are less insistent, more distracted. It is the day of Ignacio's First Communion. He will make it a bit early; he is six and a half years old, but special permission has been granted so he can make it with his cousin, Fernanda.

He was given his gifts a week before, because they would be needed for the ceremony. A lacquered prayer book, a gold cross on a gold chain, a bow the size of a dinner plate with images of the Eucharist embroidered onto it in blue silk, a white suit, white socks and shoes. The socks are silk; the shoes, a leather soft as the kid leather of the gloves she once wore, once treasured.

For months they had prepared, Ignacio and his grandmother. Marian remembers her own preparation, which was equally ardent, Sister Trinitas drawing on the board the image of the soul (not exactly a heart, but close) and then coloring spots inside it in red chalk, wiping them out with the eraser to suggest the radical effects of confession. Marian had been serious about her first confession, although she had only one sin to confess: anger, fighting with her brothers, wishing her brothers harm. And then, on the day, her white dress, a simple drop-waist organdy, and a simple veil. A prayer book almost identical to Ignacio's. Like his, white gloves, white shoes. And her terror that she would mistakenly eat or drink something after midnight and render herself unable to partake of the sacrament, and her fear, that if she did it, she would not admit to it. Refusing to brush her teeth for fear that toothpaste could be counted as food, spitting continually on the ground on the way to the church, in case some food had lodged in her teeth and she would inadvertently swallow it. The hymns, the incense, *"Pange Lingua, Tantum Ergo"* and she had felt a lightness that she treasured. She remembers her father telling her that Napoleon told people that his First Communion was the happiest day of his life, and her father saying that he hoped for the rest of her life, when she was asked the question, she would answer the same way as Bonaparte.

And yes, it was a happy day, a day of lightness. Why can she not feel some sense of kinship with her son, why does she not share some of these memories with him? But the question is a false one; she knows the answer too well. To say that there was anything of value in that part of her past would be to betray Johnny, to betray the thousands killed by the fascists in the name of God, the thousands imprisoned after the war to keep the nation pure, the jewel in the crown of the Catholic Church.

At the dinner table one night, Ignacio asks his grandmother (but not his mother) if he may have permission to wear the penitential knotted cord around his waist that the visiting Jesuit who has been educating them has spoken about as "the privilege for the person who wants to give his utmost for purity, the hero of God." Pilar jumps up and kisses him. "I think we have the makings of a little saint here." Marian is horrified, and only a bit relieved when Pilar says, "But no, such measures are not for you, you who have nothing to atone for. They are a way to God for those who have turned their faces from God. But you, my little one, have always lived with your eyes on God. Anyone can see it in your eyes: they are full of the light of the angels."

Marian knows there is nothing she can say, particularly as, when she looks in her son's eyes, she does not see light, but, too often, a self-satisfaction, a calculation. Does he know that suggesting that he wear the penitential cord would gain him favor with his grandmother, but that she would forbid it? Did he ever have the intention of wearing it, or was he just trying to be seen as a heroic penitent? Why could she not believe in her son's innocence? Is it because she cannot believe that anything in this country at this time, anything touched by the finger of the Church, can be innocent?

It is not possible to separate the Church from the government of Franco; she sees she is right as she stands outside the church watching the First Communion procession, the priest in white vestments, holding aloft the gold monstrance containing the host; the banners, "Viva Cristo Rey!," the favorite motto of Franco; the trumpets and drums of the Falangists in their blue setting the tone, left, right, left, right, for the marching children. And in the back of the church: a photograph of the pope blessing the kneeling Generalissimo, the slender Italian in his ascetic rimless glasses looking with admiration at the squat Spaniard with his epaulets and soldierly moustache.

Marian watches the children walk reverently into the church, their hands folded, their eyes downcast. The incense is particularly thick in the air today, and she finds it difficult to breathe. Everything seems too much: the girls' dresses have too many petticoats, their veils have too much lace. Except for the large bows on their shoulders, the boys are spared this obvious excess. Some are wearing long pants, some shorts. She wishes Ignacio were wearing long pants, because when she looks at his legs she thinks of an oversweet pastry: the spongy outside, inside custard perhaps, yellowish, gelatinous. Her eyes fall on the backs of his knees and she thinks, I should love the knees of my son. I do not love my son's knees. What is wrong with me, Ramón? I loved you above all telling. Why am I unable to love our son, who was conceived, I know better than anything, in great love?

The Jesuit who has been brought in to train the First Communion children gives the sermon. He speaks of their duty to do something extraordinary, for God and for Spain. With no connection Marian can imagine, he then launches into a discussion of the perfidy of the miners during the Asturian strike a decade earlier: the miners enjoyed huge salaries and had no real reason to complain, but they became revolutionaries because "they lacked morality"; while their wives and children cried from hunger at home, the miners would complete their shifts and immediately rent taxis to take them to the cities of Oviedo and Gijón, where they stayed at the best hotels and ordered champagne.

He hunches over the pulpit, his voice grows high and urgent: "What does it matter, a new distribution of wealth, while consciences remain deformed? The solution to economic problems is, before anything else, the solution to moral problems, and this is only possible in the name of God and through Christian religious education. And this Christian education must not be neglected because these little angels have now made First Communion, or even later when they are confirmed. No, parents, and you, my children, you must pledge yourselves to the pursuit of knowledge of the Truth, the Truth of Mother Church, the breasts from which you may drink and drink, and take your fill so you may be nourished for your great work, defenders of the Church and of the honor of Spain. Clothe yourselves in the armor of God so that you may be, boy and girl alike, knights in the service of the great Lord Jesus and our beloved Caudillo."

It is unseasonably warm for the middle of May, and Marian is afraid she will faint, but she would prefer to faint than to run out into the street for air and risk the accusation of disrespect for the Church of God. There are only five children making First Communion—she wonders what has happened to the children of the poor, whose parents cannot afford petticoats and leather shoes. What is their First Communion? Does it take place without pomp, without celebration, in the secure knowledge that nothing more is owed to them? She thinks of Lucia's cousins, eating boiled grass, eating carob pods.

This is all she can think of at the home of Pilar's brother, when course after course is offered in honor of Ignacio and Fernanda. The children are presented with boxes wrapped in white and gold paper with a gold ribbon. Fernanda opens hers first; she presents it to the family, and the women ooh and aah as if it were a real baby, being introduced for the first time.

The famous doll. In every newspaper, stories about the doll Mariquita, symbol of the economic miracle of the New Spain.

In 1939, a young mother married to a member of Franco's cabinet, won a prize in a raffle. The prize was a German doll, a perfect little Aryan, with golden ringlets. The mother devoted herself to making a wardrobe for the precious doll, and the women in her circle coveted it, ordered their own from Germany, and it became the prized First Communion gift. The mother, seeing the possibilities, created a new doll that would look like her daughter. Fashionable Madrileños spent fortunes on these dolls and their endless outfits, and a brother is provided for Mariquita, Juanín, so that little boys may have this doll as their First Communion gifts as well.

Fernanda and Ignacio are posed together on the couch, for pictures, the dolls in their laps, holding hands like a honeymoon couple.

This is too much; she cannot stay another minute. She says she is feeling unwell, she must go home. The blond child Fernanda and her child, Ignacio, cradling the blond dolls, relics of a Nazi past that she knows is mourned by too many of those around her. The doll costs more than what a poor family has to spend for six months of food, and this sickens her, as the excessive food here on the table sickens her, perhaps in part because she has eaten more today than she has in a very long time, and maybe this is why she is feeling suddenly sick.

She runs down the street, glad to feel the cold rain that has broken the unseasonable heat.

She is wearing high heels, which she rarely wears, but Pilar has told her she must dress up in honor of the great occasion. So she is wearing heels and unlovely cotton stockings, a shapeless grey skirt, a violet blouse with a mannish collar. The stones are slippery from the rain, and she feels unsure of her footing. But she feels the compulsion to run, to be as far away from the spectacle of what she believes is an evil excess, far from her son, on what she is sure will be forever the happiest day of his life.

Her heel catches in a crack between two of the cobblestones. Her head strikes the wet stones; she hears a snap; her leg bends in a way she knows must be the source of this blinding pain. The white houses appear before her eyes and disappear; the noise of the rain drums, then goes silent. She hears, but distantly, the words of two women who bend over her.

"It's the American. The daughter-in-law of Pilar."

"Don't move her. You must not move," she hears them say. She supposes they are talking to her.

I haven't the slightest intention of moving, she wants to say. No movement has been possible for me for as long as I can remember.

"No one knows anything about her," one woman says to the other. "No one knows who she really is."

Marian wants to laugh, because it does seem comic, her escape into the open air, her pratfall in the middle of the street, the attention of curious strangers. Everything is growing dark now, and she stops herself from saying what she would like to say: You're right. You're perfectly right. No one knows who I really am. Including me. Particularly me. You must understand, she stops herself saying to the woman who stays after her friend has gone to get more help, you must understand, I have no idea who I am.

AVONDALE, RHODE ISLAND, 2009

I DON'T KNOW *who you are.*
  Your past.
  I want it now.

My past.
  Who am I?

When had it begun, that she had become a person who would not allow the past a place in her mind? Its proper place, some might say. For the first time, she's being called on to be one of those people she's always disliked, dredging up the past, taking it out like the family's old tarnished silver, or a moth-eaten ball gown, *real silk, you know, you'd never see anything like it now.* Designed for a great-aunt, half a century dead.

What's the use of it, what's the use of it, it's of no use. Move on, get on with the thing, keep going forward. Always, there is something that must be left, fled, run from. Her family home. The war: Valencia. Then Spain itself: a whole life there. And if you were going to flee, and the flight was to be real, you had to travel light. You couldn't be carrying the weight of the past in a pack on your shoulders. You had to believe that the leave-taking was for good, or it wouldn't have been a real leave-taking. You couldn't be holding in your mind a contingency plan for going back. A complete refusal was necessary, if you were going to get away from the thing that seemed like death, or a real death, or a series of them. Or something of which people would say, "That's a fate worse than death."

But now that she is actually dying, she understands (perhaps she has always understood, but now the understanding is more immediate) that there are many fates worse than death. Because, of course, death is the fate of all the living, and a fate seems unbearable if you feel that you have been unfairly singled out, disproportionately punished. And was there just one fate, or a series of fates? Now, death was not only her next fate, but her only one; there would be no others intervening. Of all fates, perhaps the kindest: to die at ninety-two, cared for by those she loves, who love her.

Cared for by Amelia. The lovely face, always with a hint of puzzlement or surprise, like an animal lifting its head after drinking in a stream, startled, confused by the arrival of a stranger. But who is this person who has spoken with such authority, in such a clear, demanding tone?

I don't know who you are.

Your past.

I want it now.

If there is any point to it, to speaking of the past, it must be that it will be of use. Something like a cloak, a protection from a certain category of mistakes. The ones that have been made before. But why? So that the young will have the luxury of a fresh crop of mistakes?

What is the way to speak of the past so that it might be of use?

She can't create anything of the past that might be called a story. Starting with "Once upon a time . . . ," finishing with "THE END." What does it even mean: Once upon a time? How could you be upon a time? Is it like a mountain that can be climbed or sat on? And what does it mean: THE END? Nothing is ever really finished, and it seems unlikely that anything of any importance happened only once. Birth, perhaps, is the exception. And then, death. But birth and death are not a story.

The past doesn't come to her in a line, or even a series of images that can fit together to make a satisfying whole. Each image comes to her separately, like the bubbles in a pan of boiling water. You can't "tell" a series of images. Telling presupposes connection. Therefore, meaning. Impossible. For every word, there are a thousand images, too quick, too darting, minnows in a stream that a child might try to catch in her hands, but, of course, that would be impossible. Soon the child would give it up. But standing there, so still, not moving at all, not darting, is Amelia, wanting to know. And does Marian owe it to the past that it should not die with her?

Is it possible to speak truthfully? Is it possible to believe you will be understood? To provide a backdrop, a whole set of references and associations incomprehensible to someone who's been deliberately—and, in no small measure, by her—kept from the resonance and pull of just those associations?

And what's the point of it? What's the good? She has kept silent for just this reason: she hasn't believed that people's knowing would do any good. And how could you speak about a kind of horror that caused your mind to shut down, to shatter first, and then turn to stone?

She looks at Amelia, whom she thinks of as still a child. The person she loves most in the world. Standing with the dish towel in her hands, just having dried a glass, an ordinary position, as if the words she has just said were ordinary. Different now, with a new hardness. Has she, against all odds, inherited something of the Taylor family hardness? How odd, Marian thinks, I am afraid of her.

"I don't know where to start. I don't know what to say to you, Amelia. I don't know what should be said. I want to be of use to you, and I don't know what to say that would be of use."

For the first time in her life, Amelia is older than her grandmother. Her grandmother, who has always seemed so solid, so sure, as sure and solid as the stones in the wall around her house. But now she is unsure. Is it because she's ill, because she's dying? Are the ill and the dying always our children, Amelia wonders, slightly at large, in need of someone to rein them in and take hold of them, before they wander off?

The responsibility is great and strange. The opposite of most kinds of responsibility, where action is required. Her responsibility is to be still, and yet, in her stillness, to communicate the utmost attention. Of course, she learned to do this in school. But then, nothing was at stake, or very little: a poor grade, at worst a failed exam. But now, a lapse in attention could have real consequences. Fatal, really, because the death of something would be involved, the death of a memory, of a whole swath of the past.

"You've always been of use to me, Meme. There's nothing you could say that wouldn't be of use. There's nothing you could say that could possibly be wrong."

"Well, at least let me sit down," Marian says. They move to the kitchen table, where they have sat together so often, for so many private meals. The porch light is still on; Amelia had it on so Graham could make his way easily to his car. Its yellow, garish light disturbs Marian.

"Turn the porch light off, will you?" she says. She knows she is stalling for time.

Does this child understand that, in her ability to say the words she said so easily, or at all, there is the evidence of the destruction of a whole way of life, a whole way of being in the world, the world that Marian was born to?

Right and wrong. What can be said, and what cannot be said, words that cannot be tolerated, even for a second, statements, even offered tentatively, that cannot be forgiven. Some things must be laughed at, but, of course, there are some things at which it is forbidden to laugh, words that need to be repeated, repeated, repeated, and other words that cannot even be whispered. *Don't you know, don't you know, what's wrong with you? Don't you know the difference between right and wrong?*

And now, this child is saying there is no wrong way.

Because of this, her life has not been, she sees, for all its errors, a mistake.

"But I forget so much, Amelia. So much of what happened when I was involved in the war, the Spanish Civil War. I worked in hospitals, I carried stretchers, sometimes I drove an ambulance. There were bombs. I was horribly afraid."

"I didn't know you were in Spain during that war," Amelia says, swallowing her shock, keeping her tone as light as possible.

"Yes, yes, I was in that war. But most of it I forget."

"Forgetting is a part of remembering, Meme. I learned that in a psychology course I took. We forget what we need to forget in order to make room for what we need to remember."

Is this some kind of new-age nonsense she picked up in California? Or can Marian hold on to it, this mercy from a girl she has always considered merciful, in whom she has discovered now a vein of iron?

Lord, have mercy.

Child, have mercy.

"Just begin anywhere, Meme. The first step is the hardest."

C'est le premier pas qui coûte. It's the first step that counts. She learned that from Mother Kiley, whom she adored when she was, perhaps, fourteen. The thing is to begin.

The thing, then, is to begin with something that is clear to her, something she knows to be true, that hasn't disappeared in shadows. Something that she always returns to, from which everything has always started. Johnny. The first love. The purest. Purity, she thinks, is something the young no longer believe in. That must be a good thing. The first meaning it had for her was sexual purity. Don't touch your own body, don't even look at it. Later, among the comrades, preserve the purity of the idea. Worth dying for, worth killing for. A good thing, then, that the young have lost it. The ones still looking for it are looking for something from the dead past, as if they'd taken to wearing epaulets.

And yet, she can't entirely celebrate the loss. Purity of intention: that was something Mother Kiley stressed. A pure line. A pure form. Johnny spoke about it in relation to music. Is all that lost, too? It doesn't matter. The good and the harmful. Gone. There's too much mourning. Some things are better let go.

But one thing stays: she knows she had a brother whom she loved. *I don't know who you are.* Well, I am Johnny Taylor's sister. Everything is measured against that, against the questions. *What would this mean to Johnny? Would Johnny have enjoyed that? How would this person react to Johnny?* One of her earliest certainties: that cruelty was so often directed at him, and that he couldn't bear it. That she could bear it better, and therefore must protect him. Cruelty dropped on his head like a bucket of filthy water dropped from an overhanging window. Because it could be done, it was done. Her understanding of the world was formed by this. So she can say something now that she knows is true.

"I had a brother whom I loved. He was very musical, a very gifted pianist. He was gay. He killed himself. It was because of my family that he killed himself. I will never forgive them."

It is impossible to do anything but sit still, in silence. Something enormous has happened in the room, a birth—Amelia has a great-uncle she never knew of—and a death—he killed himself, and it was because of his family. All of them related to her. All of them, until seconds ago, unknown.

"I didn't love my family. You think that's a terrible thing to say, but they were cruel people, and if you loved them, you would have to love cruelty. And I refused."

Does she have the right to ask a question? Her grandmother has gone silent. Perhaps, then, a light question, one easy to answer, so that she'll keep going.

"Were they cruel to you when you were little?"

"I didn't see much of them when we were little. My brother and I were the youngest of nine, and by that time, I think my parents had gotten tired of the whole idea of children. They traveled a lot. My father had lots of business enterprises. His fortune, or his first fortune, was made in the sulfur mines of Ontario. And then there were the years in Argentina; he raised beef cattle. That was where they hired Pablo and Jacinta, they were our cook and our gardener. Our parents brought them to America. I learned Spanish from them. They were more parents to me than my parents. In the evenings, we would be brought down to my parents—if they weren't traveling—to say good-night. We had to be clean and quiet, not too affectionate— they didn't like what my father called 'slobber'—and then we would be sent to bed. I have no idea what my mother did all day: we never saw her before sundown; she may have been a vampire for all I know."

"I don't know where you lived."

"New York. New York and Newport."

"Newport, Rhode Island? Close to here, then."

They could be near, Amelia thinks. Rhode Island is a small state; she could have been bumping into relatives at any time, none of them having the slightest idea. Not that it was likely that people from Newport would come to this part of the state. South County is poorer, less glamorous. But they might have come down in the world, or they might, for example, have read about Amelia's cupcakes and made an outing on a rainy day to try them. Amelia might have been baking for her family and never known it.

"Imagine my distress when your grandfather told me we'd be moving to Rhode Island. The smallest state in the Union."

"Did you ever run into them? Did you ever go back to your old house?"

"No, I wouldn't have dreamed of it, and anyway, I wouldn't have been welcome. It isn't far from here, though, you're right. Beech Haven, it was called. It was surrounded by beautiful beech trees, that's where the name came from. But even the name was chosen because it could make a fool of some people. 'You live near the beach?' 'No, dear, not that kind of beach.'

"I suppose I could take you. But I won't, of course. It's a bunch of condos now ... I read about it in *The Providence Journal*; it was a big deal when it was sold. Because of my brother Vincent. Did you know Vincent Taylor was my brother?"

"I don't know who Vincent Taylor is."

Marian hoots. "Well, that's a good one, wouldn't it kill him, if he weren't already dead, to know that his fame was so limited. I guess that's the benefit of being brought up in California, among people like your parents and their friends. But in certain circles, my brother was quite a celebrity. The thinking man's conservative. He had his own radio show; this was before all this talk radio; he'd like to think he was different from that lot, the Rush Limbaughs, but he wasn't really, he only had a better vocabulary. A lot of famous people went on it to debate with him, mostly to be humiliated by him. I don't know why; he actually wasn't that intelligent. He had only two ideas: the virtue of the free market and the evil of communism. Oh, yes, and the absolute superiority of the Roman Catholic Church; he didn't bring that up much on the radio, however. But he had a lot of what used to be called ten-dollar words. I wonder what they'd be called now, with inflation."

Amelia knows that she will Google "Vincent Taylor" when she leaves Meme. A conservative celebrity. Not what she would have chosen ... she's more comfortable with the gay uncle who killed himself.

"If you saw the house, Beech Haven, you'd probably think it was beautiful. Was it beautiful? I was so uncomfortable there, I wouldn't know how to answer that. It had a lovely view of the bay, and real old stone walls ... like mine, but much, much more extensive. So many rooms, Amelia, eighteen rooms. Do you know what it is to live in a house and feel it doesn't want you there? More than feeling that you don't belong, that it refuses to do its job of sheltering you. For as long as I could remember, I had a sense of shame about that house, about its excesses; the excess of rooms, of land, even the excess of air, made me feel I would suffocate. I know what you think: you should feel suffocated because you feel constricted. But I felt I couldn't breathe because the ground I was standing on was too thin, that I could fall through it at any moment, that it was like a crust covering over some pit I could fall into, that I could break through the crust with one false move. So I was always holding my breath.

"I don't know where it came from, the idea, but for as long as I can remember, I knew we had too much. That the Taylors had too much. That it was wrong to have so much when some people had too little. I felt it even before the Depression, but when the Depression began—I was eleven in 1929, Amelia, you can't begin to understand the despair most people lived with then. They were terrified that they would literally starve, and, worse, they were ashamed, ashamed, some of them, to the point of death, at having to admit that they had nothing now, that they might be 'on relief,' or seen as a shiftless pauper, a bum. We never saw any of that in Newport, but when I went back to New York, I had to see the bread lines, and the people selling apples, selling anything. I couldn't not see it; I didn't understand how my family could. Then I really knew that my family, having so much more than other people, was the wrongest thing in the world, and that all the wrong things in the world were connected to that.

"If I took you to my old house, you'd be impressed. Modest, certainly, it was, in comparison with the great houses, the great mansions, the Breakers, Rosecliff, built to look like châteaux, ridiculous in New England, fortunes spent on houses to be lived in six weeks of a year. No, Beech Haven wasn't like that. It was a working farm. And it wasn't made of stone, it was made of cedar shingles; my father saw that it conformed to the landscape, my father had more taste—he said it of himself all the time—than the Vanderbilts. Oh, it was perfect for him, an Irishman living in Newport beside the wealthy Yankees, feeling he'd outdone them in good taste."

So now she has told the child about Johnny, and she has described the house. The first step has been taken. What now? So much needs to be explained. What should she work to make her see, and what can be left out? Should she try to make her feel the atmosphere of the house, and hope that will explain things? Silver pheasants on the table set for thirty, gold-rimmed plates and cups, candlelight, damask, priests with their white hands, their special white towels. Furniture polished till it shone like mirrors, little tables covered with pictures of monsignors and bishops, gilt-framed. The view in winter from the dining room window, the white expanse of snow, the moonlight falling straight onto that flat whiteness, the famous trees, budding, then lush, all of it, she knew from a very young age, was for her, and she wanted no part of it. But is that the case now? Now that she's started to tell—if not a story, whatever it is—she's not so sure.

How can she possibly re-create a world so entirely alien to everything Amelia knows? The Catholic Church, really the Holy Roman Empire. A way of being in the world, a system based not only on the belief that what was at stake was life and death, but *eternal* life, *eternal* damnation. Can she even convey what it was to believe in eternity? To believe in an eternity of flame, burned flesh, a thirst without end? The fear that if you ate a hot dog on Friday or overslept on Sunday, so that you missed the last Mass, that fate would be yours. Can she really convince her granddaughter that perfectly intelligent people lived their lives like that? And believed that the Church, *the* Church, was the bulwark against all the evils in the modern world. But if Amelia is going to understand her, going to understand the war in Spain, she will have to understand the power of the Church, something most of her comrades didn't understand. The war was so much about the Church. The Church that was hated because it had always been on the side of the rich, so that the burning of churches, the killing of priests, was justified, was celebrated. Franco and his followers killing in the name of God, in the name of the Church, justifying everything because the reds wanted to destroy the Church. In defense of their brutality, they quote Bakhtin, who they believe is a hero to all communists—although like so much else, they got that wrong. The communists had no use for Bakhtin. Only the anarchists invoked him. "No one will be free until the throat of the last priest is strangled in the guts of the last king." Half of the Spanish people seeing the Church as the monster devouring the poor, the other half seeing the modern world as a fire-breathing dragon wanting to annihilate all truth, all purity, all that is eternally valuable—whose embodiment was the Church—and so it is worth the lives of however many it took to safeguard it.

"If I'm going to tell you who I am, I have to explain a whole way of life that has, thank God, vanished. The world of the Catholic Church, the way my family knew themselves before anything. They saw themselves as Catholics, not really Americans. Oh, we lived among Americans, but we had THE TRUE FAITH and so it was our mission to convert everyone in the world. They were right in some ways; the way we lived wasn't exactly American. We didn't celebrate holidays like the Fourth of July or Memorial Day or Thanksgiving. Those holidays were for Protestants. No, we had feast days. Ash Wednesday. Pentecost. Assumption. Immaculate Conception. Oh, I can't even remember them all, thank God. The 'Church Militant,' they called it, with so much pride. They loved the idea of being always ready for a fight. They wouldn't have recognized a God of love; theirs was a warrior God, a God of righteousness; heaven was known as the 'Church Triumphant.' They loved having enemies. They loved naming something, someone, some group as outside the fold. Their greatest pleasure was humiliation. They believed they had the right to punish anyone anytime they wanted and for anything they thought deserving. Do you know what it was like always to feel you were in the center of a rifle sight, which could blast you—as it *did* blast my brother—to smithereens, whenever they thought it was the right time? Sometimes, they would speak in a civilized, sorrowful tone. 'I regret this deeply, but I am acting in the name of truth, in the name of eternity. It is necessary, in the name of truth, in the name of eternity, that you be entirely destroyed.' Or sometimes they hissed at you, 'You are in the devil's grip, I am destroying you in order that you will be saved.'

"Oh, they thought they were more European aristocracy than Americans, but at the bottom of it, there was a particular kind of Catholicism that was uniquely American. They combined the worst prejudices of the worst Americans with the worst of being Catholic— the conviction that whatever you did was in the name of the one true faith."

Slow down, slow down, Meme, Amelia wants to say. This is all too much. This is all too fast. But she's afraid that if she says anything, her grandmother will just go silent, think she can't handle it, that she's not quick enough, is perhaps too young, too weak. She clasps and unclasps her hands.

"I think I was about thirteen when my mother did something that upset me terribly. Racism. There wasn't even a word for it then. You could say 'prejudice,' but it wasn't a very strong word. I don't think they came anywhere near many black people, but they were obsessed with the corruption that contact with Negroes brought about. Oh, it had a lot of faces, from my mother's physical reaction, as if she could be infected, to my brother's genteel protectionism of Western culture.

"With my mother, it happened in the church we went to in Newport. My father had a lot of contempt for it; he was right, it was ugly. He said it was built by and for 'Greenhorns.' His life in Newport was devoted to differentiating himself from the Greenhorns, the Irish who didn't share his taste, or even his money, and the Yankees, whose wealth he believed had nothing to do with their having deserved it.

"That Sunday there was a visiting priest, an African missionary. I remember the name of the order: the White Fathers. Even then I knew that was a problem, because the priest was black, an African priest, one of the first 'native clergy' to be ordained. Of course, he was there to ask for money. He moved beautifully; I remember feeling a little guilty because you weren't supposed to have such thoughts about a priest. He spoke about his village, about children who were starving but who brought their pennies to church and sang out their catechism. At Communion time, my mother didn't join the others at the altar rail. She stayed in her pew, a handkerchief to her mouth, then holding her silver bottle of smelling salts to her nose."

Now there is someone else for Amelia to know. A great-grandmother. Fragile. Needing smelling salts. Smelling salts: she's heard about them. Perhaps not heard: only read about them. Now they are connected to her. If she ever encounters the words "smelling salts" again she will think immediately "my great-grandmother."

"I was frightened. We were always told that our mother was fragile, heroic for having borne nine healthy children, a true Catholic mother, but it had taken its toll. I asked her in that particular whisper we used in church if she was all right. She closed her eyes and waved her hand.

"Later at home she said, 'It was simply not possible for me to take Communion from a black hand. I may be wrong, but I simply couldn't do it. It would have been an offense against my ancestors.'

"I knew with everything in me that what she had done was an offense, not only against a higher moral good, but against the law of the Church, and that I would be wrong—that my soul would be in danger, you see, I'd absorbed their thinking in my own way—not to speak out. I had that impulse to martyrdom in me, too. I'd loved reading the lives of the saints; I was very big on virgin martyrs. Do you know what the word 'martyr' means? It's the Greek word for 'witness.' And I was ready to be martyred as a witness to the truth."

"Since 9/11, Meme, everyone knows what martyr means. Of course, it has a bad name now."

"It's why I understand the 9/11 bombers—of course, the martyr-dom I was interested in didn't have any victims. But I understand that kind of outrage you believe to be the only right response. I felt myself filled with it, like a balloon that is just going to have to pop.

"I told her that if taking Communion from a black priest was an offense against her ancestors, not taking it was an offense against God. I had all the legal language under my belt, and I used it with that real satisfaction you feel, that click, when the word perfectly fits the situation. '*Ex opere operans*, Mother,' I said. 'Don't you remember the law of the Church: Not the worker but the work?' I reminded her that it didn't matter if the priest was drunk, insane, a criminal. The sacra-ment was still valid. 'The priest did nothing wrong, except to be born in Africa. How could you have so little regard for the sacrament of the Eucharist as to refuse it from a lawfully ordained priest?'

"There was silence at the table. My mother crumbled her bread. My father wiped his mouth with his napkin. 'I think Marian might take her luncheon in her room,' he said.

"Thank God I didn't cry. I walked out of the room with my head held high, but as soon as the dining room door closed, I could hear the sound of male laughter. My brothers, especially Vincent, thought my performance was hilarious."

Something new is in the room's air now. A crack, a flash. Anger, perhaps, she thinks, something powerful, direct, and sharp.

"What I want you to understand, Amelia, what I want you never to forget, is that there is a malign force in the world, the desire to humili-ate, which you must always be on your guard for, which you must always resist."

Does this girl have it in her power to resist, having had to resist nothing? The world has been made comfortable for her, a world in which she could feel safe putting one foot in front of the other. Then Marian remembers Amelia's father's death. But that was nothing that could have been resisted. Did you have to have been the victim of some kind of tyranny to have the power to resist? No tyranny has been allowed to touch Amelia. What, then, could resistance mean to her?

"You must resist." The words: thick, shining, fall on Amelia's head; she feels herself anointed, ready for anything. Meme has trusted her, Meme has singled her out. But of everything her grandmother has said, Amelia knows what the most important thing is.

"Will you tell me more about your brother?"

"Fairest of them all is my winsome, handsome Johnny."

Her grandmother is singing, and her grandmother is not singing well. It's a family joke that Meme is tone-deaf. But the toneless melody is piercing, like a song from a dream.

"He never lost patience with me. Only once, when I said I didn't like Bartók. His eyes were a grey color, a color I've never seen on any one again. He had light brown hair, 'dirty blond,' we called it in those days, it was always falling in his eyes. That always annoyed my mother. One day, with her long red nails, she pushed his hair out of his eyes and left him blinded for a moment. A scratch on the cornea. But he couldn't say, 'You hurt me. You can't do that.' We could never say anything like that to our parents.

"But he was safe from them, from everything in the world, in his music. It was safe because my father, for all his monstrosities, was a man of culture. Playing Bach on his gramophone, a bit guiltily because he preferred him to Monteverdi, choosing the Protestant over the Catholic. He liked having one musically gifted son, because music was important to him, but it was also an embarrassment, because it was the weakly son, hopeless on the tennis court, uneasy. Once I heard him saying to our mother, "What the hell's the matter with the two youngest? Perhaps we were away too much." But my father couldn't withhold his regard, because Johnny's music gave him terrific pleasure. It was a gift he had to acknowledge, and when experts (my father was a great believer in experts), the teachers at

Juilliard especially, acknowledged that Johnny had a gift, well, he couldn't ignore them.

What more should she say about Johnny? How much should she let Amelia know about Johnny's death? She can't bear to make a scene of it, a little playlet, discovering her brother hanging from the ceiling, cutting him down, feeling the weight of his body on top of hers. No, she won't do that. No need to create images that will be impossible to eradicate. Some images are too strong; it is best that they be kept back. She will tell the part of the story that will strengthen in Amelia the will to resist.

"My family was absolutely horrified by even the idea of homosexuality. The whole world—all the experts, doctors, psychiatrists—was calling it a 'disease' that could be cured. So it was perfectly possible for my brother to be put in a mental hospital because he was gay; being committed was the alternative to going to jail. Perfectly possible to ruin his mind with those primitive shock treatments, perfectly possible to take everything from him that he was."

She won't go into details about Johnny's letter. She doesn't want Amelia to consider the possibility that life is not worth the living of it.

"And so I don't want to hear, ever, how much better the old days were. Some things have got much better; you mustn't ever fall into the trap of that nostalgic nonsense."

"I would never, Meme," Amelia says, wondering what in her history might have given her grandmother a suspicion of that. "You're right not to forgive them. Your family. What they did was terrible, disgusting. I'm glad I never had to know them."

Marian has a new regard for her granddaughter, the regard of an adult admiring another adult. How did she know how to say exactly the right words? The rightness of abandonment, the proper snap of breaking off the branch, not quite rotten, but rotting at its base. Terrible, disgusting. Not "I'm sorry." Not "How sad." The story of Johnny can take its proper place in Amelia's life, framed by outrage. *Terrible.* *Disgusting.* Angels preventing entry to Paradise with flaming swords.

"It was because of Johnny that I went to Spain. He had a lover, Russell, he was wonderful, we were great friends. He was a doctor. He was going to Spain to serve as a medical volunteer. I talked him into marrying me. It wasn't a real marriage, of course, but in a way, I loved him as much as my real husbands."

Her grandmother fought in a war. Her grandmother had many husbands. She had asked for her grandmother's past; she had said she wanted to know who she was, but she had no idea of the extent of what had been hidden, or what was behind the door she'd knocked on, innocently imagining that she would find a set of interesting but unalarming relics: a snood, antimacassars, finger bowls. Instead, she found something she now knows she could never have begun to imagine.

She will ask her grandmother an easier question, something that could be found on an official form. Number of marriages? Husbands' names?

"How many times were you married, Meme?"

Marian laughs, and the relief is, for both of them, disproportionate. "You'd think that would be an easy question to answer, but actually it isn't. Probably the only truly proper marriage, both legally and physically, was to your grandfather. Russell and I were legally married, but the marriage was never consummated, so I guess it wasn't really legal. And my Spanish husband, Ramón was his name, we were married by a judge in Valencia, under the auspices of the government of the Republic, but later, when Franco took over all marriages not performed in the Church, all civil marriages under the Republic were declared invalid. And then I sort of feel I've been married to Graham for thirty years, or twenty of them, at least, but of course he was married to someone else, and then, by the time she managed to get herself to the great beyond, it seemed a little absurd. We were both so old."

"You had a Spanish husband? During the war? You were telling me you got to Spain because of marrying Russell. What happened to Russell, did you stay in touch?"

"Well, after he left Spain, I didn't know where to find him. And then, in 1955, when the Salk vaccine, the polio vaccine, was announced, I saw his picture in the paper among the doctors who were working with Salk. I found out that after he left Spain, which was before I left, Russell volunteered in the American Hospital in Paris, then he was in the army . . . then he went to work with Salk. He moved to California, and we didn't see each other much; when he came to New York or Boston, I'd go and visit him, but he never came here. I think he didn't want to know the details of a life I had after Johnny. We spoke on the phone every year on the anniversary of Johnny's death. Russell died of lung cancer. Imagine, a brilliant doctor smoking himself to death."

"But you went to Spain, to the war, together," Amelia says, impatient now, although it was she who'd asked about Russell. But the war, the *war*: as a subject, it looms and presses its demands too heavily to be ignored.

"I talked Russell into marrying me. I had to get away. I was shattered because of my brother's death. I couldn't bear to have anything to do with my family, and the only way I could be sure of being outside their control was to be married. I had no money; I had never worked a day in my life; if I stayed at Vassar, it would be taking something from them.

"Of course, when I first mentioned the plan to Russell, he thought I was kidding. He said, 'Honey, what can I say, you're not my type. You're missing a vital part of anatomical equipment.'

"But I wouldn't give up . . . I guess I was relentless—yes, I know I was—and he hated my family for what they'd done to Johnny, and the thing with Russell was, he always had a deep strain of dark irony, and his marrying me appealed to that.

"Russell was going to Spain and I was determined to go with him, determined to do something I knew was important, where I knew

I could be on the side of unquestionable good, where I could be of definite use. Russell knew *he* could be of use; he was a doctor, and they needed doctors badly. But he said, 'I don't think there's anything for you there.' I told him he was wrong. I had Spanish—which he didn't—because of being brought up by Argentine servants. And I was a whiz at cars. Driving them. Fixing them. I loved cars.

"I guess it was a rebellion against my family, to prefer cars to horses. And Johnny was really afraid of horses; he'd had a bad experience on one, and he never got over it. So, you see, everything in my life goes back to Johnny. I got to Spain because of Johnny. Marrying Russell and being good with cars, those were because of Johnny. I went to Spain because of Johnny's death, and Johnny died because of the way our family was. And that had a lot to do with horses. Horses and uniforms. It sounds like some kind of nineteenth-century operetta, but that was how my family would have liked to live, in a nineteenth-century operetta—or, no, an opera. Shedding blood for the faith and singing triumphant arias, sword in hand. When I turned against horses, it was the first turn away from the family, and when I first lost respect for my father, it was about uniforms."

Horses. Uniforms. Operas. Operettas. Amelia is losing the thread. She wants to hear about the war, the Spanish husband, and her grandmother is talking about horses and uniforms. She begins to be frightened. Suppose it's too late, that her grandmother's mind is just too old.

Marian sees that Amelia's attention has wandered. "Am I being a bore? Of all the things I fear—believe me, death is nothing to it—I most fear being a bore. You know how I hate being bored; it makes me feel like someone's holding my head underwater, trying to drown me. Graham says being bored turns me into a savage."

"Of course you're not boring me, Meme. I'm just a little confused, about the horses and the uniforms."

She sees that her grandmother is struggling not to be irritated because Amelia has confessed to being confused. Marian pats her hair, as if to straighten it, but it is perfectly straight, as always, absolutely in place. She opens her hands and closes them.

"Well, horses," she says, and Amelia sees that she's forcing herself to be patient. Perhaps she should ask if her grandmother wants to stop. But having just got to the point she finds most interesting, she won't give her grandmother the option of not going on, and she fears that she's becoming cruel, as the Taylor family—her ancestors, after all—were cruel.

And Marian seems willing to go on. "Their world, the world of my family, was very much centered around horses. I think it was because they really feared and despised the modern world.

"I think they thought if they were horse people, they were putting down stakes in the camp of the past. And, of course, taking a place in what they called the Yankee world, which tried to keep them out, but couldn't quite if they could ride well and owned the right horseflesh. Oh, the to-do about the Newport hunt. The hunt breakfasts, and the outfits and the saddles and bridles and bits and all the talk about bloodlines. It bored me to crumbs. I never wanted to be any part of it.

"And the people my father hired to attend to the horses weren't kind. Johnny was afraid of the horses, but the man in charge, an Englishman, Stillingworth was his name, made Johnny ride when he was afraid and tried to make him get up on the horse again after he was thrown off and badly hurt. Well, I stopped that."

Amelia sees that her grandmother is proud; she has the face of a girl talking about executing a perfect dive from the high board.

"I was seven years old, and Stillingworth was afraid of me, because I reminded him that my father had the power to fire him, and I suggested that with one word from me, he'd be out of a job. Which was the opposite of true . . . but it was my first lesson about the power of money, how false it was, and how unjust. It was one of the most important things I ever learned.

"It just occurs to me now that maybe I was wrong. Isn't it one of the oldest clichés in the world: that you're supposed to get right back on the horse? Supposing Johnny had, and it had gone all right. We might have had a very pleasant life with horses. We might have been able to find some place for ourselves in the family, instead of being the outsiders we were. Maybe everything would have been different then. Maybe a life with horses would have made Johnny stronger, and I wouldn't have always felt I had to protect him from the family. Maybe they wouldn't have felt free to do what they did to him. Maybe he'd still be alive. He'd be ninety-four. A lot of people are still around at ninety-four. Maybe I wouldn't have felt so desperate to get away from the family. I might never have gone to Spain."

"The butterfly effect," Amelia says.

"What's that?"

"It's part of chaos theory, or random causation. A butterfly flaps its wings, and it changes the air around it, so there's a tornado two continents away."

"I like that," Marian says. "I like that very much. It's as good a way of explaining life, or of acknowledging that there's no real explanation—none that you can trace, anyway. So what would have happened if my father had hired someone kind to run the stables and someone unpleasant to be in charge of the cars, instead of Luigi?"

"Who was Luigi?"

"Oh, Luigi was an angel, although no one ever looked less like one. He was very small and very dark, and he moved very clumsily. He often looked angry, but it was because he was nearsighted, and he didn't like to wear his glasses. I told you he was in charge of the cars. He would drive our parents back and forth from New York and Newport, and then drive them around New York, and he took care of all the cars in our Newport garage. How did we ever make our way down to the garage? I can't imagine. It was at the far end of the property. I have no memory of meeting him for the first time, none at all.

I have no memory of his not being one of my favorite people. I have no memory of how I discovered that I loved cars instead of horses, which was what I was supposed to love.

"Every day in the summers when we were in Newport, Johnny and I would make our way down to the garage to be with Luigi. He never made us feel we were in the way, and although Johnny had no interest in cars, he was happy with Luigi, he felt safe with him, and Johnny didn't feel safe with many people. Luigi sang snatches of opera, and Johnny would sing along with him, and all the time they were singing, I was learning about how engines worked.

"I was just crazy about cars. I cut pictures of cars from magazines like other girls cut out pictures of dresses or movie stars. I loved the names. Bentley. Rolls-Royce. Aston Martin. Hispano-Suiza. I don't know why I was allowed to do it; I guess no one was really paying attention. And I guess, despite himself, my father admired my interest—my father was an engineer, and none of my brothers and sisters had the slightest interest in anything mechanical. For all his faults, my father never suggested that there were things I couldn't learn because I was a girl. It's difficult for me to give my father credit for anything, but to be fair, I have to give him credit for that.

"He even let me learn to drive when I asked him. I was fourteen. Luigi was willing to teach me. I promised I wouldn't go off the property. Of course, my brothers Vincent and George—George was enthralled with Vincent, although he was older, and he'd go along with anything Vincent wanted, anything he said—they thought it was another great joke, another sign of my unfitness for what they considered the proper world. 'Marian's going to get her livery license,' Vincent said. 'A good thing for her; she's probably unmarriageable, and she can get a job as a cabdriver, and we'll always be sure of a ride.'

"They knew they could use their racism to get at me. Their racism was like some cheap toy that amused them to take out whenever the occasion arose.

"I'd spent the day working with Luigi, and when it was time for dinner, I noticed there was grease around my fingernails. I was in a panic, trying to make my hands presentable before dinner because I knew black around my fingernails would offend my mother, but I also knew it would offend both my parents if I were late. I sat in my place and bowed my head for grace, leaving my hands in my lap. My father walked over to me and picked up my hands, held them for a second, lifted them to display them to the family, and dropped them with a disgusted look.

"And Vincent said, 'Oh, you see, Marian's sympathy for our suffering black brothers has gotten out of hand. She's trying to turn herself into one of them; it begins at the fingers, and God knows, sooner or later she'll be a dead ringer for Mahalia Jackson.' And he and my other brothers started singing 'Sometimes I Feel Like a Motherless Child.'

"My father told me I must leave the table. I could take my dinner in the kitchen and perhaps one of the servants could provide something so that my hands could be acceptable again, fit for a civilized table.

"By then, I wasn't even hurt by their jokes. I'd lost respect for my brothers. There was nothing in them I admired, in the way that there were still things I admired about my father.

"So Luigi taught me to drive and told me about all of his cousins who were active in the unions in New York, and his cousins who were anarchists—this wasn't long after Sacco and Vanzetti, do you know about Sacco and Vanzetti?"

"Yes, Meme, I know about them."

"Well, I never know what you know and what you don't know. Your education is a mystery to me."

Where has this come from, this sharpness, this unkindness? Is her grandmother tired, or does talking about her family make her one of them?

She goes on, as if this new turn, so painful to Amelia, were nothing.

"Later, when Luigi trusts me, he tells me that some people in his family are communists and some are anarchists, and they scream at each other about it all night long. He thinks they are both right and both wrong. He is a fan of FDR.

"He asks if he can bring me to visit his family in the Bronx, and somehow my parents find the whole thing amusing and a source of jokes and stories, also of noblesse oblige—our eccentric daughter, the youngest, the tomboy, but you can't get her on a horse. I never tell them how much I love it there, that this is what families should be, being urged to eat the food, not to use it as a lesson in deportment, not to show how a fork is properly held, lips properly wiped by the napkin held properly on the lap. The delicious food, so plentiful, and the kissing and the shouting, political arguments ending in more kissing and more shouting, so I always felt, when I came back to Newport, that I needed another sweater, that I'd entered a less temperate climatic zone.

"The worst of it was that my father fired Luigi because a cousin of his had been arrested in a plot—unsuccessful, it turned out—to blow up a factory in Brooklyn. And then—perhaps I should have known better—I lost my composure completely. I clenched my fists and stood too close to him—it was important in my family to keep the rules of proper distance—and I said, 'You know Luigi had nothing to do with it, he was nowhere near Brooklyn; he's been here in Newport for months.' And I pulled at my father's cuffs, and he pulled away from me as if I were covering him with filth, and he said, 'You don't know those devils. They're everywhere. Insinuating. Diabolical. I only feel grateful we were able to be rid of him before something terrible happened to us.'

"I never saw Luigi again. I knew, of course, where his family lived, but I was too ashamed to contact him. But when I was able to say that I'd be of use in Spain because I was an excellent driver and I knew how to fix cars, I thought he'd be happy. That was why the party let me go. That and my Spanish."

"The party?"

"The Communist Party. All the medical aid to Spain was organized by the communists, although they tried very hard not to make that clear."

"Were you a communist?"

Marian laughs. "Was I? I don't know. I was never what those horrors called a 'card-carrying communist,' although Russell was. I never had the kind of mind that could latch on to political ideas the way you were supposed to. What I knew was that it was right to be on the side of the poor, and wrong to be on the side of the rich and the people who were being supported by Hitler and Mussolini. It all seemed very obvious: there was a good side, and a bad side, and communists were on the good side. I didn't have a lot of patience with people who made it all so complicated. Were you for Stalin or Trotsky? How did you think the revolution would best come to be realized? I didn't have any appetite for the demand for unquestioning loyalty. It reminded me too much of the Catholic Church. But what would it mean to you if I said I was a communist?"

"I'd think it was interesting," Amelia says. "I'd want to know more."

"'Interesting.' Amazing that you would use that word. Amazing how a word and idea—'communism'—which for generations was one of the strongest words in the world, the purest truth or the greatest evil in the world, now has so little weight, so little force, an anachronism of a word, like 'astrolabe' or 'alchemy.' I was certainly sympathetic to communism, I still am to the dream it represented, but you would have to be a fool or very wicked not to have seen that it, too, was the source of horrors."

Neither of them wants to go on talking in this way.

"What were you saying about uniforms?"

"I suppose in a way it is rather funny," Marian says, and Amelia hears her pronunciation of the word "rather"—*RAH-thah*—and thinks again that her grandmother has no idea how her diction and her timbre give her away as the daughter of privilege.

"Except that they didn't think it was funny, they thought it was dead serious, and, of course, that makes it funnier, though it was, as I'll tell you, a terrible breach to think it wasn't dead serious. You see, it's all about some fantasy of the past, some glorious past that never existed. I've always thought that's the difference between the extreme right and the extreme left. The right has a fantasy of an impossible past, the left has a fantasy of an impossible future. And, of course, no one can know either one. But I've always gone with the left because at least there's some hope. If you romanticize the past, the present will always be a disappointment. And disappointment makes people punitive. The future has the advantage of not yet existing. But, of course, there's always the possibility of punishment because of an imagined blockage of the nonexistent future. You see, I believe there's an endless appetite for punishment, one of the strongest appetites of our species."

Of all the things her grandmother has said to her, this is the strangest. Amelia doesn't recognize in herself an appetite to punish. Perhaps it's because she has no connection to the past. And no sense that the future is anything on which she can make a mark.

"I've never seen you give up hope, Meme."

"Because I have in the past, and I know what it's like, and I will never allow it in myself again. But we were talking about uniforms.

"The time I realized I had lost all respect for my father had to do with uniforms. But my very saying I lost respect means that at one time I had it. To lose something, you have to have had it first. I guess I did have it, and my first step toward losing it happened because I laughed at the wrong thing.

"They all knew when it was all right to laugh, and they knew when laughter would be a punishable offense. What was called kidding, and what was called downright rude. Some of the things they thought were funny upset me a great deal. Like the time they got into trouble for what they did in the Episcopal church. Vincent and Bridget and Laurence and George. They broke into the Episcopal church and spread a thin layer of honey over the pews. The honey was the same color as the wood, so it wasn't visible. Only when, as Laurence said, 'the Prots put their fat backsides down and got quite a surprise when they tried to get up.'

"The police came to the house; nobody knew how they found out. My guess is that my brothers, who were great braggarts, probably went to a bar to celebrate and recounted their exploits, not realizing how many people disliked them in the town. They were fined and told to spend the day cleaning the church, which they did, raucously scrubbing and singing Latin hymns, while the priest looked on. 'I'll be damned if I'll call him a priest,' Vincent said. 'He's a minister; he has nothing to do with apostolic succession.'

"Poor Reverend Chamberlain; he was a very gentle man, and he was probably too afraid of my brothers to suggest more quiet in the house of God. When they got home, my father ordered lobsters and champagne and at dinner everyone was in a marvelous mood. But all I could think of was Mrs. Chamberlain, the Episcopal priest's wife, who was the librarian in the local library that I loved. She always saved books for me, she knew I liked biographies of nineteenth-century women. A proof of how nice she was is that she didn't change the way she treated me, but I never felt comfortable in the library again, and that was a great loss to me.

"There must have been a time when I still thought I could kid my father. Does that mean there was a time when I thought I knew the language, could speak it as the others did? It must have been part of a time when I still respected him. Now I guess I have to understand that, as a loss, there was a time when I respected my father, and a time when I did not. But no, I won't call it a loss; it was a mistake ever to have respected him. He was never worthy of respect. I guess the loss of respect was gradual, but the last step—the final chord so you know the symphony is quite done—wasn't gradual at all.

"I was always getting things wrong . . . or, I guess, when I was still a little child, I didn't get things wrong, or they let me get away with it—I guess my getting things wrong and getting called on it coincided with my no longer being a child. So, I guess I was still a child, or believing myself to be one, and that ended after I thought it would be okay to kid my father about his Knights of Malta regalia.

" 'Regalia.' That's a word I haven't used in seventy-five years. Thank God for some things. What a ridiculous word. 'Regalia.'

"The Knights of Malta. Crackpots, a bunch of foolish, dangerous crackpots. Or maybe they're not even dangerous anymore. Maybe they just like to dress up and pretend they're in the Middle Ages. Oh, I can tell you all about them; we had to be knowledgeable about anything pertaining to my father's glory. They were founded in the Middle Ages, a combination of going out to kill Muslims in the Crusades and providing care for lepers and plague victims. I can see my father repeating the words of their criteria for membership: 'Catholics who practice altruistic nobleness of spirit and behavior.' My father would have put a strong accent on *nobleness*.

"In reality, they were, probably still are, a bunch of rich guys who filled the Vatican's coffers. But it was all about dressing up.

"So one day, my father came downstairs in his 'regalia,' a black silk tunic with a white cross embroidered on the front. I still respected my father, and I couldn't imagine he'd take such a ridiculous outfit seriously.

"So I piped up with, 'Papa, you can star in the family production of *Dracula* in that outfit,' and I made a vampire face, pretending I had fangs and saying, 'I need to suck your blood,' in a Bela Lugosi voice.

"I expected him to laugh, or pretend to be offended, and then we could play at that for a while. But there was no pretense. Towering rage. There are times when a metaphor seems literal. He was a burning tower that might or might not collapse on me. I felt I could hear rumbling. I saw the top of the tower rumbling, and I thought, This will annihilate me. I will be crushed.

"He literally spat the words at me; I felt his hot saliva. He called me a little snot-nosed brat and said I knew nothing of the greatness of tradition, of faith, honor, nobility, service. He said, 'You know nothing, and you never will.'

"Who got me out of that room? Was it Johnny? How did I make it up to Aunt Dotie's room? Was it Aunt Dotie who got me out? Surely, she wouldn't have been allowed to absent herself from one of my father's command performances. Maybe it was both of them. Johnny and Aunt Dotie. It doesn't matter. I don't think that was the time she told me tears were sacred. I think she said, 'Some things are important to some people, and we don't always know why.'

"I was told by Vincent that I was required to make a formal apology to my father in front of everyone who'd heard my words. My God, how he enjoyed delivering that news. He was gloating. He was glowing with his gloating. You could see it on his face. It was shining; he was *anointed* by his gloating. I don't think I was made to kneel before my father, but I felt as if I was. And then I felt his hand, the wide, dry palm on the top of my hand. And it felt wonderful. A blessing. A solace. The end of anguish. I had never loved him more.

"But later when I thought of it, I realized that I understood the voluptuous appeal of tyranny, in a way most of my comrades never could, and so I feared the fascists in a different way. Perhaps I feared them more."

More than anything, Amelia wishes she could have been there to comfort that little girl, so humiliated by an egomaniacal . . . well, tyrant was her word for it, and she was right. She can't see the humiliated little girl, she has disappeared; a fearless girl is in her place, because somehow, she has turned the poison into something that can't harm her. She has inoculated herself, and the inoculation has made her stronger. Stronger, Amelia knows, than she herself will ever be. And she wonders, if she had been in the room with all of them, would she have had the courage to stand up to her great-grandfather, defend her grandmother, the humiliated child? Or would she have been too frightened, too weak, letting it all happen without lifting a hand. "Fascist"—how easily, how loosely people used the term. But to her grandmother, it was a reality that it could not have been for any of her own generation. Her grandmother had fought the fascists. Her grandmother had lost.

"By the time of what I think of as the second regalia episode, I knew how to keep quiet, to savor my contempt. I was in my senior year at Noroton, I knew I was going to Vassar, I'd spent time in New York with Johnny, I had friends who took me to the Catholic Worker—I still wanted to be a Catholic then—well, anyway, I had friends whose parents voted for Roosevelt, and even that was a revelation; that my family wasn't in charge of the world.

"My father was insisting that he show us his latest. He'd been vested as a Fourth Degree Knight of Columbus. Of course, you probably have no idea what the Knights of Columbus are. I didn't really either, except that it was a bunch of men who liked marching in the St. Patrick's Day parade in their outfits and being militant about what they considered the enemies to the Catholic Church.

"So, we were all waiting in the living room. My father walked down the stairs like he was minor royalty. Wearing his tuxedo and, across his chest, a white sash and, at his waist, I could hardly believe it, an actual sword. The hat, you can't imagine it, a tricorn with white plumes. My father's chest was puffed out, and he couldn't stop fingering his sword. My God, he loved that sword, that hat, that sash. And I thought, This is the most ridiculous thing I've ever seen. But then he said the words that were the proof I needed that he was worthy of my contempt: 'We Fourth Degree Knights have earned the right to address each other as "Sir Knight."'

"By this time, I knew better than to say, 'What are you talking about, Sir Knight, nobody was ever called Sir Knight, you've got it all wrong, somebody has some half-baked understanding of some tradition that they invented, that never existed. It is embarrassing. You are embarrassing.'

"But I said only, 'Congratulations, Papa.'

"And with those words, all my respect, most of my fear, dissolved."

Amelia is doing something with her phone, and Marian is annoyed that her granddaughter, who is never rude, seems to be taking a phone call while her grandmother is telling her something important.

She hands the phone to her grandmother. "Look, Meme, I've got them. I've Googled them. The regalia. The Knights of Columbus. The Knights of Malta. I can see exactly what you're talking about now."

Marian looks at the picture: an image of what she'd been trying to describe. She had been afraid that her words weren't sufficient, but that the insufficiency should be made up so easily by this troublesome device is something she can't take in without displeasure.

"I think I understand what you were trying to get away from, what you had to escape."

But did the words create the understanding, or the picture on the phone? It would be childish to ask, childish to care . . . But Amelia is laughing, the kind of laughter Marian wanted from her father, the kind of laughter she was forbidden.

Men prancing in uniforms. Ridiculous. Nothing to fear. "I was right. They are ridiculous."

"Yes, Meme, you were absolutely right."

"I'm not sure I was right about the horses."

·

A week passes before Marian continues where they left off. They are making grape jelly, squeezing the transparent green insides from the dark purple skins, dropping them gently into the lobster pot, speckled blue and white. Both of them thinking what they will not say: Marian won't be alive when the jars of the preserves are opened. Preserves, Marian thinks. My life has been preserved, but not for much longer.

"So, tell me about Spain," Amelia says. "How did you decide to go?"

"How did I get to Spain? Well, in a way it's very difficult to explain, and in a way it's very simple. So much happened by chance, the ones I happened to meet, the ones I happened to like, Luigi and his family, going to the Catholic Worker for a while, although I could never fully get on board: I knew I wasn't a pacifist, among other things. And then I was afraid they wouldn't approve of Johnny. Not to mention, the most important thing, the Depression: it made everything so clear, in some way. People devastated by it, losing everything, and my family carrying on as if nothing in the outside world could affect them. It was a time, Amelia, when everything seemed clear. Hitler and Mussolini, and then Franco, trying to overthrow everything progressive in Spain, all of them talking about democracy as if it were something to be wiped away, some clammy little excrescence under their great heroic boots. In a way it was so easy: the people I liked and admired were on one side, and people like my family, whom I no longer loved and certainly didn't admire, were on the other. And then, of course, there was my brother's death. I needed something that would allow me to believe there was more to life than his death. I was in so much pain from his death that, although I was too much of a physical coward to kill myself, I would have been happy to die. I used to make lists of desirable ways of dying: being struck by lightning was at the top of my list. Or an aneurism. Something quick and clean, nothing for anyone to dispose of."

Why is her grandmother doing this, speaking so flippantly about her own desire to die? As if it were an affectation she'd grown out of, like a cigarette holder or a fake English accent.

"You were so young, Meme. Younger than I am now."

"Yes, younger, and, at the same time, more knowing and more

ignorant. But, my God, if I had the fire in me now that I had then . . .
I'm even amazed at myself, thinking of those years, how I just did
what I thought needed to be done . . . wild things, like talking Russell
into marrying me and talking the recruiters into taking me because I
could speak Spanish and was an excellent driver and could fix cars. Of
course, when I got to Spain, the men would almost never let me near
one of the cars because I was a woman. How did I do it? I was nineteen years old, and I convinced everyone—Russell and the recruiters
for the Spanish medical volunteers—that it was a good thing for me
to go to Spain.

"Despite everything, Russell was glad to have me, because, as I
said, we loved each other, and also it gave him cover as a gay man.
We were very close. We clung to each other after Johnny's death. We
believed in things, that we could change the world. Of course, we
didn't change it, not really . . . or maybe we did, but not in the way
we thought, and probably much less than we hoped. There was so
much we didn't know. But it saddens me that people your age know
so much that I don't know. So much that it's impossible for you to do
anything."

Does her grandmother know what she's saying, what her words
might mean to Amelia? Wiping out a whole swath of the population,
consigning them to irrelevance, to paralysis. She may be right. She
probably is right. But how can she say these things so lightly, as if her
words had no connection to the way Amelia is trying to live her life?

"What can I say to you about Spain, about the war in Spain? I've
forgotten so much. People think forgetting is simple, only one thing,
that it's remembering that's difficult, that forgetting is just the opposite, effortless and natural. But no, I think forgetting must be a kind
of labor, sometimes you have to will not to remember, so yes, it is a
work, some kind of work, even if you don't know you're doing it. I
don't know, some labor of relinquishment. But it's not as simple as
people think.

"And then, even if I work hard at remembering, things fly off or fly away, and no matter how hard I work, the forgetting takes over. That's why I'm doing such a bad job at this. I begin the telling in my mind, and then it's gone, the picture of what I wanted to say. And when the picture is gone, the words are gone. It's as if I were on a horse—there I go with horses again—a pity I don't like them, because they do come in handy as metaphors. It's as if I were on a horse, feeling all right, secure even, and then I'm thrown, lying on the ground, and then another horse comes by and I jump on its back, and it's okay, I think. I'm going to get there, wherever it was I thought I was going. But then I'm thrown again, and then there's another horse and another, but I'm just exhausted and I get off. All I want to do is sleep."

Her grandmother seems to be growing agitated, and Amelia doesn't know how to calm her down. To calm her down, but keep her going. And she, too, is agitated. Her grandmother has become a stranger talking, talking in this way about large ideas, about what can't be seen or touched or smelt or tasted, her grandmother, who has always made a point of talking about what was to hand, or about political ideas that had nothing to do with abstraction, that were local and practical. Who is this grandmother whom she thought she knew? And she wonders if it's possible to say we know anyone, are all of us keeping from sight the important things that make us who we are?

"Do they still show slides? Do they still have slide shows? Well, I never liked them either, any more than I liked horses. Slide shows. They always seemed 'educational' to me, which is another word for boring, and you know how I hate being bored. Or boring because they're too personal, too particular and too common at the same time: 'There's Aunt Tillie in front of the Eiffel Tower,' and you haven't the faintest idea who Aunt Tillie is, and you've seen the Eiffel Tower a million times."

Amelia is wondering whether it's worth it to explain the new kind of slide show to her grandmother. She decides she won't. Anything having to do with the digital world throws her grandmother into a kind of angry despair.

"What I mean to say is that remembering and forgetting are kind of like slide shows, only not educational, because you can't learn a thing from them, they're just too fast, and I just want the projector to go off and the lights to go back on."

Clearly it disturbs her, this gap between the pictures and the words, and Amelia wonders if she's being greedy, maybe she should just say, Never mind, Meme, it's all too hard, just let it go, just let it go. But what if her grandmother wants to keep doing it, needs Amelia's encouragement and support to go on? Is she, perhaps, being of help? She wants to believe that it's a possibility.

"You want to know what it was like, the war in Spain? It was like nothing because to say it was like something else would be, well, just wrong. It was only itself, terrible, terrible, terrible, don't they say war is hell, everyone says it, even when they're trying to talk you into another war; but I think it wasn't like hell because everything that I've ever heard about hell suggests that it's just one thing, just terrible despair and agony, but in the midst of all the terrible things that were happening, there were marvelous people doing things so self-less and so heroic you couldn't even have imagined it, and moments when you felt more alive than ever, and then moments of complete nullity when you couldn't even remember what it was like to think, you were just tending the overwhelming numbers of the wounded and the dead, you were a kind of machine, and then you were more exhausted than you can possibly imagine. And remember it was a civil war, half the country was on the other side, the fascist side, and it wasn't even our country, and we were there for some ideal we probably didn't even fully understand ourselves. I don't know how much you know about that war?"

"I did my thesis on Lorca," Amelia says, and she hates the sound in her own throat. It sounds so juvenile, pathetic even, bringing up her college work, written in the safe haven of the UCLA library, as a way of telling her grandmother that she has some understanding of what she went through on the bloody streets.

"Well, isn't that wonderful. Why did I never know?"

"I didn't think it was that interesting."

"Everything about you has always been of the greatest interest to me. You must always have known that."

"Well, Meme, everyone is terrified of boring you, you know."

"I guess I deserve that, and it's probably a good thing. And I'm glad I don't have to go into the boring details of all those initials: POUM, FAI, CDA, all that alphabet soup people were killing each other over, I don't even remember what the initials stand for. And do you know I don't remember a word of my Spanish?"

"We could practice, Meme. You know I was a Spanish major; I can speak it pretty well."

"I wouldn't dream of it. I'm sure my brain lost it for a reason."

Once again, Amelia is abashed at her own naive eagerness. But Marian has never liked apologies—they are high on the list of the boring—and Amelia doesn't want to interrupt her grandmother, who now seems eager to go on.

"Obviously, war is about death, it's about inflicting death, but when you're in it, you have a very strange relationship to death. You don't believe you'll die; you're ready to die; you're terrified of dying; dying seems like just nothing. And you're surrounded by it, and the physical horror makes you wonder if anything in the world seems worth it, and at the same time, giving up seems unimaginable.

"How funny I'm thinking about the smell of oranges on the hands of the Spanish girls who worked for us. They'd apologize for the smell, they'd just come from picking oranges for their family and when you said, 'No, you smell wonderful,' they'd think you were a crazy American who had no sense of what's what.

"'What's what'... What's what. That's a funny expression. But the words fit, because most of the time I didn't know what was what, I was so distant from my own body, I would look at my hands and wonder whom they belonged to, or I would see my feet and feel as if I were looking at myself from the top of some barricade, some very high barricade, very far away. And at those times, I didn't know who I was or whose hands were folding those bandages, or whose feet were taking those steps—they seemed to be doing things in some world I was very far from.

"And there was another kind of being alive that made you understand what it is to be alive for most of the people who have lived on the earth. Being hungry, so hungry that you thought about food all the time, afraid you'd do something dreadful, something you'd be tormented by for the rest of your life, maybe you'd grab food from a child or kill someone because they took your hunk of bread. And being dirty, your sheets so dirty you almost couldn't stand to get into your bed, even though you were so exhausted you thought it would be fine to die just there, and the way your hair felt when you couldn't wash it, my hair, which I'd always been so proud of, became like some cheap, synthetic wool stuck to my head, like one of those dolls you see at Woolworth's but couldn't imagine anyone buying, those stiff bodies and that stiff, false hair. Oh, I forget you don't know what Woolworth's was. Woolworth's, the five-and-ten, the five-and-dime, another thing you never thought wouldn't be there forever, the red-and-gold signs and the slanted wooden floors smelling of awful candy and perfumes people like my mother had never even heard of, they kind of made you sick, they were so sweet, but the names were fascinating. Evening in Paris. Djer-Kiss. What did that mean? Was it supposed to suggest some kind of Scandinavian glamour, Greta Garbo or Ingrid Bergman, maybe? But, you see, you don't even know what Woolworth's was, so how can I expect you to understand?"

The tone is growing wild again, and Amelia feels the need to rein her grandmother in. "I do understand. I promise I'll tell you if I don't."

"Well, you probably won't, you'll be afraid I'd think it's boring to have to explain."

"I promise. And besides, you're describing things very well. I can almost feel them in my own body."

"What I hope you never have to feel is being infested by lice. How can I explain the horror of that? Something crawling on you, tiny, insidious, and you can't be swatting at yourself all the time, you're working with the wounded and the dying. At night, Russell and I would go over each other's skin and hair, raking each other's scalps like monkeys. When people say, 'It made my flesh crawl,' I'm always tempted to say, 'My dear, you have no idea.'

"The sounds you thought you would never get away from. The sounds of people in agonizing pain, the sounds of different ways of dying. And the bombs, day and night. And the radio broadcasts.

"Sometimes I think the worst thing of all—of course it wasn't the worst, the worst was the endless wounded and dead that we could never keep up with—but something that made it all less bearable was the fighting among people you thought were all on the same side. The constant arguments, at first it seemed exhilarating that people would be so passionate about ideas, but then you had to come to terms with the fact that the people you thought were brave and fascinating were talking about it being all right to kill people who you might very well think were brave and fascinating. You thought all of us fighting fascism were comrades, but no, everyone was convinced that their way was the only right way, nobody agreeing about what they were fighting for. The anarchists said that society had to be changed as you were fighting the fascists, or even if you won, you would have won nothing; the communists said no, this is a war, social change will happen when we have won. That was Russell's side, and I remember he'd get so impatient with the anarchists, I remember him saying, 'Jesus, it's not the time to question hierarchy when you have to obey orders, you're in the business of people who are willing to follow orders to the letter without questioning, it's not time to reorganize the factories when the point is to make enough bullets to kill your enemy.' It was kind of a relief to hear him say 'kill your enemy,' because everyone was using other words, as if it weren't all about killing. And everyone despised the people who tried to bridge the gap, people like Prieto, the defense minister, they rolled over his words asking people to forget their differences, they just rolled over them like some roller flattening a tennis court. The Russian secret police were everywhere, though you had to pretend you didn't know what they were up to, and you had to pretend the anarchist's romance of blood wasn't blood lust, just a passion for justice."

Her grandmother goes silent, and Amelia feels she has to guard the silence. The silence is a relief, because the way her grandmother is talking frightens her. It is so strange, so unlike Meme. The word she uses most often is "terrible." Terrible, terrible, terrible. Her speech is rushed and pressured, as if a wall of water had suddenly broken through, washing over Amelia, taking her up, rolling her, throwing her down, water full of boulders, filthy water you had to be afraid to swallow: what if the poison made its way inside you, what would happen to you then? And what if the force proved too great for her grandmother's diminished strength, what if it killed her, talking this way? It would be her fault; Amelia would have to live with that forever.

The silence, though, has slowed Marian down. Her voice is different now, slower, softer, more like the voice Amelia has always known.

"I think you have never had a faith, so you can have no idea what it is to live through a loss of faith."

She needs to understand what her grandmother means by faith. Why faith is to her a word that matters, a word with heft and shape. Certainly, her grandmother knows Amelia has been brought up with no religion; she brought Amelia's father up with none. The word "faith," for Amelia, is only a relic, frightening or beautiful, insubstantial to the hand. Is it the same thing as belief? If it is, what is there that she can say she believes in?

Of course she believes in things. There are things that she would not think to question. First and most important, she believes she has been greatly, even extravagantly, loved. By three people: her father, her mother, her grandmother. That one is dead and one is dying has nothing to do with the power of it, that it—being greatly loved—is something she can stake her life on. But is there nothing larger than that?

She believes that everyone should have enough food, clothing, and shelter to live a decent life. She believes that everyone should work to preserve the earth. She believes that no race is superior to any other race, and that no one should be discriminated against because of race, color, creed, or sexual orientation. She believes that men and women are equal. But she has never been able—this has been the problem—to connect these things with any actions that she thinks can change anything at all.

Because she also believes there is darkness underneath everything, stronger than everything. That it is too late: the earth is doomed. That there is a hatred as deep in humans as the taste for meat, a hatred for anything different. That the wealthy will not share their wealth, that they would rather people starve and freeze than they should give up their luxuries. That between men and women, there is an unbridgeable wall of incomprehension at best, and at worst glass shards of mutual hate. And that nothing, nothing she could ever do is as strong as all of that.

So, her grandmother is right, she is not a person of faith. Her beliefs have led to nothing. And yet her grandmother is speaking of a faith that she herself lost for good, that was not replaced, regained, or found.

"After a while, after 1938, you'd have had to be a fool not to know that everything was hopeless for our side. But you had to go on because people were still fighting and dying, and no one wanted to give up, that would have been the worst, we all knew that, in the same way that we all knew that going on was hopeless."

Something in the air changes; the charged, heated atmosphere has lifted and cooled. Her grandmother, lately unrecognizable because of her loss of equanimity, her grandmother who always seemed so clear, like a lake you could see to the bottom of, is now looking vague and dreamy; her sharp, sometimes piercing eyes are cloudy now, and she is focusing on some place Amelia knows is not quite here.

"And, in the middle of it all, I had my love story."

Whatever Amelia expected next, she would not have predicted love.

"I suppose I wouldn't have had it if Russell hadn't gotten disgusted with all the infighting and packed up and left. I don't know why I decided to stay. Maybe it was because I couldn't imagine any kind of life for myself in America. Maybe it was because of the girls whose hands smelled of oranges, who had learned so much, so quickly, who had never been off their family's land and now somehow were tremendously skilled at quite complicated procedures. Or because of the people I was working with at the hospital, so much devotion, so much patience, the hospital that was so beautiful in spite of everything. I can see it clearly now, how odd, a place of terrible suffering, and yet a place I loved."

"Why did Russell leave?" Amelia asks, not wanting to let her grandmother's dreaminess take over, eager to hear about the love story . . . but first wanting to bring her back to something harder, something that needs to be finished off.

Her grandmother shakes herself like a dog that has just gotten out of the water.

"Why did Russell leave? Oh, well, so many things, but one thing in particular. What a strange time that was."

Amelia wonders what exactly her grandmother means by "that," because everything she has said seems strange. But was there some firm ground that seemed ordinary, normal even, and then earthquakes, smaller or larger? Perhaps one of these is what her grandmother is calling "strange."

"You see, I was very different from him. He really was political—politically sophisticated, I mean. He had read so much and gone to so many meetings, he could quote Marx and talk about all sorts of things in terms of class conflict, but for me it was: Well, these are the good people, this is the best way to be for most people, this is a good way to live, the others are evil. His faith had a creed, and mine was just, I guess, a bunch of impressions. So when he saw the people who he believed were his people betraying what he believed was a great cause, a holy cause—although, of course, he would never have used that word, but I knew what it meant to consider something holy, and I knew that was what communism was for him. And, you see, I always knew that alongside ideas, or, I guess I would say, hiding themselves under the cloak of ideas, were personal experiences that made one person see the world one way rather than another, and he left because of the betrayal of a great idea, but really he left because of love and friendship. Because a friend of his, a man he admired, had been taken by the communists, his reputation ruined by a lie, and then he fell in love with a young anarchist, and when he understood that the boy, who was really quite simple, was in love with violent bloodshed, that it was that love that fueled everything he did, not a desire to redistribute wealth or reorganize society, that was why he gave up.

"After Russell left, it was a strange time—not strange in the sense that the whole time had been strange because times of war are strange, but strange in a rather ordinary way, almost a domestic way. I'd been tolerated at the hospital Russell worked at because they needed Russell, but then Russell was gone, and it was known that he'd questioned the behavior of some of the people in charge, and it was uncomfortable for them that I was staying on. They didn't know what to do with me, so they sent me to another hospital, which was much less fraught. That was the hospital I said I loved. It was by the sea, and it was very beautiful. I loved that place, I loved the people I was working with, and, for the first time in my life, I fell in love."

Despite herself, Amelia feels a kind of cheap thrill, as if she were watching a love scene in a movie. Her grandmother is in love. Her grandmother, nineteen, or maybe twenty, is in love for the first time.

"Ramón was his name. Ramón Ortiz. I had absolutely no experience. I was surprised at how attracted I was to him, because any words you'd use to describe his body don't seem very appealing. He was stocky, you might say. Stout."

"'Stout,'" Amelia says. "That's a funny word. I don't think I've ever heard anyone use it."

"'My rock,' I used to call him. He always knew what he thought. Before he spoke, he would have looked at all sides of a question and said the thing no one had thought of. Imagine, Amelia, he was twenty-five, not much older than you, he'd just finished his medical studies and he was in charge of a whole hospital, grotesquely understaffed, grotesquely undersupplied, and he was always steady. He never seemed to get rattled. I could tell him everything, tell him the truth, everything I thought, and he would see the truth of what I was saying and cut away what wasn't true. That was when he was pointed and sharp, he could cut away the untruth, he could untangle the knots of words and ideas. It seemed to me he could make sense of everything.

"Of course, we didn't have much time together, and I often wonder what would have become of us: if I would have kept my admiration over years. Admiration is one of the hardest things to hold on to."

Where has that come from? Amelia wonders. Whom has her grandmother stopped admiring, and why?

"I admire you, Meme. I have always admired you. I will admire you all my life."

"Well, that's somewhat foolish, but I'm grateful nonetheless." Marian reaches, absently, for Amelia's hand, as if she weren't sure quite where she is.

"Ramón had this wonderful solidity, but I'd come to know later that what was comfortingly solid in Ramón was murderously rigid in his mother. But, of course, I thought nothing of that at the time, I really didn't know much about his past, where he came from, I knew it was somewhere in the province of Valencia. He was solid, he was serious, he was entirely truthful and wonderfully incisive, but he had a playful side, even a silly side. All the time we were together, we clung to each other, like people thrown overboard in a violent ocean because these were the months of the terrible defeats. Teruel. Belchite. The Battle of the Ebro, which seemed to go on forever. And we would hold each other, and in our happiness in each other's arms ... life seemed possible."

It makes Amelia very happy to hear her grandmother talking about a happy love. That she had a good time in the arms of a man she admired, that they laughed together. It gives her hope for herself, because she has not yet experienced what she believes being in love is. Her times with men never included anything like admiration, not much laughter, and not nearly enough play. When she was with a man, she often felt that she was looking down at herself from the ceiling of whatever bedroom she was in, watching herself acting the part called "the lover," watching from some other place, remote and safe.

But Amelia's happiness doesn't last long because her grandmother's next words are, "Then I got pregnant. And then he died."

The sentences hit the ground with a dull force, a rock falling from a low place, low but invisible. Her grandmother goes silent then. She looks through the hill of unpeeled grapes for what can be salvaged.

Amelia doesn't know whether she should ask a question now. And what would the question be? Certainly not "What about the pregnancy?" And "How did he die" sounds brutal, raw.

"Was it a bomb?" she asks, thinking it more seemly to ask a question that can be answered with a yes or a no.

"Sepsis," her grandmother says. "He was infected while operating on a young soldier.

"It all happened at once. I realized I was pregnant. My periods were very irregular, we were eating very little, and I was exhausted—to say I was tired and under stress, that would be a ridiculous understatement. I didn't find out I was pregnant till I was five months gone. I said I'd have an abortion, but Ramón said it was too late.

"Not for one second was either of us happy about the coming of this child. It's a terrible thing; I think my son knew, even in my womb, that his coming into the world involved no joy. I think that's why he turned out as he did, or why I turned out to be the kind of mother I was for him. Ramón and I hadn't really begun to think about what we would do, and then Ramón fell sick. He died a horrible death . . . terrible fever and chills and an awful thirst that nothing could quench. All preventable if we'd had the proper equipment.

"I was seven and a half months pregnant. There wasn't enough time for me to travel back to America, even if I could have gotten on a ship. I had nowhere to go. I didn't know where Russell was. Letters were impossible. Later, I found out he was in Paris in the American hospital. I had no one else to go to in America, even if I could have gotten there.

"After Ramón died, I became catatonic. I knew he had told his parents that we'd got married; he said his father was kind, his mother displeased. But he said, 'It is my mother's nature to be displeased.' I would learn about that, I would certainly learn about that. And he had scrawled a note to them just before he died—that they should take me in, care for me and the baby. Somehow, someone, I don't know who, arranged it, put me on a truck, and I arrived at his parents' door."

"And the baby?" Amelia asks, frightened of what she'll hear.

"I had the baby. He survived. You could say he grew and thrived. I left him behind when I left Spain. You see, I never loved him. He was never really mine."

SPAIN, 1946

"WE'LL SPEAK ENGLISH," the doctor says.

Strange, Marian thinks, strange to be spoken to in English. There is a dull pain in her leg, and she remembers now: her fall on the wet street, being carried somewhere on a stretcher, and she remembers thinking it odd that she is being carried on a stretcher, having carried so many herself. She'd been carried to the doctor's office. This is the doctor, a woman, speaking English. With an accent she can't quite place. Irish, maybe, but not like any Irish accent she has ever heard. Two odd things: a woman doctor speaking English, and here in this small town in Spain where she has been marooned, incapable of movement or decision, her brain a dirty frozen pool, or a bowl of filthy water left out somewhere and frozen through. Almost visible at the bottom: sediment, grit, the skeleton of dead leaves. For quite a while now, she has been someone she cannot recognize. There is no one whom she loves.

"Do you remember what happened?"

"The street was wet; I lost my footing. I believe I fell."

"You fell and broke your leg. But the miracle is that nothing like this has happened before. How long have you been taking this drug?"

It's happened to her before; it happens quite frequently. She puts it down to missing something in a language not her own. But the woman is speaking English, and her words still make no sense.

"I don't take any drugs. My mother-in-law, who's a pharmacist, as you know, gives me a tonic because she thinks I'm anemic. But that's the only thing I take."

"Your mother-in-law," the doctor says, lighting a cigarette, the match striking the box with a contemptuous fury. "'Head of bone, heart of stone.' That's what I called her when we were in school. I would say it in English behind her back. She didn't know what I was saying. It drove her crazy. I suppose it was a little sadistic."

"You know my mother-in-law?"

"Everyone in this town knows everyone. But especially, yes, I know your mother-in-law. She was not unintelligent, not uncourageous. Unusual for a middle-class girl to train as a pharmacist, although her father was a pharmacist. But then, my father was a doctor. But even as a girl, she was fanatical. Of course, in this country, to be fanatical is not unusual."

The doctor laughs, and Marian notices her teeth: uneven, greyish, and yet not taking away from her attractiveness. This is a face you want to look at; you can't help it. It has an aliveness that the faces she has known in Spain no longer have.

"What a relief it is, to be able to speak things aloud. I hardly know you. But I feel free to speak. Perhaps because, of course, I know something of your history. Perhaps because it has been so long since I could speak free of anxiety that what I said was being taken down, could be used against me somehow, by anyone, by someone I might least suspect. How long has she been giving you this 'tonic'?"

"Since my child was born. Seven years."

"Well, my dear, the news is you've been drugged for seven years. Phenobarbital. Didn't you notice that your reactions were dulled, that you felt fatigued all the time, confused, in a stupor?"

"I thought it was because of what I'd been through in the war. And so many people around me seem vague and confused and in a stupor. I guess I thought it was the way we would all be now. Something in the air we breathed."

"You're right, of course, but not in your case. In your case, you were being drugged. I can only imagine why. The question is: what do we do about it? I can't send you home, back there, because taking you off the drug, of course, will have an effect, what effect I can't pinpoint exactly. Most likely, you may find it difficult to sleep. Your dreams may be troubling. You may find yourself irritable, surprised that the slightest thing will set you off. But don't be surprised; remember, this is the effect of the drug. Or the cessation of the drug."

Once again, the words confuse her. A way of speaking she hasn't heard for years. A belief that something might be changed. Changed for the better, that there are problems that might possibly be solved.

Somehow, it has been agreed (but she doesn't know how; she hasn't been consulted) that she will be staying in the part of the doctor's house that is set aside for convalescents. This is a house that she can breathe in. It stands a hundred yards up from the Calpe Road, and every window opens to the sea. The furniture is vibrant and comfortable: the sofa covered with a rough fabric, a saturated yellow gold; the rush-seated chairs; the long plain table, pine, its slender base and legs painted an apple green. A glass bowl, cobalt blue, filled with fragrant oranges. No brocade, no dark benumbed benumbing wood. Pots of flowers—terra cotta, blue enamel, blue and white porcelain; she wakes to shades of purple, orange, shocking reds. It is so unlike the house of her in-laws, where she has lived for seven years, that it seems wrong to call them both by the same word: *house.*

The house where she lived. But how was it that she lived? She understands now, the fog that seemed omnipresent, only to be expected, the slowness of limb, the longing for the bed, sleep the only thing to be desired. It was not, as she had thought, the natural outgrowth of events. She had been drugged. She cannot begin to imagine what will follow now, what she will call her life.

The servant, who explains nothing, brings her food and a bedpan and helps her bathe. For five days, she speaks to no one but the doctor. In the evening, the servant brings two plates of food on a tray, glasses of wine and water. It is understood that she and the doctor will eat together.

"I was fond of your husband, Ramón," the doctor says, "very fond. He was a rose among thorns. His father is a kind man, but with no curiosity; I don't know where Ramón's curiosity came from. God knows not from his mother. Before the war, before the madness started, when neighbors could speak to each other freely, without fear, he would come here to the surgery, and we would talk about medicine and science. And when my brother was around, he would take Ramón into the country with him on his expedition to collect specimens."

"Your brother is a scientist?"

"Yes, a botanist. But also a priest. You may meet him if you like."

Marian is confused. A priest. A scientist. But not living in the rectory. She has never seen him saying Mass, the Mass she is told she must attend if she doesn't want to risk imprisonment. He must be the one whom no one sees, who hears confessions but does not say Mass. "The wounded priest," he is called; she has never known why. A priest who lives with his sister. But she is beholden to the doctor; she won't say anything to offend her—this is Spain, country of easily taken offense—by asking a question that might be considered prying.

"I would like to meet him if it's convenient."

"'Convenient.' What an American word."

Marian feels ashamed of her Americanness, the old shame of an undeserved privilege. Her face colors—the curse of the Taylor skin. The word made flesh, the skin turned pink from anger, shame, or love.

But the doctor doesn't seem to notice.

"Tell me about how you came to Spain."

Not a request; a command. Earned, of course. The doctor has

tended her, the doctor may, perhaps, have given her back if not her life, then her clarity of mind.

She doesn't speak about Johnny or Russell. She suggests that everyone of goodwill in America was on the side of the Republicans, and that she felt she had a duty to be of service. She describes her work in Valencia—only her work. It would be unseemly, she thinks, to speak more personally.

"Well, that's very interesting. Are you a comrade?"

Marian feels pressure in the word: the demand for absolute loyalty. Which she cannot, has never been able to, give.

"I am certainly sympathetic. But it's not in my nature to align myself so exclusively."

She feels, for the first time since Ramón's death, a spark of her old identity. She is able to say who she is, what she might or might not do. "Those kinds of fealty remind me too much of the Church."

The doctor laughs. "That's what my brother says. Perhaps it's time for you to meet my brother."

Once again, a decision made for her without consultation. The doctor stands up, walks as if she's just been given a command no one else has heard, but that must be instantly obeyed. Marian lies back, her head spinning, but not now in the old fog, and tries to understand what has just happened.

The doctor comes into the room, accompanied by a man, lumbering in his walk, so different from the quick *tap tap* of the doctor's heels on the stone floor. Marian thought the doctor said he was a priest, but he's not in clerical clothing. She thinks it's almost comical that they are brother and sister. He is tall, large boned. There is something birdlike about the doctor: darting, ready to take to the air. Her hair is wild, carelessly cut; Marian imagines she cuts it herself without looking in the mirror. His hair is thick and wavy, his eyes are such a deep blue that she imagines in some lights they appear black, or grape colored. The doctor's are light brown, with flecks of orange. Her brother's upper lip is long; his lower lip is very full; his lips are unusually reddish for a man. He has not been cursed with the doctor's uneven teeth. But before she has made sense of the face, begun to categorize it, she thinks, "This is the saddest man I have ever seen."

"You see," the doctor says, "my brother got the looks in the family."

"Which is not true," the priest says. "My sister is a beautiful woman. And of the two of us, she has the beautiful character."

"And he inherited the Irish habit of exaggeration, to say nothing of falsification."

"You're part Irish, then?"

"Our mother was Irish. Did I not tell you that? It's why we both speak English."

No, Marian wants to say, you told me almost nothing.

"Shall we have a brandy to help us sleep?" the doctor says.

"Lovely," Marian and the priest say, and then they laugh at their simultaneity.

"I'm Father Tomas," he says, offering his left hand. And then she sees: he is missing the second and third finger of his right hand. Marian hopes she's betrayed no reaction.

"I don't actually know your sister's name. She never told me."

"That is Isabel. Sometimes she moves so quickly she fails to notice what she's left behind in her rush."

The doctor, Isabel now, carries a wooden tray with brandy and three small glasses.

"Isabel, you failed to tell Señora Ortiz your name."

"Well, she'd have found it out anyway, Tomas. Or are you accusing me of bad manners?"

With his good hand, he ruffles her messy hair. "God forbid. You know I think you're perfect."

For a few minutes, they speak about the weather, the progress of Marian's leg, the kindness of the servants. But Isabel has no appetite for small talk.

"I have to get her out of that house. She's being poisoned. Pilar, the poisoner. She gave her a tonic that's laced with phenobarbital. This woman has been drugged for seven years."

Never had Marian seen anyone look so distressed. Marian wishes the doctor hadn't told him. Nobody should be so distressed.

"I'm so terribly sorry," he says. "This is a mad country, and I regret that you must be a victim of its madness."

"It's a mad country, and she's a stupid, tyrannical bitch."

"What do you *really* think of her, Isabel?"

The doctor rolls up her napkin and throws it at her brother. Marian sees that this is an exchange they've often had, and risks laughing. She understands that, for the first time in a long time, she knows it's all right to laugh. And she has it right: there's no risk. The lifting of the burden is so enormous that she laughs, she knows much too loudly. And then the three of them are laughing.

"So, little brother, this is where you come in. I have to let that bitch know I'm on to her. But, of course, I have nothing to hold over her head, and she knows she could report me to the Guardia at any time."

"But she'd hesitate doing that because of the mayor. And our uncle. And your brother-in-law."

He understands, unlike his sister, that Marian needs more information. "Isabel saved the life of the mayor's daughter, an appendix was about to rupture, so he protects her. And our uncle is a bishop, and he is feared."

"And then, my dear brother-in-law is one of the fat midget's economic advisers."

"Nevertheless, Marian, although I, and particularly my sister, are probably safe from major effects, we are always liable to petty harassment. Particularly from the Guardia."

"So this is where you come in, *Father,*" Isabel says, with a not entirely benevolent inflection. "She knows you collect plants, she knows you're interested in medicinal plants. I'm going to tell her to give you the tonic so you can analyze it, perhaps use it in your studies."

Now Marian feels free to express her puzzlement. "I don't quite understand," she says.

"I don't want you trapped in that house. I can keep you here for a while because that house is all stairs, and you can't climb them. But even when you move back, I want to be able to keep an eye on you. Now, Tomas, you know I don't believe in a benevolent God, or any God at all, or even Providence, and any fate I believe in is only cruel. But I think I can make something happen that will be good for all of us. Tomas, you're going to have to use your clerical authority. I want you somehow to hint at mortal sin."

"I wouldn't do that, Isabel."

"Well, never mind, I will."

"She wouldn't believe you."

"She might believe a sinner would know the ins and outs of sin."

"We don't need to bring sin into it."

"Why not? She will."

"You know what our mother would say: 'You must show that you are that much better than they.'"

"I always hated that as a child. I hate it now. But I'm going to go on. I think what could be a good thing for us all is for you to hire Marian as your assistant. She can help you collect and catalog specimens. You need someone who knows both English and Spanish . . . and do you have Latin, Señora Ortiz?"

"Enough," Marian says. "Please call me Marian."

"If we have to bring the bishop in, we will. And I am, of course, Isabel."

"I know he'll think it's an excellent idea."

"The old hypocrite."

"Isabel, he's a good man in many ways, within his limits. And I would not have my life as a botanist except for him."

"Yes, yes, but that doesn't make up for everything. Never mind. Does your father-in-law really need you in the ironmonger's?"

"I don't think so. I just think he lets me work there to be kind. And I'm not bad at bookkeeping. But I can do that anywhere, anytime."

"He is a kind man, poor sod; God knows how he got the bad luck to end up with her. The story is that she had a great love who disappeared and ditched her, and she married poor Ramón out of desperation. And then he learned what desperation might be. You know, he had smallpox as a child, and he must always have felt unattractive. Whatever you want to say about Pilar, she's good-looking. Maybe he thought he hit the jackpot. Instead of the pisspot."

Marian wonders if Tomas will remark on Isabel's language, or her lack of charity, but he says nothing.

"So then it's settled," Isabel says.

"Isabel, I think you've forgotten something," Tomas says.

"What?" Isabel says, impatient, ready to be off.

"You haven't asked Marian."

She puts back her head and laughs. "Oh, that little thing," she says.

Marian doesn't know how she can convey the extent of her gratitude, the extent of her amazement at the prospect of a new life. Of any life at all.

"I'd be more than honored," she says.

"Good. Now we have to beard the lion. You'd better wear your cassock, Tomas. Bring the biretta too, just in case."

Tomas says, "This has exhausted me. I'm going to bed." Marian wonders if he'll bless them, the leave-taking of every priest she's known. But he doesn't. He kisses his sister; he lays his unmutilated hand on Marian's head and wishes her a good rest.

Isabel sits down and lights another cigarette. "It's not just good for you and Tomas, don't think that. I need someone to talk to, someone I can feel free with. With Tomas, one has to be careful not to be too dark. You'll be giving me a great gift."

"I've done nothing," Marian says.

"Well, perhaps we've all simply done what we were meant to do. By whom, of course, I have no idea."

•

Marian had thought that the touch of Tomas's hand on her head and the effects of the brandy would put her right to sleep. But she can't sleep; she's excited. And Isabel has warned her that sleeplessness might follow being taken off the drug. But for the first time in a long time, she is hopeful, and the new feeling pierces through the old dead skin of hopelessness that had become so customary that it was no longer noticeable.

It happened so fast. Too fast? She had been carried to the doctor's surgery, the doctor had given her an injection, and when she awoke, her leg was in a cast. Then she'd been carried to another part of the house—a servant explained that some patients were taken there to convalesce. She had been fed and bathed. She had slept, been fed, and bathed again. And then, arriving like an army on the march, the doctor: We will speak English. And without consultation or hesitation: We will change your life.

She's afraid. Having been offered this possibility when she thought no possibilities were open to her, she can't bear the idea that it will be taken away. That she might have to go back to her old life. The old fog. She has always been afraid of her mother-in-law. Will the doctor, Isabel, be strong enough to counteract Pilar's strength? An iron woman. A woman of stone.

She thinks of the old children's game. Rock, paper, scissors. Rock breaks scissors. Scissors cuts paper. Paper covers rock. Her mother-in-law is the rock. Isabel, so sharp, so determined to cut through things with her every word and gesture: she is the scissors. And Tomas—is he the paper, his role to cover over, perhaps with the authority of the

Church? She doesn't like the analogy. Rock paper scissors, scissors paper rock, paper scissors rock. It's an endless game, and it can never be finished, never really won.

·

Señora Ortiz has been told to arrive at eleven o'clock. At ten minutes to eleven, the servant—whose name, Marian has learned, is Teresa—arrives, carrying a pitcher of orange water and, next to it on a wooden tray, four glasses. Isabel and Tomas settle themselves in two chairs near Marian's bed. They place the third chair between them, but farther from Marian, closer to the center of the room.

"Don't tell me you've got the jitters," Tomas says.

"She's everything about this country I hate."

"She won't defeat you."

"Why, do we have God on our side this time?"

"We have each other."

Señora Ortiz is wearing her best clothes; a tight-fitting wool suit and black suede shoes with thick high heels and open toes. A small hat, pressed close to her head, in the shape of a crescent moon.

"Father Tomas, I hope you're feeling well."

"Yes, thank you, Pilar. And you? And Ramón? And little Ignacio? We were hoping to see him here."

"He's very susceptible to germs. I didn't want to bring him to a place where he would be exposed to possible infection." She still has not addressed Isabel, but her remarks jet out and land on the doctor like a squid's ink.

"Let's get to the point," Isabel says. "Your daughter-in-law says you've been giving her a tonic."

"She's anemic."

"In fact, Pilar, she's not. The tonic has had a soporific effect; perhaps that's partly responsible for the fall. What's in the tonic?"

"A traditional Spanish medicine."

"That would interest me, Pilar," Tomas says. "As you know, I'm particularly interested in medicinal plants. I'd appreciate it if you'd allow me to analyze it."

Señora Ortiz snaps her head back: an animal afraid that the trap set for her will not be one she can avoid.

"I'll get it to you at some point, Father. I'm rather busy now."

"Good, good, thank you, Pilar. What I was hoping, Pilar, is that it would suit you if I could hire your daughter-in-law as my assistant in working on this botanical project I've been trying to complete for years now. I really need someone to help me with collecting and categorizing plants. It has to be someone who knows both Spanish and English."

Señora Ortiz's eyebrows come together, as if a wire had been inserted into the skin of her forehead and then pulled tight.

"It seems to me, Pilar," Isabel says, "that Marian should stay here until her leg is healed. I know how busy you are, with the pharmacy, and your grandson, and I'm sure you don't need the extra burden of having to care for someone who can't go up and down stairs by herself. Of course, her son will miss her."

"Ignacio is fine with me," Señora Ortiz says, opening her mouth as little as possible, as if begrudging, Marian thinks, even the sound of the child's name in this room.

"Perhaps you'd like some time to think it over, Pilar."

Señora Ortiz stands up and takes a snowy handkerchief out of her pocketbook. She wipes her mouth with it, replaces it, and shuts her pocketbook with a vengeful click.

"That isn't necessary, Father. I think you've worked it all out for yourselves."

"God will reward you, Pilar," Tomas says.

"May I have your blessing, Father?"

"Of course," he says.

Señora Ortiz falls to her knees, a gesture of such habituation that she needs nothing to lean on. The sight of such rote abjection sickens Marian, and she sees the reflection of her disgust on the face of Isabel.

Father Tomas blesses her with his wounded hand, but lays the good hand on the top of her head.

"You know where to find me if I'm needed," she says. She places a dry kiss on Marian's forehead, and it's all Marian can do not to wipe the spot as soon as the lips are removed.

"I'm wondering, Father, if I might ask the favor of your accompanying me to my door."

"I'd be pleased," Father Tomas says. No one meets anyone's eye.

Isabel paces up and down.

"I hope she doesn't talk him into anything. He can be easily threatened. He can be easily made to feel moral responsibility for something that has neither morality nor responsibility attached."

They hear the door close, and he walks into the room. "You must understand she's not really a bad person."

"Tomas, you wouldn't have thought Caligula was really a bad person. But go on. I take it this was not said to you under the rubric of the sacrament."

"No, she made the point that she was not confessing because she had not sinned, but she thought, of all of us, I would understand because I was the only one who had been, in her words, 'true to his baptism.' She's not a bad person, but I do believe she's guilty of the sin of idolatry. But, thank God, I'm not her confessor, so it's not my responsibility."

"What the hell are you talking about, Tomas? And you're wrong. She *is* a bad person. Look at what she did to Marian."

"Idolatry. The worship of a false god. In the Middle Ages, it was grounds for being burnt as a heretic."

"Some customs should be revived," Isabel says.

"Isabel, stop," Tomas says, and remarkably, she bows her head, chastened.

"She worships the Church, not God, and she worships fascism. And I think, Marian, that she worships your child as if he were not a child of God, but a little jeweled god himself."

"I find the way they are together disturbing," Marian says. "And there's no way I can be with him because of the way she is with him."

"I know, Marian. I know you're right. I'm very sorry. But by her lights, what she did to you was to protect you and, particularly, little Ignacio. She was afraid if she didn't sedate you, you'd be indiscreet, that you'd say things that no one should be saying, that because you were American, you wouldn't understand the need for silence, and that they'd take your child away from you and put him in an orphanage. She's not wrong; they did do that, they still are doing that to the children of people they call 'reds,' and it's very easy for them to label you a red, therefore outside the protection of the law. Really, Marian, she believes that what she did was the best thing to protect you and Ignacio."

"It is grotesque, Tomas, that you don't think it's evil, what she's done," Isabel says.

"I'm very reluctant to use the word 'evil' . . . I've seen what happens when people use it casually. It's real, I know it's real, but probably rather rare. Mostly, people are in impossible positions, and they act impossibly."

"Well, she's not going to act impossibly anymore."

"Because your intelligence and imagination are more powerful than her idolatry. Try and pity her. She has lost her son; she lost him before he died. She felt quite alone in the world until this little boy, and now she's in danger, in her worship of him, of loving him in a way that will distort his growth."

"What can I do for him?" Marian asks.

"First, you must save yourself. Or allow my sister to save you. You will be with us every day, you will help me in my work, Isabel will bring you back to health. You see, my sister is a formidable woman. I often think if she'd been in charge of the Republican army, she'd be running the government from Madrid."

"Except for one little problem, brother. The lack of a penis."

Isabel lights a cigarette, enjoying, Marian can see, her role as the bad girl, the daring big sister. Marian feels she has been caught in a whirlwind. What is the right thing to be feeling? Outrage? Relief? Anger at Tomas's pity of the woman who has caused her and her son such harm? When the whirlwind stops, she is left with a feeling of amazement. For this brother and sister. One who can make things happen. One who insists that we forgive.

•

Now she wakes in the mornings knowing that she is alive, that there is a difference between aliveness and deadness, and that she is on the side of the alive. Now colors take on their old vividness; things have points; things have edges, have outlines; there are spaces between them through which light strikes, clear, an arrow or a knife. Why had it meant nothing to her that at the edge of the town there is the sea, the Mediterranean? *Mare Nostrum.* Our sea. She had never thought of swimming; now she will think of it. She will have to buy a bathing suit acceptable to the priests and the Guardia. Perhaps that means it will be impossible for swimming.

But with the gift of aliveness there is a price. Isabel had warned her. You may have trouble sleeping. You may become more irritable.

Not a gift, not a gift at all, the theft of a refuge or sleep, this new quotient of wakefulness. Sleep had been her refuge; something to long for, the bed however hard, the blankets however resisting. Now what will her refuge be? The world, she has long known, does not provide her refuge.

Now she notices the streets, not as white monochromes but as peeling blocks interrupted by complex and often rusting black gates. Now she must make the effort to turn her eyes away from the malnourished children, their heads too big for their dwarfed bodies, the dogs that she dare not pet, their thin triangular heads, their backs embossed with weeping sores.

·

After six weeks, she returns to the place she must, despite herself, call home. But it is impossible to think of it as home, this place where she has no place.

Home. Not home. A place, but no place. Not surprisingly, this is where irritability—the symptom of which Isabel had warned her—takes hold. The abject passivity of her father-in-law, which once she pitied, now creates in Marian the desire to slap his face. That face: pockmarked, ruined, unlovely. Wake up, fight back, can't you move faster? His kindness to her, which in her fog had been a slender branch she clung to, now is cause only for resentment. Did you know what your wife was doing? she wants to shout at him. But even if he had known, he would have done nothing to stop her. He has never been able to say the slightest word of anything but acquiescence to his wife.

But the center of Marian's irritability is her son. She hears, on the streets through the open windows, mothers shouting at their children, and for the first time she understands. She would like to take her son by the shoulders, to shake him. "Wipe that look off your face or I'll wipe it off for you." Where has she heard those words? Certainly not from her genteel, absent parents, from the well-paid servants.

So where do they come from? She had hoped that her new clarity would allow an opening for ordinary mother love. But the opposite has happened.

She tries to do things with her son, but it's too late. She wants to take him into the countryside, even on short walks to the seashore, but her mother-in-law says he is weak, he suffers from allergies, he is prone to asthma, the woods would be a danger to his lungs, the sea breeze would cause him to catch cold. She tries to teach him card games, but his eyes travel always to his grandmother, who stands behind him, ready to snatch him if his mother's nearness should do him any harm.

She gives him books about animals and ships and children who live in treehouses or the forest, but the only books he likes are about the lives of the saints. He particularly likes child martyrs. His body is flaccid, with none of the liveliness that makes the bodies of all boys beautiful. When Marian suggests that her son might be eating too many sweets, the cheap sweets his grandmother feeds him till his flesh is pale and fat, Pilar tells her she knows nothing about raising a child, a Spanish child; the home is the source of sweetness, a refuge from the bitterness of the world.

There are reasons, of course there are reasons, why the flaccid body of her son causes her to pull away, why his simpering sloth-ful manner makes her want to strike him into some swift boyish life. But the reasons are not good enough. She is an unnatural mother. A casualty of war. Too late for her, as it is too late for the amputees, the beggar woman crying in the street for her assassinated lover.

With the new clarity, there is the great gift of work. Tasks that are absorbing, pleasant, unlike the work of the war, they have a kind of leisure folded into them, a place left for understanding. She enjoys being in charge of tending Tomas's equipment. Making sure every-thing is properly packed in the rucksack before they start out on their day's collection. The delicate silver scissors, the plain-faced knife, the lethal-looking shears. Cellophane envelopes. Small cloth bags. Tomas carries the rucksack with the care of a mother carrying a child. At home, he takes over: placing the specimens in the plant press, brought home from his student days in Ireland. Then placing the specimens between sheets of newspaper, to be glued the next day onto special acid-resistant paper, with just the right amount of glue—he insists on doing this himself, as he does the labeling and the transfer of notes from the field notebook to the specimen book.

He praises her care. It has been a very long time since anyone praised her, a very long time since she has done anything she believed worthy of even the slightest praise.

They leave early in the mornings, just at sunrise. On their walks, they are silent. Then, alert as a fox, he will stop, stoop, gesture for the scissors. She provides them, as she provided scalpels to the doctors (two of them her husbands) in the dreadful but heroic operating rooms. She opens a cellophane envelope, hands it to him along with the tweezers, then the sky-blue leather field book, in which he writes a brief note on what he's found.

Each season delights him, but most especially he loves the early spring, particularly the pink almond blossoms with their unpretentious but insinuating smell. The hundreds of wildflowers that he snips with tenderness, determined that each should be classified, given its proper name. Her favorites are the wild narcissus and wild lilies. He is particularly fond of the carob tree, with its graceful shape; he reminds her that in the worst days of the war, people stayed alive by eating its pods. In the fall, they pick the delectable mushrooms; the cook will make an omelet with the precious morels.

He has a great interest in medicinal plants, and together they prepare tinctures and ointments. He makes a tincture of St. John's wort, which he tells her with pride is native to this part of the world: it is meant to cure melancholia, although he says it has not been of help to him. Marinated in olive oil, it is a disinfectant. He considered distributing a small pamphlet on medicines that could be made from local plants, but then he reckoned that the old women of the town probably knew far more than he would ever know, but they wouldn't share their knowledge, even with a priest. And Isabel was contemptuous of herbal remedies. So he decided against it, as he often decides against completing certain projects. A large part of Marian's job is to convince him that he should keep going, that what he is doing is worthwhile.

They walk the dry roads, and she is so often struck that here, unlike in America, there is no wilderness, nothing that has not been inhabited for centuries. Even the caves in the rocks have, from time to time, served as dwellings. They pass the ruins of houses centuries old, fields that have been terraced since the time of the Moors; terracing, he tells her, is a skill learned from the Moors, like so much that is beautiful in Spain. "They had a genius for anything to do with water. They knew that in a dry land, it is as precious as gold." They pass men who cut blocks of ice from a pit where water freezes in the brief winters; the men haul the ice to the town on the backs of their donkeys; half of it melts on the way. Sometimes dry winds from Africa blow dust that fills the sky and stains the white houses reddish brown.

On the way home, he speaks easily. Sometimes he sings Irish songs, Spanish songs, Gypsy songs, songs in Catalan and Basque. A sweet, low voice. This is when she sees the boy in him.

He rushes through lunch. Isabel pretends to chide him from eating too fast, but his enthusiasm pleases her. He can't wait to get to his desk. Marian lays out the papers sent from Ireland for mounting.

They always try to get home before noon, before the broadcast of the Angelus.

Tomas's distress at the blaring Angelus is nearly unbearable to watch. He stands still, prays, or pretends to pray. Marian pretends only. Then he rushes into the house, sits with his head in his hands, and rocks. "They poison everything beautiful. They beat the ploughshares into swords."

And Isabel says every time, "Never mind, Tomas. We're all right here. Come and have lunch."

But he will not; he disappears into his room. Isabel has charged Marian with being sure they are inside the house well before noon. Almost always, Marian succeeds, and she's proud of this. Fortunately, they work in his study in the afternoons; there's no chance for them to be in the street when the later prayers are blasted.

•

It is nearly a year before Isabel speaks freely to Marian, although Marian is pretty much living with them. She takes most of her meals with them, nearly all her days are taken up with Tomas's work: she goes back to the house of Pilar only to sleep. Isabel had said that speaking freely was what she most wanted. But even in English, she whispers, although the Guardia, if they heard, would understand nothing. Still, she whispers. The Guardia have the habit of walking into Isabel's surgery if it is empty, or if they know that Tomas isn't there and she and Marian are alone in the house. They open the door without knocking. They ask for a glass of water. And then they just sit in the front room, their feet planted far apart, their legs open, saying nothing, but saying with their bodies: We will do this whenever we want; we can do this whenever we want. You think you are safe, but you are never free of us. Isabel refuses to change anything about her behavior; she goes about her business as if she didn't see them. But after they leave, she pours a brandy for herself and Marian; then she allows her body the luxury of trembling.

Isabel begins the first time with a simple sentence. "My husband and I met at university." She considers herself hardheaded, a realist, but in fact Marian thinks Isabel is the most romantic person she has ever known. Her romance is not the simple romance of a lost youth: the memories of all-night discussions, cheap wine, endless cigarettes, no need for sleep. Perhaps, Marian thinks, she treasures it because it is a past like many others, a past that many young people all around the world have shared. You didn't have to be in Spain at a particular moment; it was possible to have had experiences unshaped by disaster. She knew she would marry her husband, she says, the first time he walked into a café where she drank with her friends. She was one of the two women at the table; he chose to sit beside her.

"Before I met him, I was a political naïf, an economic idiot," she says.

He was a lawyer. They planned to serve the needs of the poor; he would work to bring them justice, she to bring them health.

Her romance of the years 1931 to 1935 has the deepest tincture. She and her husband moved to Cádiz, where his family was from.

"We had a small, perfect house by the sea. The Republic had been elected. Real democracy for the first time in Spain! It was easy to believe that the dead hand of the past would be amputated without bloodshed. Oh, we were foolish, but we were intoxicated, because, in no time at all, the Church had lost control of education, the fat priests had to give up their fat salaries, people went to meetings instead of to Mass, they joined unions instead of sodalities. Women were allowed to vote; divorce became legal. We had the luxury of despising the socialists; we threw around threats and slogans like balloons; we couldn't believe the country wouldn't be thrilled to follow our lead.

"And then began the first of the series of shocks: the losses of elections, the crisis of the Asturian miners, when the government, the government we believed in, turned against the striking workers, and we saw our own side shedding our own side's blood. That was the first we saw of the fat midget, Franco . . . no one would believe he could be of importance.

"Then the greatest shock: the coup, led by the fat midget, who enlists the help of the German and Italian armies. And the Moors, trained by his soldiers to a particular brutality. We had prided ourselves as Marxists as being free of race prejudice, but we couldn't stop our terror of the Moors ... and maybe it was worse for us because, partly, we believed we deserved brutality at their hands since our hands were covered in the blood of their people."

When she speaks about what was done to her husband, she becomes another woman. She spits her words; she grinds her cigarettes into the ashtray as if she were grinding them against the faces of her enemies.

"I was working in the hospital in Seville when he was killed. He and a group of others known to be Republicans were taken to Falange headquarters, in a former casino, a very luxurious casino, where they were subjected to particularly sadistic torture. They were forced to ingest a liter of castor oil and industrial alcohol mixed with sawdust and bread crumbs. They were in acute abdominal pain, they continually soiled themselves, and then they were savagely beaten.

"It was a terrible death, an agonizing death, but also a humiliating death, a disgusting death, a death you wouldn't want anyone to see you dying. His brother called me, his brother whom they had called to claim his body, his brother, not me, because he was a member of the Falange. I think he was frightened of me, he was right to be frightened of me. Of course, they had cleaned my husband up. He looked beautiful, my beautiful Antonio, but I knew he didn't look beautiful as he was dying. And what his brother said to me was perhaps the worst thing of all. 'It was a mistake,' he said. 'If they'd known who he was, if they'd known he was my brother, they would not have done this thing.' He wanted to turn the horror into a private tragedy, a singular accident ... and that seemed to me the worst betrayal of Antonio, of what he had lived and died for.

"When he said that, I heard myself making a sound that was not a human sound, it was an animal sound; it frightened everyone, even myself. My brother-in-law, who I suppose is not a wicked person, only someone in love with order above all, was frightened of me, that I was a wild animal that might turn on him. What made me make that terrible sound was the word 'mistake' and the idea that it was a mistake only because he was connected to someone whose power they honored, and that, without that connection, it would not have been a mistake, it would have been an act of justice.

"Sadists, torturers, taking their hats off to me, afraid of me, afraid of Antonio's brother, assuring me that those responsible had been punished . . . did they think that mattered to me? I did go mad, I suppose. I stayed only long enough to try to prevent them from burying him in the Church, but then I went home, I gave up, because his parents wanted that, and whatever else he was to them—a disappointment, a shame, although they really weren't political, but they were religious, and it was nearly impossible to be close to the Church and be anything but a fascist—whatever else, he was their son; he had been their son longer than he had been my husband. So I gave in; I couldn't refuse them that consolation. I was beyond consolation, and so I felt it mattered less that I should get my way."

It is another year before she feels secure enough that Marian understands her brother and treasures him as she treasures him, that she tells Marian the history of Tomas's mutilation.

"In that mad time, the time of the country's madness, and my madness, I did a terrible thing. I did the thing that I regret more than anything. It was a wicked thing, but I must believe I did it out of madness rather than wickedness. I wrote to Tomas; he was studying in Ireland; our uncle, the bishop, supported his desire to train as a botanist, he wanted Tomas to come back and teach here, and he didn't believe he could get the training he needed in Spain.

"Tomas was away from the madness, safe, protected, studying. I think he was happy. Until I began writing. I told him everything I saw, every terrible thing. I shouldn't have done that. I knew him, I should have known what it would do to him, but he was the only one I had, and he was far away—I must admit that there was part of me that was angry that he was safe in the bosom of the Church—and so I wrote compulsively, letter after letter, fifty, a hundred, I don't know, and so what he did, what happened to him, was my fault, because I should have known.

"I hope he really burned them, those letters, as he says he did, because they should never have been written, they should not be allowed to exist. All my despair, my rage, my absolute loneliness, shot like a bullet to my brother so far away, telling him everything but insisting that he not come back, that he stay where he was in safety. Safe except for me.

"I wrote about all the terrible things I saw, but I concentrated on what the Church had done in the name of God. The priests who blessed rebel flags, adopted fascist salutes, cartridge belts slung over their cassocks. So many priests joined the rebels that many of the faithful had no one to perform the sacraments. I sent him the speech of the archbishop who praised the bombing of Guernica. I told him about the bishop who bragged that he had watched without emotion as the Moorish soldiers carried on their bayonets the ears and noses of Republican prisoners, describing the scene as merely 'the natural excess of all wars.' I wrote pages and pages about the brother of one of the nurses I worked with, the mayor of a small town, a union organizer, who was shot in the stomach next to an open grave in the cemetery. The soldiers got drunk while they watched him die. And they thought it would be funny to put their empty brandy bottle in his mouth so it would look like he'd drunk himself to death. The priest that was with them just stood by and let them do it; he himself laughed. And the wife of a soldier I treated, a young woman of nineteen with twins, the Civil Guard was willing to spare her, but a priest who was with them encouraged them to shoot her because 'with the animal shot, there is no more rabies.'"

She beats her fists against her forehead and says, "I should have known, I know him better than anyone, I have always known him better than anyone, how could I have done it?"

She has become, Marian thinks, a cutout figure of a woman, an outline only, emptied by the words she says.

"And then I got a letter. This letter. I can't even say the words; you must read it for yourself."

She hands Marian sheets of paper that have obviously once been rolled into a ball, then straightened out, but nothing could disguise the violent treatment the pages once received.

Marian wishes she had glasses so she could pause for a moment, postpone reading words that she knows will be terrible. She thinks of the letter Johnny wrote to her, "My dearest girl . . . Life is not good enough for me to live it."

Dearest Isa:

I know you will find my actions horrifying. I must believe that you will understand. I have done what I have done with great deliberation; it is something I believe I had to do. The alternative would have been to take my own life.

I cannot forgive myself for staying here in safety while you and so many others I have loved have suffered the unspeakable things you have described. I am grateful to you for providing me with this information. Nothing I heard here suggested anything but the nobility of the Rebels, the knightly character of Franco, the holiness of their cause, the chivalry of their every act. "Nuns are raped; priests are killed." That was the only truth they were interested in our knowing; perhaps it is the only truth they believed in. But I believe you; I have always believed you of all people in the world, and your letters shook me out of my dream world, and I have explored what has been written about our country elsewhere; without you, I wouldn't have had the courage for this. As you have been outraged by what has been done in the name of God, you must believe that I am even more outraged. But I have always known of the two of us: your outrage leads to action, mine to despair. I know I am too late to have put my body in the place of justice, but I can use it to witness, if only to myself.

You know—or perhaps you don't—that in canon law a priest can only consecrate the host if his right hand is intact. He must have a proper thumb and middle finger, or he is considered unfit to touch the Host. I got the idea for what I have done when I was working on Billy Devlin's farm, my friend Billy, the one mad for studying new varieties of corn. He has an uncle who made a fortune in America and then came back to Ireland, bringing with him up-to-date American farming equipment. The old farmers didn't want to use it, so he convinced Billy and me—you know I always liked fooling with machines—to learn about the new inventions, and as we were priests, if we were using them, maybe the farmers would think it was God's work and they should use them, too.

I felt I was going mad, listening to what people in the seminary were saying about what was being "done to God's holy Church by the vicious reds," and I knew they would call you a red, you and your friends, but I knew that you were all on the side of the poor. I found out that the rebels were given endless arms by Hitler and Mussolini, whom I know without doubt are evil. And I knew that you and people like you and your friends were in danger. And when you told me about what had happened to Antonio, and that it was happening again and again, and the Church was triumphing in it all, refusing to speak out or even acknowledge the horror, to say nothing of helping people mourn it . . . I felt I had to do something. I had to put my body on the line as you and so many people I loved had done.

As I said, I was working on Billy's uncle's farm. Working the combine harvester. Do you know what a combine harvester is? Probably you don't, why would you? I'm sure there aren't any in Spain.

There's a blade that cuts the hay; it looks like an eight-foot-long pocket comb, but with two rows of teeth, each tooth shaped sort of like a pointed kitchen knife, but one side is thick and smooth, the other side is like a knife, it does the cutting. The blades open up like scissors. The knives slide back and forth in short strokes.

As I watched the machine, I decided what I would do. When the work of the day is done, the driver has to bring the blade back up to a vertical position because you can't go through gates and down roads with an eight-foot blade sticking out to the side. The blade has to be lifted by hand and pushed to its vertical position. We'd been warned that when the machine is off it looks safe to pick up the end of the blade and then push it the rest of the way up, but that, as it's pushed up, the knives can get pulled by gravity and resettle themselves. Well, I didn't leave it to gravity. I gave the blades a jerk; I knew they only needed to move a couple of inches to do the work I wanted. I put my fingers, the two middle ones, in the right place; the blades cut them off.

Of course, everyone was horrified, and it was quite painful, and you know I'm not a stoic, God knows, you understand that better than anyone. But at the same time, I was relieved of the terrible pain I'd been feeling, my shame for staying safe, my shame for the Church I love. I know you don't love it, but

I trust you to understand what you can't understand in my beliefs as I understand what I can't understand in yours.

I asked the people at Maynooth to contact our uncle, the bishop. I made my confession to him. I told them that I wanted him to be sure that I would not be given a dispensation to consecrate the host. I know you don't respect him, but you must, because although he said that I had committed a grievous mortal sin, he believed that I was not in my right mind. He said he believed I was not in my right mind, but he no longer knew what a right mind was, so he would do what I asked: make sure that the dispensation was denied.

I will come back to Spain. I will live with you in Altea. Together, we will bind up wounds, because in all our suffering, we are not alone. I'm not talking about God, don't worry. I'm talking about you and me, the love that we have for each other that is part of what Dante says moves the earth and the stars.

Marian puts the letter down. She can't meet Isabel's eye. What possible response could she give to this letter, this extraordinary letter, most of it taken up with physical details, the justification of an unjustifiable action; the explanation for what must be inexplicable.

Only two words come to her mind, and she knows they are the right ones. "I understand." She feels the rightness in her spine, on the palms of her hands. But what does it mean to understand something like this? Perhaps, that the motivations are traceable; they can be connected like points on a map. What she doesn't know is how to name an action such as this. Madness? Heroism? The categories seem clumsy, inflexible, but the alternatives are far more unsatisfactory. What comes to mind is a word from a way of life she will no longer allow into her understanding: martyrdom. She will refuse, then,

Adam's task. She will not name. All that is required from her is this physical sensation she calls understanding. She tells Isabel the story of Johnny.

Isabel nods. "Your brother. I understand."

"Will you tell Tomas that you have told me and I understand?"

"I will," Isabel says. "And then there is no need for us to speak of it again."

·

What she learns from the brother and sister comes to her in different modes, at different tempi. Isabel's words about her past rush out in torrents: there would be a deluge of revelations, and then nothing, perhaps for months. But what Tomas tells her comes in trickles, usually when they are on their way home from collecting. And some things she learns almost casually, a calm stream, because the brother and sister speak freely in front of her. She isn't sure always if they know she's there.

Tomas asks her, when she is writing the Latin name of a species, how she learned Latin. "Is it because you had a Catholic education?"

"The Madames of the Sacred Heart."

"Ah," he says. "The aristocracy."

She tells him about Mother Kiley and Mother Gomez and Mother Labourdette, and in return he tells her about his uncle.

"I owe him a very great deal. He was the first to interest me in botany; he's a rather fine amateur botanist, and he arranged for me to study in Maynooth. Isabel has no use for him, but Isabel can be—though she could never admit it—too hasty sometimes. She doesn't like to believe that he uses his power to protect her, that he has said words in the right places so she can practice medicine here, so she can live in whatever freedom is possible in this country. She doesn't like to admit that she can live as she does because she is under the

238 · MARY GORDON

protection of the Church and the state: our uncle, the bishop, and her brother-in-law, an economist in the Franco government. It's important to Isabel that she forget these things. It's important that she not be reminded."

Tomas is the only person in Spain who asks Marian about her personal life. When he inquires about her family, her words, like Isabel's, come out in a torrent.

"I don't love my family. You think that's a terrible thing to say, but I don't. I never felt they were really connected to me."

She tells him about Johnny.

On his face is that look of bottomless sadness. Usually, when she sees that look, she wishes that whatever has been said to occasion it had not been said, that whatever has occurred to prompt it hadn't happened. But now his sadness is a comfort to her; it accompanies her own; he says nothing to suggest that the sadness will pass or that it somehow should be pushed away.

"I am very sympathetic to suicides; sometimes, I think they are the most courageous ones.

"I know that I myself am drawn to it, but I am a physical coward, and I wouldn't do it to Isabel now; she's suffered too much. I might have done it when I was younger, but then I was more pious; I questioned then very little of what I was taught. But I understand your brother, please know that I understand. I'm sure suicide isn't a sin, I'm sure Jesus would never punish anyone for their sorrow. I know that Judas is in heaven, in heaven because of his sorrow, and I hope that I will be someday because I know I am a Judas. I betray the just men who died fighting injustice, who were tortured and killed by monsters. I protect the monsters. I keep the secrets they tell me in confession, and, because of me, they are safe from their secrets, as those who fought for justice were never safe. And on the other side, I keep the secrets so they can tell someone that they know their life is false, that they participate in the great lie—but I don't encourage them to fight again, because I believe that would be hopeless. And so, I am a Judas in that way; I betray them, too; I betray them to hopelessness."

"No, Tomas, you give them whatever hope there is. You give them consolation. But who can console you?"

"I am distractible by the natural world. That is my consolation."

One night after they have finished dinner, a night when Isabel isn't home, he says to her, "There is nothing sadder than seeing something you were born to love degraded."

On Saturdays, at confession, the line in front of his box is huge, and after three hours, he comes out, sweaty and exhausted. Aged. Once, when he looks particularly spent, Isabel says, "Maybe sometimes you can tell Father José you can't do it. It takes too much out of you."

He turns to her with the nearest he gets to anger. "You don't know. You can't possibly know. No one can. You don't know what I've heard. I no longer have the comfort of believing that the brutality was only on one side. You say you've seen horrors, heard about horrors, but you have no idea what people have confessed to. I can tell you about fascists starving nursing mothers, so they had to watch their babies die before them; I can tell you about Republicans shoving a crucifix through a priest's eardrums so they broke, and then choking him with a rosary; I can tell you about fascists holding children in front of their own bodies so they themselves will not be shot, and shooting teachers just for being teachers—would they have shot our mother?—and I can tell you about Republicans digging up the skeleton of a nun, dressing it in whorish clothing, and dancing with it, and where does it end, where does it end, will you tell me how it is possible to bear this, even to think of it? And yet, I come back to Guernica: the planes, the animals, the frenzy of the mothers, the killers safe in the air; nothing the Republicans did was as terrible as that. But maybe it's only because they didn't have the arms. Perhaps if they had, they would have been no different. But, in fact, they didn't have the arms, so there is a difference. I think . . . but how do I know what makes a difference . . . I don't know . . . I don't know."

"Go to bed, Tomas," Isabel says. "You must sleep. You must try to wipe it from your mind."

"Forgetfulness would be the greatest betrayal. I must remember."

"But you must live your life."

His voice goes uncharacteristically bitter. "My life," he says. "My life."

He leaves the room. Isabel and Marian sit silently, terrified that in the morning they will find him dead, because it seems impossible that someone should suffer so much and live.

She only hears Isabel angry at him once. She is in the kitchen, and Tomas is in the sitting room, talking to Marian. "I love the Spanish people because of their suffering."

A glass breaks. Marian hopes that it's just an accident; just something slipping from a wet hand. But Isabel comes into the room, pulling at her wild hair. She speaks in Spanish. Is Spanish the language for anger, as if it were their childhood tongue?

"I hate to hear you talk like that. This goddamn Spanish worship of suffering. The cause of so much suffering."

Then she looks panicked and says to Tomas, "I'm sorry. I shouldn't speak like this."

"You mustn't worry, Isabel. You can say whatever you like to me. Your words can't hurt me; the words that hurt me are the cold words of cold hatred, that's what kills the spirit. Your words are words of outrage, and your outrage is holy."

She throws the towel she was holding to the floor. Her face is nasty as she says, "Holy, holy, holy."

And suddenly, the two of them start howling like wolves. They sit down because they're laughing so hard, they can't stand up.

They tell Marian the story of the parish priest's dog who would wait for him outside the church, and when the bells rang for the Sanctus, the "Holy, holy holy," the dog would start howling, and the priest would just talk louder to try to pretend it wasn't happening.

Marian feels a piercing envy that this sister has a living brother, who, however much concern he causes her, still breathes and moves beside her. Isabel has Tomas; Marian has lost Johnny. There is no one with whom she shares a private language. There is no one for whom she comes first.

·

It is the beginning of her understanding that she won't stay in Spain forever. She grows more determined when, knowing she has no choice, she attends the ceremony of Ignacio's induction into the Young Falangists just after his confirmation, when he is twelve years old. The morning of the ceremony, she hears her son and her mother-in-law twittering like birds with delight and excitement.

She stands next to her father-in-law, whose sadness is unlike Tomas's: his defeat is entire; he has no distractions; his humiliation is complete. The sound of the bugle and the drums, which the others applaud, makes her wish she could run raving through the streets and tear down the grandstand that has been built for the leaders of the party. They stand together in their blue uniforms, giving the fascist salute. Flags snap in the cold wind. She looks down the line of young boys in their Falangist uniforms. It is all she can do to stand still next to her father-in-law. Forced to applaud, she will not cheer.

For years, she and her son have barely spoken. They are polite, strangers who pass each other coming and going in shared corridors, the sharing not their choice. The only gifts he gives his mother are holy pictures with swoony-eyed saints on clouds that look like the kind of candy he loves best: marshmallows, garishly dyed pink. For Marian's birthday, he presents her with a scapular and the indulgences attached to it if one wears the cloth with stamp-sized images next to the heart and prays special prayers each morning. She pretends gratitude, looping the string around her neck, tucks it into her bra, and promises falsely that she will pray daily.

For his confirmation name, he chooses Tarcisio, after a Roman child beheaded because he would not surrender the sacred host he carried in his bosom. Tarcisio allowed his young head to be separated from his body, and the soldiers fell to their knees, instant converts.

The Christmas he is thirteen, Ignacio writes a play and organizes its performance in the nave of the church. It is called *The New Tarcisio*. She asks to be spared the details of the play, pretending that she wants to be surprised, but fearing that she won't be able to keep silent. She asks Tomas to accompany her; she demands that Isabel stay away.

Ignacio appears in the front of the church, dressed in his young Falange uniform. His classmates, his costars, are dressed in rough, ragged clothes; around each neck is a red bandanna. They threaten the young Tarcisio with their broomsticks, the points sharpened to look like bayonets. "We are the soldiers of the Republic," they cry. "We understand you are carrying the host. Give it to us so that we may feed it to our dogs. Or we will cut your head off in the name of the Republic, for we hate with every fiber of our bodies all that is sacred, all that is holy, all that is dear to the Catholic Church."

The young Tarcisio bows his head, offering his neck to the swords, which are not bayonets after all. "I will die rather than allow you sons of Satan to touch the sacred host."

The broomsticks fall on the young head. Tarcisio is covered with a sheet, his legs and feet left visible. He twitches and expires. The audience breaks into wild applause.

Marian vows that she will leave the country.

·　·　·

That spring the stranger appears. The almond blossoms are at their most beautiful.

On one of the old Moorish trails, they see him: a young man standing in front of an almond tree, sketching. His blondness shocks Marian: it is out of place in this dry country; it has been, she thinks, years since she has seen such light blue eyes. She wonders what language he will speak. He greets them in Spanish.

"You're American," she says.

He laughs. "I travel thousands of miles for the experience of Spain, and I meet an American."

"I, however, am not American," Tomas says. "Half Spanish only, I'm afraid. The other half Irish."

Of course Tomas invites him to lunch.

They discover a greater coincidence. The young blond, whose name is Theo (is this a visit from a god?), is from Rhode Island. But not, Marian is grateful to hear, from Newport, but from the other side of the state, a village called Avondale, near the ocean, abutting Watch Hill, an enclave of the second-best rich. Watch Hill, whose houses are grand but merely mansions and not, as in Newport, châteaux.

After lunch, he asks if they would like him to play some American songs on his harmonica. Tomas, who loves all songs, says yes; Isabel and Marian share a doubtful glance. Marian hopes he won't play "Camptown Races" or "Old Black Joe" or "Home on the Range."

What he plays touches them all. There is no way, of course, for him to have known its place in Marian's history, sung as a mockery by her brothers: "Sometimes I Feel Like a Motherless Child." Asked for another—by all of them, with no reservations—he produces "Swing Low, Sweet Chariot."

Not a hint of American swagger in these songs. This is the music of suffering, mournful but refusing defeat. Marian sees that Isabel has decided to like the stranger. Theo.

He is invited to spend the night, as it is obvious from the bedroll he carries with his knapsack that he was planning to sleep outdoors.

He is a real American, Marian sees, unencumbered by the immigrant fear of taking what is not rightly his, of being tricked into thinking it is his right and then humiliated. He says he is delighted to stay with them, delighted with their generosity, delighted with their company. She can tell that delight is, in some way, not surprising to him. Is it the romance of a hospitable Spain, or the reflex of the privileged, assuming favors are due to them, that they have only to open a hand to accept what is rightly theirs? She knows that Isabel and Tomas don't have these thoughts; it is the work of one American judging another American.

He is the youngest person in the room. Marian is twenty years younger than Isabel and Tomas; she is thirty-four, and she reckons Theo to be ten years younger. He seems untouched, unblemished: the fair skin, the straight shoulders, the unbowed spine. He has no impulse to whisper.

Marian imagines for him a past of ease: summers of sailing, winters of red-cheeked tobogganing, skating, and hot cocoa, ready for him in a warm kitchen where an old retainer cheerfully presides. She is fighting against his ease; something in her would like to punish it, or at least expose it. She is horrified to recognize in herself the family appetite.

He has been with them for a week, accompanying Marian and Tomas on their expeditions, drawing the landscape and then small, precise renderings of their specimens, ten, twenty to a page. "Tell us about your family," Marian says, when they are sleepy after lunch, about to separate, she to go home, the others to their room for the siesta. "Are you part of the old Rhode Island nobility?"

"Well, perhaps back a ways, but I'm from the rebellious branch.

My mother was a debutante but ran away to Paris to study painting. My father wasn't American at all. He was English. I was born in London. My parents sent me to Rhode Island to an aunt when the war heated up. They stayed; my father worked for the Ministry of Finance; he felt he was needed. They died during the Blitz."

Shocked, ashamed at her misperception, she sees over his head, as in a cartoon bubble, "Sometimes I Feel Like a Motherless Child."

"And so, of all of us," Isabel says, "only you were affected by the Big War. What people think of as the real war, as opposed to our war, which was only a dress rehearsal. You see, we were kept out of it by Franco, it went over our heads, like bad weather in another part of the world. We had our own tragedies to absorb us."

Isabel tells her story, or a version of it. Tomas says nothing about his wound, which, self-inflicted, must be kept in shadow.

Marian no longer needs to fight against Theo's ease, because it is not ease but resignation. One of the categories that allows, for her, desirability. She is able to enjoy his long strides, so different from the Spanish walk, marked by its verticality. She likes his clothing: what are called dungarees, workman's trousers, which he tells her are all the rage in America now. A shirt of a tough, blue cloth, the shade of a winter morning sky, which he tells her he buys in an army-navy store. He amuses her by naming the items for sale in an army-navy store; he describes all kinds of knives, compasses, indestructible thermoses, a hundred different kinds of rope. The catalog of abundance makes her, for the first time, homesick.

Does she desire him or only the end of a Spanish life, the threat of starvation, the threat of imprisonment, the threat of betrayal taken in with every breath? For the first time ever, she allows herself girlishness; she combs and pins her hair carefully now. It has been years since she's owned a lipstick, and she considers buying one, but lipsticks are for sale only in her mother-in-law's pharmacy, and she will not expose herself to the scrutiny that the simplest purchase— aspirin, witch hazel—inspires in her mother-in-law's implacable eyes.

She loves the smell of his fresh, young sweat; when he takes off his shoes to bathe them in a stream, she is enchanted by his long, narrow feet. "How beautiful on the mountain are the feet of the messenger of the Lord." For once, she doesn't reject the words from the discarded past. He is a messenger from somewhere, some better place, but he has not been sent from the Lord, who has, for her, the slight problem of nonexistence.

Isabel and Tomas are shameless about throwing them together. Marian understands that her desire for Theo is part obedience, and this, mixed with his representation of a freer life, makes her wonder how much of what she calls desire is pure. She makes herself believe that he honestly likes her, he is drawn to her in a way that is not tainted, because sometimes he feels to her like a motherless child, and she is ten years older.

But she has no strength to resist his loveliness, his sweetness, the ripple of her skin, like a horse's flesh in a light wind, when he puts a hand on her shoulder, her flattered pleasure when he presents her with a pencil sketch of herself in which she can, for the first time in years, imagine herself as beautiful.

"That can't be me," she says, mortified by her own coyness.

"I wonder who it could be, then," he says, with a feigned punch to her shoulder, the American boy's gesture no one in Spain would dream of applying to a woman.

Inevitably, then, the first kiss, the first chaste embraces. How different his body is from Ramón's. Ramón's solidity, his closeness to the earth, and this, this creature whose bones are light and palpable under their less ample covering of flesh, whose muscles are long and smooth, whose hair is straight and fine and fair, who towers above her with the vitamin-fed height of North America.

Slowly, they tell the stories of their lives.

"My aunt is a lovely woman," he says, "my aunt Amelia. One of those women who always has a little piece of fine lace at her neck. I always felt that I had to be careful that my presence in the house wasn't too much for her: too noisy, too dirty, too male, too healthy. She'd never expected children in her life; she had arranged her life so that it was very orderly, there would be no surprises. And then she had the surprise of me. How anxious she was. Every time I left the house, she imagined a disaster, a broken leg, a car crash, a kidnapping. I think it was a relief to her when I went off to Choate; oh, I know she missed me, but I think it was a relief. When I came back from the summers, I couldn't help chafing against her anxieties, and I felt like a monster for feeling like that. I've been away for a few months now and I write her all the time. I think she doesn't sleep nights, imagining me being knifed and my body cut up into small pieces and thrown into the ocean. You'll like each other, I think. She's serious, and she was a mad Roosevelt supporter. Now all her energy goes into hating the Wisconsin senator who's created the communist witch hunt."

"McCarthy," Marian says. "Our papers call him 'America's Savior.'"

How different from her imagination: the orphan boy raised by a gentle aunt, sent away to school, home for summers of watchful, anxious indulgence, tentative, half-fearful ministrations, left to himself in honor of the space needed to mourn his loss. And what was it he said, "You'll like each other"? Does that mean he thinks they will see each other in America? Foolish boy, she wants to say. I am trapped here for life.

Remarkably, he seems to understand the crashing aggression of the Taylors. "I did spend six years in boarding school," he says. "I understand bullies." She had been reluctant to tell him about Johnny—you never knew how people would react to an announcement of homosexuality; recoil could come from the most unexpected places. But his anger at her family's treatment causes her to make a fist and pound it against a tree. She confesses her false marriage to Russell.

"Well, that was a pretty damn smart way of getting to do what you believed in."

"I guess you're still legally married to Russell," he says one day, blushing as she has seen no one in Spain blush.

"Well, I suppose I am. I don't know where he is."

"What would you do if you wanted to get married again?"

"I never thought about it."

"I would like you to think about it now."

She understands he is proposing.

"Of course, I would be willing to adopt your son."

Ignacio. She hadn't thought about bringing him to America before Theo said he would be willing to adopt him. But there is no question in her mind what her response will be.

"No," she says, "Ignacio will stay here."

They understand she has accepted his proposal.

"Are you sure you can live with that?"

"Perhaps, Theo, this will make you love me less. But I feel nothing for my son."

She sees that he is pretending to understand, but he has no will to make a judgment. They have decided on a life.

The rest of their love affair, which they keep secret, even from Isabel and Tomas, consists of letters back and forth between America and Madrid. She believes it will be impossible for her to get a passport, impossible for her to leave the country. He says he knows that it will not be. What he hadn't told her is that he's named for Theodore Green, the senator from Rhode Island, his mother's uncle.

"He likes me," Theo says. "He was thrilled that I chose Brown over Harvard."

"Well, everyone likes you, honey, that's your problem. I suppose it will be mine." It feels luxurious to take a teasing tone, unused since the first days of Russell's anger.

"But I'll never be able to get a passport, even if I weren't married to Russell, with the political climate in America, all this Red Scare hysteria, all this McCarthy mess."

"I don't think you understand my great-uncle's position. The things he can make happen. Besides, the Spanish and Americans now have to pretend to be in love so the Americans can build submarines here and Franco can take Eisenhower's dollars. They're about to sign a cooperation pact."

She could never travel from Altea to Madrid without arousing her mother-in-law's suspicion. So Theo travels back and forth to Madrid. He has meetings with the new American ambassador, a crony of his great-uncle Theo.

Everything is done in secret. It will not be difficult for her to leave Spain, but to leave Isabel and Tomas will tear her heart. She and Theo speak endlessly about what to tell them and when. Marian doesn't want them to be harassed by her mother-in-law with her connection to the Guardia, pumped for information, threatened for withholding it by some force that her protectors cannot keep her from.

And then it comes to Marian: a strategy foreign to Protestant Theo. She will tell Tomas in confession; he will be bound by the seal to reveal nothing.

She begins with the familiar form: "Bless me, Father, for I have sinned, and I am about to sin. I'm not here for absolution; I don't believe that what I have done will be erased. But I need your help, and the help of the authority of the Church. Theo and I want to get married."

How wonderful, he says, and claps his hands. She wonders if that is the only time anyone has ever applauded in the confessional.

"But to get married he'll have to be baptized. So will you baptize him?"

"My dearest friend, I can't do that, even for you, unless it's something that he wants."

"I'll talk to him. I'll make him want it."

"No, you can't make him want it. We have to find something about it that will have meaning for him, that will not make it a farce."

"Leave it to me."

"No, Marian, leave it to me."

Tomas meets privately with Theo for many hours, behind closed doors. He gives Theo books, which Theo reads with the concentration of a schoolboy preparing for an exam. Marian is a little annoyed that he is taking the whole thing so seriously. Tomas arranges with his uncle, the bishop, that the banns be published in another parish, far from Pilar's eyes.

The eyes that Marian cannot meet are Tomas's. Their separation will be a grief to both of them, and she knows how he lives with grief. This will be a separation forever. What would you call the kind of love we have? she wonders. Brother and sister, no, she wouldn't put herself in the place occupied by Isabel, not even in a back corner of it. They are partners in something: a work, the living of a life. She knows that she will never have a love like this again.

Isabel refuses to express sadness; she absorbs herself in the legal details and says, not entirely kindly, "Once again, we are saved by our connections to the powerful."

Marian takes nothing with her from her in-laws' house. Theo says he'll buy her everything she needs in Madrid. A friend of Isabel's, a comrade, probably has access to a car. Marian slips out of the house at three in the morning. She takes one last look at her sleeping son. No feeling accompanies the look. The wish that the body of her sleeping child engendered some ripple of tenderness remains a wish only.

The car is waiting for her behind Isabel and Tomas's house. The parting, they all know, will be final. Isabel allows herself tears. "Now I will have no one to talk to," she says. And Tomas says, "Only your poor old brother."

"Oh, you," she says. "Sometimes you're just too good to talk to. I mean I have no one to talk to about all the terrible things I think about people."

"I'll try to be more terrible," Tomas says.

"Yes, Tomas," Theo says. "You work on that."

Marian is afraid that if she opens her mouth to speak, she will release a howl of grief so loud it will wake the town and ruin their escape.

Tomas puts his good left hand on her head. "Go with God," he says.

Marian is surprised that Isabel makes no objection.

In Madrid, they stay in the luxury of the Palace Hotel. They drink in the elegant bar. Over their heads is the fabulous glass dome: sparkling blue-green glass, as if you sat beneath a peacock's fan, spread full, shot through with silver. She knows that this room, because of the plentiful light shining through the glass dome, was used as an operating room during the war. How strange, a bar is an operating room and is then a bar again, a bar where the wealthy raise their glasses to each other, perhaps the same wealthy men whose guns ruined the bodies of the men operated on under the high, light-giving dome. She is pretty sure that Theo doesn't know the room's history, and she doesn't want to tell him. The war is over. The war is in the past.

After years, ordinary married love. For the first time, clean sheets and a soft bed. The boyish body of her new, third husband. Passage booked on a ship, not now in the company of ardent comrades, thinking they would change the world, but leisured Yanks, on their way home from holidays newly available to them in the New Spain, now a friend of all Americans.

AVONDALE, RHODE ISLAND, 2009

MARIAN walks out of her bedroom and into the living room, where Amelia is sitting. How slowly she walks. In only a few weeks, she has become what she has never been: an old woman. A dying woman. She is carrying two shoeboxes, and they are a burden to her.

"Can I carry these for you, Meme?"

"Please, my dear, I'm not quite that pathetic yet. The worst thing you can do is to make me think I'm weaker than I am."

Then she sits down and Amelia is safe, because her grandmother laughs.

"What I mean is that you mustn't make me understand that I'm as weak as I am. You're very good to me, Amelia. I hope it isn't too difficult. Though you wouldn't say if it were."

"It's not difficult, Meme. I'm quite happy."

Marian wonders how she can believe this. But how can she not believe? Amelia has never developed the habit, or skill, of lying. Lying puzzles her; it disturbs her; she doesn't quite understand its place in the world. This, Marian thinks, is the luxury of being a child not raised on a diet of shame. Raised almost without censure, a censure so rare and so light that it need not be questioned much or fought against.

She opens the boxes. The cardboard looks insubstantial. It has done its work, and now it wants to give up, to fall apart, to crumble into uselessness. She takes a pile of letters and puts them on the floor. "This isn't what I want. I was looking for pictures."

Amelia sees that her grandmother is ready to talk about her past again. She's longing to ask, "What happened to your baby?" but she knows she can't. There is nothing to do but wait.

Trying to fix her eyes, her mind, on anything else, she sees her own past handwriting with unease, as if she were watching herself rise from the dead. A pile of envelopes tied with a light blue ribbon. Letters from her to her grandmother. At the flap of each envelope is a blood-red spot, and she remembers now her devotion to the seal that her father gave her for her tenth birthday.

She found it in a flea market in Davis, California. What ugly places they were, those flea markets, how ugly most of the things were, except the rare ones that were beautiful, and some people who were selling things cared enormously about them. Everyone set their tables out on the hot asphalt. Packages of batteries, car parts whose function she couldn't begin to imagine, leather coats and jackets that frightened her with their suggestion of criminal or wrongheaded ambition, mugs with pictures of dogs, of cats, of birds, of rainbows, beads that were the color of nothing you'd ever seen anywhere else.

Everywhere there was the smell of food you knew you wouldn't like once you were eating it, but that you still wanted: cheese or caramel popcorn, sugar-coated roasted almonds, hot dogs, cotton candy. She can't remember how she became so fixated. It was lying on a table that belonged to the vendor whose space at the market was next to her father's. Somehow she found herself fingering it: a seal that was really a Victorian watch fob, a small, brass piece that looked like something from a board game, a hole in its top through which a watch chain was threaded, the bottom, the actual seal, half the size of a dime. A circle of orange stone—she would learn its name: jasper— into which had been carved the words "Forget me not," and a flower whose shape delighted her.

"That's really taken your fancy, hasn't it?" her father said. And after they finished packing up, he slipped it into her hand: a small black velvet pouch; inside it, the brass piece that she had coveted.

"The woman selling it told me something very interesting about it. About the way it's carved. A special process called 'intaglio.' We'll look it up in the encyclopedia when we get home."

The minute they got home she ran to the encyclopedia, a souvenir of her father's childhood that no one in the family consulted, but that was given pride of place—though hidden—in a cabinet. Opening the doors in the secret, unmarked spot, she sat on the floor and copied the definition of "intaglio" into her diary. It is one of the memories that has not been blurred or diluted. She could wake up, even now, at three o'clock in the morning, even with a hangover (which she has experienced twice), and tell you the definition of "intaglio":

A technique of engraving on stone. The opposite of relief, the stone is cut into and a design is formed below the surface. Often they were used for seals, so the image was actually the opposite of what would be reproduced in wax. A sharp tool, a small whirling wheel, is powered by a pedal the carver must keep activating, pumping with his foot at the same time as he does the delicate work of carving his design, stopping occasionally to sluice the stone with cool water so that the pressure and heat won't cause the stone to crack.

The next day, she and her father bought the sealing wax: flattened candles, in peacock blue, emerald green, ruby red. Amelia became obsessed with sealing all her letters with her wonderful seal that said "FORGET ME NOT," repeating the message with a picture of a flower. The person she wrote to most often, the only person she wrote to regularly, was her grandmother. And now she sees that her grandmother has saved all her letters. There they are, in a pile at Meme's feet.

She looks at the ruby and peacock and emerald circles that are the seals, broken so her grandmother could read whatever silly thing Amelia had said. And it comes to her: a fit so perfect that she feels she must distrust it. *I am being intaglioed.*

This is it, this is it. She is the stone, and her grandmother is the carver. Always she believed there was about her some blankness, not emptiness, a smooth flatness whose failure to have been marked rendered its value null.

The blankness was her lack of a history. And now her grandmother would create it, pushing hard and fast with her foot, carving painfully with her skillful hand, using the tool whose end point was a diamond, sluicing with the relief of a reminder of love. And what is the result of the labor? An image incised, the negative of what would be another image when the seal was pressed into hot wax, and another image, high rather than recessed, was formed. Sent out into the world. Now the part of her that had been blank would hold the image that she would use to create another image when she pressed down. This is who she would be. Finally, she knew her work. What she had been waiting for all along but had no idea how to ask for.

Her grandmother hands her a photograph. The cardboard backing is ripped; the image is faded.

"This is my friend Isabel," she says. "Isabel saved my life. Well, I guess you could say there were many people in Valencia who saved my life, taking me into safe spaces when the bombs were going off. But Isabel saved my sanity. When she found me, I was not in my right mind."

Of the things Amelia had imagined about her grandmother, losing her mind was not one of them. What had she imagined? She had not allowed herself to imagine anything. Her mother's warning had been so stern. "Your grandmother keeps her past very secret, and she must have good reasons for that, we must respect them. Remember,

Amelia, they were a generation who believed in privacy, they made something of a fetish of it, maybe. I think they overdid it. But it was the only way they knew, it's the only way she'll permit any kind of closeness at all."

The thought of not being close to her grandmother was so frightening that she had shut her imagination down: no speculations, no theories, not a single image. She would admit nothing; the risk was, simply, too great.

Marian is troubled by the task of bringing Isabel to life so she is real to Amelia. Of course Isabel is dead, but Marian has no idea how she died or when. None of the words she can think of saying seem adequate; they seem categories only; she is tired now she is nearly always tired; she is shocked at the number of hours she sleeps; she doesn't have it in her to summon whatever would be necessary to bring her friend into the room.

She is dissatisfied with the words she uses. "She was a doctor, which was very unusual at that time for a woman in Spain. She was a communist during the Franco years, and that was very, very dangerous. She was the bravest woman I ever knew."

She passes the picture to Amelia and begins to laugh. "That wild hair," Marian says, "that absolutely wild hair. I think she liked it, though she pretended it vexed her. In that world, a woman's hair said so much. Some of the women's hair was evil."

She shivers and brushes something invisible off her shoulder.

"You think it's strange to say that hair can be evil. But it was. Stiff, aggressive, punitive hair. Unnatural curls, nothing that moved, you'd never dream of touching it. Fascist hair. I always think of it as fascist hair. And the hair of the poor had lost its luster, the famous lustrous hair of Spanish women, you never saw it; women wore it pulled back tight, tight, and pressed down. Only the very youngest had hair that had any shine or sign of life. The war had taken it all, the war and the years of terrible poverty."

Amelia looks at the photograph. She has never seen a face like this one: it's so entirely of its time. And yet it's a modern face. The hair is completely unstyled, which makes it modern, but no one would have that face now. Is it just that the photograph is faded? Or that most of the people Amelia knows no longer have imperfect teeth? But there is something in that look, so ardent, such a mix of grief and will, that makes it of its time. The smile is simple, but seems hard won . . . insisting upon something despite the evidence of the eyes. A brave smile that inspires a particular kind of sympathy, so clear is the effort behind the smile.

"I had a fall in the street; I broke my leg, and she treated me. And in the course of fixing my leg, she discovered that I'd been drugged. At first, she suspected that I was drugging myself. But very quickly she realized that my mother-in-law had been drugging me. My mother-in-law was a pharmacist.

"I was drugged for seven years, and I didn't know it. Every morning for seven years, Pilar gave me what she called a 'tonic' laced with phenobarbital. Seven years of my life lived in a stupor. But even now, seventy-five years later, I can't say for certain whether she did it out of hatred or out of love."

Amelia should be used now to receiving shocks. First, the suicide of a great-uncle she never knew she had, then a half uncle in Spain, abandoned by her grandmother, and now the information that someone to whom she has, thank God, no blood relation drugged Meme for seven years.

"How could it possibly have been out of love?"

"Because in a world of insanity, a world of nightmare, it is often impossible to distinguish love from hate. Oh, I don't mean that she did it out of love for me. She hated me for everything I represented and everything that had caused her son to fight on what she thought was the wrong side, to give his life for what she believed was a great error, no, she would have called it a grave sin. But she loved my son. Ignacio, his name is. I don't know if he's still alive."

"You haven't been in touch with him."

"No, I have not. You see, we had almost no relationship. He despised me; he thought I was a sinner; he didn't want to get too close to me for fear of being infected by my sin ... my sin of not believing in fascism and the Catholic Church. That's what his grandmother taught him, and he was much more hers than mine. After a while, we didn't even bother to pretend.

"And when my mother-in-law looked at my son and my son looked at her, the air they breathed in and out was a more concentrated version of the unhealthiness that was the general air. They had their own language, like lovers. They only wanted to be with each other. They would share these black, malevolent glances, like a pair of executioners biding their time. You think I exaggerate, but I felt when they looked at me—yes, I know it's my own son I'm talking about— that they would have preferred me dead, that they would have taken pleasure in my death. Every other look of theirs was cold and judging, that was who they were to the world, judges, but to each other, their eyes were soft; their looks suggested a kind of rottenness. They had the same kind of soft rottenness in their eyes when they looked at someone in authority: one of the Guardia, one of the priests, best of all a visiting monsignor.

"I could say that she took him from me, but that wouldn't be quite right, it wouldn't be quite fair. He was never mine. My body rejected him from the first. He was three weeks premature, and my milk never came in properly. You must believe me, Amelia, I loved his father. But I never saw his father when I looked at Ignacio, only his father's mother. And my own father: they had those same kind of dark, tight curls. My brother Vincent had them, too. Ignacio was conceived in love, but born in a time of horror, and he represented all the horror that I had wanted to put far from me."

Amelia feels that an enormous boulder has come rolling down a hill, flattening her. Stop, Meme, please stop, she wants to say. This is too much too quickly. Let me lie here, still, and quiet, let me try to lift this weight that stops my breath. Don't you understand what it might mean to me, what you just told me? That you were drugged for seven years. That you had a child who you never loved. You, the person whose love was always the unquestioned firm place on which I could stand when I was afraid of being swept away. A mother who cannot love her child? Who are you, did I ever know you? Does it mean nothing to you that you had a child you never loved, a child you left behind? Abandoned. A child whom you mention only by the way, of much less interest to you than your friend the doctor.

"We could talk freely to each other, Isabel and I . . . I can't begin to tell you what a luxury that was, how rare it was in those days. Partly because we both spoke English, but we had an important bond: we both had brothers whom we loved above everything, brothers who were not as strong as we were. Her brother—Tomas, his name was—lived with her, he was a priest, but also a botanist."

Marian takes Amelia by the hand, surrounding her wrist like a tight bracelet, like a cuff.

"I must make you understand. You must understand Tomas. You must."

Amelia nods. She's frightened. She has no idea who this person Tomas is. And she's never seen her grandmother like this, all her tenderness, all her good humor melted away, exposing a single, cold blade, ready to draw blood. She even smells different; the mild powdery scent that is Meme, the smell of the lavender soap she's always used, is gone now; a bitter smell of unhealthful sweat enters the air. Does her grandmother think Amelia knows who this person Tomas is? She is frightened in a new way, now. Perhaps her grandmother can no longer keep things straight.

"I will not allow him to be dismissed as a madman. Not by you. Especially not by you."

"I would never do that, Meme," Amelia says, not knowing what she has pledged to refuse.

"Oh, Amelia, what am I doing? What am I doing to you? I always thought I got it right with you, that I paid attention and understood. I thought I was a better grandmother to you than I ever was a mother. I never loved Ignacio. And your father, well, he was so easy to love, he never seemed to require much of me. I was always afraid I hadn't given enough, that I hadn't been able to figure out what he really needed because he never seemed to need anything. He was like one of those flowering desert plants that seem to provide their own sustenance. But you, it was different with you. I thought I could see what you needed, and that I knew how to provide it: quiet and the time and room to understand things in your own way. I was proud that I'd given you that. And now, what am I doing? Insisting that you have to understand something in exactly my way, in exactly my time. A mission that needs to be accomplished. No questions asked. No time to look around."

Marian takes her hand from around Amelia's wrist. She lays it in her lap; her two hands lie slack, palms upward.

The word "mission" makes Amelia think of *Mission Impossible* movies. Does her grandmother even know about those movies? Perhaps a change of frame of reference will be good. The air needs lightening; they need to breathe.

"Well, maybe it's a mission that I choose to accept, like those movies, you've probably never seen them, Meme, but never mind. They always have some guy jumping out of a plane onto a moving train. Only I don't want to be the guy jumping out of planes or on top of moving trains. I want to be your knight in shining armor. Your Joan of Arc. Remember that Joan of Arc book that you gave me, with the wonderful old pictures? I always loved those colors best: teal and dusty rose and ochre. When I painted, those were the colors I always wanted to use. I wanted to make everything I painted look like the world in that book and the world I saw when I looked through the red glass panes around your front door," Amelia says.

"That was a lovely book. And the trees do look lovely through that red glass, through our old windows. They were put in by your grandfather's family. Maybe that's a useful past for you, a lovely past, not like the one I'm thrusting on you now."

Amelia can see that her grandmother isn't really paying attention to her own words. But then, she's back. "You're being like a little Joan of Arc now, aren't you, charging at me, making me tell the truth, making me do what I was afraid to do. I always thought of Isabel as Joan of Arc. I was always afraid they'd burn her at the stake."

Amelia wants to say: Don't say that to me, don't put me beside your friend Isabel, your brave friend, the doctor, the one who saved your life. If I stand next to her, in her light I'll be blotted out; I'll be the one in the picture you can't quite see, the one in the shadows. Coldly, she decides to press a claim that Isabel could never call on.

"But it's because I want *your* past. Because it's mine. Because you're the one out of everyone who's most mine and I'm the one out of everyone who's most yours."

It's out now, the secret never spoken before, saturated with betrayal, the casting aside of the blood mother, the responsible mother who kept the child alive. Does it make it less of a betrayal that she needed to go to her grandmother because her mother didn't understand her nearly so well? Perhaps. Perhaps not. But for the moment, they can share the thrill of this uncovered truth, their secret sin.

Now Marian knows that there is no longer any need to question whether or not she should be telling Amelia all these things. Whether it's a selfish desire to have her own past kept alive. A putting herself forward, as if she overestimated her own importance, the importance of her life. A fear drummed in by her mother: the southern woman's false claim of modesty, a kind of holding back that Marian always knew was only another kind of display, different from her father's insistence on revealing nothing: the Irish passion for holding back.

But the memory of Tomas carries with it no doubts, no reservations. It is vital that this should not disappear, and if she doesn't speak—and she came so near to not speaking—the disappearance will occur. Newly, this is unbearable. There was no one like him. There never will be again. He was the best of his kind, and his kind will not be seen again. Perhaps that is a good thing; no one should suffer as he suffered. But it isn't good for the rest of the world that there should be no more like him. People were better for having known Tomas. Of all the things she has questioned in her life, this she has never questioned, as she has never questioned her love for Johnny and his love for her. She wonders, wondering as well why it took her so long to consider this, that what she was best at was being a sister.

How, though, can she make Amelia understand categories that have long seemed to exist? His story will be, for Amelia, incomprehensible. Marian has seen him always as someone who fulfilled an ideal that had once seemed not only possible but also the most desirable. The saint. Can she make up a story, like the parables of Jesus, to explain what it was that makes her call Tomas a saint? The Good Samaritan? She hears the words thrown at her by her family, *Who do you think you are, Jesus Christ?*

Well, she will just begin with something for which categories are still to hand. A time. A place. A family origin. Perhaps it would be best to begin with Isabel, a more familiar type. Hero. But never saint.

"They were older than I, Isabel and Tomas, Tomas was her brother, did I say that? Twenty years. I think they were around fifty, but I never asked, and it never came up. They were only half Spanish; their mother was Irish. I think that's important, there was something in diluting—oh, I don't know what you'd call it—that Spanish insistence on everything being black and white."

Marian knows she's rambling. Get to the point, get to the point, she hears a voice berating her. She knows that voice; it's her father's, but despite her first impulse to ignore it just because it's his, she doesn't ignore it, because it's speaking sense.

"I worked as Tomas's assistant. He really seemed to need my help; he needed someone with some education, who could speak Spanish and English. Even my mother-in-law couldn't refuse him, because he was a priest, you see, and also wounded."

"Was he wounded in the war?"

"No, he did it to himself. And to explain why he did that, I have to explain who he was. If I use the word 'saint,' Amelia, what would that mean to you?"

Amelia feels a kind of panic: the examination that happens in all school-based nightmares, the question for which you are not, could not ever be, prepared.

"I guess it would mean a very good person."

She sees by her grandmother's face that the answer is not right.

But she will not give up.

"I guess it has something to do with religion. So, maybe not Nelson Mandela. But what about Martin Luther King?"

"Maybe, maybe," Marian says, "maybe King. But I think a saint can't be particularly concerned with victory, with a particular outcome, a particular success, and King was certainly strategic."

"So what you're saying is a saint is someone who has no strategies."

Her grandmother's smile is so extravagant that Amelia ducks her head, closes her eyes, as if a blinding light were falling on her.

"Yes," Marian says, "yes, that's exactly right. My poor Tomas had no strategies. It's as if he was missing a protective skin that kept him separated from people, from their griefs, as if the layer separating him from other people was completely porous. He would absorb other people's sorrows, he would become saturated with them, and somehow the grief was lessened for the other person; he had taken it in, it had become his."

"Was that because he was a priest, because he had faith?"

"Oh, I guess he did have it. Faith. Although he said he wasn't a person of faith, he was a person of hope. But he was never optimistic about things turning out well in this world. He did have some sense of another realm where things would turn out well, where, as he said, every tear would be wiped away. You see, Marian, he said to me once, 'I believe in pie in the sky. Or, at least, I hope for it. A piece for everyone.'

"He knew that for someone like me, who had no faith, who had lost all faith, or had renounced it deliberately, what he believed in was ridiculous. He admitted it was ridiculous, and he never tried to make anyone believe anything that he believed, particularly when, at that time, anyone speaking in the name of faith had so much blood on their hands. I don't believe in God, I couldn't believe in God after what I'd seen. My brother hanging from a rope, unbelievable cruelties inflicted by people on each other, often with the greatest pleasure, unbelievable suffering as a result of these cruelties or in defense of something believed to be the good, maybe even actually the good. But I believed in Tomas, or I believed in something he had access to that I refused to call God. It was a dimension that added a kind of depth to everything he did, a way he had of being *with* someone, of giving more than anyone could possibly ask anyone to give of themselves, giving his utmost, of wearing himself out, and then somehow going on, not from any kind of hope that we would recognize, but because he'd been somehow refreshed or refilled at some well I could never approach. I never met anyone like him; I don't think there will ever be anyone like him again.

"Are you beginning to understand, Amelia?"

"I think so," Amelia says, because there is nothing in her that would say she doesn't understand; she's afraid that it would create a breach between her and her grandmother that would be impossible to repair. She is not being untruthful, there are parts she understands, although she is frightened of what is to come, frightened of her own potential failures at understanding.

"I need to believe you understand because when I tell you about what he did to himself, it's going to be hard for you not to be revolted."

"Revolted," Amelia thinks, remembering her Spanish and its Latin roots, means to turn away. And whatever else, she knows that she will never turn away.

"He was tall, large, somewhat lumbering, he had very thick, very black, wavy hair and his eyes were a deep, deep blue. When you saw him, what you always saw first was sadness.

"Which isn't to say he was never happy. He took great joy in things. He would say, 'Look at the charm of that' . . . about a flower, or a bird, or a seed.

"He was a priest, but he was also a scientist, and you couldn't separate the two because the natural world was a great source of his faith. And what threatened his faith was his awareness of what people suffered, and that was what his priesthood was about: to be of consolation. But his consolation was in the natural world. He went to Ireland because he knew he could get the kind of training he needed there, but he came back to Spain for the same reason that Isabel stayed—because he knew that people were desperate and that he was needed.

"For all his sadness, there was nothing more joyous than walking with Tomas in the countryside, helping him collect specimens. That was my job. It was all Isabel's doing, she could do that, find solutions to things that seemed impossible, then shrug when you told her she'd done something impossible. 'Nothing's impossible if you have brains and guts,' she'd say, not apologizing for claiming them for herself.

"Tomas had the Seeing Eye; he could spot the differences in species when I couldn't until he pointed them out, and the variety of the world delighted him. People were drawn to him as if they were living in a frigid climate and he was an open fire always available for them to warm themselves in front of. He would never judge; it was as if he felt judgment wasn't an interesting category, or occupation. That's another reason he liked getting out to the countryside, to get away from people. Because they were always after him, always wanted to be near him, always wanted to tell him something.

"I said that what was most important about him was his sadness, and it was, in a way, but in another way, it was most important that he was a priest. How can I explain to you what a priest meant in that world, at that time? Now when you hear 'priest' the first word that comes into your mind is probably 'pedophile.' But at that time, both in Spain and in the world I grew up in—I mean the part of it that was Catholic—even though it was America, priests were like movie stars and generals and Supreme Court justices. Mothers wanted nothing more than for their sons to be priests. People deferred to them, they listened to them, even though a lot of them were fools or drunks or bigots . . . That kind of power, that kind of glamour, has to be corrupting. Some of them, a few of them, actually were what they were supposed to be, 'servants of the servants of God.' They were at the bedside of the dying, or they'd be the one to tell a mother her child had been killed, but most of them were spoiled and harsh and not very bright. So the whole idealized image of the priest, humble and self-sacrificing, is based on a few of them, the way the idea of the prostitute with the heart of gold is probably based on a few, probably there are a few whores with hearts of gold, but mostly they're just hard and jaded."

"I don't think anyone but you would come up with that analogy, Meme."

"I wonder what my father and my brothers would think of it. Well, they're all dead. And all those priests with their well-cut suits and their white collars and their white hands. There was a kind of fetish about priests' hands, we always had pure white linen towels available in the bathroom when priests came to visit, so that's why the thing that Tomas did made so much sense, in its dreadful way.

Marian goes silent. She doesn't want to tell this story, or tell it wrong, so that Amelia will think Tomas is crazy or pitiable. She wants to tell her granddaughter that, even though what Tomas did goes against everything in the world she believes, it was a great act, a heroic act. The act of a saint.

"Remember, I told you how important a priest's hands were, how they were a kind of fetish, but it was a fetish that had been locked into law. Remember Tomas must have been in torment, absolute torment. He loved the Church, he really did see it as a mother. He was in torment over the horrors committed in the name of the Church he loved. But more than anything, he loved his sister, and he believed in her absolutely, as he believed in nothing and no one else, even the people in the Church in whom he was bound to believe under pain of sin. He also believed that being a priest, staying a priest, having kept away from the horrors safely in Ireland, he was complicit, complicit by his silence or his absence. So he decided that he had to do something with his own body to witness the horror and his complicity in it. Simply that. The only judgment would be against himself for being complicit and silent."

Marian wonders how much to tell. Should she describe the combine harvester, should she explain, as Tomas did in his letter, how he came to the decision, how he made it all happen? No, she will say it simply: "He deliberately cut his two middle fingers off in the workings of a farm machine. It was a part of a canon law that a priest had to have his thumb and middle finger intact to be able to consecrate the host."

Marian realizes that she's using words that require translation.

"To 'consecrate the host.' Let me see, how I explain this. You know that Catholics and some Protestants go to communion."

"Yes, Meme, when we lived in Mexico I used to go to church with my friends sometimes. I always wished I could go up to the front of the church with them and get whatever they were getting."

"Well, what they were getting was a little piece of bread, usually a flat, white wafer, which a priest said some words over, and people believe, they have to believe, that it's not really bread anymore: it's the body of Jesus. People killed each other over whether it was still bread or not, whether its nature had been completely transformed. God knows what people will kill each other for."

"So, because he couldn't make communion he couldn't be a priest?"

"You don't say 'make communion.' You say 'consecrate the host.' And no, in fact, he had thought all that out. What he did would prevent him from participating in the ancient ritual, the public ritual that was a communal celebration. But what he could do, and what he did, and it nearly took his life, was hear confessions. That would be private. You were allowed, even in that awful environment of fascist surveillance, to go to confession to whatever priest you wanted. And the local priest in Altea, who was a perfectly nice, rather stupid, frightened man, was glad to have Tomas's help, because he knew he would have to hear things in confession he didn't want to know about, and he was glad he didn't have to live with Tomas, because he was a very intense guy, Tomas, and brilliant, and the other priest was glad he didn't have to try to keep up with him. You've probably heard of the seal of confession."

"No."

"No? You've never seen those movies about priests who won't give up murderers to the police? Montgomery Clift, I think. Oh, never mind. Or in a million cop shows, the cops want the priest to give them the clue that would nail the man who hacked up ten women in motel rooms, but the priest won't 'break the seal.' So people knew they could tell Tomas everything they'd done, and they knew his kindness and that he wasn't someone who would judge them, and they knew he would keep their secrets till his death. And in that time, in that place, people had dreadful secrets. It nearly killed him."

Her grandmother had warned her that she might be revolted, and she had promised herself that she wouldn't, she had promised her grandmother. But how can she understand what she's just heard? Nothing in her life has prepared her for this. Her grandmother is right; she is, if not revolted, then appalled that she can only see it as a pathological act, a masochistic act, but that is what her grandmother, grabbing her wrist like a cuff, has said she must not do. Perhaps this is the time to lie. Her grandmother says that in a situation of two bad choices, one has to choose the least bad. But she has no practice in lying, and she's sure her grandmother will see through her. She must think of something to say that has at least something of the truth in it.

"It's a very sad story. It might be the saddest story I've ever heard."

Her grandmother looks up: startled, pleased. "Yes," she says, "yes, that's exactly right. The saddest story. A story that happened because of a time of insanity and violence. In another time, in another place, Tomas would have been the kindly priest who disappeared into the mountains to collect specimens, maybe something of a joke among the people because of his devotion to weeds. And, of course, you can say that what he did was mad, but maybe madness in a mad time isn't madness. Maybe it's the only alternative to silence, to the silence that allows you somehow to prosper from the defeat of the innocent, the victory of the guilty. Because I know that the right were more guilty, that they were always on the side of the rich against the poor, and that the atrocities they committed—maybe it was only because of the accident of being better armed, but I don't think so—were greater than the other side, the numbers were greater, and, to my mind, and certainly Tomas's, they were worse because they were performed in the name of God. So, yes, the saddest story. Sadness is difficult; people will do anything rather than be sad. Anger is exciting, it's enlivening, and judgment is bracing: your spine straightens, your head is up, and you walk with a new purpose. But sadness—you must just be still with no idea how to move anywhere. That's why it's important to me that you don't use terms like 'sick' or 'self-hating' to explain what Tomas did. Those words are off the mark, given the times. But sadness, I think maybe when it comes to the history of the world, sadness is always the right thing to say."

Amelia sits at her grandmother's feet and puts her head in her grandmother's lap. Marian strokes the fine, fair hair. Her father Jeremy's. Her grandfather Theo's.

"I thought I'd stay in Spain forever, and then one day, when Tomas and I were collecting specimens in the mountains, a blond angel appeared. The angel was your grandfather, Theo, who was, of course, not an angel, just an adorable young man.

"He was only twenty-four, ten years younger than I, walking through Spain with his notebook and pencils, sketching. This man, who was so much a boy, lifted my heart, and I came alive again, although Isabel and Tomas had done most of the work—I'd been with them for seven years. But your grandfather's sweetness, his beauty, his wonderful hands and feet, and the smell of him . . . which I could never get enough of . . . well, that brought me to life in a new way.

"I was ready to leave Spain, and it wouldn't have been possible without your grandfather.

"We came to this house; he became a cabinet maker. I met Helga, and we started the nursery. We were very happy. We didn't exactly mean for me to get pregnant. Or maybe we did—I don't know. And then I had your father. And the last part of my life was given to me. I knew I wasn't a monster. I could love a child. I could marry a good man, have good work, make sense of the world. We were very happy for thirty years, your grandfather and I, and your father—he went off to college and your grandfather and I had ten years alone together in this house. And then he died, just there; see that apple tree, he was pruning it and he had a heart attack. I found him, just at the foot of the tree. So like him, to die without a fuss, to die in a place where he had just been useful and happy.

"And there you are. You wouldn't be here if I hadn't lived my life exactly as I did. And so this is the end of the story, Amelia. The story you wanted to hear."

But what is the story? That Meme went to Spain to support the Republic, that she married a man who died, that she had a baby, that she was drugged, that she lived in terror in Franco's Spain, that she had two friends whom she loved, one of whom mutilated himself ... but she is calling him a saint ... that she met the angel Theo, my grandfather, that my father was born. But what about your son? Amelia wants to ask. Do you know what happened to him? Do you know where he is? Did you ever try to get in touch with him? Is he still alive? Is he just one part of the story? And maybe not the most important part? How can that be, Meme? It can't be. That you have forgotten a child.

Her grandmother looks at the photograph of Isabel one more time, then replaces it in the cardboard box, covering it with a kind of finality, satisfied that something has been finished. But Amelia knows nothing has been finished. No, Meme, she wants to say. Nothing is finished. Something, I think, has just begun.

SPAIN, 2009

AVONDALE, RHODE ISLAND, 2009

A VOICE is saying in a language that is not hers, but that she understands, that the plane is about to land in Madrid. Only half awake, she is confused. It doesn't seem likely that she would be arriving in Madrid. Then she remembers: this is the thing she has to do. She knew it almost from the beginning, from the time she knew who her grandmother was.

Amelia knew that she would have to lie. There was no choice. She must go to Spain, find Ignacio Ortiz, her uncle, Meme's son, and bring him back for reconciliation with his mother before it's too late for both of them.

She has saved five thousand dollars. It wasn't very difficult. She didn't pay any rent; Meme provided most of her meals; she did her laundry in her grandmother's washer. Occasionally, she'd have a meal out with her friends. She'd bought herself a shearling coat and a pair of sheepskin-lined boots. She'd bought Meme a cashmere shawl, a deep red with a pattern of bronze roses, and her mother a silver brooch in the shape of a dragonfly. Other than that, most of her salary went into her savings account.

She found Altea on the map. She would fly to Madrid and take a plane from there to Alicante. From there, a bus to Benidorm, and then a taxi. She hadn't done it herself. Rachel had helped her. Rachel was the first she tried her lie on, or one version of it. She told Rachel her friend from California was getting married in Altea. She told Meme that her friend was getting married in Madrid. In the middle of the night, she woke up in a sweat: suppose Rachel and Meme spoke and discovered the difference in the stories. Then she remembered: Meme was very sick; she couldn't drive anymore. She wouldn't be going into town, and it wasn't like Rachel to visit a sick person. Sickness of any kind "just creeps me out," she said, knowing herself to be a hypochondriac. It was one reason she was very careful about the ingredients in her breads and cakes. She wouldn't, for example, let Amelia use anything but natural food colorings. Sometimes this frustrated Amelia, but she went along with what Rachel wanted.

"I'm going to be gone for ten days, Meme," Amelia says. "Josh said he'll call you every day, and I have ten days' worth of soup and stews in containers in the freezer. Josh will bring the rest. And Rachel will provide bread and muffins."

"She won't bring them herself. She'll find someone to do it for her."

Amelia kisses her grandmother's papery forehead. Her lips notice that the surface is moist, as it has never been, as if her grandmother were in a constant state of exertion, as if the ordinary business of living were a strain, an effort, an event.

"You're a pretty sharp cookie, Meme," she says, "although I know you don't like cookies. So what should I say: you're a pretty sharp leaf of arugula?"

They both laugh more than Amelia's comment deserves, because they are both worried that while Amelia is away, something terrible might happen.

Amelia's other trips abroad have always been with her mother. Naomi was much in demand by the governing bodies of the cities of the world; they got to fly first or business class, and someone always made their hotel reservations. This is the first time Amelia has flown economy, and the first time she has had the job of finding a hotel. She always felt uneasy not flying economy as all her friends did, and the discomfort of crushing her long legs is a small price to pay for the freedom from guilt she has always had when observing her less fortunate fellow passengers. But she hadn't understood how much more difficult it would be to sleep, and she arrives in the Madrid airport, which seems to her the size of the whole town of Avondale, cramped and groggy, exactly as all her friends always say they are when they land in Europe.

She makes her connections with no trouble, and the cabdriver in Benidorm drives her to her hotel at what she considers a breakneck speed.

The idea of being in the place where her grandmother was young, where her grandmother gave birth, was victimized, then rescued, and then escaped makes her feel she is on a pilgrimage, and every stone seems sacred. The houses are white; the dome of the cathedral is indigo blue; but most of what her grandmother said about the town does not apply. There is no hint of starvation; there are tourist menus everywhere; signs are in several languages, including Asian characters and Arab script. This is not a place of bare survival; it is a place devoted to the perhaps questionable pleasures of strangers.

She found the hotel on the internet, or Rachel did. The room itself is unremarkable. The hotel is a chain, and the room could have been anywhere in the world. She's surprised that it really is close to the sea, that her room really has a view of the Mediterranean, surprised that the Mediterranean is actually there, that it isn't something in old books that no longer exists, like the library at Alexandria, surprised that the Mediterranean looks like the Mediterranean. Bluer than any water she could have imagined. It seems to have no coldness in it; the blue is uninflected by grey or green or silver . . . it is simply blue. She thinks of her grandmother standing at the Atlantic, and she remembers her childhood fascination with messages that were sent in bottles. She would like to send her grandmother a message in a bottle. "Dear Meme, I love you, and I don't want you to die feeling that anything important has been left unresolved." And then she realizes that she has forgotten to pack a bathing suit.

She walks on the esplanade and almost immediately sees a sign, painted in yellow on a white stucco wall. "Bikini Heaven. Everything for the beach."

She doesn't want a bikini. She has always worn a one-piece. Not out of modesty, but because she loves to swim and one-pieces are more comfortable. She wore a bikini once; she bought it in Westerly the summer after her junior year in high school. She doesn't know why she doesn't swim in LA, but Rhode Island is the place where she swims—the grey, calmer waters draw her as the wild waves of Malibu do not. She bought a bikini, fuchsia colored, perhaps cerise. She put it on and wore it under an old work shirt of Meme's. It was the first time she'd ever seen Meme's eye fall on her with anything but the purest pleasure, the purest approval. Meme didn't like the bikini, she didn't like Amelia in it. She didn't say anything, but Amelia knew.

And so she hopes there's something in Bikini Heaven other than bikinis. She doesn't want to be wearing a bikini, which is a frivolous garment, wrong for what she's doing here: something serious, really a matter of life and death. But the sign said, "Everything for the beach." There's hope in that, she tells herself, it said *everything*.

She walks up the steep street. She imagines women carrying jugs on their heads; she imagines donkeys, their dainty hooves gracefully negotiating the stone paths. She had always wanted a donkey; she imagined that in their patience, in their slowness, they'd be very comforting.

The minute she enters Bikini Heaven, a voice in her head shouts: Everything you will see from now on will be dreadful.

The store is large and dark. No attempt has been made at decoration; bathing suits hang on metal racks, separated by sizes indicated by plastic discs with numbers written on them in black marker. The saleswoman, who Amelia guesses is younger than she, doesn't look up at Amelia; she seems absorbed in studying her fingernails—long, and painted navy blue. Amelia makes her way to the area that indicates her size. How distressing it all is, this display of bad fabric, bad design. Why, she wonders, do they think everything has to look like something else? They're bathing suits; why do they have to have gold rings or clear plastic brooches in the shape of daisies, or sequined letters, or even animal-print trim? And they all seem so small; they make the bikini she bought in Westerly, the one her grandmother didn't like, seem positively puritanical.

She doesn't know the Spanish word for a one-piece bathing suit. The salesgirl's lack of interest discourages her. She riffles through the suits, trying to find something that doesn't lower her spirits more than she can bear. She tells herself: It doesn't matter, you don't know anyone here, and if this is the standard, no one will judge you. But she would judge herself. The look of things matters to her; it always has. Not that she cares for fashion, but ugliness hurts her.

A middle-aged woman with glasses on a string around her neck (Amelia feels reassured by the maternal or librarian-like accessory) smiles encouragingly at Amelia, as the younger woman did not. She asks, in English, if she can help. Amelia replies, in Spanish, that she wants something that's not a bikini.

"One-piece?" the woman says. "But why? You have such a lovely figure."

"I'm just used to a one-piece."

The woman's ankles look painful in her wedge espadrilles. She sighs, disappointed that her expertise—after all, it *is* her field—is being ignored. She indicates a section in the back of the dim room. She points to a small rack of bathing suits that all seem to be made of fur or foil.

Amelia will have to try them on. Only two are even possible: dark brown velour with gold appliqué, and a silvery one that reminds her of the containers her juice came in when she was in grade school. She takes both into the dressing room, hoping for a miracle when she tries them on. But there is no miracle. She decides on the velour: it will draw less attention.

Miserably, she pays from her stash of euros. Miserably, she walks down the hill, her eye falling on nothing that seems desirable or even acceptable. She wonders if anything in the town has been made anywhere near it. There seems to be an endless succession of stores selling flimsy, Indian-looking skirts and blouses, giving off a smell she decides is a mix of fish and motor oil.

She's too dispirited to think of lunch. She goes back to her hotel and lies on her bed. Outside the window, the water seems too blue to think of swimming in; she thinks that if she dives in her skin might be stained or bleached. She closes her eyes and tells herself that these reactions are a common by-product of jet lag.

When she wakes, she puts on her bearskin bathing suit; it makes her feel hot. Her jeans and long-sleeved T-shirt are too warm; she hadn't reckoned on the heat at this time in October. She has no lighter pants; her T-shirts are all long-sleeved; and she can't bear the idea of buying anything in the stores she's seen.

She makes her way to the beach. Why hadn't she noticed that the beach was rocky, rather than sandy? She slips her sandals off; the rocks hurt her feet. She notices people going into the water wearing special shoes. The prospect of exposing herself in her ugly suit and exposing her tender feet to the sharp rocks seems overwhelming. She must get herself lunch. She tells herself that she's probably overreacting because she's hungry. Possibly, she thinks, I will never swim in the Mediterranean.

The esplanade, which Amelia guesses is a relatively recent development, is made up almost exclusively of restaurants and cafés. Amelia chooses the one that doesn't have its menu translated into English, that isn't advertising mojitos or cheeseburgers or English cream teas. The café's sign pleases her; it suggests the playfulness of Miró: a red sun superimposed on stylized black script with the name of the café, l'Espril. She doesn't know what that means, and she tries not to let that disturb her.

Her waitress greets her with an unfamiliar term—*Salve*—but Amelia can see that her intentions are friendly. She orders a tortilla español, a café con leche, and a mineral water. It's one o'clock, but no one else seems to be eating lunch.

She hadn't realized how hungry she was. With the first delicious mouthful, the soothing egg and potatoes and onions, she allows herself to acknowledge her disappointment. She wanted the town to be as it was when her grandmother left it sixty years ago. She wanted to swim in the Mediterranean. She looks out at the sea, the unmixed blue, the palm trees swaying almost theatrically in the light breeze. She must take herself in hand. How ungrateful, how wasteful: she is lucky to be where she is. The bubbles in the mineral water seem comical and friendly, and the waitress, asking if she'd like another coffee, seems to be genuinely concerned, if not for her larger welfare, then at least for her temporary pleasure. She says yes to a second coffee.

As she is finishing it, a young man wheels an old woman to the front table of the café. The woman in the wheelchair doesn't look frail; her hands are twisted, gripping the armrests, but her expression is lively and she is far from thin. Meme is much thinner, she thinks. Meme looks frailer. But Meme is dying.

The waitress kisses the young man and the old woman. The young man orders pastries and orange juice. He sits across from the old woman; they seem to be enjoying themselves, though Amelia can't hear what they're saying. His cell phone rings; he apologizes to the old woman and walks up the esplanade, where he paces up and down in animated, pleased conversation.

A sudden wind blows the napkins off Amelia's table and then

takes the white cotton sun hat of the old woman in the wheelchair. The hat blows down the esplanade. The young man is walking in the opposite direction of the hat; he doesn't see it. The old woman seems distressed, and makes gestures of anxiety and loss. Amelia springs to her feet and runs down the esplanade. The hat, playful, taunting, keeps escaping her, but finally she steps on it to stop it, then picks it up and dusts it off with her fingertips. Her sandals, she is pleased to see, have not made a dirty print on the white cotton of the hat.

She makes her way to the old woman's table, triumphant. She can't seem to modulate her smile. And she is greeted by a smile as unmodulated as her own. The old woman sees her and says, "I know it's foolish, it's a very old hat, not really expensive, but I'm fond of it. I'm very grateful to you."

And then the young man is at the table. He takes Amelia's hand and kisses it. "You must join us," he says. "Allow us to buy you a coffee."

She's had two coffees and knows that a third will make her jittery, but she has no impulse to refuse. The young man is exceptionally handsome. He is handsome in such a predictable way for a Spanish town—as the Mediterranean is predictably blue and the palm trees are predictable in their regular swaying—that she wonders if she's in a dream, but a dream that disappoints because of its excessive clarity.

"My name is José," he says, in heavily accented English. "I am called Pepe. But nearly every man in this town is named José and called Pepe. So you can't make a mistake. Or maybe you are always liable to make mistakes."

"We can speak Spanish," she says in Spanish.

"But I like to practice my English. Only, maybe you like to practice your Spanish. So why don't I speak to you in English, and you can speak to me in Spanish?"

"Pepe, you are a clown," the old woman says. "You see, my dear, my grandson is a clown. Which means that I always have something to laugh about—not such a small thing at my age. I am seventy-six last April. Let us speak Spanish, as my English is pathetic."

So she's much younger than Meme, Amelia thinks, proud of her grandmother's youthfulness and vitality.

"I am Amelia. Thank you for the coffee."

She feels like she's saying sentences from an elementary Spanish textbook, but she doesn't know how to make her speech more natural. She doesn't know what to call the old woman, and she doesn't know how she'll explain what she's doing in the town. She will have to lie. In the last month, she has lied more than she has in the twenty-four years she's been alive.

"I hope you've had a swim," Pepe says. "It's exceptionally warm for October."

"Well, I'm afraid I couldn't cope with the stones on the beach."

"You need bathing shoes. Give me your foot." He falls to his knees and grabs her foot. He pulls her sandal off.

"Stay here," he says, holding her sandal in his hand. "Well, I guess you have to stay here. I have your shoe. You see, it's a good way of keeping you here so we can spend more time together."

He runs down the esplanade, her sandal in his hand.

The grandmother laughs. It is clear that everything her grandson does delights her. Amelia recognizes the brand of delight.

The inevitable question arrives: "What are you doing in Altea?"

Amelia is prepared with a version of the lie: the lie of the friend's wedding. She thinks it's best not to add an entirely new lie, but thriftily to tailor the old one. She doesn't think lies are precious, or even fragile, but they aren't trivial, and she doesn't like to be careless with them. She has two versions of the lie: the Rachel version and the Meme version. It seems right to present the Meme version, otherwise she would have to come up with a local bride and groom.

"A friend of mine is getting married in Madrid. And another friend spent time here, quite a while ago, and said it was wonderful and I should come here to rest from my flight, rest from my work, rest before the festivities in Madrid."

"And what is your work?"

It occurs to Amelia that her work might be something to be embarrassed by. Embarrassing to a certain kind of person, a different embarrassment from her mother's and her mother's friends, whom she is used to embarrassing, but to a hardworking person who had wanted education for the next generation and would find someone with a college education baking fancy cupcakes an incomprehensible failure. So she decides to lie again.

"A friend and I own a restaurant."

"Oh, that is very hard work. My son and his wife and his wife's parents own a restaurant in England. In Brighton. It was too hectic for Pepe, that's why he came back here."

"And what is his work?"

"He has a little shop. He'll take you there very soon, I'm sure. He's very proud of it. Everyone who goes in there leaves happy: that, he says, is his goal."

Pepe runs up the esplanade holding what Amelia thinks are two huge, pink marshmallows. But they are plastic bathing shoes; he holds them over his head. He twirls, a victory dance.

"The last in your size. Such a quiet color for a quiet girl. You are a quiet girl, I know. But perhaps you will find another side of yourself in Altea."

He waves to the waitress and dramatically pantomimes wiping his sweaty brow. She brings him a glass of mineral water, which he swallows in a gulp.

"Now, *abuelita,* what will we do with our guest, whose name I do not even know?"

"She told you, but you weren't listening. Amelia."

"Yes, Amelia. What will we do with Amelia for the rest of the day?"

"You will take me home for my siesta, and then you will swim in the sea."

He kisses his grandmother and straightens the shawl around her shoulder. "And you will look at us from the balcony, my *duenna.*"

"Heaven forbid. *Duenna*. No. And you know perfectly well I've never thought I had to forbid you anything since the day you were born."

Amelia feels her tiredness and worry fall away. But perhaps, free of them, she realizes for the first time how ill-considered her errand is. How did she think she would find Ignacio? She realizes now that there were ways she could have learned about him, ways that anyone of her generation would have gone to right away. She suspects that she didn't want information, didn't want to know anything that might have stalled her determination. She realizes now that she had thought nothing out, that she had acted purely on impulse. Now she would pay for that. What would she say to him? She assumed that the right thing would come to her. She wonders if Pepe will be able to help her. She wonders how she'll explain what she's up to, or if it will require another lie.

He says he will come by for her in half an hour. Her only thought is: I think I can get a new bathing suit in that time. It is all right to wear the bearskin one-piece when she is by herself or among strangers. But with Pepe, Pepe of the beautiful skin and shining hair and light, light step—she can't wear something that ugly. There has to be something in Bikini Heaven that's just plain. She hadn't looked at the tiny suits. But there has to be something . . . black or blue or red . . . something simple, something not pretending to be something else.

The woman with the glasses on a string is behind the counter. "You're back," she says. "A change of heart."

"I guess, or maybe a little courage. It's just that I thought my boyfriend in America would be upset if I wore a bikini without him, and then I thought, 'He'll never know.'" She acts a conspiratorial giggle, which the woman joins in with pleasure.

What a liar I've become, Amelia thinks. But she knows it's better to say she was worried what her boyfriend would think than that she was worried what her grandmother would think. On the other hand, she could have come in cold, imperious, answering with silence any possible question. But she didn't have that in her. On the other hand, she hadn't thought she had it in her to lie so easily.

Her eye falls on a plain black bikini, claiming nothing for itself. She doesn't try it on. "Must run," she says, "meeting someone on the beach."

It's likely, she thinks, that everyone in the town will know it's Pepe, and she wonders what her status will be tomorrow. But she will not be coming back to Bikini Heaven. Three bathing suits in two days would just be too much.

She stands in front of the mirror to try on the suit. It's briefer than anything she's ever worn, but, as she's small breasted and boyish in the waist and hips, it's far from scandalous. She tells herself that Meme would realize that in a world of no good choices, she has done her best.

"I hope the wind won't make you shiver," Pepe says. "I could never swim in England, never once. It was just too cold. This is pushing my limit."

"In Rhode Island, where I'm from, this would be considered ordinary."

"But we are never ordinary here. Come, we must run in not to prolong the misery. Of course, if it seems too cold for you, there's no need to stay in. We can just lie here and chat."

"Oh, no, I always go in . . . I always make myself if I'm feeling reluctant. It's something I promised my grandmother, that I'd never refuse a swim in the ocean if there was any chance for it at all. She says, 'You never regret a swim in the ocean.' She says all the time, 'You don't regret what you did, just what you didn't do.'"

"I would like to meet this grandmother. You didn't tell me you have a grandmother too."

"Yes, I live with her now."

"Ah, so we are members of a small, select club. Grandchildren who are tenants of their grandparents. Tenants and caretakers. Only, I love my grandmother, sometimes I think more than anyone in the world."

"Me, too," she says, and squeezes his hand, because it so pleases her that this handsome young man can say the sentence, "I love my grandmother, sometimes I think more than anyone in the world."

She has already begun to lose her summer tan, and since she doesn't usually wear a bikini, her midriff has been untouched by the sun. She's embarrassed by the whiteness of her skin. Pepe doesn't seem to be looking at her; he's running to the water like a boy, his bathing shoes not slowing him down at all. She feels she must run in as he did, although usually she enters the water gradually.

He is puffing and shouting. "It's ice water. I am not a polar bear." He splashes and turns over on his back and spits water into the air. She can tell that he has no intention of really swimming. She'd like to join him, to be his partner in this pantomime, in which the water itself plays only a minor role. But even more, she wants to experience this water, understand its difference from the Atlantic and the Pacific. She floats on her back, then lowers her head under the water just enough so she won't hear Pepe's noises and expostulations. Her eyes rest on a rocky formation—"a minor Gibraltar," she would like to write in a postcard to her grandmother. But her grandmother mustn't know she's here. Not till her mission's accomplished.

There has been no outcropping like this in any water she has swum in before, and she wants to give it time to make a deep enough impression on her brain so she'll be able to call it back with confidence that she hasn't made it up.

She tries to imagine Meme as a young woman here, older than she is, but not by much, a new mother, soaked in grief and almost paralyzed. Did her mother-in-law worry that, drugged as she was, it would be dangerous for her to swim? Or was it part of her plan that this troublesome girl would drown and be out of their lives for good? Her death an accident and good riddance? She wants to weep for Meme and weep in rage at the mother-in-law who made her life a living death, and then she remembers what Meme said, that possibly she was doing what she thought was best. "In a time of insanity, insanity is normal."

Did she swim here with Isabel and Tomas, Isabel, whom Amelia would have liked to know? And Tomas, a trouble to her. Despite the promise she made to her grandmother, she can only think of him in the terms she swore she wouldn't use. Self-mutilating. Masochistic.

Did she swim here with my grandfather, Amelia wonders, did she move through this water, thinking of his body, as I am thinking of Pepe's?

Amelia sees that Pepe has taken himself out of the water; he's speaking to a man in some kind of uniform. Some coins are exchanged, and the man produces two blue canvas chaise longues. This is the kind of thing Meme would never allow: she would insist that they lie on their towels, even though the beach is rocky.

He holds a big beach towel for her. "You'll freeze," he says, rubbing her shoulders vigorously.

"No, Pepe, you forget. I'm used to the cold."

"No one is ever used to the cold. They just pretend they are."

In fact, though she was warm in the water, the breeze has begun to chill her. She puts on her jeans and shirt, but they'll be uncomfortable soon on top of her wet suit. She'd like to leave and change, but Pepe has paid money for the chaise longues, and she feels she must lie there, not to seem ungrateful.

"So will you tell me why you're here?"

"Not now," she says. "I'll tell you later." She closes her eyes and pretends to drift off to sleep. She will tell him, she wants to, badly, but she will have to know him better to determine how the telling will be done.

While she pretends to sleep, she looks at him through three-quarter-closed eyes. He is doing something with his complicated phone—iPhone, BlackBerry—Amelia doesn't really know the difference. She takes her cue from Meme, who loathes all new technology, but she can't afford to be so disconnected, and Meme needs her to have at least a little expertise. She thinks it's funny the way people use their thumbs now on these new gadgets. Thumbs are such comical fingers, she thinks. And yet now everything seems to require a very specialized dexterity of thumbs. Thumbnal dexterity, she wonders; perhaps thumbnal, not thumbnail, will become a word.

She sees that Pepe is getting restless. What would Meme say to that? She is critical of people who are incapable of stillness; she has no understanding that when she wants to be on the move, no one else's stillness is taken into account.

Amelia opens her eyes lazily: she is feeling lazy, so she's glad that at least this gesture isn't false. But she uses her eyelids to indicate that she is ready for sexual involvement. Or she intends this: she hopes he has understood.

"I must go back to work. But I'm hoping you have no plans for the evening. It's a cliché that Spaniards never invite you to their homes, but I've spent a lot of time in England. So I would like to invite you to my home. Actually, my grandmother's."

"That would be so kind. May I bring something?"

He kisses her hand. "Your pale and lovely self."

· · ·

She takes a very long shower in her ugly but convenient hotel room, guiltily pleased at the comfort of the unlimited hot water against her skin, which she failed to protect sufficiently from the strong sun. She has brought very few clothes with her, and so the decision of what to wear is painless. She will wear the gauzy turquoise skirt, the white T-shirt, the dark blue pashmina she bought for ten dollars on the streets of New York. She hopes that both Pepe and his grandmother will like what she's wearing, or at least find it acceptable. She's always known that she is pretty, that her looks are the kind that people like and are drawn to; but she knows they are undramatic, and feels fortunate that people have never resented her looks, never have taken against her because of them. She is never threatening. This is one of the truest things about me, she thinks: I threaten no one.

She thinks of her grandmother's swans: exotic, dramatic, a danger to anyone who comes close. She is not a swan. Perhaps, she thinks, I'm one of those sandpipers who skitter along the shore. She is bothered by the comparison. Everyone likes sandpipers, but they barely make an impression on the sand. Perhaps she is too light, she makes too little impression on the surface of the earth. She doesn't want to be a sandpiper, but what *does* she want to be? Nothing really heavy, nothing really slow moving. But is there such a thing as excessive lightness? Not settling in. She has done nothing so far about meeting her uncle Ignacio.

Since she has met Pepe, the town seems to have transformed itself. Before, she was distressed by everything: the cheap Asian imports in the clothing stores, the cheap menus offered to unadventurous tourists. But now she concentrates on the whiteness of the houses, the vivid pink and purple flowers climbing up their walls. Bougainvillea, she remembers from California. A woman is watering a pot of blue-grey flowers, ones Amelia has never seen; she is attracted by their modesty in relation to the vivid others. She asks the woman what the flowers are called. Moonflowers, the woman says. The exchange pleases both of them, and they wish each other a very good afternoon.

She wonders how the old or disabled cope with the endless flights of unforgiving stone stairs; there is no other way to get from the seashore to the main parts of the town except to climb and climb. A year ago, she's sure, Meme would have had no problem. Now she wouldn't be able to get around here very well. Meme is suddenly old. Meme is dying. But that, after all, is why Amelia is here.

She passes a store that sells ceramics, and in deference to her father's memory, she goes in. Her first response is distress at what is on the shelves. It isn't a careless ugliness; it is considered. The woman behind the counter is the potter; a flyer on the counter makes that clear, and stresses that she is devoted to the idea of angels. Almost everything in the store has something to do with angels. There are pitchers with angels' wings attached to their sides, mugs with angels hanging off their handles, bowls with images of angels pressed into their bottoms. The potter also invokes the sun: the walls are covered with nonfunctional sun shapes in yellow and orange with overexcited rays emanating from their centers. What is it about this place that makes people want to make something that looks like something else, something it has no right being? Bathing suits like animal skins or foil, pitchers with feathery spouts, mugs with wing handles that would be a problem when you tried to drink.

She thinks of her father and the simple, useful things he'd made. His quiet glazes: blue greens, mauves, ochres. Everything with clarity of line and form. She wants to rush up and embrace the woman behind the counter, the potter. Thank you, thank you. Because of your vulgar work, you have given me back my father, or given him to me in a new way. She used to be embarrassed because not enough people loved her father's work, passing it by for the work of others, for objects more loud-spoken, more daring. Now she loves her father with a sharp, invigorating love. A proud love with a new tint of aggression. She wants to say to the potter: My father was a real artist, and you are not. Because of her harsh thoughts, she feels it's necessary to buy something from her. She buys a small bowl with the imprint of an angel on its base. At least its design doesn't get in the way of its use. She'll give it to Pepe's grandmother.

The grandmother's house is halfway up a narrow, cobblestoned street. Some of the doors seem not to be doors but curtains made of metal chains. Some doors are heavy and ancient, suggesting the idea of fortifications. Number 17 is one of them. She is pleased to find a brass door knocker in the shape of what she believes is a pomegranate.

Pepe is wearing light, loose trousers, grey blue, and a thin, semi-transparent, white shirt. His feet are bare; she is aroused by his long, slender toes, which are the color of the crust on the bread Meme has made for as long as Amelia can remember.

He indicates a small entry hall behind a green painted gate that stands in front of another large, fortified-looking wooden door. "When I was a child, there was no crime in Altea, but now, I'm afraid, this is not the case. Which is why we have this other door, which I keep locked all the time when my grandmother is alone. People seem to have no moral sense. I don't think they'd stop at the idea of robbing an old crippled woman."

Pepe's grandmother is sitting in a large, wooden chair in a small room that has, in addition to her chair, a love seat covered in a rough, dark orange fabric, a table, and three small chairs, intricately carved and rush-seated. On the white stucco walls are plates with scenes of farmers or hunters.

"I love your plates," Amelia says. "My father was a potter. And I've brought you a little bowl, which is not nearly so lovely as the things you have."

"Thank you," she says, opening the package with her crippled fingers. "How delightful, this little dish, with an angel at the bottom. How wonderful to be able to think of angels when you finish your fruit."

Amelia worries that the grandmother might prefer this bowl to her father's.

"A potter," she says. "What a fine thing to do with one's time. I won't rise to greet you because that is difficult for me now. Pepe will bring us some drinks. Does white wine suit you? I hope you're not one of those Americans who never drink because all they think about is their waistline. But you don't need to worry about that. You are slender and long-legged, with your lovely long white neck, like a swan."

Swans again! She wants to tell Pepe's grandmother about Meme and the swans, but it would be too difficult to explain. And it might put her grandmother in an unflattering light.

"I'll get the drinks," Pepe says, and she can hear the sound of his bare feet on the tiles, though she can't see through the doorway.

What will she speak to the grandmother about? Most old women are not like Meme and her friends. But she doesn't know what this woman is like; she is much younger than Meme; Amelia can't begin to guess her interests or what she would find disturbing.

"I also live with my grandmother," she says, knowing that would be reassuring to the old woman. "So, Pepe and I have that in common."

"Well, that is very unusual, a fortunate accident, you might say, because it is not, in fact, a common thing, two young people who live with their grandmothers. Where are your parents, then?"

"My father is dead. My mother lives in California. In Los Angeles."

"That is where Hollywood is, isn't it? When I was younger, I adored the movies. Now there is not so much I like to see, and it's difficult for me to get out. But when I was younger, I was in the movies all the time. The movies were very important to us in Spain then. The country was very poor, and it was one thing everyone could go to for entertainment, and sometimes, in the winter, people would go just to get warm. The government was very strict about what we could see. *Gone with the Wind*, for example, we had heard about it, but we weren't allowed to see it. And they would make cuts in movies of parts they thought were objectionable . . . I remember one film where an unmarried couple was living together, and the dubbing made it suggest that they were brother and sister, so the whole movie made no sense. Oh, I remember when Rita Hayworth came to Spain; we were all beside ourselves with excitement."

Amelia wonders what this means about the grandmother's politics.

Pepe comes into the room carrying an oval wooden tray. On it are three glasses, a bottle of wine, a dish of olives, a dish of almonds, a plate with small meatballs, and another with small, fried fish.

She's hungry; although the sky is still light, it's nearly nine o'clock. She eats the savory foods with great pleasure, enjoying the saltiness alongside the gentle sharpness of the wine. When Pepe offers her another glass, she takes it happily. Happiness is in the air, in the fabric of the love seat, the complicated carving of the chairs, the farmers and hunters on the plates, the terra cotta tiles. She feels happy and she feels safe. She will tell them the truth about what she's doing here. She will ask for their help.

"I'm really here," she says, "because my grandmother lived here. A long time ago. The nineteen forties. She lived here for a dozen years. She's American. I wonder if you knew her."

The grandmother's expression that was so lively goes suddenly blank.

"Those were bad times, very bad times. Dark times. We were very poor then. The accident caused so much heartache, so much suffering."

Amelia wonders what the accident might have been. Was there a fire, an explosion, a bus crash killing children?

"My grandmother, though, do you remember an American woman who lived here? She was married to a young man of the town, he died in the war; she lived with his parents. His father owned an ironmonger's; his mother was a pharmacist."

"I don't remember those times. They were not good times. Pepe," she says, rubbing her twisted hands, "I think I have gotten very tired. Will you help me to bed?

"I'll say good-night then, my dear," she says, offering her cheek to be kissed, but not meeting Amelia's eye, and not suggesting that they meet again.

Amelia feels she's done something wrong. But what else could she have done? Fear lodges in the place in her chest where the large bone halves. Perhaps this was not just an unwise but also a harmful journey. But harmful to whom? In America, everything had seemed possible. But that's what people say about Americans, she thinks, those who like us like us for it, those who despise us condemn us as ignoramuses: only in America would people think anything is possible. And she isn't in America now.

What was her fantasy? Meeting Pepe and his grandmother so nearly fit it exactly. A romance with a young Spaniard, an elder opening the shut doors of the past, inviting her into the history that she had come to take her part in. But Pepe's grandmother shut the door with the fixed purpose of someone who is trying to keep out a thief. Her look seemed hunted. Did Amelia have to understand herself now as the hunter? She has always disliked the idea of hunting, men dressed for the kill, the prey so drastically overmatched. Is that who she is? The hunter? The thief?

"I'll be twenty minutes at the most," Pepe says. "I'll just give my grandmother a light supper and see that she's tucked into bed. Perhaps you'd like to go upstairs onto our roof? You can see the sea from there; you'll be just in time for the sunset." He hands her the bottle of wine and her glass. "Please," he says. "Enjoy yourself."

She climbs the narrow stairs onto the roof. In fact, she's missed the sunset. The sky is smoky; deep violet clouds are solid globes, disappearing before her eyes into a darkness that creeps up, allowing her only a glimpse of the dark sea. The chorus of birds grows incrementally silent; she wonders which species go silent first and how each knows when to be quiet. Swallows wheel and dive, then disappear, absorbed into the growing darkness.

Then, timidly, two stars appear, and she becomes conscious of a three-quarter moon, reflected in the water that has, newly lit, become newly visible. She sits back on the white plastic chair, the same chair she has seen on every sidewalk in front of every restaurant and café she has seen in every city she has been to in America. A soft breeze blows the curls that have escaped from the tortoiseshell clip she's caught her hair in. She pulls her scarf more closely around her shoulders. A light winks—is it a lighthouse? How has she not seen it before? She sips her wine, holding it against the moonlight, looking through the gold to the dark evening air.

She hears Pepe's light step. "I hope you've been happy on your own here. I have the feeling that you understand the kinds of things that must be done when one has, as we have, a grandmother."

"Yes, of course."

"This isn't the easiest house for an old woman who has trouble getting around. The kitchen is in the basement and my grandmother's room is upstairs. Sometimes I have to carry her downstairs because she doesn't want to give up cooking. In many ways, it makes no sense. But she loves her house, she's lived here since she was a young bride, and if you just don't think about it in terms of what's sensible, it's a good arrangement, certainly good for me, and for her as well, even if it means I have to carry her up and down the stairs rather than her having to give up the house she loves."

"It's a lovely house," she says, "and you're so kind to invite me. But I seem to have upset your grandmother, I'm very sorry. What was the accident your grandmother referred to? I gathered she didn't want to talk about it."

"The accident? Oh, that's what my grandmother's generation calls the civil war. As if it was no one's fault, it just happened. For years, no one would talk about it at all. You must remember that when you and I were born, Franco had only been dead ten years. It's only recently that people would talk about it."

"What side was your grandmother on?"

"My grandmother is as political as a grapefruit. But the town was divided, I gather, half Falangist, half Republican. My grandmother probably did whatever her family did, but I have no idea, as I said, she never talks about it. My grandmother is not an educated woman, and she dislikes any kind of discord. Also, she is not particularly adventurous. It was my parents who left the town; no one had for generations."

"She's a delightful woman. I'm sorry that I distressed her."

"Oh, it's nothing. I will tell her stories about how kind you are to your grandmother—you can give me facts, or I can easily make them up—and tell her you are a tender, young girl who inspires tenderness in me, and she will love you and forget all about it. She's very good at forgetting unpleasantness."

He pours them each another glass of wine. They are sitting on a bench attached to the white wall. He puts his arm around her. She inclines her head toward him so he knows she wants to be kissed.

Perfect, she thinks, this is perfect, to kiss this lovely man with his warm skin, and his glossy hair, and his wonderful, huge eyes, and his smell of soap that might be sage or rosemary, who carries his grandmother up and down stairs. But she knows he's wrong, that his grandmother has not forgotten the unpleasantness, and that, like Amelia, he's been raised not to be part of the darkness of the past. But he is not like her, because her father's illness and death made the darkness impossible not to fear. He's someone who doesn't fear it, because he hasn't yet met it. He's devoted to pleasure, not only his own, but the pleasure of everyone. And he is not like her because she has something in her that he does not, a kind of force that made her grandmother tell the story of her past.

This is who he is; this is who he will be to her. Not a part of her mission: a part of her holiday. The breeze cools their skin; they kiss and kiss, as if it were the only activity open to them as a man and a woman. She has never enjoyed kissing so much; it's not a prelude to anything, not just something to be got through, but a delightful activity valuable for its own sake.

"Perhaps tomorrow we can spend more time together," he says, and she knows what he means. "Right now, I feel it is best to do nothing that might disturb my grandmother."

His decorousness arouses her as mere ardor would not. He leans against the white wall, brilliant in the darkness, and she leans against him. What a great pleasure it is: this light leaning. Something, she thinks, like getting into a hammock and letting yourself be supported by something as light as woven cords, the air beneath you, you're not on the ground but not far from it, and you feel safe, safe enough to fall easily asleep. But she can't fall asleep. She needs his help to find her uncle. She must have a clear enough brain to invent another lie. She knows she's getting better at it, but she's not quite expert. She wonders when lying will come easily to her, another skill grown automatic, like ice-skating or crochet.

"I actually haven't come to Altea for pleasure. I'm here to look for someone who's a relative, related, actually, to the man my grandmother was married to when she lived here."

It's not really a lie, she tells herself; nothing she has said could be counted as a pure untruth. She understands that this kind of calculation is what could easily be called the "slippery slope." The slippery slope that lands you right in the waterfall of automatic deceit.

"How thrilling," Pepe says. "A search for your roots. What's his name?"

"Ignacio Ortiz."

Pepe whistles. "Well, as they say in England, you might just find a pot of gold at the end of this rainbow. Señor Ortiz is very wealthy. A very prominent businessman. Of course, I've never met him. He sells expensive cars to people who don't really live here."

Amelia shivers, excited by the discovery, and he feels her shiver and puts his arm more tightly around her. She imagines this is what it's like when a detective finds his—what, his prey?

She hates having to use these hunting terms. And she doesn't want to use the pronoun "he." She is the girl detective, Nancy Drew, from the books she devoured in the summers spent with Meme in the attic room that is hers again, where everything important to her now is kept.

They are both reluctant to move. She tells him she's actually too tired for supper, the tapas were enough. He apologizes, but she says, "No, actually I prefer to eat lightly at night," which is, miraculously, not a lie.

The square is bustling with young people. Rock music blares from the bars; boys and girls their age stand, holding full glasses, swaying—and smoking, Amelia is surprised to see, as if no one ever told them this might not be good for their future health. Everyone greets Pepe, and he greets them but doesn't stop to talk. She hopes there'll be more kissing at the door of the hotel.

In front of the cathedral there is a temporary wooden structure, a kind of castle. The young people lean against it; there's a doorway that only a very small person would be able to enter.

"What's that?" she asks Pepe.

"Oh, that was for the festival. The festival of the Christians and the Moors. The children dress up, some as Spaniards at the time of Isabella and some as Moors, and they reenact the Battle of Granada. The children who are playing the Spaniards chase the Moors from the street, wielding their swords. The Moorish children are carrying scimitars."

Amelia doesn't know how to respond. She doesn't know how to understand that Pepe is speaking of this as if it were normal, acceptable.

"Don't you think that might be offensive to Muslims?"

Pepe looks at her with genuine puzzlement. "But there are no Muslims here. And besides, the part of the Moors is the coveted part. All the children want to be Moors. The costumes are much better, and the scimitars are much more fun."

She knows there's something dreadful about all this, but she doesn't want to spoil the night by arguing about it. He sees nothing wrong with it, and it is his home. She was right not to tell him the whole story of Meme's time here. He would be the wrong person to tell it to; there would be no category for it in his understanding of the world. She leans back into the arm that Pepe has put around her and enjoys a voluptuous yawn.

She sleeps dreamlessly, but lightly, with the lightness she associates with Pepe, and she wakes rested. She has breakfast on the hotel terrace, tostadas and café con leche, which seems to her the perfect thing to be eating for breakfast on an October morning looking at the Mediterranean. Pepe has told her that he must work today, that she must go for a swim without him, but that she should come to the shop at about five, and he will take her to meet her uncle.

She knows that the time here is unreal, that it can't be said to serve as a model for what ordinary life might be. But, having learned to turn her back on the recent horrors imposed on the town, like a bad haircut on a beauty, she has seen the pleasures of daily life here: the white walls, the ornamental gates, the climbing flowers, the kindness of the waiters and waitresses, the children playing late at night, surrounded by their parents, their grandparents, people living in the benevolent outdoors, enjoying each other publicly, strolling arm in arm: all this is impossible in the chilly North or in car-infested California. She allows herself to imagine what it might be like to live here for a little while; she could get some kind of job—perhaps in a bakery, though she hasn't seen any bakeries, but it doesn't matter, she's sure she could find some kind of job, she isn't very choosy or demanding about what work, in her imagination, she might do. She would perfect her Spanish. She would read about the history of Spain. She allows herself to imagine that she would be living with her uncle Ignacio. Every morning she would shop, sometimes in the covered market, on Tuesdays and Saturdays in the open market. She would cook only fresh, seasonal food; she would learn more about cooking fish; she would learn to clean a fish. She would help Pepe with his grandmother: it would be a real service when the *abuelita* became more crippled. Amelia wouldn't mind helping her bathe. It would be a simple, unhurried life, but every act would have a finished, a polished quality.

Then she remembers: to live here, she would have to be far from Meme. But soon Meme will not be in the world, and what had seemed only minutes before a desirable lightness now seems not desirable at all but dangerous. Without Meme in the world, how will she attach? She will fly off into a space that is intolerable in its lack of boundaries. There is, of course, her mother, but her mother presses down: too much gravity. Meme's touch is light; she holds but does not press. Amelia begins to weep, and she allows herself a childish, a ridiculous gesture: she opens her arms and cries *Meme, Meme*, like a child running for comfort. But there is no comfort to be found.

She knows what Meme would say: Go for a swim, it will restore you. But restore her to what? To a living body, a young body that will live in the world long after her grandmother is no longer a part of it. And that is what Meme would want, for her to live happily ever after.

Without Pepe, she is in a different relationship to the sea. She can plunge right in and swim without a goal for as long as she likes. The salt of the sea becomes indistinguishable from the salt of her tears, and she feels free to weep there for her beloved grandmother, who taught her to swim, with whom she has been happy swimming. She opens her eyes under the water; looks at the ribs of rippling sand, spies a few scant, silver fish who hurry to be away from her. She rolls over on her back, focuses on the rock formations. On her right side, an emerald hill; on her left, its cousin, bare rock, barren. And she wonders how these two can be so different and so near. This, she thinks, is the kind of thing Meme would inquire about and find an answer for. And she knows that she will not.

She showers and walks back to lunch at the café l'Espril, and the waitress greets her like a regular, points her to what is understood now as "her table." Again, she orders the tortilla and some grilled vegetables. A glass (one only) of white wine. The vegetables are not, as she imagined, simply grilled, but breaded, and she enjoys a transgressive pleasure in what is surely not grilled but fried, although the meal lies heavy on her stomach, and she wants a nap. She allows herself another shower and lies naked on her bed, enjoying the warm breeze on her nakedness, and she allows herself to think of Pepe and what, she is sure, is in store for them tonight.

She wakes at three and walks along the esplanade. Pepe has told her she must have a *horchata*, the iced almond drink that is a Valencian specialty, at the café of a friend of his, who makes a very good one. She mentions Pepe's name and the owner, a slight, elegant sixty-year-old man in grey trousers and a short-sleeved blue-and-white-striped shirt, serves her seriously, formally. He seems not depressed but worried, or perhaps only congenitally fatalistic, as if he had a secret knowledge that he is making the last *horchata* in the history of the world but must keep that information quiet. It is a cliché about the Spaniards: that they are fatalistic. She doesn't believe in sentences that begin with "The Spanish people . . . ," but she can only see fatalism as he turns to the refrigerator and then presses the buttons on a machine that makes a drink that is nothing but delightful, suggesting nothing but that life is pleasant, nourishing, and sweet.

She enjoys the sound of her sandals on the stone steps, the clean light on the white buildings. She stops midway up the hill to savor the view of the seashore stretching out from the uneven levels of the reddish-brown tile roofs. She takes her hair out of her clip, shakes it out, and clips it again. Tonight she will be with Pepe.

She finds his shop easily; it is on a small side street closer to Pepe's grandmother's house than to the esplanade. The metal sign that hangs out into the street has an orange-yellow sun and underneath it, in English, "House of Sunshine."

Pepe is behind the counter, engaging a woman in her fifties in a conversation centered around which of three silver bracelets she might buy. Amelia wouldn't dream of interrupting him. He suggests to the woman that she buy all three, and this seems like a good idea to her. He concludes the purchase by leaning—it's more of a jump—over the counter and kissing the woman's cheek.

Amelia smiles when she catches Pepe's eye, but she knows she must wait till the customers are gone before she approaches him. A German couple seems to be buying something that Amelia can't see. She looks at the earrings in the display case; they're unremarkable. She can imagine herself buying any of ten pairs and not being distressed if they were lost. She walks into the next room. All pleasure drains from her body.

There are a series of figurines on glass shelves; they seem to be wizards and dragons. The dragon's eyes are startling red and green stones; the fire breathed from his mouth is a violent orange; his outsized tail is encrusted with vaguely leaf-shaped, metallic plates of an even more violent green. One dragon is approximately the size, she thinks, of a two-year-old. All the wizards seem to have what is supposed to be natural hair, wheat-colored wisps that fall down to their midnight-blue capes with patterning of metallic stars. They range in size, but the largest matches the size of the largest dragon. She can't imagine who would desire such things; she can't imagine why Pepe would sell them.

There are pictures of bullfighters and Gypsies painted on wood, and a large oil painting of a buxom *señorita* in a peasant outfit. On the far wall there is more of the cheap Indian clothing that, in America, only stoners wear; she can smell, as she approaches them, that combination of fish and motor oil, with an overlay of ink. The wall beside the Indian clothing is devoted to clocks; a quarter hour strikes, and she hears the Bobby McFerrin tune: "Don't worry. Be happy." As she comes closer, she sees that on each side of the pendulum is a white square shaped like a traffic sign. One says "Don't worry." The other says "Be happy."

Her body is uncomfortable in this room. I ate too heavily, she tells herself, but she knows that isn't it. It's the ugliness, the cheapness of everything in Pepe's store, and she can't stop her physical reaction to it. She tells herself that it isn't important, that Pepe is a wonderful person, kind to his grandmother, tender and attentive to her as a woman, but her eye falls on the picture of the bullfighter and her heart contracts.

Two customers enter the store, a father and a son. At first, Amelia thinks they're American, but then she realizes they're English. The boy, who is very blond, is wearing shorts that reveal, worryingly for Amelia, his thin, milk-white legs. "It's here, Daddy, this is the one I want." He pulls his father over to the shelf of wizards and dragons.

"I say, that's rather a size," the father says, picking up a wizard. "Do you think it would fit in your bedroom?"

Pepe stands next to them, tactfully not hovering, although Amelia imagines he's worried about what would happen if the wizard, priced at 250 euros, fell out of the father's hand onto the tile floor.

The little boy starts hopping up and down; Amelia wonders if he needs to use the bathroom.

"Please, Daddy, please, I want it more than anything. I want it more than I've ever wanted anything in my entire life."

The father hands the wizard to his son and makes a gesture of helplessness, his palms raised toward the ceiling.

"I suppose you'll have to have the dragon, too."

"Oh, Daddy, it would make me ever so happy. Happier than anything."

"Well, then, it's settled," he says to Pepe. "Wrap them up, if you please, safe for travel. We're back off to home today."

"They will be, as you say in your country, safe as houses."

"Your English is very good," the father says.

And Pepe tells them about his years in Brighton, and the father recounts seaside holidays and wonders if he's ever eaten in Pepe's parents' restaurant. "I'm sure you haven't," Pepe says. "You would remember our wonderful calamari. But next time, you must go and tell my parents you were in Altea, and they will treat you like one of the royal family."

"Oh, can we go, Daddy, can we go?"

"You never know what will be in the cards, Simon."

They're very happy, the three of them: Simon, his father, and Pepe, and Amelia is ashamed of her own unhappiness. When they leave the store, Pepe runs from behind the counter, lifts Amelia in the air, spins her around, and kisses her.

"A wonderful sale. I think it was because you were here, you brought me luck. We will go out to a very special place tonight for a very special dinner. This is a great success. Jorgé, my supplier, was right: wizards and dragons are very big now, very big."

"That's wonderful, Pepe," Amelia says, but his hands on her shoulders don't arouse her as they did the night before.

"I've drawn a map for you. It's not difficult, but you should give yourself time. I'll pick you up at your hotel at nine—unless, of course, you'll want to be spending time with your relative."

She walks down the steep hill, enjoying the austere white walls, the grey cobblestones, the invasions of color: the well-cared-for flowers in pots or trained on trellises. She has to acknowledge how much of her decision to come here has been fueled by fantasy. But for an American thinking of Europe, fantasies are superabundant: bad movies, great novels, spreads in cookbooks or fashion magazines. Meeting Pepe and his grandmother, the warm sea, the warm breeze, the waitress who treated her as an old friend, all these seemed to suggest that the fantasies were not junk food but the necessary nourishment for an unusual but sound decision, an adventure, a rescue. But now she's feeling only disappointment. Pepe is a nice man, an attractive man: she enjoyed kissing him. But there was too much he didn't understand. That the past had marked his grandmother indelibly. That it wasn't all right to make a kiddy show out of the annihilation of a people. That you mustn't add to the ugliness of the world by how you make your living. She knows it isn't his fault. Altea endures through tourism, and to survive in the tourist trade, you have to cater to the taste of tourists. She wonders if she'd like Pepe more if he knows the things are ugly and cynically sells them, or if he thinks they're just fine.

But none of this is important. The time for fantasy is over. The person she will meet is not a figment of her imagination. He is Meme's son.

She stops at her hotel to dress. She looks at herself closely in the mirror, regretting that she hasn't brought the right clothes. She should have something like what her mother habitually wears to work: a pantsuit, at least something with a jacket. She needs to be more like her mother now, certain that what she's doing is right, that there is one right thing, only one, whose claims entirely drown out whatever might be its opposite. She thinks of her gentle father, who died too soon.

She looks through her makeup and decides that nothing she has will endow her with the authority she craves, and she doesn't think it's the right time for experimentation. So she thinks of her father, and how he prized simplicity and plainness. She knows she isn't plain. She knows she has, for all of her life, been called pretty. And it has helped her, she knows, being a pretty girl, the kind of pretty that doesn't seem to exert pressure. She can't make herself over in the half hour before she enters her uncle's showroom. She'll try to use the gifts she has; she'll approach him as a simple, pretty girl on an errand of mercy. What could be simpler? She'll present herself, and then simply speak the simple truth.

The showroom is on the busiest street in the town. Cars whiz by her in a way that she hasn't experienced since she's been in Altea. She pulls open the heavy door; it seems to resist her and makes a whooshing sound, ushering her into a new climatic zone. The air-conditioning is on too high; she feels goose bumps prickling her skin, and she's worried that this will compromise her small store of authority.

Nothing in the overlarge room seems ever to have been alive. The tones are metallic. Silver grey predominates: the deliberately industrial ceiling lights; the chrome desk fixtures; the floor, nearly without color, polished so highly that for a moment she thinks it might be a large mirror. The cars are larger than any she has seen on the streets here; the room is larger than any she has been in; the temperature is lower; and the music, piped from somewhere, is untraceable to any time or place. She feels as if she's stepped out of her spaceship into a new planet, inhospitable to any life she's known.

A young man in a grey suit, white shirt, black tie, is sitting behind a desk. Suddenly, Amelia is frightened. Suppose Ignacio isn't here. Suppose he's on vacation. Why hadn't she thought of that? Well, it's too late for her now. She must be her mother: just do what needs to be done. Or her grandmother: jump right into the ocean, you'll be glad you did.

She asks for Ignacio Ortiz. The young man asks if she has an

appointment. She speaks a sentence that she knows is a bald irrelevance but thinks might carry, because it might suggest the press and
weight of dollars.

"I've come from America."

The sentence works. The young man nods. "But you speak Spanish.
Your accent is very good." He enters an office, then returns to his desk.
A few seconds later, another man approaches, his hand extended, a
look on his face meant to be both welcoming and quizzical.

He doesn't look the way she had imagined. The first word that
comes to her mind when she sees him: fleshy.

He is around her height, five seven, short for a man, she thinks,
and his shoulders are broad: they are the only thing about him that
suggests hardness. Everything else about him is soft, not a pillowy
softness, a confectionary softness, coated with a hard sugar shell of
inarticulate demands. On the pinkie of his left hand, he wears a silver ring with a dark blue stone. His tie is silvery, his lips are very full.
His hair has been moussed or gelled into a cap of luxuriant curls; it
matches, she can see, his tie. His eyes are dark and large; they look as
if, at any moment, they might spill over into tears.

He shows her into his office.

"How can I help you, young lady? Let me see if I can guess: you
are relocating here. This is the town of your dreams. You have met
someone and fallen in love. You need a car that will make you feel
safe and happy."

She sits in the chair across from his wide, silver desk and gathers her skirts around her. She pulls her pashmina closer around her
shoulders. She smiles the smile that, for all her life, has made people
want to give her things.

"Actually, I'm not in the market for a car. I'm sorry if I suggested
that. I'm actually here because we're related."

The liquidity in his brown eyes hardens, freezes, not into ice but
into a kind of lusterless metal. "That is impossible," he says. "I'm
sorry, young lady, but you are mistaken."

His hardening creates a reciprocal hardness in her. "I am not mistaken," she says. "I'm your niece. Your mother is my grandmother."

"My mother died when I was very young."

"I think, sir, that what you say isn't true," Amelia says, her hands trembling so hard that she grips the edges of her seat. "My grandmother is Marian Taylor, an American who lived here from 1938 till 1953. She was married to your father, who died before you were born. She lived with you and your grandparents until she left for America; I understand that you were quite young."

"You understand nothing."

"She's very old now," Amelia goes on, as if he hadn't spoken. "She's dying. I thought perhaps that you would like to see her."

"You thought incorrectly, miss. My mother died to me when she left, when she left me, her only child, and the family who had sheltered her in a time of desperate need."

He rises from his chair and walks toward her. She tells herself there's nothing he can do to her: they're in a public place; three salesmen, two customers are in the outer office. She understands that he would harm her if he could. But he can't make her leave without some show of physical force, in which, as there are customers in the showroom, she imagines he'll be reluctant to indulge.

"She's dying, Señor Ortiz. Your mother is dying."

"My mother has long been dead. She died of the disease of her perverse beliefs. She was poisoned by the filthy ideas of the communism she put above everything. She was poisoned and became diseased. This country was too strong for her, too healthy; she had to go back to America, where she could breathe the air that nurtured her disease."

"My grandmother isn't a communist," Amelia says, not knowing why this is the idea she's landed on. "She never has been."

"You can't believe anything they say. They are children of lies. They all lie to better spread their poison."

"My grandmother is a good woman. She has done great good in the world." How, she wonders, could she talk about Meme's work for the environment, the preservation of wetlands, the creation of public gardens, transportation for the elderly? How puny that all sounds, pathetic, even. How can she tell him that her grandmother has loved her in a way that made her feel safe in a world that, she now understands more than ever, has never been a place of safety?

"She was a diseased creature that spread her disease. The disease that eventually infected this country, that has turned it from one of the healthy spots on a dangerous earth to just another disease-ridden outpost of error and perversion. Oh, she would be happy in the current Spain, where everything goes, everything is allowed, now we are a culture of pornography and drugs and divorce and homosexuality and abortion. Where we were once the crown of virtue."

Amelia knows that, for the first time in her life, she is truly angry. Furiously angry. The sensation is so foreign to her that she thinks she may be having a seizure. This heat in her face, this racing of her pulse . . . perhaps it's a fever, the highest fever she has ever had. Perhaps it's feverish delirium that allows her to rise to her feet, stand face-to-face with Ignacio Ortiz, pull herself up to her full height so she is actually the taller, move closer to him than good manners would permit.

"My grandmother was right. She said you were born a fascist and you would always be one."

"I suppose you think that is an insult. For me, it is an honor."

"An honor? To be associated with people who violated the freedom of millions? Who executed millions in the name of order?"

"Order, yes, but, most importantly, truth and honor. You understand nothing of truth and honor. You Americans, you can only speak in small words, written in small letters."

She has never been even remotely patriotic, but now she is determined to defend America.

"Life, liberty, and the pursuit of happiness. They are not small words."

"Pursuit of happiness? Compared to a devotion to truth and honor? You speak of happiness. As an idea it is nothing but paltry, lukewarm, mediocre. Pursuit of happiness. These words do not speak to the blood. Which is why, in the end, we will triumph."

"Well, you won't triumph, but you will shed blood. Much more blood has been shed in the name of honor than in the name of happiness. And life and liberty: liberty is nothing to you, and you don't love life; it's death you love."

"Yes, thank God, we are not afraid of death. As I imagine your precious grandmother, who was, after all, baptized in the faith but renounced her faith for the poison faith of communism, is facing it now with terror."

"You couldn't be more wrong," she says, but his words frighten her. She has never asked her grandmother if she is afraid of dying.

"Leave these premises or I will call the police."

"And say what? That they should arrest me for introducing myself to my uncle? But I'm happy to leave. I don't want to breathe the same air as you any longer than I have to," she says, flinging her shawl over her shoulders, enjoying the cliché.

If with Ignacio she felt for the first time the seizure of anger, running down the streets she feels for the first time what it must be to be insane. She sees herself running, her hair falling out of her clip, hears the *flap flap flap* of her sandals' leather soles, but she sees and hears from a distance, as if she were on a high place, what might be called an observatory. Her face is flushed; sweat is pouring down her back, she feels the stream of it traveling down her spine. She has only one thought: she has to get out of here, she has to be home. With her grandmother, who may be afraid of dying.

She can't imagine why she was ever so foolish as to undertake this errand. Why she thought she could simply arrive and say to someone, "Your mother, who abandoned you while you were still a child, is dying. She doesn't know I'm here to find you, but if you will just come with me, I can bring you to her."

Shame sluices her being as streams of sweat sluice her skin. You are a fool; you are a ridiculous person, she says to the reflection in the mirror. She throws her clothes into her suitcase, not stopping to fold them. Briefly, she contemplates leaving a message for Pepe. But there is nothing to say.

She checks out of the hotel and asks them to call her a cab. The woman at the desk tells Amelia it will cost a hundred euros. She agrees. She knows she couldn't have done what she's doing before the age of credit cards.

She has no idea when the next plane to Madrid might be, or, after that, the next plane to New York. It doesn't matter; she doesn't mind spending the night in the airport as long as she's out of this town.

The old Amelia would have felt it necessary to make some excuse to the hotel owners. But not the new Amelia. The old Amelia would not have run away. The intermediate Amelia, who came into being when she hatched this plan, the Amelia who lied: she would have made up a story. But the Amelia she is now feels no need to make an explanation. None at all.

There is a plane to Madrid an hour and a half after she arrives at the airport, a seat if the *señorita* is willing to go first class. The *señorita* is. There is a way of getting to New York tonight if she is willing to fly through Oslo. It will take thirteen hours. She agrees.

All she wants to do is sleep, not to be conscious until she arrives in America. There are too many things to understand. Too much has happened. There is too much for her to know about herself; how can she be both the person she was only a few days ago and the person she now knows herself to be? It's as if she is a nursling and, because of extraordinary circumstances, has been abruptly and rudely weaned. And the necessity of the weaning has forced her suddenly to grow teeth. She feels it in her mouth: the new sharpness, the cutting through the pink tender gums. This is who I am now, she thinks. I am grateful for everything that happened, everything I saw.

For the first time, she knows exactly who she is. She is a person who will refuse some things. Will refuse to allow them to go by while she keeps silence. The sense she always had of floating above her life has disappeared. Because she knows she will refuse lies—and she knows it because she has refused lies about someone she loves, about ideas she didn't even know she believed in. And so I must, she wants to tell her grandmother, be a person of faith. To be a person of faith means to be willing to say yes and to be willing to say no, not counting the cost. She did this in the cold room with the man who spoke words that were evil. Was he evil himself? He frightened her, but she said no. She loved her grandmother, and to what her grandmother's life meant, she said yes.

She rents a car in New York and drives the three hours to Avondale. Exhausted, she stops for a coffee near New Haven and gulps it down with a McDonald's hamburger, which she is ashamed to admit she enjoys. She adds an order of fries, which she enjoys even more.

She passes the great houses of Watch Hill, built by millionaires, probably including her great-grandfather, whose existence, only weeks ago, she couldn't have imagined. She drives up the dirt road to Meme's house.

She opens the door quietly in case her grandmother is sleeping. But she isn't sleeping. Amelia hears her voice; she's speaking on the phone. "I know you were interested in opposing the swan-egg-addling program. We weren't able to make our case a few months ago, but we're trying again. We're going to meet and marshal our facts and be sure we have a well-articulated argument. They thought it was all over. But there's another spring coming just around the corner. We need to get organized now."

And then she hears Helga's voice. "They don't know who they're dealing with, but they'll know soon enough, by God."

And now Rosa is saying, "You shouldn't sound so angry. You don't want to appear rude."

"We won't give up without a fight," Marian says. "They don't know who they're dealing with. They don't begin to understand who we are."

"My darling Meme," Amelia, standing in the hall, says to no one who can hear her. "I think I begin to understand, I think I have at least begun to understand who you are. And now I must begin to understand who I am. I must begin to understand how to live a life."

But there is one thing she knows she understands: Ignacio is wrong, as wrong as everything else about him, as wrong as everything could possibly be. Her grandmother's life was good and right. It was a life of meaning. A life that made sense.

And she knows now what she couldn't tell him then for certain. But she is certain now: her grandmother is not afraid to die.

·

In the next weeks, Marian grows steadily weaker. Amelia spends most of her days sitting beside her grandmother's bed, giving her sips of water, holding her hand.

It is early morning; not yet five. A few stars hang in the dim sky; the moon, a crescent, can still just be seen, and the sun, weak, silvery, seems unequal to the effort of providing warmth and light. Marian raises herself up to take a drink, puts her head back down, and takes Amelia's hand.

"I'm dying. I know I'm dying, but I don't know what that really means."

Amelia puts her head on the pillow beside her grandmother's.

"I don't know what it will be like," Marian says. "Sometimes I think it will be nothing, sometimes I think it will be like music, sometimes I think I'll be with everyone I love who has died before me."

"Oh, Meme, I will miss you so much."

Marian's head thrashes on the pillow. "You see, this is the kind of thing that steals my peace. I can't tell you that I'll miss you. I don't know. Do the dead miss the living? Or are they only with the other dead, the living so far away that they can't be remembered or believed in. Can the dead say 'I miss you'? Can the dead say the word 'I'? With what mouths could they form words? Or is it all just nothing?"

Marian begins to weep, and Amelia weeps too, fearing that she has troubled her grandmother, stolen more of her peace.

"I wish," Marian says, "that I could say to you, believing I was speaking truth: I know that we'll see each other once again."

The tears gather more thickly now in Amelia's eyes and the dim light turns everything indistinct. What she knows to be the furniture of her grandmother's familiar room seems now not chairs, tables, a dresser with bottles—perfumes, medicines—but trees in a deep mist. She guesses only at their shapes. The most she can say is that some are taller than others, some more slender, some perhaps only bushes, squat, pressed low to the invisible ground.

Her eyes strain to distinguish them. And then she understands, they aren't trees; they move toward each other, turn away, then toward each other, move farther back, then nearer. Can these be the beloved dead? Can one of them be her father? Is the empty space to his left the space for Meme? And on her father's other side, another empty space, this one for her? Yes, this is possible, and so she will choose to believe that it is true.

She knows just what to say. She knows the words that will bring comfort to her grandmother, words they both can trust.

"One day, you know, Meme, I will be among the dead."

Marian laughs. "Yes, I suppose you will. Somehow I'd never thought of that."

"So it's possible we'll see each other again. You must admit it's at least possible."

"Yes," Marian says. "It may be possible. Yes."

ACKNOWLEDGMENTS

Like everyone who has even approached the rocky territory of the Spanish Civil War, I am indebted to the work of Hugh Thomas and Paul Preston. I am particularly grateful to Hugh Thomas for providing the authority for my suspicions about the reliability of George Orwell's *Homage to Catalonia*. Paul Preston's *Doves of War*, which traced the role of four women in the Spanish Civil War, was of particular use to me.

Angela Jackson's groundbreaking work on British women in the war opened many doors, most especially her biography of Patience Darton, *For Us It Was Heaven*.

Peter Carroll's work on the Abraham Lincoln Brigade and Anthony Beevor's clearheaded historical writing widened my perspectives and the range of my understanding.

Julia Newman's splendid film *Into the Fire* brought to life the stories of heroic women who were faceless names only.

Fredericka Morton's archive in the Tamiment Library of New York University provided invaluable material, much of it firsthand accounts of American nurses.

Mary Bingham de Urquidi's *Mercy in Madrid* was a treasury of particular information about the lives of nurses in the wartime hospitals.

For a writer, theft is the sincerest form of flattery, but it should not go undocumented. I want to acknowledge the use of some phrases and images from Josephine Herbst's *The Starched Blue Sky of Spain*, and Dorothy Parker's "Incredible, Fantastic . . . and True," which were also invaluable sources.

My most particular thanks go to Professor Carme Manuel of the University of Valencia for her extraordinary generosity in opening the city for me . . . accompanying me on walks, introducing me to people with precious information, and pointing me in the right direction again and again.

My thanks to Isabel and Juan Antonio Yáñez, for their hospitality, the depth and breadth of their knowledge, and their generosity in sharing it with me.

My conversations with Angela Cassanova of Kovington, Kentucky, who lived through the Franco years as the daughter of a left-leaning mother, were an incredible treasure.

When I try to remember why I felt the urge to write this book, inevitably I return to the work and life of Simone Weil, her letter to Georges Bernanos, and his searing *Diary of My Times*.

Closer to home and no less dear to my heart are my translators, Mei Li Johnson and Adam Zapades, and my dear helpers, Rebecca Kelliher and Cecelia Lie, who civilize my feral typing.

A NOTE ON THE TYPE

This book was set in Albertina, the best known of the typefaces designed by Chris Brand (b. 1921 in Utrecht, the Netherlands). Issued by the Monotype Corporation in 1965, Albertina was one of the first text fonts made solely for photocomposition. It was first used to catalog the work of Stanley Morison and was exhibited in Brussels at the Albertina Library in 1966.

Typeset by Scribe, Philadelphia, Pennsylvania
Printed and bound by Berryville Graphics, Berryville, Virginia
Designed by Maggie Hinders